The Dead of Jura

By

Allan Martin

TP

ThunderPoint Publishing Ltd.

First Published in Great Britain in 2020 by
ThunderPoint Publishing Limited
Summit House
4-5 Mitchell Street
Edinburgh
Scotland EH6 7BD

Cover Image © Annmarie Young / Shutterstock.com
Cover Design © Huw Francis

ISBN: 978-1-910946-67-1 (Paperback)
ISBN: 978-1-910946-68-8 (eBook)
Printed and bound in Great Britain by Clays Ltd, Elcograf S.p.A

www.thunderpoint.scot

Acknowledgements

Many thanks to all who played a part in bringing this book to publication.

To all the readers of The Peat Dead who asked for more of Angus Blue.

To those who read versions of The Dead of Jura and commented. To HB for advice on police plausibility. To fellow authors who offered encouragement. To Val Renehan for great conversation.

To Olga Wojtas and Marion Todd who not only read the final version and gave positive feedback, but also allowed me to quote them.

To Seonaid and Huw Francis at ThunderPoint, who've seen it through to publication.

And, above all, to Vivien, who's been with it from start to finish, and persuaded me to take out the scene with the aliens.

Dedication

To Vivien, with love.

Note on Places

Dunrighinn is fictitious, as are all the characters who appear in the book. However, my own ancestors did farm at Ardmenish and run the mill at Craighouse. The rest of Jura's geography is more-or-less accurate.

Prologue

A discreet beeping woke the man up. He silenced his watch and checked the time. 6.15 am. No rose pink dawn presaged a day of sunshine; instead, thin cloud filled the sky. That was good. No reflections and shadows to confuse things. And dry too. He smiled – yes, perfect weather. Time to prepare.

The waterproof sleeping bag had kept him warm and dry through the night. He crawled out of the bag, wiped it dry and clean, rolled it up carefully, stowed it in his rucksack. All of this he did without standing up, keeping low in the rectangular cutting he had made in the heather, just below the top of the ridge. As he worked he noticed a couple of deer watching him from further up the hillside. Eventually they lost interest and turned back to grazing.

He'd been careful in preparing. He worried about ticks, which multiplied here thanks to the island's swollen deer population. His boots, camouflage trousers and dark green jacket were waterproof and treated with permethrin-based insecticide. He'd also sprayed his hands, neck and head with a DEET-based insecticide. Despite these precautions, he would nevertheless have to check himself thoroughly once he got back. He also wore a dark green woolly hat and had smeared his face with brown camouflage paint.

From a dark green waterproof bag he extracted the elements of the rifle, and assembled it with the smoothness born of much practice. The final piece was the telescopic sight. He fixed an ammunition clip into the slot below the plastic stock. Eight bullets. More than he needed.

He crawled forward to the top of the ridge. Looking over the edge, he could see the big house below him, several hundred yards away. In front of it a wide lawn ran down to the shore of the small bay. About two-thirds of the way from the house to the water he could see the helipad, a square black patch of tarmac with a large white circle on it and a cross at the centre. That gave him a frame about sixty yards wide to cover. He opened up the bipod fixed to the rifle's barrel and set it carefully at a spot where, with the rifle resting on it, he could easily pan the weapon across the space between the house and the helipad. Then he tested the telescopic sight, so that the grey path leading from the front door of the house to the helipad was perfectly in focus.

Now to wait. He glanced at his watch again. 6.40. Plenty of time. Be patient, keep as still as possible. Nothing must be out of the ordinary.

At 6.55 he sensed, rather than heard, the beating of the rotors on the heavy air of the morning. Then the sound came too, and now he could see the small helicopter coming over from the east, from the mainland. As it neared the edge of the land the helicopter seemed to hesitate and hang back from the shore.

Then his eye caught another movement. The door of the house had opened. A man came out and waved to the helicopter, signalling it to land. It moved noisily forward and down, and then gingerly settled itself on the helipad. The man on the ground ran, head bent down, over to the helicopter and pulled open a door in its side. He held the door open. No-one got out. The man seemed to be talking to the pilot. After a couple of minutes, he went back towards the house. As he neared the door, he waved to someone inside.

Now the house-door opened again. More people were coming out. He eased the sights gently away from the helicopter and focused on the figures. He recognised the man as soon as he appeared. His face filled the sight. Now it was essential to keep calm. Focus on the task. Focus on the target.

Day 1. Monday

1

A late morning in May.

Inspector Angus Blue was in his office in the Oban Police HQ, on the ground floor, at the back of the building. He was contemplating two books on his desk, one a German dictionary, and the other a paperback, *Die Toten ohne Schatten* by Hubert Valkerius. Since meeting the translator of Valkerius's crime novels, Blue thought it was time he polished up his rusty German. He had worked out the title – *The Dead without Shadows* – and was working through the blurb on the back, when the phone rang.

"Police Scotland. Inspector Blue here. How may we be of assistance?" Police Scotland was very concerned about its image, not without some reason, as the years since unification had not been easy. Procedures had been put in place at the behest of expensive public relations consultants to enable every contact with Police Scotland to be a positive one. Blue was not always so punctilious in using the prescribed form, but since he could see from the display on his phone who was calling, he chose not to omit it.

"Good response, Blue, and picked up in only three rings. Well done."

"Thank you, sir. I am here, of course, to be helpful, and not only to the general public."

"Yes, yes, of course. Can you come up for a minute. Something important, very important."

"Yes, sir, right away. I was naturally extremely busy, but at your summons all is put aside."

He heard a harrumphing sound at the other end, then the line went dead.

Three floors up, Superintendent Campbell's door. He knocked and entered.

"Angus, come in, do take a seat," said the Super, motioning towards an upright chair facing his expansive desk. "The truth is," he went on, as Blue sat down, "that this is a really tricky one. Needs to be handled very carefully."

"Like skinning an eel, sir?"

3

"YesI suppose so. I didn't know you were a fisherman, Blue. No, sadly this has nothing to do with fish. There's been a shooting, on Jura."

Like a discreet butler calling for attention, a low burbling sigh gave Blue the news that Campbell's top-of-the-range Italian coffee machine had been activated. The plus side of a visit to the CID chief.

"I don't want to seem flippant, sir, but there's always shooting on Jura, isn't there? Or does it only happen in the autumn?" Was this one accidental? One rich idiot shooting another, instead of the wildlife. Blue almost hoped so.

"Ah, yes, very good. But this is people, Blue, people."

"Is the wildlife fighting back then? An old dear with a grouse?"

Campbell was not amused. "People, Angus, important people."

"So, more than one?"

"No, no. Just one. Isn't one shooting enough, Blue?"

"One is surely too many, sir."

"Of course, of course. Nevertheless, there's been a shooting. Thankfully not fatal. The victim is in hospital at the moment."

The warm, earthy aroma of top-of-the-range coffee wafted in Blue's direction. He breathed it in and savoured it. The smell of the coffee was always so much better than the taste.

"And we're sure it wasn't accidental?"

"No, no, clearly targeted. Attempted murder, at the moment, that is. The victim was shot by a marksman some way off. A sniper. And it does look like there's a political angle. The victim is not just anybody."

"A good point, sir, everybody is somebody. No-one is just anybody."

"You know what I mean. We need to focus here, Angus. This is going to be a difficult one. I got a call ten minutes ago from ACC Harkness, reporting the incident to me. She had it from the CC himself, and he, the CC that is, was informed by one of the high-ups at the Met."

"Isn't that unusual? Don't people normally call 999 and the message comes to a lowly operator in Glasgow, and up to us?"

"Exactly, Blue, that's exactly how it should be. But not this time. This time the people at the scene phoned the Met and asked them to come and investigate. But as you know, and were no doubt about to tell me, they can't do that. Naturally, of course, it's not their patch. That's why our friends at the Met followed the normal protocol and passed the matter on to Police Scotland. Well, not exactly the normal protocol, as someone high up at the Met went directly to the CC"

"How did he react?" The previous Chief Constable, brought in from London's Metropolitan Police, had left not long since under a cloud. His style hadn't worked in Scotland. The new CC was a local man.

"I wouldn't care to speculate, Angus. Coffee?" The chief did not await Blue's response, swinging round in his top-of-the-range executive chair to collect two small cups from the base of the machine. The name reminded Blue of an Italian footballer.

"Thank you, sir." Blue fetched himself a sachet of brown sugar and a small teaspoon from the tray on the windowsill. "So, when did this incident take place?"

"This morning, about seven o'clock. In front of several witnesses, I'm told."

"And it took four hours for the message to get to us?"

"Quite so. It seems no-one was in a hurry to bring us into it."

"Have you any idea why that might be, sir?"

"Probably because the victim was a cabinet minister, albeit a junior one. Lord Steppingham. Minister of State at the Defence Ministry."

"Wasn't he the one who said we should bomb the migrant boats in the Mediterranean, to stop them getting to Europe? 'Show them where they belong!' I think those were his words."

"Ah. Yes, that would be him."

"What was he doing on Jura?"

"He owns an estate."

"Don't they all. Do we know what happened?"

"It seems he was walking from the house on the estate – Dunrighinn it's called – to a helicopter, which had come to take him off, when a gunman, ensconced somewhere up on the moor overlooking the place, started shooting. Thankfully, he was only wounded, though we don't know how badly yet. Seems no-one else was hurt. Efforts were made to catch the gunman but he couldn't be found. That's all I know."

"And you want me to take it on?"

"You know the score, Angus. You get the ones that require a bit up here." Campbell tapped his right temple with one finger.

Blue was perfectly aware of the score. Anything that looked weird, complicated or, especially, difficult, went to him. He didn't mind that too much. It made life interesting. So when a drug-crazed ned bludgeoned his girlfriend to death with a chair leg in Lochgilphead, Inspector Carroll was despatched to the scene, and got the credit for the arrest. Ditto with the drunken forester who decapitated a colleague with a chain saw, then proceeded, following correct forestry practice, to trim the arms and legs off the corpse, slicing off one of his own kneecaps in the process.

"Do the local police there know about this?" He remembered the team he'd worked with on an earlier case on Islay. Good cops all of them.

"No, not yet. So we need to move fast or we're not going to look good. This is going to be high-profile, Angus, so we need to solve it. And be seen to be doing so. And being highly professional about it. ACC Harkness hinted that the Met could be called in anyway, if it turns out to be a political or terrorist matter."

"As opposed to an everyday attempted murder. Can they do that?"

"Oh yes, if 'national security' is deemed to be involved, London can overrule the usual protocols and put in whoever they like. Which usually means the Met. If they're itching to do that, we'll have to be very careful."

"Well, I'd better get over there then."

"Good!" Campbell looked relieved. "Now, we can get you over there in the launch in no time. I'll get a car to take you home to get your overnight stuff and then drop you at the harbour."

"OK. What about Scene-of-Crime?"

"Take a couple with you to get things moving. The others can go with the van to Kennacraig for the ferry."

"I'll take Steve Belford and Jill Henderson, if that's OK. And as there's been shooting, I'm afraid we'll have to take Dalvey too." Ex-Sergeant Kevin Dalvey had been a SOC team-leader, but a series of incidents arising from his drinking and bad temper had resulted in his being demoted, and confined now to ballistics work, for which he had considerable expertise.

"I suppose so. He's been warned to be on his best behaviour. And claims he's off the booze. Keep an eye on him, Angus. We don't want him causing an incident. Again."

"And I'd like Sergeant McCader on this with me too."

"Yes, I rather expected you would. I'll ask the local force to be put at your disposal too – I think you know them – and if you need more people, let me know. But that could be tricky with this Royal Progress coming up. No doubt every man, woman, horse and dog are going to be deployed, even if there's no-one there to watch it."

As part of its 'Bringing the Nation Together' programme, the UK Government had decided that the monarch and other members of the royal family should make a 'Royal Progress' through Scotland, Wales and Northern Ireland. The plan was that the royal party should pass along selected routes, and appear in most parts of the country, showing the citizens how valued they were as part of the UK. 'The monarchy,' the prime minister had announced on TV, 'is a unique and age-old symbol of British identity.' Demonstrations against this unique and historic symbol were to be banned during the course of the event, in the interests of national security. Political parties opposed to the monarchy were warned that any activity by them relating in any way to the Progress would be dealt with severely under terrorism laws.

"I think I'm going to be well out of it then, sir, if I'm not needed to hold back the hysterical crowds of royal devotees."

"Quite. There's a further complication. You'll probably have to deal with people from the Political Protection Unit, from London – they may even have been there when it happened – so be diplomatic. And if you feel that this needs someone more senior to intervene at any point, get in touch with me right away."

"Will do, chief."

"And keep me informed as often as you can. I suspect the CC will want to be fully informed as this develops. He's also keen that Police Scotland demonstrates both its skill and its professionalism."

Blue got up to go.

"One other thing, Angus."

"Yes, chief?"

"If you do have time to get over to the distillery on Jura, and you can, get me a couple of bottles of the 21-year-old. There are two expressions, one's called *Time*, and the other *Tide*. Yes, I know, a bit pretentious. But if you can get me one of each, I'd be very grateful."

2

An hour later, Blue was on the police launch, leaving the shelter of Kerrera, and heading on south west, with the grey mass of Mull further away on the right. The sky was grey, there was a chilly breeze and the water was choppy. Most of the passengers preferred the relative comfort of the cabin, but Blue liked to sit out in the open air at the back of the boat. He had the right clothes for it, tending always to dress for the outdoors. The journey would take over two hours, but there was no point speculating about the case until he was at the scene. Arrive with an open mind. And there was plenty to see on the way.

They hugged the coast, continuing south-west, and passed on their left the rocky summit of Seil Island, with the two green humps of Insh Island on the right. Then south past Easdale, where Blue remembered the huge cavities left by the once-booming slate industry. Now on the left came Luing, another slate island, and then a seascape of rocky islets and skerries as they passed between Luing and Lunga, and then rounded the faded green-brown bulk of Scarba into the Corryvreckan Strait.

To reach Jura they had to cross the whirlpool itself, not the comic-book giant spiral of moving water sucking ships to its centre before swallowing them whole, but rather a wide stretch of strangely choppy water masking the complex and powerful currents which could draw a boat where it had no wish to go. Crossing the Corryvreckan was an oddly unnerving experience, as if you sensed the hunger that lurked beneath.

It was at this point that the bulky form of PC Dalvey emerged, white-faced and groaning, from the cabin, and made for the side of the boat, where he leaned over and vomited into the sea. Eventually he let his overweight body slump down on the bench beside Blue, wiping his mouth and moustache with a handkerchief.

"Fucking boats! I bloody hate them!"

"Don't worry, Kevin, we'll soon be there," said Blue.

"I bloody hope so. Fucking islands! Er, sorry, boss."

Sergeant McCader came out next, in his usual jeans and black leather jacket. A small man who could vanish in a crowd of three. "Hi, Kevin," he remarked cheerily, "You only got half way through your Mars bar. Do you want the rest?"

Dalvey turned again to empty his stomach into the waves.

"I guess that's a no." McCader turned to Blue. "So this is the whirlpool, sir. I didn't imagine it like this at all. But you do get a real sense that if you fell in you wouldn't get out again."

Blue pointed to the land that lay ahead of them, steep rocks around the coast and the tough grasses on the hills almost yellow. "That's the top end of Jura coming up now."

"I thought so. I was hoping to see George Orwell's house."

As they came round the snub end of the island, keeping it to their right, they could see a rectangular oasis of lush green between two rocky outcrops, and at its top edge a white house, two storeys in the middle, with the gable end of a single-storey room abutting on each side. Like a farmhouse without a farm.

Blue pointed. "That's it. Barnhill. Orwell went there off and on between 1946 and 1950." He passed his binoculars to McCader.

"Can't have been easy to get to. I suppose he must have come in by boat, with everything he needed."

"People overlook the extent to which canning transformed everyday lives. Corned beef and tinned peaches, any time of the year!"

Dalvey gazed with them at the house. "Is that where we're going, chief?"

"No," said Blue, "We've a way yet, about half way down this side of the island." Dalvey groaned again.

"The place looks pretty barren," remarked McCader.

"It wasn't always. The Clearances made it what it is now. Most of the island is deer-hunting estates. Where the rich and powerful can kill for fun."

"Makes you fucking sick," commented Dalvey.

"My people lived here," said Blue. "Further south, mainly. My grandmother's family, they were called McIsaac, they were the millers in Craighouse. The mill's still there today."

"So this is a bit of a home-coming for you," said McCader.

"I suppose so. There are still one or two Blues there, I think, cousins of my grandfather. My great-grandfather left in the 1870s for Greenock, then moved to Glasgow. There was plenty of work there then. He became a stonemason, helped build the Central Station."

"Do you think they missed the island life?"

"They made the best of what they had. But they never forgot their origins."

The sun had broken through the thin cloud, and the others emerged from the cabin to stare at the rocky shore as it slid past. Steve Belford, SOC team-leader, tall and gangly, his curly brown hair and glasses making him look like an American academic. And Jill Henderson, shorter and even slimmer, her hair cut short, pixie-meets-Cleopatra, a glossy shade of dark blue. Her steely gaze, which deterred even the most confident would-be Romeo in Police HQ, fixed on the landscape.

Blue took the opportunity to address them: "OK, everybody, listen carefully. There will be people at the crime site who will be watching us very carefully, maybe looking for any signs of carelessness or ignorance. So we've got to be on our best behaviour, and totally professional. Whatever you find, report it to me."

"Where are we staying?" asked Steve.

"I haven't a clue, Steve," said Blue, "That's been left to the local police to organise. But there's not much accommodation on Jura, so we may well have to stay on Islay and come over to Jura every day."

"Not another fucking boat!" groaned Dalvey.

"Mr Dalvey," warned Blue. "Be very careful what you say. You may not be among friends."

The boat turned into a small bay. On its left side, the land sloped steeply down to the water. Towards the right however, there was an area of relatively flat land, a half-moon clinging to the foot of the hills. At the rear of this area a house was almost tucked under the steep hillside: stone-built, two storeys, and Velux windows in the roof. At the centre of the ground floor was the main entrance, with an open porch jutting out, supported by stone columns. On either side of the door were four tall windows. The upper floor was similar except that the windows were not so tall, and there was one over the entrance. The roof had a steep pitch, to accommodate the attic rooms. To the right of the house was a courtyard surrounded by smaller buildings; to its left an open area used as a car park. Two black Range Rovers were parked there.

Rough grass, cut short, covered the space between the front of the house and the shore. From the front door a gravel path crossed the grass to a helicopter landing pad. On the pad sat a small helicopter. Further to the right, nearly at the western edge of the bay, a jetty stood out by the blackness of its water-lapped stone. That was where they must disembark.

An old man in overalls and wellies was waiting on the jetty. He took the line thrown to him and expertly tied it to a small black-painted iron bollard. Then he took the various bags passed to him and laid them on the jetty, and finally assisted each of the passengers getting off the boat. The choppy water caused the boat to rise and fall unpredictably; for the passengers it was a question of taking a step into space at the right moment. The old man was silent throughout this operation. When it was over he untied the rope and cast it casually back onto the deck of the launch, and then signalled to the launch that it should depart.

Blue was rather puzzled by this. He'd expected the police launch to wait, in case anything or anybody, needed to be taken back. The launch's captain looked at him for instructions, then his other crewman, who was picking up the mooring rope, shouted across: "What'll we do, sir? We dinna seem very welcome!"

"You may as well go!" Blue shouted back. "We're all staying here, at least till tomorrow, and we'll be coming back on the ferry. Thanks for the ride."

The captain waved, and the launch swung its nose away from the jetty and set off back towards Oban.

They made their way off the jetty, clutching their overnight and equipment bags and stopped when they reached the path leading to the house. Without a word, the old man made off towards the outbuildings. Then they noticed two figures striding purposefully down the path. One was tall and slim, with dark hair lightly gelled back and a moustache of which Clark Gable would have been proud. He was wearing a brown Barbour jacket. The other was shorter and stockier, in a shapeless parka, with a shaven head and an ugly expression.

As they came up to the Oban officers, the taller man moved into the lead. Blue stepped forward to greet him. The tall man smiled thinly and extended a hand.

"Good afternoon. Philip Ffox-Kaye, from the Met. Chief Inspector. Glad you're here to assist us."

Blue shook hands with him. Ffox-Kaye's handshake was firm and reassuring, albeit a little overstayed.

"Hi. Angus Blue. Inspector. Police Scotland. I hope you're here to assist *us*, Mr Kaye." He saw the other stiffen slightly. The polite smile waned and vanished.

"Ffox-Kaye, please. Did you say Blue?"

Blue did not answer. He knew that Ffox-Kaye had heard him perfectly well.

"Your name is not unfamiliar to us at Special Branch," said Ffox-Kaye icily. "Anyway, as the senior officer here, I believe I'm in charge, Inspector. Shall we get on with this?" He began to turn away, but Blue did not move. His team remained standing motionless behind him. It was clear to them too that they were not welcome.

"I'm sorry, Mr Ffox-Kaye, but you are mistaken, and I think you know it. As a visiting officer from another force, who may have an interest in this case, you will be treated with civility and respect, and we will do our best to help you with your own concerns. But you have no authority here. This is Scotland, and Police Scotland is the police force here. Dealing with crime here is our responsibility, not yours." Blue was for the first time grateful for the *Who are we?* training courses which all officers, Inspector and above, were required to attend soon after the unification of Scotland's police forces. Role-play on meeting officers of other forces as well as journalists had been a central part of the course. Thank goodness Blue's role-play partner had been an awkward old bugger from Edinburgh with a well-used face and a puzzling name.

Ffox-Kaye paused and turned his cold gaze back on Blue.

Blue was not daunted. "I've been sent here to investigate a case of attempted murder. Perhaps you could explain to me how you come to be here?"

"I am an officer of the UK Political Protection Unit. I am here in that capacity to protect the body and the interests of a UK Cabinet Minister, and by extension, the British Government."

He stared at Blue. Blue stared back. "Is that it?" he said.

Ffox-Kaye's face twitched. His moustache looked as if it were glued on. Blue resisted the urge to give it a tug.

"All right, Blue. I acknowledge that, as the local police officer" – he sounded the words as if he was really saying 'country bumpkin' – "tasked with investigating this incident, you have a right to do so. But I do have a role here, whether you like it or not, as a member of a UK-wide national unit. I am entitled, as an officer of the PPU, to observe your investigation, and to be given all information pertinent to the case. I will of course offer you any information which I deem to be relevant, provided that it does not conflict with issues of national security. I am empowered to deny officers of provincial police forces such as yours access to any information, persons or locations, if that access may, in my judgement, conflict with the interests of national security."

It was clearly a well-practised and oft-repeated speech, thought Blue. Ffox-Kaye must have attended a *Who are we?* course of his own.

"I am also required to liaise with my colleagues in the Anti-Terrorist Unit, and with the Security Service. And if I judge that the case is terrorist- or security-related, I can request that it is taken out of your hands and passed to the appropriate UK national agency. Don't you think that an attack on a cabinet minister is pretty close to that point already?"

"Thank you, Mr Ffox-Kaye, that's a very succinct summary, if I may say so. Being merely a provincial policeman, I'm not an expert in these matters, and will have to confirm what you say at some point with my superiors. But I don't see any reason why you should make it up, so for the time being I'll accept it. And your kind offer to help."

Blue looked over Ffox-Kaye's shoulder to the other man, who was scowling at him from behind the Special Branch man. "I don't think we've met, either. Are you a colleague of Mr Ffox-Kaye's?"

The man moved to Ffox-Kaye's side, almost jostling him off the path onto the grass. He did not offer Blue his hand. "Matt Plaistow. Inspector. PPU. Before that, the Met. Serious Crimes Squad."

Blue nodded to Plaistow. "I'm glad to meet you, Mr Plaistow. I can see we're going to have lots of fun together, gentlemen. But first, is there somewhere we can put our bags? I'd like to get the forensics under way as soon as possible."

"You can dump them in one of them outbuildings," said Plaistow. He turned in the direction of the courtyard and shouted, "Hey, Jock, get your lazy ass over here! Now!"

The old man reappeared round the corner of one of the buildings and looked expressionlessly at Plaistow.

"Show these people to the Kit Store!" shouted Plaistow, jerking his head in the direction of Blue and his team. "You can leave the stuff there," he said to Blue, then turned on his heel and walked off. Ffox-Kaye studied Blue for a moment, a faint smile on his thin lips. Then he too turned away.

"Charming pair," said Sergeant McCader.

"Wankers!" said Dalvey.

"Language, Kevin," said Blue.

They walked across the dry grass to where the old man was waiting for them. He motioned them to follow him and went back into the courtyard. It was paved, with a range of single-storey conjoined buildings on three sides, the fourth side being formed by the gable end of the big house. The courtyard buildings began some two or three metres from the house, so that vehicles could get access at both the front and the back.

The old man led them to a small wooden door in the right hand range and opened it with a key. He went in and beckoned the others to follow. It was indeed a store room, with two rows of wooden lockers at one end and a row of coat hooks along the other end, waxed jackets and long waterproof coats hanging from them. There were windows in the middle of the other two walls. One looked onto the courtyard, the other onto the grass, and the concrete pad where the helicopter sat. There was no sign of Ffox-Kaye or Plaistow.

"You can put your things here. This room's no used very much. Only when there are shooting parties. The door at the other end, that's a toilet ye can use."

"Thank you," said Blue. "Pleased to meet you, I'm Angus Blue." He offered the man his hand.

The old man studied the hand, as if it were a specimen of some strange creature, perhaps turned up unexpectedly whilst digging for peats. Then he grasped it firmly. "Tam McGowan. Just ca me Tam."

Blue introduced his team.

"You'll be from Oban, then?" asked Tam.

"That's right. Do you know it?"

"Ach, I used to go there quite often, when the wife was still alive. We'd go just for the weekend, stay at that wee pub by the harbour, it has a couple a rooms. Very cosy too. My wife liked the shops, and on the Saturday night we always went to the pictures. That was a rare treat. Sunday morn we'd go to the Free Kirk up the hill – there was always a powerful sermon there." He suddenly peered out the window into the courtyard, then seemed to relax again. "I've to be careful with ye. Yon London polis have said I'm no to talk with ye, or I'll be in real trouble. So if ye meet me outside, dinna say anything, they're aye watching. I'd better no be too long here either. I'll give ye the key to this room, so's ye can leave anything ye want here."

He removed the key from a large bunch. There was green tape round the shaft. Blue noticed that some of the other keys had other colours.

"Tam, did you see what happened here this morning?" asked Blue, as the others were sorting out the scene-of-crime kit.

"I'm no supposed to say anything to ye, Mr Blue."

"Why not?"

"They said it wis a security matter. Whatever happens here is secret. They said they'd tell ye all that ye're needing to know."

"Did you see anything this morning, Tam?"

"Well," – Tam glanced again at the window – "no really. I didna get here till after. I'm no supposed to start till eight, so I was still at home when it happened."

"Where's that?"

"I've a wee cottage two miles or so up the road, the other side of the hill. Mind you, I heard the helicopter comin in, as I was having my breakfast."

"Did you hear the shots?"

"I couldna rightly say, Mr Blue, yon machine's awfa noisy. It kinda spluttered a few times after it landed. Maybe that was the shots."

"Could you say how many splutters you heard?"

"I don't know, two or three, maybe more. I wasna really listenin that much."

"Did you come right over then?"

"Naw, the helicopter coming in was fairly normal. That's how his Lordship usually came in and out. Didna want to mix wi poor folk like you an me on the ferry, eh? I got here at eight. I come in round the back, so I didna see what was going on at the front. As soon as I was out the car, Mr Seymour – he's the estate manager – told me to go up to the hide at the wee lochan and check the roof was no leaking. I didna get back till just before you arrived. So I canna be much help to ye."

"Not at all, every little bit helps to build up the big picture. By the way, where do come from originally, Tam? You don't sound like a Diurach." Blue guessed that native Jura folk probably sounded like the Islay natives he'd met.

"Naw, ye're right. I'm from Ayrshire myself, no far fae Girvan. His Lordship disna believe in hiring local folk. He says ye canna trust them, they're aye gossiping. I don't know, they dinna seem very talkative to me."

Tam glanced out of the window again. "Ach, there's Mr Seymour now. I'd better go. I'll see ye later." He slipped out the door and was off.

The two SOCOs and Dalvey were struggling into their white overalls.

"Right, everybody," Blue announced, "this could be difficult. I don't know what agenda these two guys have, but 'helpful' doesn't seem to be part of it. They may even be looking for excuses to get us off the case. So do everything by the book, and if there are any problems, tell me right away. Steve, the first thing is obviously to find out where the shooting happened so that you and Jill can set up a perimeter and start examining the ground. Kevin, we need you to see if you can find any bullets. Tam mentioned two or three shots, and I'm assuming they're not all stuck in his Lordship's body. Sergeant McCader and I'll see if we can get an account of what happened, hopefully find some witnesses."

"If they haven't been got at by Laurel and Hardy out there," said Jill Henderson. "Those two are a real pair of smartarses."

"Try to avoid communicating with them," advised Blue. "If they ask anything, or tell you to do anything, refer them to me."

4

Back outside again, they could see that an area two thirds of the way down the path from the house to the helipad had been marked out with white tape tied to stakes. It included about ten yards of the path and two or three on either side. Ffox-Kaye was standing by it. He smiled broadly, showing his perfect teeth. How many thousand plastic micro-beads, so destructive to the marine environment, had made those teeth so white, thought Blue.

"Angus, glad you got sorted out there. As you can see, we got the site marked out for your SOCOs. Anything you need to know, just ask me." Rank hadn't worked, so now it was charm.

"Thanks Mr Ffox-Kaye…"

"Please, call me Phil."

"Thanks, er, Phil. Before we start, could you just give us a brief rundown on what happened?" The SOCOs paused by the tape, and McCader stopped next to Blue.

"No problem. I wasn't here, you understand. Matt got on to us as soon as it happened, and I was on the next plane to Glasgow, then on to Islay. I got here about eleven. Anyway, what seems to have happened is this. Jason Van Kaarsten had come over for the weekend to discuss with Giles – that's Lord Steppingham – some business stuff. This morning they were due to take the chopper to Glasgow airport, then head on down to London City. The chopper was due in at seven, that's the usual time. It landed without incident. Matt, who was here with Giles's security detail, went to the chopper and checked the IDs and manifest. Then he went back to the house to OK Giles and Jason to go. They were just about here when the shooting started. There were only two or three shots, fired from up on the moor somewhere. One of them hit Giles, knocked him down, so I think the shooter thought he was dead. Then he shot the rear prop on the helicopter. That was a neat trick, meant we couldn't get the chopper up to spot his getaway. Clearly a professional job. That was it. All over in a few seconds."

"What happened next?"

"Well, no-one knew that was it, so Matt and the other two PPU chaps returned fire, though they couldn't pin down the shooter's position. Then they got Giles into the house. Thankfully he was still alive. Matt called us right away, and naturally we passed the information on to your CC."

"Did anyone examine the site at that point?"

"No, not at all. Matt knows his stuff. He got the area taped off as soon as it became clear the gunman had made off."

"Good. OK, Steve and Jill, can you get started here? Kevin, can you hang on for a minute?" Blue lifted the tape so that the two SOCOS could enter the cordoned off area.

"So what happened to Lord Steppingham – did he get medical aid?"

"There was a nurse in the house – Giles has a heart condition, so prefers to have medical skill to hand, just in case – and she treated him immediately. The wound was in his shoulder, broke a couple of bones. She treated it and bandaged him up. Then they got him out of there as fast as they could."

"Why was that?"

"Isn't it obvious? If he was the target, which looks pretty likely, the gunman may have realised he'd failed to get him, and come back for another shot. Giles's safety took precedence over everything else. He's a cabinet minister, and that makes his wellbeing a national security issue. When they phoned me, I told them to get Giles out ASAP. The chopper couldn't be used, so they got him into a car and onto the first ferry over to Islay. We had a plane collect him there and fly him to hospital in London. He's still there now. His condition's stable at the moment. Bullet did more damage than we'd thought. Seems to have been diverted by his shoulder-blade down into his chest."

"And Mr van Kaarsten?"

"He wanted to go with Giles. He's a close friend – from Cambridge days – so I thought it would be good for Giles's morale to have him there."

"That's very helpful, thank you. We'll need to speak to witnesses. And the local police from Islay will be here to offer me their assistance." Blue gestured to McCader, "This is Sergeant McCader." Ffox-Kaye nodded vaguely in McCader's direction. Evidently sergeants didn't qualify for a handshake. "And Mr Dalvey here is our ballistics expert. He'll have a look at the ground, see if he can recover any bullets. By the way, what happened to the bullet that hit Lord Steppingham? Did the nurse extract it, or did it pass right through?"

"I'm not sure about that. We'll have to ask Matt about it. I've asked him to give you his account of events once he's free."

"That would be useful. And I appreciate him getting the site taped off."

Blue glanced over to where Belford and Henderson were already on their knees in the taped-off area. Then he asked Dalvey to see if he could locate the bullet that had damaged the helicopter. He didn't want Dalvey getting into a spat with the SOCOs. Dalvey scowled, and set off towards the landing pad.

"Who took charge here after the shootings?" Blue asked Ffox-Kaye.

"Matt. He's a natural leader, you know, good man. He sent Sergeant Steele and PC Corning – the other two PPU men – off with Giles, to make sure he got to London safely. It was lucky we had someone here who could make the decisions."

"Yes, I see what you mean. What about witnesses?"

"Matt made a full list, and talked to each of them to see how much they'd seen. I'm afraid there aren't many and they didn't see anything, apart from Giles and Jason getting shot at and Giles being hit. No-one got any sort of sighting of the shooter. If you talk to Matt, he'll point you to them. We haven't taken any statements, didn't want to step on any toes, of course." The corner of his mouth twitched, as if it couldn't make up its mind whether it was going to smile or not.

"Of course. I'd like to speak to Mr Plaistow now, then, if that's possible."

"I think he's up at the house at the moment. Just one little point about that. I'm afraid we can't let you or your people into the house itself. That's a national security issue. We're still going through the place to make sure Giles didn't leave any confidential documents around. That could include notes scribbled on bits of paper, so you'll appreciate it could take some time. Once that's done, you're free to examine the place if you need to. By the way, there's a kitchen in one of the courtyard rooms you can use. I've cleared it with Jack Seymour – he's the estate manager."

5

As they approached the house, Blue noticed there was a plain-clothes officer on guard at the front door. The door opened, and Matt Plaistow came out, shuffling himself into his parka.

"Matt!" called Ffox-Kaye. "Mr Blue wants to know about witnesses."

As Plaistow came up to them, Ffox-Kaye nodded to him. "Well, I'll leave you to it." Then he went up the short flight of stairs to the entrance to the house, pausing to have a word with the guard at the door, and disappeared inside.

Plaistow gave Blue an I'm-a-hard-man look and said nothing.

"I'm looking for witnesses to this morning's events. I take it you were one?"

"Yeah, that's right," growled Plaistow.

"Perhaps you could tell me what you saw yourself."

"Doesn't your sergeant have something to do?"

"Yes. Right now it's listening to you," said Blue. "Is there a problem with that?"

Plaistow shrugged. "Whatever. Here's what happened. The chopper was due in at seven to pick up his Lordship and Mr van Kaarsten. There's a security protocol to this. We all wait in the house till it lands, then either me or one of the other PPU guys goes out to check out their IDs, the schedule, that stuff. Once the all-clear's given, the passengers can leave the house and go to the chopper. This morning I waved the helicopter down, then went over and checked it out. Everything was OK, so I went back to the house to bring them out."

"Where were they going this morning?"

"Glasgow Airport. Anyway, everything was OK, so I led them down the path towards the chopper. Sergeant Steele and PC Corning brought up the rear. So his Lordship and Mr van K were in the middle."

"What were they doing at this point?"

"What do you think? Talking to each other. Anyway, we'd almost got to the chopper, when suddenly there's shooting."

"How many shots, would you say?"

Plaistow shrugged again. "Two, maybe three. Fired in very rapid succession. The first, or maybe the second, took out his Lordship.

21

I'm armed, of course, so I took a few shots at where I thought the shooter was. But I couldn't see anything, and his Lordship needed help – he'd gone down as soon as he was hit, we thought at first he was dead. Anyway, Sergeant Steele and PC Corning got him into the house and called the nurse to look at him."

"What had Mr van Kaarsten done when the shots came?"

"Dropped to the floor straight away. Army training. Low profile. He was OK."

"What happened next?"

"I got Mr van K into the house and found his Lordship was alive. Then I came out again to see if I could spot the shooter. I thought if I could get up in the chopper I'd be able to see him on the ground, as he tried to get away. So I ran over there, but the pilot says one of the shots damaged the tail rotor, so he couldn't control the chopper in flight. I urged him to have a go, but he refused. Bloody coward. D'you know, when I got there he was still cowering behind the seats. Mark of a professional, I'd say."

"You mean the pilot refusing to fly?"

"No, of course bloody not. I mean the shooter, thinking ahead, taking out the chopper so we couldn't see him escape."

"OK, so what did you do then?"

"Went back to the house. Nurse was dealing with his Lordship by this time. He was wounded, in the shoulder, it didn't look good at all, but she said it weren't life-threatening. She bandaged it up as best she could, but said he needed to be in hospital soon as possible. Then I phoned Phil, the DCI that is, to report. He ordered us to get his Lordship out of there pronto. We couldn't use the chopper, so we decided to take him by car to the airport on Islay. Phil would organise a plane to pick him up and get him to London, then an ambulance to the hospital. I sent Steele and Corning with him. And Mr van K insisted on going too."

"Why didn't they send another helicopter over to collect him?"

"We didn't know whether the shooter was still around, or whether there was more than one of 'em. So we thought it less risky just to get him out of there right away. It was a risk taking him in the cars too – they could have ambushed them – but we had to get him somewhere safe. In fact, there was no trouble on the road, we got him safely over to Islay, and onto the plane."

"So Sergeant Steele and PC Corning were witnesses too?"

"Yes, obviously. But they've gone back to London with his Lordship. I'm sure Phil can get statements from them for you. If you ask nicely." Plaistow smirked.

"So who else saw the attack? What about the pilot?"

"That idiot? He didn't see much, he was hiding. Dived to the floor, he said, inside the chopper, when the first shot came. Even then he was in a bit of a state afterwards, so the nurse gave him a sedative. Jack Seymour took him over to his place to calm down. I'm sure he's still there now."

"Mr Seymour. The estate manager?"

"Yes."

"Did he see anything?"

"No, he'd spoken to his Lordship earlier, and was in his office – it's one of the rooms on the courtyard. At the back."

"Where does he live?"

"About four miles up the road. One of the smaller lodges. Stag Lodge, it's called."

"OK, thanks. Did anyone else see anything from the house? From the windows, for instance."

"Nah. The nurse was having breakfast in the kitchen – that's at the back of the house. So was Mr James."

"Who's he?"

"His Lordship's secretary. Him and the nurse – Rogers was 'er name – were going to get the ferry later this morning, then the scheduled flight from Islay to Glasgow, and on down south. They left at about ten, so I guess they'll be well on the way by now."

"Where are they going?"

"Where do you think? His Lordship's place. They work for him."

"Where's that?"

"Bedfordshire. Near Luton. Steppingham House."

"Don't tell me. In Steppingham."

Plaistow looked suspicious. "How did you know that, eh?"

"Just a guess. Who else was in the house?"

"There's a cook, she was in the kitchen too, so she didn't see anything. And a housekeeper, but she was making up the beds. Then there's that old guy, Jock, or whatever his name is, the handyman, but he hadn't arrived yet."

"So you and the pilot are the only people still here who saw anything?"

"Yeah, that's right." Plaistow smirked again.

"Well, thanks very much, Mr Plaistow. By the way, who laid out the tape here?"

"I told Sergeant Steele and PC Corning to do that. Before they set off with his Lordship. I've been in the Met for twenty years, so I know the ropes. Real police work there."

Blue ignored the jibe. "Thanks, that's very helpful. What are your plans now?"

"I'll need to report all this to the PPU in London."

"I don't suppose they'll be too pleased."

Plaistow shrugged. "Not much we could have done about it, was there? And at least his Lordship ain't dead. Anyway, they told me to get down to London pronto to report. I was going to get off earlier, but Phil asked me to wait till you got here, so that I could give you an eye-witness account. It would be a bit unfortunate if all your witnesses had cleared off!" He laughed loudly, with an odd braying sound.

"I'm grateful to you for that. By the way, Mr van Kaarsten, who does he work for?"

"Company called AvK Matériel. Well-known."

"What was Mr van Kaarsten's role in the company?"

"Some sort of sales director I think."

"Is he married?"

"Nah. Divorced. Aren't we all? Come on, you're not suggesting he was the bloody target. It's pretty obvious to me, and to Phil for that matter, that Lord Steppingham was the target."

"We can't rule anything out at this point. You know that."

"Yeah, yeah, whatever."

"And you think the first or second shot hit Lord Steppingham?"

"That's what I said, ain't it? You think I didn't see?"

"You may have been leading them to the helicopter, walking ahead of them."

"I'm telling you I saw it!"

"It's also possible that both men were targeted. What was Mr van Kaarsten doing here?"

"Having a business discussion with his Lordship."

"What do AvK Matériel do?"

"Bloody hell, you jocks do live in the Styx, don't you? Arms, mate, and lots of 'em. They supply the British Army, the Saudis, and plenty others too."

"So this was about defence procurement, then?"

"I'm not at liberty to tell you that. That information is classified. And it ain't relevant to what happened today, take that from me."

"Did you come over with Lord Steppingham?"

"Nah. I came over earlier, on Saturday morning, to check out the house. His Lordship and Mr van K came over on the chopper that afternoon, they arrived about four."

"So they were here from Saturday afternoon until this morning?"

"That's right."

"What did they do? Apart from talking?"

Plaistow paused. "Yeah, they did a lot of talking. And eating. And some drinking too, I suppose. I don't know, I wasn't with them. My job's security, not snooping. Me and the other guys were keeping an eye on the house."

"Did you ever see anyone hanging around, or looking interested in the place?"

"Nah. I'm pretty sure of that. Look mate, we're professionals, we know exactly what we're doing. And the shooting, that was professional too, take it from me. And we'll get the fucker who did this, believe me." He looked at his watch. "Bloody Hell! I've been yapping to you for ages. I've gotta be off. If that's everything, of course. If you need to talk to me again, just contact PPU."

"Thank you for your help, Mr Plaistow," said Blue. But Plaistow had already turned his back, and was making for the house.

6

"So one of our witnesses didn't see anything, and the rest have cleared off!" said McCader. "That's helpful."

"Hmm. Once we've got transport, we'll have to get over and talk to the pilot. Meanwhile, can you go and see if Kevin's got anything, and I'll check out the SOCOs."

Blue walked down the path until he reached the tape. "How's it going over there?" he called to the two SOCOs, still on their knees. They both got up and came over.

"There's something odd here, boss," said Steve Belford. "No, on the contrary, there's nothing here at all."

"Well, there are certainly plenty fag-ends, rabbit droppings, and footprints on the grass," added Jill Henderson, "but no blood, no bullets, no impact marks from bodies falling."

"It didn't happen on this stretch of the path," said Belford. "No way."

"Unless they hosed it down and blow-dried it!" said Henderson. "And then replaced the fag-ends and bunny shite."

"OK," said Blue. "Do a walk up and down the whole path and see if you see anything. Maybe they taped off the wrong section."

They heard a car revving up, and looking over to the car park, saw one of the black Range Rovers spurting gravel as it headed off onto the drive. That would be Plaistow making his getaway, thought Blue.

He went down to the helicopter, where McCader and Dalvey were talking.

"Got the bullet, boss," said Dalvey, "but it's stuck in the bloody machine. Take a look."

He handed Blue what looked very much like a telescopic gun sight, and pointed up to the small vertical rotor at the rear of the machine. Blue squinted through it, but couldn't see anything that looked like a bullet. He gave the sight back to Dalvey. "I guess you need to get a ladder and retrieve it."

"I didn't bring a ladder."

"Go and ask Tam McGowan for one. I'm sure there's a few around here." Dalvey scowled, and headed for the courtyard.

"I think the cavalry's arrived," said McCader, and pointed towards the southern end of the bay. Blue noticed there was a gateway there, with white-painted steel gates, six feet high, attached to solid brick gateposts. On either side of the gateway, a steel fence of a similar height, topped with tight coils of razor wire stretched away.

Stopped beyond the gate were two police cars and a large white van. A figure got out of the leading car and tried to open the gates, without success.

"It's Inspector Nicolson, sir," said McCader. "Looks like no-one's letting her in."

They could now see a guard inside the gate, talking to the Islay police chief through the gate. Finally he turned and walked unhurriedly up to the house, talking on a radio as he did. The house door opened, and Ffox-Kaye strolled out and waved Blue over. As he approached, Ffox-Kaye pointed towards the gate.

"There are some people claiming to be police at the gate. Who are they?"

"Isn't it obvious?" said Blue.

"Good God!" exclaimed Ffox-Kaye, "Now we've got the local plods at the door too. Next we'll have the peasantry lining up to stare through the bars like monkeys, eh?" He chortled at what he fancied a joke. No-one else was laughing.

"Would you mind opening the gates now?" said Blue, in the calmest voice he could muster, "Those are my colleagues from the Islay police station who are here to assist me, and the van is our mobile scene-of-crime unit. They are both essential to my enquiries."

"I can't let all these people into my site. There's a national security issue."

"You said that only affected the house itself. Why does it affect the grounds too?"

"We can't have them tramping all over everything, and poking their noses everywhere. I'm finding it hard enough to monitor what you and your team are doing. I don't have enough people to watch this lot as well."

Blue could see at the gate someone was waving at him. He recognised Inspector Moira Nicholson, chief of police for Islay and Jura. He waved back, then turned again to Ffox-Kaye.

"Perhaps you'd like to phone my Superintendent, and explain your problem to him. I've really no idea how Police Scotland personnel can be a threat to national security. Here's his name and phone number." He took a card from his inside pocket and held it towards Ffox-Kaye, who contemplated it for what seemed an age.

"All right, I'll let them in," he said, as if referring to animals or inferior beings. "But I'll need a list of names, including yourself and all your people, and I'll want their IDs checked by my people, for national security purposes. And you, Mr Blue, must accept responsibility for them."

"I'm willing to do that, as a normal courtesy. I hope you will reciprocate that courtesy by supplying me with a list of your people here, yourself included, in order to eliminate them from our enquiries."

Ffox-Kaye stared at Blue.

"Mr Ffox-Kaye, I don't have time for a staring contest right now. I have an attempted murder to solve. Please open the gates. You will get your list once they're in."

Ffox-Kaye brushed his arm as if getting rid of a troublesome fly, then spoke into his own radio. "Dragon3, Dragonmaster here, open the gate. Out."

The gates began to open slowly, the wheels at their bases crunching on the gravel. Blue realised they were controlled from the house. The convoy passed through and headed along the drive towards the car park, drawing up alongside the remaining black Range Rover.

Blue took out his notebook and scribbled the names of his team on a page. He extracted it carefully and handed it to Ffox-Kaye. "These are the police personnel who accompanied me. You know my name so you can add that. I'll give you the rest once I know which local officers and SOCOs have just arrived. I'd like, as I said, a list of your people here. I may also have to take shoe prints from them. By the way, your officers seem to have put the incident tapes in the wrong place. So the actual locus of the shootings may have been compromised. Can you explain that?"

"You'd have to ask them. I wasn't here at the time."

"And they're conveniently gone, aren't they?"

"Are you saying it was deliberate?"

"I'm expressing puzzlement at what seems an elementary scene-of-crime error. I'm assuming that PPU personnel are specially selected and highly trained, and wondering how this could have happened."

"We've got it, boss," came a shout from Steve Belford, and Blue turned to see the two SOCOs standing on the path about twenty yards nearer the house than the taped area. Ignoring Ffox-Kaye, he went over to them. Belford was pointing to an area just off the path.

"Looks like it happened here, chief. We've got impact marks over there, and just beyond them there's what might be a blood-spatter. We'll shift the tape right away and get this area cordoned off."

"Good work," said Blue. "You've got the rest of the team to help you now." Two figures were struggling into white overalls by the white van.

A female uniformed officer strode over the grass to him. Tall, short brown hair, hazel eyes, a smile of recognition. Inspector Moira Nicolson. Blue noticed that Ffox-Kaye had vanished, presumably back into the house, which now had two guards at the entrance.

Blue shook hands. "Hi, Moira, how are things? Haven't seen you since the Peat Dead case last year. Everything OK?"

"Yes, we're all surviving. Nothing quite as exciting as that, of course, until today that is. I've been asked to give you support, and at least two officers. Will Arvind and Deirdra do? They're keen to work with you again." PCs Arvind Bhardwaj and Deirdra Craig had assisted Blue in a difficult case the previous year.

"That would be great. Thanks. Have you got much on at the moment?"

"Not really. We caught a couple of guys who'd brought drugs over on the ferry. Red-handed, in the act of handing them over to a local who was planning to sell them to the kids at the school in Bowmore. We knew who he was – news gets round Islay very quickly about anything out of the ordinary. That's the plus side of being on an island. What about yourself?"

"Oh, this and that. I'll tell you over a meal if I get the chance. It's my turn to treat you and Alasdair. Oh, by the way, I'm not sure where we're supposed to be staying. We came over in rather a hurry."

"Don't worry, Angus, I'll get something sorted out. And you can use one of the cars, too, that's why I brought them both."

"That's great, thanks."

Inspector Nicolson was peering past him. "Er, is that Mr Dalvey I'm seeing over there by the helicopter?" Dalvey was at the top of a tall stepladder poking at the helicopter's tail rotor, whilst McCader and Tam McGowan stood by the ladder watching him.

"Yes, I'm afraid it is. But he's been warned to be on good

behaviour. He's only here for the ballistics, and with a bit of luck he'll be off back to Oban tomorrow."

"Good. I wouldn't want another run-in with him. Well, what have you got?"

"I'm not sure. One person wounded by a shooter up on the hill somewhere. All the witnesses bar one have legged it, the wrong locus was taped off, and there's a Special Branch guy who'd probably like us all to clear off. Am I being paranoid if I think there's something fishy about it?"

"Tell me more."

Blue brought Nicolson up-to-date.

"What happened to the shooter?" she asked, when he had finished his account.

"Don't know. We haven't got round to addressing that yet. You know the island. Where do you think he'd go?"

"You're assuming he's not local. Gamekeeper with a grudge, neighbour annoyed about the noisy parties, that sort of thing?"

"That's always possible, of course. And we'll have to check where any locals with shooting skills were this morning. The shooting was good, apparently. Accurate, although not fatal. And taking out the helicopter was an added touch that an amateur would be unlikely to think of. So at the moment I'm inclined to think some sort of professional. But whether it's criminal or political, I don't know. Yet."

"OK, we can check out the locals for you. I'll get Arvind and Deirdra to do that. Do you need to set up an incident room?"

"Yes. But I don't want that to be here. It would be too close to DCI Ffox-Kaye – that's "Ffox" with two F's by the way – and his gang. I'm not sure I trust them."

"Leave it with me, I'll see what I can find."

"Thanks. About the shooter getting away. I'd guess he's either gone to ground somewhere on the island, or more likely, tried to get off it as soon as he could. 'He' being generic human being, by the way. But statistically more likely to be a he. There are simply far more men who're trained to shoot well. Gamekeepers, soldiers, sport-shooters"

"Not forgetting policemen," added Moira.

"Quite. So, what are his options to get off the island?"

"There are only two ways off – take a boat or fly. Flying would be tricky. There's no airstrip here, but a microlight could take off from the road or one of the fields. Or even a beach. However, they're noisy creatures and someone would be sure to notice it. He'd also have to park it somewhere while he did the job. Same goes for a helicopter. So flying's very unlikely."

"What about boats?"

"He could have a motor-boat hidden in a cove somewhere, then yomp across country, do the job, and go back to it. Wait till night-time, then make off. Chug into Oban early in the morning as if he's been out fishing, leave the boat, disappear."

Blue nodded. "That's certainly a possibility. Anything else?"

"He could hire a boat somewhere to bring him to Craighouse and fetch him off again. We can check with the hirers at the places he's likely to do that. The most likely place would be Tayvallich. We can check the Islay and Jura boat-owners too."

"Worth doing, though I suspect, unlikely. That would leave a witness."

"Unless there's a body, lying in a boat somewhere."

"Hmm. Let's not go there for the moment. But anything hired would come in to Craighouse, wouldn't it, and tie up at the pier there?"

"You would think so. Though there are a few little jetties here and there."

"OK, Moira. What if he takes the ferry to Islay? That would enable him to bring a car, and make a quick getaway."

Nicolson considered. "Well, he'd have to get off the hill, then make his way to his car, and get back to the ferry, without anyone noticing. And that's unlikely, given there's only one road, up this side of the island, and folks tend to notice anything unusual, even a strange car, especially when we're not yet at the holiday season."

"Is there CCTV on the ferry?"

"Only at the pier at Port Askaig. But what are we looking for?"

"Probably worth checking all of today's traffic, just to see if anything looks suspicious."

"Rifle propped on the passenger seat?"

"That sort of thing. How far are we from Craighouse?"

"About ten or twelve miles. A fair walk if he left his car there. At least two hours. But that still means he could be on the Jura ferry at half past nine, and could probably just make it to Port Ellen to get the 11 am boat to Kennacraig. And then he's away."

"There's CCTV at Port Ellen too?" asked Blue

"Yes. I see what you're getting at. If we see a car on the 9.30 from Jura which then turns up for the 11.00 at Port Ellen, it could well be our man. There won't be many cars that do that, and we can simply check them all out."

"That sounds good. Vans and lorries too. A small van might be less noticeable than a car."

"Oh, sorry Angus, but that's not all. This is May, so there's also a passenger boat that comes over from Tayvallich in the morning and evening. A small catamaran, pretty fast. He could leave his car in Tayvallich, come over on the cat in the evening, camp out on the moor somewhere, do the job, then take the boat back this morning. There's no CCTV covering that one. But at this time of year – the service only runs from May to September – there won't be that many passengers, so there's a good chance the boatman might remember someone who did the trip."

"And I'd guess coming over to Jura in the evening then leaving in the morning is not the usual trip. He'd be kind of running against the tide, as it were."

"We'll check that out, too. So, looks like we've got plenty to do! We'd better get the troops moving."

"I'll come over and say hello to Arvind and Deirdra."

7

Blue went over with Moira Nicolson to the police cars. He greeted the two extra SOCOs, Andrew McGuire and Dennis Johnstone, as they passed him on their way over to the taped area. McGuire was carrying his camera and tripod, whilst Johnstone had brought a bag of assorted bits and pieces.

Arvind Bhardwaj and Deirdra Craig greeted him with enthusiasm, Bhardwaj smiling, Craig more serious. She was a little taller than him, slim, her brown hair in a ponytail.

"Great to see you again, chief," said Bhardwaj, "we could do with some excitement. I haven't had a chance to really stretch these new cars. Both the old ones were so bashed up after that case last year that they had to be replaced. Dacia Stepways – the budget was limited, but they're great vehicles. Best that Romania's auto industry can produce. Designed for the African savannah, so very tough. And the high wheelbase is useful for rougher ground."

The two cars were identical, white, with the police transfers very carefully applied. Blue asked Craig what she thought of them.

"Aye, chief, right enough, they're very nice."

"Good. Well, here's a trip for you, Arvind. Can you find a place called Stag Lodge – it's up the road a few miles – and see if there's a helicopter pilot there. If there is, and he's not still sedated, can you bring him back here. I'd like to have a chat with him."

"On my way, chief."

"I'll go back to Craighouse, and make some arrangements," said Moira Nicolson. "Can I take Deirdra to give me a hand?"

"Of course."

"I'll give you a ring when I've got the incident room set up."

The police cars left the car park and headed for the gate. This time the gates swung open as if by magic as they approached. So someone was watching their every move. Through the gate, the leading car turned right to head further on up the road, whilst the other turned left to go south to Craighouse.

Blue noticed that Dalvey was off the ladder, which Tam was carrying back towards the courtyard. He went over to where Dalvey and McCader were standing.

"What have we got then, Kevin?"

Dalvey held up a small see-through evidence bag, with a lump of grey metal inside. "Bog-standard 7.62 x 51mm NATO bullet. Very common type, fits loads of sniper rifles. This one's got pretty deformed as it hit the rotor drive, but we can still recover the rifling marks, so should be able to link it with some probability to a particular gun. Have a look." He pulled from his packet a geologist's loupe, a small but very powerful magnifying glass, flicked it open, and offered it to Blue. "Can you see the tiny grooves across the side?"

Blue was surprised by the scale of magnification, and took a while to get his eye, the loupe and the evidence bag close enough to get a sharp image of what now looked like grooves chiselled across the side of the bullet.

"That's good. Thanks, Kevin. Could you go and ask one of the guys at the door of the house if you can have the bullet from Lord Steppingham's shoulder? Mention my name. They won't let you into the house – that's out of bounds apparently – but someone should go in and fetch it. If there's a problem, let me know."

As Dalvey set off for the house, McCader pointed up towards the hillside.

"We need to establish where the shooter was located, sir, see if he left anything, and what routes he took onto and off the moor. Without a whole line of people it's going to be hard work. Pity we couldn't have taken the helicopter up and got a look from the air."

"You're right," said Blue, "One or two people wandering about up there could spend a lot of time and not find anything. But I think I know a man – or rather a woman – who can help. Give me a couple of minutes."

Blue checked his mobile; thankfully there was still a signal. But then he thought, if a cabinet minister lived here, he'd need a signal. All he'd have to do was suggest it, and the phone companies would be falling over themselves to provide it. He selected 'Alison H' and pressed the *Call* icon. After several rings, a voice responded.

"Hi, Angus, good to hear you. Are you just phoning to see if I'm OK. How sweet."

"Er, well, actually"

"So that's how it is. You want something. Well, I'm very busy. I have a paper to write for the Forensic Archaeology conference in Tallinn in September. So it had better be good."

"You've got a camera drone, haven't you? I've seen some of those pictures you put on Twitter."

"Shh! Don't tell Police Scotland about that!"

"Do you want a chance to play with it?"

"Hmm. Beats writing a paper, I must say. Where are you?"

"Jura."

"Now you're talking. Tell me more."

"Attempted murder. Victim shot by a sniper up on the moor. I want to find out where the shooter was situated and how he got to and from the spot. Can your machine help?"

"Absolutely! Even if it didn't, I'd be up for a visit to Jura any time. I'm guessing you want this done by yesterday."

"Yes, soon as possible. Is that OK?"

"No problem. For you, Angus, anything. What's it now? Just after three. Not sure if I can make it in time for the boat today. I'll check the timetable. If not, at least I can pick up the drone and be ready for the first boat tomorrow. I'll call you when I know more. Bye."

She hung up before Blue had a chance to say anything else. He turned back to McCader.

"OK, Enver, we've got a camera drone for tomorrow. Dr Hendrickx is coming over with it." Dr Alison Hendrickx was Police Scotland's forensic archaeologist, with a Europe-wide reputation. She'd helped Blue out before, and almost been killed in the course of doing so.

"That's good. It'll save a lot of time. By the way, sir, it's almost tea-time. Shall I get the kettle on?"

"Good move. See if you can find that room Ffox-Kaye was talking about. In the courtyard. I'll let the SOCOs know, and see how they're getting on."

Three of the white-clad figures were on the ground, and one taking photographs, as Blue approached. Steve Belford came over to the tape.

"Hi, Steve, how's it going? What have we got?"

"Got a definite blood and tissue splatter over there. We've got samples and Andy's taking pictures now. But the site's been messed up a lot, there are footmarks all over it. "

"I guess that was when they were getting the victim away and into the house."

"There's one bit there where I think someone's emptied out a cup of coffee. With milk. It's obscured what might be a bloodstain."

"Any sign of another bullet? There may have been three shots."

"No, nothing. We might have to get the metal detector out and search a wider area."

"Once you've finished here we'll let Mr Dalvey do that. Take a tea-break now. Enver's got the kettle on. One of the rooms off the courtyard."

8

The kitchen off the courtyard featured a pink-Formica-topped table of 1960's vintage and enough plastic chairs to seat the four SOCOs plus Blue and McCader, with another three still stacked in the corner. It was also well-supplied with teabags and instant coffee of an inferior quality, and the fridge contained two litres of milk. There was even a packet of own-brand milk chocolate digestives from a supermarket. Blue wondered if Ffox-Kaye had arranged for these supplies to avoid letting them use the kitchen in the house. The biscuits went down particularly well, as those who'd come on the police launch hadn't eaten since breakfast, and there didn't seem to be a fast food outlet nearby. Blue suspected the nearest food shop would be in Craighouse, twelve miles away.

As the coffee was being passed around, Dalvey arrived. He scowled at the SOCOs, whose respect he'd conspicuously failed to gain as a team-leader, before his demotion the previous year. He fetched himself a chair from the stack and set it as far away from them as he could.

"Hi, Kevin," said Blue. "Did you get the bullet?"

"Yes, boss, eventually. Those bloody morons at the door enjoy the power trip all right. I had to show them my ID, and then sign for the thing. Bloody crapheads."

"Have you had a look at it yet?" asked Blue.

Dalvey rummaged in the pocket of his waterproof jacket and produced the small evidence bag. Now he could pontificate.

"Yeah. It's a 7.62-51 NATO round right enough, same as the other one. But of course I won't be able to say it's from the same gun till I've seen it under the microscope."

"Do you think there were possibly two shooters then?"

Dalvey shrugged. "The bullet'll tell us that."

"The small number of shots and the fact there were was only one hit would tend to point to one," said Blue, "but we'd need to have that confirmed. Anything else you can tell us right now, Kevin?"

Dalvey relished the role of ballistics expert, and studied the bullet theatrically. "Hmm. Yes, it's very deformed. That's unusual for a single wounding shot. But it may have hit the shoulder blade then glanced off onto another bone. I'd need to know the exact nature of the victim's injuries."

"So there might be another bullet out there somewhere, depending on the number of shots."

"I'll get the metal detector onto it next," said Dalvey. "Judging by the angle of the shot downwards from the hill – I'd say about ten degrees – and the limited spread of the casualties, the search area could be quite limited. If I find anything, the location will help us pinpoint where the shooter was. Or shooters."

"There's good news on that front," Blue addressed them all. "Dr Hendrickx will be coming over with a camera drone, which should help us find the shooting position, and maybe track the shooter's movements onto and off the hill."

"That'll certainly save us a lot of poking about," Steve responded.

"Anything more since we last spoke, Steve?" asked Blue.

"Not really. The site's been trampled quite a bit."

"It's been tampered with," added Jill Henderson. "Deliberately."

They all became silent. "What makes you think that, Jill?" asked Blue.

"Partly the amount it's messed up, partly intuition – it just doesn't look right, chief."

Dalvey snorted. "Women's bloody intuition!" He grinned inanely round the table. No-one responded. Jill Henderson fixed him with a steely and implacable stare. Dalvey went red and dropped his head to examine his chocolate digestive more closely.

"What else, Jill?" continued Blue.

"We know that one person was shot, and then the body carried off. But the ground's been very thoroughly trampled. It's as if somebody spent a while just stomping all over it. Plus that coffee splash. OK, if you find your coffee's gone cold, and you're outside, you can just pour it on the ground. But right on top of a bloodstain?"

"Well, it was hardly visible," put in Steve.

"Nevertheless, I'm sure there's something not quite right."

"Maybe it's just carelessness," said Steve, "like marking off the wrong area. We can't assume there's some sort of plot."

"What if the shooting was an inside job?" said Jill, "You know, politically expedient. Set up by the secret service to get rid of Lord Steppingham. Maybe he'd become an embarrassment. Maybe he knew some secret about the prime minister. What if he was about to dish up the dirt, so" She drew a finger across her throat.

"Come on, let's not get too melodramatic," said Steve. "I think those PPU guys are just careless. No good at real policing, so they get shunted onto baby-minding politicians. Let's get the work done and see what the tests show up when we get to the lab."

"Thanks, Steve," said Blue. "And let's hold on to Jill's suggestion too. We do need to be aware of all the possibilities here, and keep an open mind. But we've only got one shot here, so it's important that we're thorough. If any of you do have ideas, don't keep them to yourselves, talk to me. Something tells me this is not going to be an easy case, and your idea might be the one that cracks it. Anything. Except aliens, that is."

Once the SOCOs were back at work, McCader washed the mugs, Blue dried.

"Enver, you've been involved in undercover stuff, so you'll know more about this than I do. Could it be an inside job, as Jill suggests?"

McCader studied the suds before answering: "It's not impossible, chief. Though I'm inclined to think it unlikely. A political elimination from the inside would normally be more discreet, and dressed up as an accident or, even better, natural causes. What we've got here would only make sense if they've already set up someone, or some group, for the fall. Maybe some suspected terrorist they want to pin it on."

"Killing two birds with one stone."

"Something like that. So you'd need to keep an eye on Ffox-Kaye. See if he starts to focus the blame before there's really any evidence for it."

"Hmm. The more we look, the more questions there are. Who was the target? How many shooters? Who were they working far? Add to that our witnesses disappearing"

"All for perfectly plausible reasons," put in McCader.

"And the site perhaps being doctored. I'm feeling it's getting muddier every minute."

"There's something else that bothers me, chief. Lord Steppingham was only wounded. A real professional would have left him dead. Put a couple of bullets into just the right places. Full stop."

"Maybe this was a budget assassin. Or an amateur."

"Well, chief, perhaps Dr Hendrickx can move things forward. If we find the shooting position, and it's not been disturbed, that might reduce the number of questions."

9

There was a knock at the door, and Bhardwaj came in, followed by a sleepy-looking man in his late forties, with sandy-coloured hair and a round, chubby face.

"This is the pilot, chief. George Conway."

"Come in, Mr Conway," said Blue, "I'm Inspector Blue, this is Sergeant McCader. Please take a seat. I'm sure that PC Bhardwaj has explained that we need to hear your account of what happened this morning, even if you've already told it to someone else. Arvind, could you make Mr Conway a cup of coffee"

"Milk and two sugars, please," interrupted Conway. "Yes, that would be good, a cup of coffee. Wake me up."

"And make yourself one too," continued Blue, "if you want one."

"Thanks, chief," said Bhardwaj, and busied himself with the kettle and the mugs.

Blue and McCader took chairs opposite Conway. Blue began. "We'll have to take an official statement later, but right now we'd just like to hear it while it's fresh in your mind."

"OK," said Conway, grimacing as if reliving a painful memory.

All at once the door was swung open and Ffox-Kaye walked in. He surveyed the scene briefly, then addressed Blue. "Perhaps I didn't explain myself clearly enough earlier, Mr Blue. As an officer of a *national* unit, involved with potential security issues, I require to be informed of *all* developments in your investigation, and to be notified *in advance* of any case conferences or interviews with witnesses. I also require copies of all case reports. An official notification of these requirements has been sent to the Chief Constable of Police Scotland." Without another word, he walked round the table to the corner seat vacated earlier by Dalvey, and sat down. In this position, he was behind Blue and McCader, and could see Conway. Blue noticed that Conway looked paler than before he had come in.

There was silence in the room. Only Bhardwaj's back could be seen moving, as he finished making the coffee, then gave one to Conway. He took the other and was making for the door when Ffox-Kaye spoke: "That'll do me nicely, thank you, constable. Then you can go."

Bhardwaj looked at Blue, who nodded. Then he shrugged and

took the mug to Ffox-Kaye, who pointed to the window-ledge. Once he'd set the mug down, Bhardwaj quietly left the room.

Blue began. "Mr Conway, you're a helicopter pilot?"

"Yes."

"How long have you been doing that job?"

"Oh, about twelve-thirteen years now."

"Would you consider yourself an experienced pilot?"

"I think so, yes."

"And which company do you work for?"

"Sandor Logistics." He pronounced it "shandor".

"I've not heard of them. Where are they based?"

"Charleroi, near Brussels. They operate across Europe, branches in most countries."

"So you didn't come here directly from Belgium, then?" Behind Blue, Ffox-Kaye made an exasperated why-are-you-wasting-my-time type of sigh, but said nothing more. But it made Conway visibly more flustered.

"Er, no, not from Brussels," he replied to Blue. "No, I'm based at Stanstead. But I came up from there yesterday, to Prestwick. That's where I flew from this morning."

"And what was the itinerary you were given there?"

"Oh, simple. To fly out here, arriving bang on 7 am. Pick up the, er, passengers, and take them to Glasgow Airport."

"Do you know where they were going on from there?"

"Er, no. I just do the helicopter flights. I'd guess there was a private jet taking them on somewhere else. But I don't know."

"How many passengers were you expecting?"

"What? What do you mean, expecting?" Conway looked flustered.

"Sorry, I meant how many passengers were you supposed to pick up and take to Glasgow?"

"Oh yes. Two. Lord Steppingham and Mr van Kaarsten." Conway glanced at Ffox-Kaye.

"No-one else? No security people accompanying them? Isn't that unusual? Lord Steppingham is a government minister. Think again."

Conway glanced behind Blue again, and after a pause went on. "Well, maybe there was another one. Yes, Inspector Plaistow. He was on the list too."

"Do you have the manifest for the flight, then? I presume that included a passenger list."

"Er, no. I gave it to the Chief Inspector." He nodded nervously towards Ffox-Kaye.

Blue turned in his chair. "Is that correct, Mr Ffox-Kaye?"

Ffox-Kaye smiled thinly. "Yes, Mr Conway is perfectly correct. We've retained it for security purposes. You'll have a copy as soon as it's been checked and appropriately redacted. But I can confirm what Mr Conway has said. The passengers were to be Lord Steppingham, Mr van Kaarsten and Inspector Plaistow. The reason Mr Conway is so, ah, hesitant with you, Inspector, is that there were in fact additional passengers. These were security personnel who for obvious reasons cannot be identified. If you like, you can call them Mr A and Mr B. I can't give you any further information."

"Would I be right in equating Mr A and Mr B with Sergeant Steele and PC Corning?"

"I'm not at liberty to confirm or deny that."

"OK. So, Mr Conway, you were expecting up to five persons, is that right?"

Conway looked relieved. "Yes, exactly, five."

"And what about crew? I assume you were not alone."

"No. There was just the co-pilot and me."

"And the co-pilot was?"

"Brian Richards." Matt Plaistow had not mentioned a co-pilot.

"Blue wrote the name down. "And where is Mr Richards at the moment?"

"Oh, he went off this morning. Got a lift from Mr James and Miss Rogers. He didn't want to be stuck here waiting for the chopper to be fixed."

"I've spoken to Mr Richards," said Ffox-Kaye. "His story matches the others. It's no different from Mr Conway's account, I can assure you. But we can certainly arrange for a statement to be taken from him and forwarded to you. Though it's pretty obvious what happened out there. I appreciate that it's easier for local policemen to cover their backs by collecting endless statements saying the same thing, but I'm still surprised you aren't out there trying to track down whoever did it."

"Don't you think it's important to speak to the witnesses of a crime?" said Blue.

"Of course I do!" snapped Ffox-Kaye, "But it's bloody clear what happened here. How many times do you need to hear it?"

"I've only heard it once so far, from Mr Plaistow. Don't you think it's worthwhile to hear it from at least two witnesses? I'm afraid that here in Scotland you need two witnesses to get a conviction."

Ffox-Kaye didn't answer, but looked out the window with a bored expression. He then noticed his coffee on the windowsill, and took a big gulp. Suddenly he choked and spat it all out. "Aaah! What the hell is this stuff? Is he trying to poison me?"

"Didn't he say, sir?" said McCader quietly, "PC Bhardwaj often puts a little chilli powder in his coffee. Gives it a bit of zing, he says." Ffox-Kaye said nothing, his mouth twitching furiously. It was evident he would have liked to rush over to the sink and wash his mouth out, but felt this would give a poor impression of a top man from the Met.

"May we continue?" asked Blue, turning back to Conway. "All right Mr Conway, now tell us what happened this morning."

"Well, we came in towards the landing pad. Inspector Plaistow waved us in. We landed perfectly. Then the inspector came over and checked the manifest, as well as our IDs. That was normal procedure. Then he went back to get the passengers. To the house, that is." Conway paused.

"OK. What did you and Brian do next?"

"We prepared the chopper for take-off. Brian did the engine and controls check, while I went to the rear of the cabin to check the seat adjustment, belts, and so on."

"How many seats are there?"

"We can take eight passengers."

"So, you were checking the seats. What then?"

"Suddenly, I heard these shots. Bang, bang, bang. I dived to the floor behind the first row of seats. I heard Brian saying, 'Christ, there's shooting!' and then next thing he was beside me, behind the seats too. Then there was another shot, and a big cracking sound right above us. We thought they were attacking the chopper then. We just kept our heads down and hoped for the best. After a while, when there were no more shots, we looked out. It all seemed to be over, so we came out. I can tell you, Inspector, I've never been so frightened in my life. The nurse had to give me a sedative – I just couldn't stop shaking. Not after what I'd seen."

"I thought you hadn't seen anything?"

"No, what I meant was, after I found out what had happened. How close I was to death? I could have been killed. The chopper's not armour-plated, you know. Once they started shooting at it, they'd soon have killed me and Brian. I was in a really bad way, I can tell you. Mr Seymour let me lie in one of his spare rooms. That's where I was when the policeman came, your policeman I mean."

"So you didn't actually see the shooting taking place?"

"No, not directly. I just heard the shots."

"How many shots?"

"I don't know, maybe three or four. Yes, three first, then the one that hit our rear rotor. Four."

"And you didn't see who fired them?"

"No, not at all. Once I looked out again, everything was over. They must have been terrorists. Al Qaeda or these Syrian people. Terrible."

"Thank you very much, Mr Conway. What are your plans now?"

"I'll wait here with the chopper till the engineers get here to fix it. I guess that'll be tomorrow morning, though they've told me they're already on the way. Mr Seymour's offered to put me up overnight if need be. Depends how long it takes to fix it. Then I'll fly it back to Prestwick."

"You've been very helpful, Mr Conway. I'm going to ask one of my officers to take a statement from you now. All you have to do is repeat what you've told me. Sergeant, could you ask PC Bhardwaj to come in and do that?"

"Certainly, sir." McCader got up and went out. Conway took a large slurp of his coffee. There was no chilli powder in it.

Ffox-Kaye stood up. Conway looked fearfully at him. "Thank you, Mr Conway," he said curtly, then as he passed Blue, "Make sure a copy of that statement is forwarded to me." And he left the room.

Conway leant back in his seat. He looked as if a weight had been lifted from his shoulders. His forehead glistened with sweat. He fished out a handkerchief and wiped it.

"What do you think?" said Blue suddenly. "Do you think his Lordship or Mr van Kaarsten was the target?"

Conway tensed again. "What?"

"Who do you think was the target?"

"I don't know. Like I said, I didn't see anything. Not a thing. I told you. And him too, Ffox-thing. He said it was terrorists, bound to be. Arabs, Islamic fanatics, I don't know."

McCader came back in with Bhardwaj, who was carrying a clipboard and a biro.

"Enver, can you sit in on this," said Blue, "just in case Mr Conway remembers anything further."

"Yes, sir," said McCader, and took a seat by Bhardwaj. "Don't worry, Arvind, I won't interrupt. By the way, Mr Ffox-Kaye liked his coffee." He smiled.

Bhardwaj only cleared his throat, and arranged his clipboard and pen on the table.

Once he was out in the courtyard, Blue phoned Campbell.

"How's it going, Angus?"

"Not easy, chief. Something's going on here, I'm just not sure what. There's a DCI Ffox-Kaye from Special Branch, says he's PPU and has a crowd of goons with him. He's not making it easy for us."

"Yes, the ACC's passed on to me a communication from them, demanding our 'full co-operation'. I must say, it's hardly co-operation when we have to tell them everything, and they only tell us what they want to. I suspect they'll try to get their hands on the case as soon as they can. Anything else?"

"Yes, chief. Most of our witnesses have vanished. All for apparently very plausible reasons. Plus the locus of the shooting was misidentified. It's very odd."

"Hmm. Have the local police got there?"

"Yes. Inspector Nicolson's going to get an Incident Room set up near Craighouse."

"What's wrong with where you are?"

"I don't want to deal with this case right under Ffox-Kaye's nose. If we're in Craighouse, at least we can see him coming."

"It's probably wise," agreed the Super. "These people always have an agenda, and it's not always to do with truth or justice. Are they actively obstructing the investigation?"

"No, just making it difficult. For instance, they won't let us into the house. Say it's a security issue. I don't know what's in there they don't want us to see."

"These people are paranoid, Angus. Obsessed by secrecy. Maybe Lord Steppingham makes origami figures of Trident missiles out of the toilet paper while he's sitting there. Anyway, how's the work on the site going?"

"The locus has been badly messed up, perhaps deliberately, but we did get some blood samples, and found two of the bullets. Still two to go, Dalvey's out with the metal detector now. Dr Hendrickx is coming tomorrow with a camera drone, which should help us identify the shooter's position."

"Ah, good, you need to find the shooting position. See if he's left anything. Are you checking the ferries, etc., to see how he could have got in or out?"

"Yes, chief, plus boat-hirers, and any CCTV footage we can find. The shooter must have made it off the island at some point. We're checking accommodation providers too. Trouble is, we don't know who we're looking for."

"OK. Stick with it, Angus. By the way, there's a news blackout on this. Our friends in London insisted on it. Said they'd throw the Official Secrets Act at any reporter who sets foot on the island. I've no doubt it'll hold for a bit, but sooner or later it'll spill out onto social media. Hopefully you'll be able to get any work done on the site before the newshounds arrive. And as I say, if you need anything, or are getting too much trouble from this PPU twerp, just let me know."

Next, Blue phoned Nicolson to find out about the incident room.

"Good news, Angus. The Jura Service Point can let us have their research room for a couple of weeks, longer if necessary, and there's a couple of computers already set up there. It's next to the primary school at Keils, that's about a mile north of Craighouse. Ten miles south of where you are now. But I'm afraid there's nothing nearer."

"That's excellent. What about accommodation?"

"All sorted out too. The Craighouse Inn was completely booked up – including a party of German whisky tourists – but we've got everyone into B&Bs in and around Craighouse. I'll give you the details when you get here."

"Thanks. There's not much more I can do here, so I'll come over fairly soon. Is there any coffee there?"

"I've been over to the shop, and got a 4-cup cafetière and some ground coffee. Plus milk, sugar, biscuits, and so on. I brought a kettle from the station. Home from home, eh?"

"Looking forward to it already. See you soon."

He'd noticed Dalvey hanging around while he phoned, so motioned him over. "What've you got, Kevin?"

"Another bullet, boss. Some way off the locus. Looks like it just missed everything and buried itself in the ground. But it helps give a line to the shooter's position. I could take a look up there now."

"No. I don't want anybody walking around up there till we get the drone up there tomorrow morning. Besides, Kevin, you'd be stepping on toes, wouldn't you?"

Dalvey scowled. He was thoroughly disliked by all the SOCOs who had worked under him in the past, and Blue knew they would waste no time in complaining if they thought he was intruding on their work.

"The bullet. Same as the others?"

"Yeah. Not so bashed up, so we'll get a better look at the rifling marks."

"Could there be any others? Witnesses were a big vague on the number of shots."

Dalvey shrugged. "If this guy's a professional, there won't be. If they're not in the area I've covered, or stuck in a body, I don't know where they could be."

"Could the shooter have missed his first shot at the rear rotor on the helicopter?"

"Possible, but I'd reckon unlikely. It's a fairly easy target. However, if you want, I can mark out the area for a near miss and check it." Dalvey's tone told Blue he thought this exercise a waste of time.

"Tell you what. Do that tomorrow morning. Once Sergeant McCader and PC Bhardwaj have finished taking Mr Conway's statement, you can come with us to the Incident Room."

"I'm not coming in a car with…"

"Don't even think it, Kevin! How much pay did you have docked for the last racism charge? There's no room in the scene-of-crime wagon, with four in it already, that means the only seat free is in Bhardwaj's car. You can walk if you prefer. It's about ten miles. Or you could call a taxi – you might get one from Bowmore by lunchtime tomorrow. Take your pick."

10

Bhardwaj drove Blue, McCader and Dalvey at a nerve-shredding speed down Jura's single-track main road, giving a running commentary on the bays and moors, estates and farms they passed. Dalvey sulked in the back seat by McCader. To their right, the moors rose purple and brown to the bleak grey masses of the Paps, to the left the land sloped down to the shore, rocky stretches and then sandy beaches, and then a wide strip of flatter land with an oval inlet, almost a lagoon, in its centre. Near it a large farm complex.

"Ardmenish Farm", said Bhardwaj.

"My ancestors lived there," said Blue, "At Ardmenish. Had the mill at Craighouse too."

"Are there any still here? On the island?" asked McCader.

"I think there's an old lady somewhere. Maybe others. I've been meaning to come here again, but never got round to it, not since…" He paused, stared at the grey farm buildings, crouched round their courtyard, protecting the sheltered space. "Not for a long time."

In a short distance the road came down off the hillside until it ran right beside the shore, and they could see on their left a long sandy beach. A few miles along the car pulled off the road onto a parking area squeezed between the road and the sea.

"Here we are," announced Bhardwaj. "Please take care when crossing the road."

As they got out the car, they could see two buildings opposite them. On the left, the primary school, serving the whole island, perhaps dating to the 1970s. On the right, separated from the school grounds by a wooden fence, a flat-roofed single-storey building of the same vintage, once the school janitor's house. Now it was announced on a sign as a "Service Point".

Moira Nicolson met them at the door and led them through a corridor to what must have been the janitor's living room, a square space with windows on two sides. It was furnished with a wooden desk in one corner, a wide shelf along one wall, with two PCs sitting on it, a long plastic-topped folding table, and half a dozen plastic chairs. In the middle of the room stood a short and well-built woman of middle age, with a round smiling face and brown curly hair. Moira introduced her as Maggie Stillman, the service point manager. Maggie explained that the service point was a point of contact with the local council, which, centred at Lochgilphead, well into the mainland, was not very local at all. The service point was the council's presence on Jura, but it was also a local heritage centre, where people could, and did, come to examine Jura's genealogical records.

"Aren't we going to be restricting your activities here?" asked Blue.

"Only a little bit," answered Maggie, her voice soft and low and slow. "All the council stuff we handle in the room next door, so it's the family tree hunters who will be a little inconvenienced. But we can always give them a corner of the office. I've moved the genealogical material out of here to give you more space, but left the two PCs for you. One has a printer, and there's Wi-Fi here too. We've a photocopier, scanner and colour printer in the office which you're free to use – don't worry, we'll send Police Scotland a bill when you're finished! I see Moira's brought in some coffee-making equipment. I've got two spare keys, so I've given one to Moira and Mr Blue, you'd better have the other. By the way, are you one of the Jura Blues?"

"Yes, I am actually," said Blue a little reluctantly.

"Well, well, I thought so. We'll have to have a chat about that. Once you've got settled in of course."

Settling in took about 30 minutes. Blue took the desk and put his laptop on it. One of the tables was moved against the wall. McCader also had a laptop, which left the PCs to Craig and Bhardwaj. While they were setting up, Blue asked Dalvey to use the table, get some paper and a map, and work out from the angle of the shots where he reckoned the shooter might have been firing from. Moira then brought Blue up to date on the accommodation. The ferries to Islay started early and ran fairly late, so Craig and Bhardwaj would stay in their homes in Islay and come over for the day. The SOCOs, Dalvey, and McCader had been booked into Bed and Breakfast accommodation in Craighouse, the SOCOs and Dalvey for one night, McCader indefinitely.

"What about me?" said Blue.

"Ah, well, I was going to put you into a B&B when Maggie said you might be related to Effie Blue. She called her up and had a chat, and the upshot is, you're staying with her. She is your great-aunt, after all. I just couldn't refuse, could I?"

Blue was lost for words. He could hardly remember his great aunt Effie. His last visit to Jura must have been nearly twenty years ago, while he was a student at Glasgow Uni, during the summer vacation. He remembered an uncomfortable afternoon in an overheated room with tea and scones. He didn't know whether to curse Moira or thank her. But then, he could always move somewhere else if there was a problem.

He put on his best smile. "That's fantastic, Moira. How amazing. No wonder Maggie knew I was related here. Where does she live?"

"They're all within walking distance of here – it's less than a mile to Craighouse – but, as I said, I'll leave you one of the cars." She fished a key from her tunic pocket and handed it to Blue.

11

Within an hour – and it was now about six o'clock – the SOCOs arrived, and piled into the room. Moira explained that she'd arranged for the cafe next to the old mill in Craighouse to stay open late, provided they arrived before seven.

Blue had to decide now whether to drive everyone for another two or three hours, which would see them tired in the morning, or stop now, and have them wide awake and sharp for the next day. He went for the latter. In many cases the first 24 hours were crucial, while the scene was still warm, witnesses fresh and on-the-spot and perpetrators possibly still nearby. But in this case all those advantages had been lost. The long delay in reporting the events to Police Scotland had by itself ensured an easy getaway for the killer. On top of that, the scene had been messed around and most of the witnesses removed to some distance and to a different jurisdiction. This one was going to be more of a long haul, and for that he needed his team to be alert and on the ball.

He got everyone round the table.

"OK everyone, we'll have a quick review of where we are now on the forensics, then meet again at 8.30 tomorrow morning. Steve, do you want to start?"

"Sure, chief. I think we're done on the casualty site. We've got samples, we've drawn the plan, and Andy's taken the pics. We're ready to move on to the shooting site, as soon as you locate it."

"Thanks, Steve. Kevin?"

"Er, yeah, got three bullets. And I've worked out from the trajectories where the shooting site is likely to be." He passed Blue a printout. A blow-up of the 1:25,000 OS map with three lines running across it, and a shaded area around two points where the lines intersected.

"Thanks, Kevin, good work."

"We could be looking for another site too," said Moira Nicolson. "The shooter may have bivouacked elsewhere on the moor, then come up to his shooting position later."

"Yes, that's true," said Blue, "and there could also be tracks where he, or they, came on and off the moor. Let's see what we find tomorrow morning. We'll meet here at 8.30. I know it's early, but we need to make the most of the day. Sooner we start, sooner we're done. And if you want to eat now, and get your expenses back, there's only one option. The cafe by the mill are staying open for us, provided we're there soon. But there could be other folk there, so no-one mentions the case. At the moment there's a news blackout on it, so be extra careful. Everybody got that?" Nods all round.

The meal passed uneventfully. To Blue's relief, there were no other customers in the room. The atmosphere was relaxed, and even quiet, unusual for a gathering of police officers. The menu was limited, haddock and chips all round, with cheesecake and cream to follow, then coffee. At times Blue was able to sit back and consider his colleagues. All good at their jobs, despite their human flaws. Steve Belford, his career set back by an impetuous car chase which ended with a colleague badly injured, the slate cleared with his recent promotion, staring into the amber depths of a 10-year-old Isle of Jura single malt. Jill Henderson, razor-sharp and always focused, taking in every word spoken by each of them, one Martini and lemonade enough for the whole evening. She'd make a damn good detective, if she could be persuaded to give it a go. Andy McGuire, well-built, prematurely balding, always amiable, and a top-class crime-scene photographer, nursing a glass of dark Islay-brewed oat stout. Dennis Johnstone, his thin face pock-marked by some childhood illness, always sad-looking, trailed it seemed by ill-luck, but a stubborn and painstaking investigator, staring into a glass of red wine. Dalvey, unable it seemed to break clear of his demons, but whose ballistics skills and knowledge of weapons was second to none, steadily drinking extra-strong lager. Blue noticed that when he was about to order a third can, McCader whispered something in his ear. Dalvey stared at his plate for a moment, lips pressed together, then asked for Irn Bru instead. Enver McCader, born in Albania and brought up in Dundee, thin, black-haired, clean-shaven, a man who could become invisible, breathing the fumes from a 12-year-old Bruichladdich. He'd been assigned to Blue the previous year from duties which were absent from his file. Moira Nicolson, highly competent, exiled to Islay for challenging the male-dominated *status quo*, swirling the white wine in her goblet. Deirdra Craig, serious and quiet, a wizard on the computer, topping up her glass from a bottle of fizzy water. She must be driving. Arvind Bhardwaj, eager, thoughtful and observant, but a natural behind a steering wheel, on his second bottle of Czech lager. Blue was not the type of policeman who spent all his free time drinking with his colleagues. He was not particularly interested in the ins and outs of their private lives. But he knew that when it came to the job they had to do, he could trust their expertise and, in most cases, their judgement.

Nicolson, Craig and Bhardwaj left before coffee was served, to catch the late ferry to Islay.

As those who remained sipped their coffees, Blue told them he hoped that if Alison Hendrickx found the shooting position, with luck they'd be back in Oban by the following evening. He also urged them to get a good night's sleep and ensure they were present for the case meeting in the morning.

"It's bloody early," grumbled Dalvey.

"No problem, sir," said Belford.

"Sooner we start the better, chief," said Henderson.

"Any other comments?" said Blue.

Then they picked up their overnight bags, piled meantime in the corner of the room, and set off to find their B&Bs. The four SOCOs were at the Old Mill, while Dalvey and McCader were at the aptly named *Tigh na Mara*, "House of the Sea". Blue set his steps for Effie Blue's house.

12

He soon found it, a tidy bungalow not far up the lane behind the cafe. It was called *Tigh na Diuraichean*, "House of the Jura folk." Was there a message in that? He rang the doorbell.

A small and very old lady, with straight iron-grey hair, cut in a neat fringe, and glasses hanging on a chain from her neck, opened the door. She was vaguely familiar.

"Angus, come on in. I wasn't expecting you so early."

"I really appreciate your offer, er, Aunt Effie, and the inconvenience I'm putting you to."

"Ach, not at all. I have the room from when I used to do the B&B. And I can't let family stay in some bleak hotel while I've room for them. Well now, let's get your things to your room, then we can have a cup of tea and a wee chat."

The tea was served. Blue had steeled himself for the topic that would come first.

"Aye," said Effie, "I remember that last time we met. It was at the funeral. Was it six or seven years back? That was a black day for you, that accident."

"Nothing's accidental," said Blue, more bitterly than he'd intended. "Everything has a cause. It was maybe unintended, but there was nothing accidental about it." He saw again the rain beating on the windscreen, as he tried to keep up with Trudi. At the next junction, he'd turn left for the police station, she'd go straight on for the hospital. The lights were at red, but as she came up to them they changed to green. She waved her hand to him in between the gear changes as she moved off. And in the next moment the black bulk of a lorry swept her car out of his vision, and her out of his life.

"You won't ever forget it," said Effie. "Don't even be trying. But you need to see it as part of the past. Part of your story, but not the end, even if you thought that at the time. Believe me, Trudi doesn't want you to be dwelling on it for the rest of your days. Don't ask me how I know that, I just do. A gift I've inherited from somewhere. She's wanting you to move on, to make your life a happy and productive one."

There was an awkward pause. "He had blackouts," said Blue, "the lorry driver. Hadn't reported it to his employers. He'd have lost the job right away. His employers said they'd have moved him to the packing area. But the pay was less than the drivers got."

"They sent him to the jail, though, didn't they?"

"He wasn't a monster, like the papers made out, just a stupid wee man, who didn't think past his own self. So, so stupid." He felt the tears come, pulled out his handkerchief, wiped his eyes, blew his nose.

"He paid for it though, didn't he? In the end?"

Blue remembered that too. The tabloids reporting with glee how the man had been assaulted in prison. During a fracas in the canteen, possibly set up, someone had slashed both his Achilles tendons with a shard of glass. He was operated on, but didn't put any effort into the physiotherapy, and left prison walking with great difficulty, leaning on a stick, dependent on powerful painkillers. There was no job waiting for him, the conviction had seen to that. He drank heavily, his wife left him, and three months later he was found dead in his flat, poisoned by a mixture of alcohol and painkillers. The Fatal Accident Inquiry concluded that it was 'accidental'.

"What he did killed him as surely as it killed Trudi," he said. "But it didn't bring her back. His death was as pointless as hers."

"But you've learned to live on. That's what she wanted, Angus."

It was his faith that had sustained him. He knew many who lost their belief when tragedy struck. But his church had not been one where people went through the motions, turning up on Sundays to get right with God, and then forgetting about Him for the rest of the week. The church had embraced him and his grief, had hugged him close until the worst was past, until he could see a future and not just a past. To those ordinary people who had taken time from their own lives to give life back to him, he would always be grateful.

"…worn."

He roused himself. "Sorry?"

"I was going to say you're looking worn. But it's the wrong word. Weathered is better. And I dare say, experienced too. You've been through a lot, I know that. But looking at you now, I'm seeing that you got through it, even if you don't quite realise it yourself. Now drink up your tea, it'll be cold. Tell you what, I'll go and make another pot. No, forget that, I've something better."

She collected the teacups, the milk and the teapot on the tray and disappeared into the kitchen. In a minute she was back, this time with a couple of tumblers, a little jug of water, and a bottle of golden liquid. "*The Diurach's Own,*" she said, "sixteen years old, and for my money you can't beat it." Blue shook his head, but she brushed his refusal aside. "Nonsense, Angus, this drink is nurture for the soul. *Uisge beatha.* Water of life. We've both earned it, in our own ways."

The golden liquid, half and half with water, smelt and sipped and tasted. Rolled around the palate, savoured and swallowed. Syrupy but far from sweet. Not smoky like some of the Islay whiskies, but rounded and smooth, tasting of the earth and the sea. He let the spirit carry him for a few moments. He drifted in the warmth of silence.

"Now I'm thinking it's time I filled you in on the rest of the Blues," announced Effie. "You're certainly not the only one, so don't go imagining you are."

Blue soon realised that Effie was far more knowledgeable about the wider Blue clan than he was. He asked her how she kept in touch with them all.

"Ach, well, yon Facebook's a great thing. I was trying the Twitter for a while but couldn't see the point o it. But Skype now, that's awfa useful, when you've children and grandchildren in America and Australia. Even in Scotland too."

"You've got a computer, then?"

"Ach, we all have. And super-fast broadband, so they call it. It was a project from the council a couple of years back. They got most of the money from Europe."

"Do you do much with it?"

"Oh, plenty. Right now, I'm putting all the family stuff onto one of those genealogical programs. Ina McNeill at the Museum on Islay, she persuaded me to do it, she was giving me the program too. Told me us old folk have got to get all the stuff in our heads recorded somehow while we're still here, and still *compos mentis*. It's not just the lists of names, you see, she's wanting the stories too, all I can remember about each one of them. And pictures. I've got lots of old photos. My grandfather was always taking pictures, he bought a little box camera sometime in the nineteen-thirties. And each photograph had to say something. You couldn't be just taking thousands with your phone then."

"How is Ina doing?" Blue had met Ina McNeill the previous year.

"Och, she's fine. As fine as us old fogies can be."

His phone pinged. A text message. "On Islay. At Moiras. Pick U up tmrw 7 am by cafe. Alison x" He excused himself to Effie and typed the reply, "OK. CU tmrw. Sleep well." He hesitated before adding an x.

Then the talk was of Jura, and how the island was changing. Effie explained that the problem, as with most of the islands, was that most young people had to leave to find work, and few came back. So the real natives became older and fewer. Meanwhile, new people were moving in, immigrants from the mainland, from England, or further afield. They were of three kinds. The first kind were those who were looking for a new life. They wanted to get things done: they were active, and sometimes vociferous in demanding more facilities and support from the council. Then there were those who were looking for a quiet life. They wanted things to stay just as they were; they were usually retired and wanted a peaceful idyll in which to drift away their final years. Finally there were those who wanted a holiday home, to visit from time to time, or to hire out to other holiday visitors. Together these three groups succeeded, without trying, in pushing house prices way beyond the means of those young folk who did want to return.

"You know," she concluded, "we welcome new people – the islands have to be populated to survive – but there are some places where there are no native-born folk left at all. That's why it's so important for us to record all that we can of the way life used to be like, before it's gone forever."

"Is there any way to slow down or stop the changes?"

"Jobs and housing, those are the things young people are needing. Everything else will follow. With the broadband people can be working from here. But of course, the landowners are against that. An island bustling with people isn't any good if you're wanting a game reserve for the rich. It's time all that was changed."

"What would you do?"

"Oh that's simple, I'd take the land off the lot of them, and give it to people who'll live on it and use it. For crofting or whatever. Another distillery or two. Farms where deer are husbanded for the meat. More tourist facilities. A brewery. A branch of UHI. Whatever works."

They both fell silent. There was a lot to think about there.

Blue broke the silence. "What do you know about Lord Steppingham?"

"Ach, he's one of the worst. His house and grounds are surrounded by barbed wire like some military base. Maybe he's keeping spare nuclear warheads there. He uses the estate purely for shooting, for his rich friends, and I suppose people he wants to curry favour with. I've heard all sorts have been there. Arab sheiks, African dictators, even the prime minister. He's tried to veto any development on the island. He even opposed upgrading the road – that's why there's grass growing in the middle by the time it reaches his gate."

"Anything special you've heard about what goes on there?"

"We've heard there's something going on up at his place. I'm guessing that's why you're here."

"I can't tell you exactly what it's about, but, yes, it's up there."

"Well, I've not heard much. Not for want of trying, mind. We old folks like to know what's going on, and we've plenty of time to talk about it. Trouble is, he avoids using local people. All his domestic staff he brings in from outside. They come in in those black Range Rovers a day or two before he arrives, and leave the day after he goes. I think they're all from his estate in England. The only local people he uses are Mr Seymour and that handyman, Tam McGowan. They live on the island right enough, but he brought them in from outside too. Seymour aye keeps himself to himself, and I'm thinking Tam daren't tell anything. Mind you, Mary – that was his wife – was more talkative. But she passed away a couple of years ago. She used to say they were having big parties, drugs, drink, whatever else you can imagine, but she wouldn't be giving any details, more's the pity. Said Tam'd be out on his ear if anything got out."

"What about estate staff, you know, gamekeepers, ghillies?"

"What I've been hearing is that they're not allowed inside the house and grounds. There's a lodge further up the hill where the shoots all start – that's where they're based, and they stay at the cottages there. They're not supposed to come into the village – all their supplies are brought in. And of course they've been warned not to gossip. Anything leaked, they're fired. Three years ago it was, one of them was sneaking down to the hotel for a pint one evening. Next morning he was out on his ear, and word sent round the other estates to blacklist him. Aye, that was his career as a gamekeeper over, right enough."

"Do you know of anything happening up there the last day or two? Anything unusual?"

"No, I can't think of anything. But I can certainly make some discreet enquiries. It's the weekly coffee morning at the community hall tomorrow, so I'll be keeping my ears open."

"Not too obvious, mind."

"Angus, my laddie, you clearly don't know your Great-aunt Effie very well. Now, here's something completely different, as they used to say. Come over and look at this."

Against one wall of her living room was a heavy table of dark wood, and on it lay a large roll of paper, tied with a ribbon. Effie untied the ribbon and unrolled the paper – heavy cartridge paper, several A2 sheets taped together at the back. On it was a family tree.

"The Blues of Jura and all their connections. I'm a Darroch, and your grandfather's wife was a McIsaac, so they're in too, plus lots more. Nine generations, back to the 1790s. All the information's in the computer program too, but it can't print it all out as nicely as this."

Blue examined the chart. His forbears, men and women who had worked this land, for whom this island was their world. "It's a beautiful piece of work. You should have it mounted on the wall."

"Aye, that's not a bad idea. But it's not finished yet. Never will be, I suppose. Look, there's you down there near the bottom, and…" Her voice trailed off. "I'm sorry, I can see it still hurts. There are some things we never get over. My John died ten years ago, and I can still see him sitting there where you are. But you have to go on. You've focused on your job. But the time will be coming when you need more than that."

Blue soon excused himself. He needed to unpack, set up his laptop and start the first draft of his case report. The document would grow as the case developed, and each night it would be updated.

By eleven o'clock it was done. He read it through. Lots of questions. Not many answers. But that was the way it often went. You had to identify the questions before you could recognise the answers. Sometimes they were sitting there all the time.

Day 2. Tuesday

13

Blue's alarm wakened him at six, and Effie served a hearty breakfast at 6.15. By 6.55 he was walking down the lane, to find Alison Hendrickx's blue Fiat waiting for him on the main road. The rear was packed with boxes. The white police car was following. He got into the Fiat, and they were instantly off.

"Hi, Angus, good to see you." She squeezed his arm briefly, then switched her attention back to the driving and put her foot down. "We're going to have to move it a bit, the sun's about to break through that thin cloud, and I don't know how long it'll last. Coming in at a nice low angle, it'll really show up any terrain anomalies. How are you?" Now they surged past the service point building, the other police car still in the car park across the road.

Blue gazed at her. The blonde hair short and bobbed, rimless glasses, fine features, frown of concentration. He'd missed her. "Fine. Good to see you too. You're staying at Moira's?"

"Didn't I say that in my text?"

"Well, yes, I was just looking for a conversational opening."

"Ah. Mankind's great quest. I could hardly stay anywhere else after last year, could I?"

"No, I suppose not. Who's in the car behind?"

"Moira, Deirdra and Arvind. Bob and Boris are manning the station. I'm glad you've got Arvind and Deirdra again. That'll be good for them, they need to be stretched. And Dalvey's here too? Last night's meal must have been a ball." Was she being sarcastic?

"He was very quiet. I just hope he didn't go on to the Craighouse Inn afterwards. You've got a lot of stuff in the back there?"

"You get a lot of room when you fold the seats down. This isn't one of those toy helicopters that were all the rage at Christmas. This is the real McCoy, wait till you see it. I had to promise Arvind he could fly it. It's a professional camera drone, don't ask what it cost. Police Scotland only have a couple, so we'd better not break it."

"Must be a month since I saw you last."

"Ah, yes, the concert. That was fun. Well, you haven't changed a bit. Isn't that reassuring? This is a great road, isn't it? I like the grass in the middle. Gives it that 'away from it all' feel. How far is it?"

They were passing Ardmenish Farm. "Another four or five miles. A big set of gates with lots of razor wire, you can't miss it."

"Sounds like his Lordship values his privacy."

"Or has something to hide. How much have you been told?"

"Phoned Superintendent Campbell yesterday, as soon as I got your call, to get the official OK. He's very sweet, in a gruff sort of way. Anyway, yes he filled me in on what he knew at that point. Is there more?"

Blue gave a quick update. By the time he'd finished, they'd come over a summit on the road and spotted the gates ahead. And the fence and the razor wire.

"Good heavens! What's he keep in there?" said Alison.

They stopped at the gate, the police car still behind them, and Blue got out. He buzzed the intercom set into one of the heavy brick gateposts. When a voice answered he said, "Police. Could you open the gates please."

There was a delay of two or three minutes before the gates swung open. They drove in and parked. Everybody piled out of the cars and Alison opened the rear of hers to get the equipment out.

"Good morning, Mr Blue! What have we got here?" Ffox-Kaye appeared as if out of nowhere behind them. He'd presumably been watching from the house.

Blue introduced Alison to Ffox-Kaye, who took her proffered hand and kissed it, holding on to it just a little longer than was necessary. "So nice to have a beautiful woman on our site."

"You have several," she replied icily, turning her back to return to the car.

Blue explained that they were going to use the camera drone to locate the shooting site.

"Hmm, I see," said Ffox-Kaye. "I'll be interested to see how you manage. Just a little warning though. No photographing of the house please, or any of the outbuildings. If the drone is obviously heading in that direction, I'll order my men to shoot it down. National security, you understand. And I'll expect you to email me copies of all pictures taken. *All* pictures. Even the duds. Thank you." He strode off again.

Blue went to the car, where Bhardwaj was waiting to help Alison get the various boxes out the back end.

"Yuk! He's a charmer," said Alison, "I wouldn't want to be stuck in a locked room with him. Right Arvind, let's get the stuff out the boxes. Start with the big one."

Once assembled, the quadcopter camera drone looked impressive, even before it did anything. It's shiny cross-shaped white plastic body measured about 80 by 80 centimetres, with a propeller blade at the end of each arm. The body perched on four spindly legs, each about 25 cm long, and within them, fixed under the body, a camera with a thick lens pointing horizontally.

"Wow, hot stuff!" Bhardwaj was clearly impressed.

"I can take HD video or very sharp stills with the camera," said Alison. "You can watch the video on the screen as it flies. We can fly it manually or use GPS to send it to a specific point."

"That's good," said Blue. "Here's where we think the shooting position ought to be." He gave her the sheet Dalvey had produced.

"OK, this looks good. Er, Arvind, do you know what you're doing?"

Bhardwaj was fiddling with the remote control unit, staring at the 8-inch screen in front of it. "No problem. It's just like the one my little brother got for his Christmas, only a bit bigger. Well, actually, a lot bigger. And it has auto-takeoff and landing, and GPS and video-streaming. Fantastic!"

"Let's get it in the air then."

Bhardwaj carried the drone well away from the house and set it on the grass. Meanwhile Alison had typed in the co-ordinates of the area Dalvey had identified. She handed the controls to Bhardwaj, and in a couple of minutes, with a louder whirring than Blue had expected, the machine rose up and hovered in front of them. After a few tentative moves in different directions, as Bhardwaj got a feel for the controls, it set off slowly up towards the hillside beyond the fence.

Blue glanced back at the house. Ffox-Kaye stood by the door watching the drone, whilst one of his goons stood next to him with a video camera trained on it. No doubt everything they did here would be filmed.

The drone skimmed over the fence, clearing it by several feet, then continued on up and disappeared over the brow of the hill. Alison and Bhardwaj were now focused on the screen, heads together. Blue edged closer – he didn't want to nudge either of them and accidentally send the drone crashing to its doom.

"Look!" Alison was saying, her finger almost touching the screen,

"There it is! Can you see that flattened area. Hold it there, don't move while I take a still shot." Bhardwaj held the control steady whilst she prodded two of the keys. "Got it. OK, now hover right over it, and we'll capture the GPS co-ordinates."

It took a while for Bhardwaj to get the drone exactly over the site to Alison's satisfaction. Then she asked him to bring the drone further back again. "We've located the site and noted the co-ordinates. Now I'm looking for signs of coming and going."

Again the two heads hunched over the little screen, and now it was Bhardwaj who spotted the anomaly. "There, is that it, running across there, almost invisible."

"Could it be a sheep or deer path?" asked Blue.

"Always possible," answered Alison, "but I'm not sure why a sheep or a deer would want to walk from the road up to this spot and then back again. I'm pretty sure it's our man. Or men. OK, Arvind, bring it back now. Careful when you land it."

"Doesn't it have auto-landing?" said Bhardwaj.

"Yes, but you've still got to get it in the right position for the auto-land to take it down smoothly."

After a couple of anxious minutes the machine reappeared over the hill, and returned to them, hovering before them lower and lower until finally it seemed to sink with a thud of relief back onto the grass, and the whine of the blades deepened and died.

"Mission accomplished!" said Alison.

"Well done," said Blue. Nicolson and Craig, who'd been watching the whole time, broke into applause, and Blue joined them.

"Now we need to get back to the incident room to download the images," said Alison. "I wouldn't advise trying to locate the site till we've got the pictures and plotted the features on the map.

As they packed the equipment back into the car, Ffox-Kaye came over.

"I take it you've located the spot?"

"Yes," replied Blue. "We're going back to our incident room now to download the pictures and plot the location on a map. Then we'll come back and get the SOCOs onto it. I'll print off copies for you too."

"That won't be necessary. Just put all the files on a disk for me. See you later." He gave Alison a smarmy smile, more of a leer, and was off.

14

They were back at the incident room just after eight, and got the kettle on for coffee. Alison asked Craig and Bhardwaj to do the work on the computer. The data was stored on a tiny 64 gigabyte memory card which Alison had extracted from the drone when it had landed. Deirdra copied the files onto the PC, then passed the video and still images on to Bhardwaj to process, while she concentrated on mapping the co-ordinates.

At half past eight the SOCOs arrived and five minutes later McCader and Dalvey, the latter stuffing the last piece of a bacon roll into his mouth. McCader apologised for their late arrival. Once everyone had coffee sorted out and got themselves sat round the table, the meeting could begin.

Blue reported on the work with the drone, much to the disappointment of the SOCOs. "We wanted to play too," said Jill. "We all want a shot next time."

Bhardwaj played the colour video from the drone on his computer whilst Alison provided a commentary. They could see the ground moving ahead of the drone as it took off, then the estate fence and gate drifted below, and the camera's eye came over the brow of the hill, to see the almost featureless moorland stretching off, gradually rising towards the west. Then the movement slowed down and the camera was focused on an area almost at the brow the hill.

"There it is," said Alison, "you can see the early sun coming in from the south east casts a shadow in that area that looks like a shallow scoop out of the hill. Almost like a giant footprint. Now look over to the left. Can you see the faint line running away from it down towards the road."

"So he came up from the road, and went back to it later?" said Steve Belford. "And didn't go anywhere else?"

"That's what it looks like."

"So he may have spent the night there?"

"It's not possible to tell from the pictures how long he was there, but it doesn't look as if there was any other disturbed area. Either he came up there early in the morning or the night before, and lurked in the spot he was going to shoot from."

"That suggests," said Moira Nicolson, "that he got himself, or somebody else got him, to the point where the path hits the road."

"Exactly," said Blue, "and somebody may have seen him coming or going, on foot or in a vehicle."

"You're talking about one person, Alison," said Jill. "Do you think there was just one?"

"I can't see signs of a lot of footfall on the main area. I feel two or more people would have disturbed the ground a bit more. But you'll be able to check that out on the spot."

"We'll need to check for sightings on the road, early yesterday morning, or late the previous evening," said Moira. "I'd suggest Arvind and Deirdra get onto that once the printouts are done. I can help there too. If that's OK with you, Angus?"

"That sounds good, Moira, thanks. Deirdra, how long before the map's ready?"

"Inside half an hour, chief, Ah've almost done wi it."

"And the pictures, Arvind?"

"Printing out right now, chief."

"OK. As soon as they're done, I'd like you to get your team up there, Steve, and see what you can find. Enver, can you take Kevin up with you? Kevin, see if you can find any more bullets, and Enver, have a general snoop round all the buildings, if you can do that without the goons getting in your way."

"I'm sure I can manage that, sir," said McCader with a smile.

Twenty minutes later, at ten, the SOC team, armed with photos and a ground plan, set off, tailed by Alison in her car. McCader and Dalvey followed in a police car. Blue had given McCader a DVD with the downloaded files on it, and the file for the groundplan, to pass on to Ffox-Kaye.

"If there's any sign that he's going to interfere with the shooting site, let me know right away. Though I don't see any point it. He can let us do the work and then just demand the results."

15

Blue invited Nicolson, Craig and Bhardwaj to sit at the table.

"OK. Arvind, Deirdra, thanks for the work so far. That's enabled the SOCOs to get moving. Now we need to see what we've got in terms of comings and goings. I doubt there's a lot of traffic on that road, so somebody may have seen something."

"And any stranger would have been noticed," added Moira. "I'd suggest Deirdra and Arvind do house to house starting up the road – last house that way is about four miles short of the gate to the estate – and then working back towards Craighouse. There are quite a few houses scattered along the road, or just off it. I think Maggie Stillman has a copy of the electoral roll here, so that'll give the names to most of them – all the ones that aren't holiday homes anyway. Meanwhile, I can make some phone calls to the ferry operators and see what we've got in the way of unusual traffic. I can also get them to assemble any CCTV footage that might be relevant."

"That sounds good. I'd better let the Super know what's going on."

Blue left the building and crossed the road to the car park, to get some privacy. The sun was still shining, and the only sound was that of the sea, a calming susurration. All at once a grey van swept past and rushed on up the road towards the Dunrighinn estate. "Avotek Aero Engineers" in purple letters, with a picture of a cartoon helicopter with a big smile on the nose. Blue watched it until it disappeared, then took out his phone.

He brought Superintendent Campbell up to date.

"Sounds like you're making a bit of progress there, Angus. That's good. Email me the pictures and map along with the current version of your report – I know you keep them up to date. Anything we can put on the CC's desk will help to show we're on this. By the way, be careful with this Ffox-Kaye. I've been asking around. Apparently he's on the way up, Super before too long I hear, and aiming a lot higher. He used to be with the RPU – Royal Protection Unit – so he knows all the right people."

"OK. I'll watch him. Anything else?"

"You clearly haven't been reading today's papers."

"No, that's right. What's happened? Another shooting?"

"No, nothing like that, thank goodness. The prime minister's finally released the text of the Act."

"Ah. And what's in it then?"

"You'd better look at it yourself. It'll be all over the internet by now. I'll talk to you later."

Blue walked back towards the incident room. The Super had sounded preoccupied. He'd better check out the Act. As he came in Bhardwaj and Craig were looking through a printout of the electoral register for Jura with Inspector Nicolson, Craig making notes in the margin as Nicolson told them what she knew of the people who lived on the main road.

Blue turned on his laptop, opened up Mozilla Firefox and typed in "National Symbols Act UK". The top item found was from the *Daily Courant*: "Government to Protect Symbols of Britishness". The article focused on the prime minister's statement to the House of Commons the previous evening that his government was "Taking steps to protect the powerful symbols that make we British a proud and united people." They were going to introduce in the next few weeks a "National Symbols (Protection) Bill". The new law, when passed by Parliament to become an Act, would make it a criminal offence to denigrate, disparage, insult, or damage any item which was listed in the Appendix to the Bill as a National Symbol. The list was short: the union flag, the institution of the British monarchy, the person of the monarch and her immediate family, the office of prime minister, and the UK Parliament. Punishments for committing an offence under the Act would range from a spot fine of £60 through higher fines up to a maximum prison term of four years. The prime minister commented further that this Act would "ensure that the things most of us Britons hold dear will be protected from denigration by the enemies of this country, both external and internal."

"That's us off, chief," called Bhardwaj, as he and Craig made for the door.

"Right. Good luck. See you later." Blue noticed that Nicolson wasn't there. She must be using a phone in one of the other rooms.

Next he turned to the *Daily Redtop* article, "PM takes on Brithaters". This told him that the union flag – incorrectly known as the 'union jack' – was to be used on all documents issued by the UK

Government, and would be displayed on the cover of all new UK passports. It was also to be prominently displayed on and within all buildings owned or used by government agencies or other public bodies. A folded union flag would become the usual object upon which witnesses in court would be called to swear. Destroying, writing over or crossing out, or covering over a union flag or its image would become offences. In particular, the paper gleefully announced that those people in Scotland and Wales who had covered the union flag on their driving licence with small stick-on images of the Saltire or Welsh dragon would be subject to a fine of £120 plus three penalty points to be added to their licence. The writer urged the "boys in blue" to get to work spot-checking licences immediately.

The *Liberator* took a different line with "Thai-style Royal Insult Law threatens Free Speech," quoting a lawyer representing a human rights organisation and a journalist, both worried that, whilst they could see the 'admirable intentions' of the proposed law, its enforcement could lead to the suppression of free speech and the freedom of the press. In particular, the apparent outlawing of criticism of the royal family worried the lawyer because it would curtail 'legitimate discussion of the functioning of the monarchy;' and the reporter added that it concerned her too, because 'we have a duty to report scandals involving royals.'

Whilst most of the Scottish papers followed the line set by their London editions, the *Cryer* voiced concern over the right of the Scottish Government or local authorities to fly the Saltire on their buildings, especially on St. Andrew's Day, while *The Nation* declared that the Act would be a major attack on an individual's right to consider themselves Scottish. Blue noticed that the latter piece was penned by John Striven, an old friend of his from their days at Glasgow University. Both papers carried the same quote from an unnamed UK government spokesperson that, 'the regions of the UK have nothing to fear in expressing their regional identity, provided this happens within a British perspective.' The Scottish Government refused to make any comment until the full text of the Bill had been published.

Blue could understand that Police Scotland might find themselves bogged down in trivial actions like checking everybody's driving licence and rear number plate, which would divert manpower from crime-fighting and, even worse, make enemies of lots of ordinary people who simply took pride in their own flag. He realised that he himself would be caught in the net of this law, as his own car had SCO and a Saltire at one side of the rear plate, rather than GB and a union flag. He had no intention of changing that, and suspected that most people in the same situation would take the same attitude. But he also wondered where the 'Britishness' drive would go next. What other 'national symbols' might be tagged onto the Act? And what about the corollary: might some symbols be banned as 'anti-British'? The Super was right to see this as a worrying development.

16

It was after eleven, and he was about to check out Lord Steppingham and Jason van Kaarsten on the web, when Moira Nicolson came back into the room, followed by a fresh-faced and smiling young woman holding onto a large red Post Office bag slung over her shoulder.

"Hope I'm not disturbing you, Angus, but I've got something."

"No, no. Fire away."

"This is Annie Clay. She's the postie here. She comes over from Islay in the morning and works her way up the island and back by lunchtime. I managed to catch her on the phone before she got the boat back to Islay. I think you should hear what she has to say."

Blue shook the woman's hand and thanked her for coming in, then invited her to take a seat at the table. He and Moira sat opposite. He turned the voice recorder on, made the introductory statement, and then indicated to Moira that she should begin. She nodded to him and faced Annie Clay, who was still smiling.

"I'm sorry, Annie, I forgot to offer you a cup of tea."

"That's all right, Moira, I've just had one. I was just on my tea break at the cafe when you phoned." Blue couldn't quite place the accent, he thought maybe somewhere in the English Midlands.

"Well, Annie, can you just take us through yesterday morning?"

"Certainly. I'd just come off the eight o'clock boat from Port Askaig – I do that every weekday morning – and driven about half a mile up the road, when I saw these cars rushing towards me, obviously trying to catch the return boat. Luckily the road up to Craighouse has two lanes, or I don't know what would have happened, but I just stopped the van where I was, and waited for them to go past. I mean, I could have just driven on, but there was something scary about the way they came at me."

"Tell us more about these cars."

"There were three of them. Big black Range Rovers. Driving really close together, but fast. Like a convoy."

"Did you see who was in them?"

"No, the windows were really dark, so I couldn't see inside. I did manage to see the driver of the first one, a man with a black moustache. I couldn't see any more than that. But he did have a rather unpleasant expression, as if, why were I looking at him. I must admit I were relieved when they'd passed."

"Did they catch the ferry?"

"I'm sure they would have, they always wait a few minutes before the return to Islay, and if they see someone coming down the road, they hang on. Ask Fergus, he's bound to remember them."

"Fergus is the boatman on the ferry," Nicolson added.

"Did you see the number plates?" Blue asked Annie.

"No, sorry."

"That's OK. Thanks, Annie, you've been very helpful "

"There's more," cut in Nicolson, "Annie, what other cars do you remember passing on the road?"

"Yes, Moira, this was later, maybe about nine, I were just coming out of the distillery shop – delivering the mail you understand – when this big grey people-carrier drove past, in a hurry too."

"Did you get a look at the people inside?"

"Well, again the rear windows were so dark, all I could see is that there were figures in the back, definitely people there. But I got a good look at the driver, she had to slow down to get round the post van. Middle aged woman, very made up, you know, plastering over the cracks. Very dark hair, dyed I suppose, round her head rather than long. Oh, and glasses, light-coloured frames, maybe pink, I don't really know. As soon as she were past the van she was off again at speed. Other folk will have seen her too, I'm sure. There were people standing outside the shop across the road."

"And this wasn't a vehicle you've seen around?" asked Blue.

"No, no. I've been doing this a few years now, I could probably recognise most of the cars on Islay and Jura by now. That wasn't one I knew. And there was no Islay wave."

Blue knew that most residents on Islay or Jura will give a wave to any car that passes them. Usually it's just a tweak of the hand or a raised index finger. "That does suggest she was a stranger," he agreed.

"Fergus will have spotted her too, if she was going for the boat," added Nicolson.

"Thanks, Annie, anything else?" asked Blue.

"Yes, one more thing. About quarter past ten I were coming out onto the road, from Ardmenish Farm, in the van. I had to wait a moment because a big black Range Rover were coming past. Like the ones I saw earlier, but not going quite so fast. There was a man driving, and a woman in the passenger seat, maybe someone else at the back, I couldn't really tell. There's only the houses on the estates beyond Ardmenish, so it must have been coming from one of them."

"That's great, Annie," said Moira. "Many thanks for your help."

Moira saw Annie out of the building, then came back.

"That's useful, isn't it?" she said.

"It certainly is. At last, a witness to something! And some corroboration of the story I got from Plaistow." He turned his notebook to a clean page. "OK, let's see what we've got. At seven we have the shooting. Then Annie sees the Range Rovers at eight."

"Was that them taking Lord Steppingham off?"

"That does sound right. And it suggests a lot more PPU muscle on the site than Plaistow or Ffox-Kaye were prepared to admit to."

"At least three, simply to drive the vehicles."

"Plaistow said that it was Sergeant Steele and PC Corning who went with Steppingham. We can ask for confirmation of that, but I suspect Ffox-Kaye will simply say that he can't reveal the actual numbers or identities for security reasons. Let's not bother him with this at the moment."

"The other black Range Rover sounds like the secretary and the nurse from Dunrighinn. And the co-pilot. On their way to the airport."

"Yes, I'd agree. We'll need to get pictures of them so that Annie can ID them. We have to rule out the possibility that it was the shooter and an accomplice."

"Who'd picked him up on the road, you mean?"

"Yes. Though I suspect he was long gone by then. But this grey people-carrier at nine, that's a mystery. That doesn't tie in with Plaistow's account."

"It's possible they were from another estate further on. There are also a few cottages rented out for holidays by some of the estates. We can phone them and see if anyone was there."

"Yes, no point in seeing a mystery if there isn't one."

"I'll contact Fergus at the ferry. He's a sharp old man, who can often tell you who crossed on a Thursday evening two months ago! I'm only exaggerating slightly."

"Good, in fact it might be worth while both of us talking to him. Not just about the cars Annie saw. The shooter may have gone that way too. We also need to contact the airport to find out who passed through yesterday morning and where they were going. And the ferry to Kennacraig, just in case someone there spotted something relevant to us."

"Leave that with me. I'll get Bob to do some of it from Bowmore. We'll also need to contact the chap who runs the passenger boat from Tayvallich to Craighouse. I'll give him a ring now."

17

Moira went off to use the phone in the other room. She was back in a couple of minutes, before Blue had come to any conclusion about what to do next.

"I've been on the phone to Alex Malcolm – he runs the passenger boat from Craighouse to Tayvallich. He's based here, and is available now if we want to talk to him. Fancy a bit of fresh air?"

It took them ten minutes to walk to the harbour at Craighouse. The boat, a sturdy-looking launch, was tied up. Not far off, in a wooden shed with a sign above proclaiming 'Jura Fast Ferries', they found Alex Malcolm, a young man with beard and pony tail, relaxing with a cup of tea.

"Hi, Moira. And you'll be Inspector Blue. For the moment you've doubled the Blues on Jura. Tea?"

"No thanks, Alex. We won't keep you. We're just interested in anyone who maybe came over on Sunday evening and went off again Monday morning."

"Sorry to interrupt," put in Blue. "How often do you run?"

"Twice a day. I go over to Tayvallich at 8.45 am and five pm, returning at ten am and 6.30 pm. That's from the beginning of May till the end of September. I also charter the boat for cruises, but there's no fixed programme."

"So what about Sunday evening and Monday morning?" asked Nicolson.

"What's this about? Has a notorious killer been visiting Jura?"

"It's just a routine enquiry."

"That's what they always say. Let me think. For a start, going over to Jura on a Sunday evening and leaving on Monday morning would be a bit of a daft trip, since there's nothing on in Craighouse on Sunday evenings – even the distillery shop is shut – so we don't get many people doing that. I'd notice it right away. And nobody did that this week. I'm sure of that."

"OK. Who was on the boat Sunday evening then?"

"Over to Tayvallich, I took a couple from Glasgow – they'd been on Jura for the weekend, walking I think, left their car in Tayvallich – and three Dutch guys who'd been doing the Islay distilleries, and then Jura to finish off. I think they'd been over about a week, a car from a hotel in Oban was going to meet them at the other side. Just as well, as they'd enjoyed a good few samples during the day. They were very satisfied with the experience, I can tell you."

"And coming back?"

"That's easy. Nobody at all."

"Well, that seems pretty clear. What about Monday morning?"

"That was a bit busier. Let me check the book." He pulled off an untidy shelf a battered hardback A5 notebook with a picture of palm trees on the cover. "Let's see. OK. Here we are. Going over to Tayvallich. Seven Germans – one of them told me they'd been over for the whisky too, two Englishmen – I think they were bird spotters, though I didn't speak to them – and two French girls, sorry, young women, backpacking round the islands. Marie and Annette – they were hoping to get a lift to Lochgilphead." He blushed. "Well, there was nobody waiting for the boat back yet, so I gave them a lift myself – I keep my car over there, you see – it only takes ten minutes."

"And was there anyone coming over, when you got back to Tayvallich?"

"Just Dave Kinsman – he's a plumber from Ardrishaig – there was a problem with the boiler at the Craighouse Inn. I took him back that evening."

"Nothing struck you as odd about any of those people you've mentioned?" asked Blue.

"Dave Kinsman's a pretty odd character. Who has a Kaiser Wilhelm moustache nowadays?" Malcolm caught the lack of response. "Oops, sorry, joke in poor taste. Has there been a murder? No, don't tell me, drug trafficking. Little boats creeping into Craighouse by night. Honest officer, it wisnae me!"

"Just a routine enquiry, Mr Malcolm," said Blue. "I don't suppose you keep the names of your passengers in that book?"

"No, just numbers and where I reckon they're from. Just to get a feel for who my customers are. Helps me to decide where to advertise. Honest, guv, I'm a respectable businessman."

"And where do you advertise?"

"*Scottish Landscape, Whisky Monthly, Schottland Illustrierte, La Belle Ecosse.* There's a Dutch magazine too, I can't remember the name. The Jura website helps, obviously. And word of mouth."

"Well, many thanks for your help, Mr Malcolm. Good luck with your business."

"Thanks, Alex, that was actually very helpful," added Nicolson.

On the way back, Blue's mobile rang. McCader, reporting that Dalvey, despite searching a wide area with the metal detector, had not found any more bullets.

"OK. And did you get a look round yourself?"

"Oh yes, no problem. Ffox-Kaye only seems to have two or three people left here."

"Find anything interesting?"

"I'll tell you when I get back." McCader was always cautious when speaking on the phone.

"Right. How are the SOCOs getting on?"

"They're still at it."

"Good. Can you come back here now, and bring Dalvey with you."

"Will do, chief. See you soon."

18

In fifteen minutes they were back in the service point building. It was about half past twelve, and Blue sensed there was something different the moment he opened the door to the incident room. A big pile of sandwiches sat on a large ashet, and next to it a plastic container full of chocolate mini-muffins.

"Where do you think these came from?" he asked Moira.

"I've no idea, I'll ask Maggie."

They soon found Maggie. "Oh yes, the food. Effie Blue brought it round about twenty minutes ago. Said she couldn't have Blues, or any of their friends, starving on their own island. Looks like there's enough for an army."

"Tuna mayonnaise with spring onion and rocket on wholemeal bread," commented Blue, as he started on one. "My favourite."

They were just settling into a couple of sandwiches each, when McCader and Dalvey arrived back from the shooting site. Dalvey seemed to smell the food from the doorway and when his questioning glance got a nod from Blue, he tucked in. Before following suit, the sergeant explained that Dalvey had taken the metal detector over the area between the helicopter landing pad and the house. After watching Dalvey gobble down his first sandwich, Blue asked how he'd got on.

Dalvey looked anxiously at the remaining sandwiches as he answered, "Not a sausage, chief! Well, not a bullet anyway. I did find several interesting bits and pieces, but I'm not sure any will be useful to you." He rummaged in his jacket pocket and produced a handful of small evidence bags, each with a date and number written on the white rectangle on the front. He laid them out side by side on the table. A bent nail; a 10 pence coin; a silver-coloured cigarette lighter; a Swiss army knife; a rusty kitchen knife; and a small brass cartridge case. He picked up the latter. "But you might find this worth a look."

"What is it? I mean, I can see it's a cartridge case. What can you add?"

Dalvey took the bag and peered at it. "It's a 9 x 19 mm Parabellum cartridge case. Still in shape, I'd guess it was fired fairly recently."

McCader glanced over at Blue. "Kevin found it in the grass, probably trampled in. Could be one of the shots fired at the shooter by Plaistow or one of the others."

"Kevin," asked Blue, "is this a fairly common type? I mean, can you tell what sort of gun it came from?"

"Not really, boss. It's the most common cartridge type in the western world. Fits a bargeload of handguns, starting with pre-World War I Lugers. This looks like what they call 'NATO standard' but it's used by armed forces as well as law enforcement in many countries, not just NATO members. In fact, the Russians even have a version of it, known as the…"

"But there is a question here," interrupted McCader.

"What's that?" asked Blue.

"If this is one of the shots fired at the shooter, where are the rest? Kevin covered a pretty wide area, and didn't find any more. So either they were carefully collected afterwards, and this one was missed because it had got pushed into the ground by someone's foot, or…"

"They didn't fire any more shots," finished Dalvey.

"Did you cover the whole area between the house and the helicopter?" asked Blue.

"Sure. Those goons stopped me getting within about ten yards of the house, so I suppose they could all have fired from there."

"Is it normal practice to pick up cartridge cases afterwards?"

"In common or garden warfare, no," answered Dalvey. "With law enforcement actions, cartridge cases are usually located and retained for evidence purposes. This also discourages inappropriate use."

"But in operations where secrecy is normal," added McCader, "cases would be collected simply to prevent knowledge of the operation leaking out. That could be the case here. Security people habitually behaving as if they have something to hide. Even when they don't."

"OK. Let's look at the other stuff. What about the lighter, Kevin?"

Dalvey picked up the bag. "It looks an expensive one. There's a curling dragon etched into a black lacquer coating, and there's a tiny word on the side of the lid." He pulled out his loupe again and flicked the powerful magnifying glass out. "Let's see, ah yes, 'Cartier'. So I guess it's not a cheap one."

"That doesn't take us very far," said Blue. "I'm guessing expensive stuff was the norm here."

"Wait a mo," said Dalvey, "I think there are some letters etched on the top, but there's mud on it." He began to pull open the seal to take the lighter out of the bag.

"Hold it, Kevin," said Blue, "there may be fingerprints too, so we should leave it in the bag."

Dalvey scowled. "Why do we want to take any prints off it? We know who was there, don't we? Besides, this has probably been lying there for ages."

"We don't know that for sure," said Blue, "but if there are any prints, we need to get them. They're probably not relevant, but you never know. Thanks Kevin, you've done well here."

Dalvey blushed, but his mouth was now full of sandwich so he was unable to say anything.

"But I think what we need now is for you to get back to Oban as fast as possible and process the bullets and the cartridge case." Dalvey's face told them this was welcome news. "But leave the other finds here for the SOC team," Blue added.

"There's a boat at two from Port Askaig," said Moira. "Angus, if we take Kevin down to Feolin and put him on the boat to Port Askaig, we can also have a chat with Fergus."

Blue looked at his watch. Five past one.

"That's a good suggestion, Moira, but I need to find out how the SOCOs are doing first. And Arvind and Deirdra. Enver, can you take Kevin to Feolin now for the ferry? Kevin, once you're across to Port Askaig, you just get the next boat to Kennacraig, then the bus to Oban. Don't forget to keep your receipts."

"No difficulty there, boss. Islands, I bloody hate them. And boats, I…"

"Right, Kevin, that's enough! Email your report to me tomorrow. Enver, once you've dropped Kevin, have a chat with Fergus. Find out when we can have a longer talk with him. When he's off duty maybe."

19

McCader and Dalvey left. Blue was relieved Dalvey had gone. He was a valuable asset when there were ballistics issues, and when he worked on his own. He was not so good at working with others, and had rubbed up a lot of his colleagues the wrong way when he had, for a short time, been put in charge of a SOC team. As a supervisor, his overbearing manner, short temper, and contempt for women and all non-white people had led to several complaints, and since a major incident the previous year, he was kept in the lab, or under close supervision.

Five minutes later Bhardwaj and Craig arrived. They too tucked into the food. Blue could wait till they'd eaten before asking what they'd found. They told him over coffee and mini-muffins.

Craig had finished eating first, so Blue asked her. "Aye, no bad, chief. Got a couple of useful statements."

"Can I check off a couple of items first? Then we'll see what else you got. What about a convoy of three black Range Rovers, probably shortly before eight am?"

"Check!" shouted Bhardwaj, almost dropping his second muffin.

"Arvind," said Moira, "there's no need to shout, is there?"

"Sorry, boss. Yes, we got them."

Craig was consulting her notebook. "Aye, a Donald Ferrier of Ardmenish was in a field taking feed to his sheep when he saw them. Driving very fast, he said. That was about 7.45 am. Then Mary Buchanan was opening up the village shop, about 7.50 she says, when they came rushin through the village. Yvonne Watts – she runs the cafe – saw them too, about the same time, from her window."

"Good. What about a grey or silver people-carrier, about an hour later?"

"Yup," said Bhardwaj, "Got that one too."

"Aye, a Raymond Slater was digging in the front garden of his cottage at Keils, just up the road from here, when it came past. A woman driving, he said, and some folks in the back, maybe women too, but he couldna see them too clear. Yvonne Watts saw that one too. And Mrs McCormack – she's the headteacher at the primary school next door here – she was lining up the bairns in the playground when it went past. That was no long afore nine too."

"Excellent. OK, what about another black Range Rover, about quarter past ten?"

"Snap!" cried Bhardwaj. "Sorry."

"We've a few witnesses for that one too. Agnes Fairlie and Mollie Grayson were having coffee at the cafe, and saw it out the window. And we've three others who saw it as well."

"That's great. What else? Leave out anyone recognised as local."

"You're going to like this one, chief," said Bhardwaj excitedly. "Tell them, Deirdra."

"Aye. At 7.15 Rachael Scrimgeour – she lives in one of the cottages in Ardmenish – was walking her dog and was on the track up tae the road, when she saw a cyclist go past that she didna ken. He was headin towards Craighouse."

"A cyclist?"

"Aye. We asked for a description. She thought it was a man, average height and build, wearing a dark green waterproof jacket, and camouflage trousers. But she couldna see his face – he had a bike helmet on – one of they ones that look like old German army helmets, she said – dark glasses, and a scarf wrapped round the lower part of his heid. He had black gloves on too. And a big dark green rucksack on his back."

"D'you reckon that was the shooter, chief?" asked Bhardwaj.

"It's certainly a possibility. The rucksack suggests equipment or camping gear. What kind of bike was it?"

"She said quite a small one. Seemed too wee for the size of the rider. She thought maybe a child's bike. Or one of yon fold-up ones with wee wheels."

"Any other sightings of the cyclist?"

"Naw, just the one. Sorry, chief."

"No need to apologise. That's a good lead. Any other sightings that might be interesting?"

"Naw, that wis it. All the other traffic was people they kent well. But I've made a list anyway." She unfolded a sheet of paper. "This is all the sightings of people or traffic on the roads, goin both ways." She handed it to Blue.

"Thanks, Deirdra. Oh, just one other thing. Did anyone happen to see another black Range Rover, around eleven? This time heading up the road, towards Dunrighinn."

Craig frowned. "No, chief, that doesna ring a bell."

"All we got is on the list," said Bhardwaj.

"Good. We're beginning to get a bit of perspective on this. We need to find out who the cyclist was, and who were in all those vehicles."

"The cyclist is a good lead, isn't it?" said Moira. "Right time, right place, right kit."

"Could be. I don't want to get too excited yet. But it's a real lead, right enough."

"So what next?"

"I need to get back up the site and see how the SOCOs are getting on. I'll go with Enver as soon as he gets back. Meanwhile can you two" – he indicated Bhardwaj and Craig – "get down to Craighouse and ask around some more about the cyclist. Ask if anyone's seen him around anywhere. Was he around the day before, or did he come some time previously to check the place out? I know the description doesn't tell us much about the man – if it was a man, that is – but the rest might trigger some recollection."

20

Now it was after two. Blue texted Alison Hendrickx to say that he was on the way. By the time he'd finished, McCader was back. Nicolson was busy on the phone, talking to Sergeant Bob Walker in Bowmore. Blue gave her a wave, and set off with McCader. Blue updated him on the cars and the cyclist as they headed up to the site.

"Sounds positive," said McCader. "Cycle up the night before, hide the bike near the road somewhere, yomp up the hill and find a spot, spend the night there, maybe in a one-man tent or bivvy bag – sorry, that's basically a waterproof sleeping-bag – do the job, back to the road fast as you can, and off on the bike again. The only danger would be that the PPU people instantly send a car down the road to look for you."

"Which on this occasion they failed to do. I wonder why?"

The SOC van was parked outside the gates of Dunrighinn, at a lay-by where easy access to the hillside was possible. McCader led Blue up a path onto the moor. Above him he could see police tape on the horizon. They reached a taped off area. Steve Belford and Alison were waiting for them.

Steve came forward as they arrived. "Hi, chief."

"Hi, Steve, how's it going here?"

"We're done! The others are in the van waiting for the starting gun."

"OK, what have you got?"

"First the positives. You can see the slightly flattened area there. We reckon that's where he had some sort of groundsheet spread out. You can see where some of the heather's been cut away with secateurs, to enable him to get as low a profile on the hill as he could. If he was here overnight he probably had a waterproof sleeping bag."

"A bivvy bag?"

"Yeah, right, that's it. Er, then, in the morning he crawled two or three feet up onto the ridge here so that he had a good view of the house. There are some marks that might have been made by his elbows and boots. He would have set his rifle up about here, probably had a bipod to rest it on. There are a couple of holes here and here which might fit the bill. Then after he'd done, he wrapped everything up very carefully, put it away and made off."

"Why do you say carefully?"

"That's the negative bit. Because he didn't leave anything behind. Nothing. No bits of equipment, no food items, no cartridge cases. He's been very tidy."

"Surely everybody leaves something."

"Absolutely. He may have sneezed or coughed. Picked his nose even. There will be tiny scraps of DNA lying around. But we can't recover them, because we don't know where they are."

"So we've got nothing?"

"No, that's not quite true. You see, he wasn't so careful on the path down to the road. He was probably in a hurry then, keen to get away. So we've got a couple of things. First, a boot print from a muddy patch, and that'll give us a size and a brand name. And then, further down, we got some more. Alison has them."

Alison pulled from her packet and held up a small evidence bag and Blue squinted to see what was in it. A couple of black hairs, about three inches long.

"How did he manage to lose these?"

Alison took up the explanation. "He was probably crouching low as he ran, and may have simply tripped on a heather root. We found them caught in a heather plant, along the path we think he followed. As well as this."

She pulled out another small evidence bag. In it was a tiny bronze-coloured disk. "It's a one Euro-cent coin. Remember that these things could have been left by another person altogether, or even two other people. But I'd guess the balance of probability is that they're from the shooter."

"We could compare the DNA to what we have of known criminals, internationally. The coin could suggest he came from, or had been abroad recently," said Blue.

"Or not," said Alison. "It could have been in a pocket for months before falling out."

"What about the number of people here? One or two?"

"We'd say the evidence points to one," said Steve. "Two people in this space would have had to be very close to each other! And almost certainly got in each other's way if they were both trying to set weapons up."

"You've got photos?"

"Yes, Andy's done all that. We've taken some soil samples too, especially around the boot print and the area where he might have tripped."

"OK. Anything else you need to do?"

"No," said Steve, "Just get back to the lab and see what we've got. The van's already packed."

They all walked back down the path and up to the van. The cabin housed two rows of seats, and the three SOCOs were lounging in a state of readiness.

"We're starving," said Jill Henderson plaintively. "Can we go now?"

"OK," said Blue, "I don't think the next boat goes from Port Askaig till four, so why not go back to the incident room. There's a pile of food there, help yourselves. Then go over to Islay, and take that four o'clock boat to Kennacraig. Get to work on the stuff in the morning. Well done, you've done a great job."

Steve jumped in and the van made a three-point turn and disappeared off towards Craighouse.

"I'd better tell Ffox-Kaye we're finished here," said Blue. "Anything else happened here, by the way?"

"The helicopter's gone," observed McCader.

"Flew off about half an hour ago," added Alison. "There were some guys in a grey van, they must have been the engineers. They've gone too."

They strolled over towards the gates, and Blue pressed the buzzer, expecting the gates to be opened. Nothing happened. A couple more prolonged buzzes produced a similar result.

"Did they all go off in the chopper?" Blue wondered aloud.

"There's Ffox-Kaye," said McCader.

And indeed DCI Ffox-Kaye was walking unhurriedly down towards the gate. When he arrived the gate remained closed. Ffox-Kaye spoke through the bars.

"Ah, Blue. I assume your SOCOs are done now?"

"Yes. I'll send the report of course. Did you have any questions?"

"No. I had a look up there before they got here. All seems pretty clear. Lone gunman, well-trained, left nothing, made off down to the road. Probably got picked up there by a car."

"Why did you need three vehicles to take Lord Steppingham to the airport?" asked Blue.

For a brief moment, Ffox-Kaye froze, then immediately the mask returned. "For security reasons I'm unable to give details of Political Protection Unit officers or vehicles."

"After the shooting, why didn't you send a car straight down the road to see if the shooter could be apprehended?"

"Lord Steppingham's safety was the first concern. By the time that was ensured, it would have been too late."

"Were you here when it happened?"

"I've already told you, I didn't get here till about eleven. And now I'm going. There's a couple of things you need to know. First, I'm closing this site down as of now. That is, the house and everything within the fence. All the buildings will be locked and security alarms set. The complex will of course still be guarded by PPU personnel. But no-one will be allowed in. That includes you and your people."

"Can I ask why?"

"Simple and rather obvious, even to a plod. Everybody's left, and they're not coming back for a good while. So the place shuts down."

"And the other thing you want to tell me?"

"I've been authorised by the UK Home Secretary to carry out a parallel investigation into these events. Not a joint investigation, a parallel one. Naturally you will give us copies of all paperwork on your investigation, we will reciprocate, although security issues will necessitate a certain amount of redaction. For the next few days I and my investigation team will be based in Bowmore, until we are satisfied that this part of the world is no longer relevant to our inquiries. After all, all the witnesses are now in England, which is beyond your jurisdiction. I will of course be interviewing them myself."

"Clearly I'll want to talk to some of them too."

"There's nothing clear about that at all. It's plain what happened. But of course, if you feel the need to duplicate my interviews, you're free to do so. To make it simpler I have arranged with the various police forces who may be involved that all contact in relation to this case shall be through me. I think your superior officer has my contact details." He turned his back on them and walked away.

"That doesn't sound good," said McCader. "Two investigations at the same time. Seems to me that somebody has an agenda."

"Cheer up Angus, it might never happen," said Alison.

"Trouble is, it probably will," said Blue. "Come on, let's get out of here. Back to base, Enver. I'll go with Alison this time."

21

"What are you going to do now, Alison?" Blue asked, as they drove away from Dunrighinn. "Want to get back with the SOCOs to the mainland?" He was trying to sound casual, but couldn't get the tension out of his voice.

"And leave you looking so fed up? I couldn't possibly do that. I've not seen Moira and Alasdair since last year, so I think I'll take a few days leave and stay on Islay. Do a bit of walking. Play with my drone. Maybe even see you too. If you've time?"

"Yes, that would certainly be good. Yes. But this case just gets more complicated all the time. And now this this so-called parallel investigation. It's ridiculous. What the hell are they playing at? Bloody Ffox-Kaye!"

Alison laid a hand on his arm. "Calm down, Angus. This is not like you. He's obviously got on your nerves. You just have to get on with your own job. You've got some leads, haven't you?"

"Well, one or two. That's why we don't need this other thing. We'll get there, I'm sure of it. If they'll let us."

"Tell me the most promising one."

So Blue told her about the cyclist seen on the road not long after the shooting.

"I didn't hear you mention that to old Foxy there. That sounds a pretty good lead. And you've got enough good people to follow it up with you. You should also have a chat with Superintendent Campbell. You've told me yourself, he takes a good overview of things. Promise me you'll do that."

To which Blue grudgingly agreed.

Back at the service point, Blue phoned Campbell.

"Angus, good to hear from you. What's going on there?"

"A parallel investigation under Ffox-Kaye. I'm not sure what's going on."

"Yes, I've just had notification of that. Unfortunately we can't stop it because of the security aspect. The CC's not happy about it, I can tell you. Thinks it's much too premature. But, for the moment, you've not been shut down. So just stick with your own investigation, and take it wherever it leads. I'll back you up. You're a damn good investigator, Angus. I wouldn't have assigned you to this case if I didn't think you could solve it. Now, tell me exactly what you've got so far."

Blue did that.

"Hmm. I think you're right, this cyclist is the key. Check all the transport possibilities. He must have come over somehow, and got off somehow. There'll be a trace, and you'll find it. I suggest you see the other witnesses if you can too. I suspect van Kaarsten is now well out of reach, but you could talk to the staff at the house. Go down to England and chase them up, see what they have to say."

"Or whether they've been told to keep their mouths shut," said Blue bitterly.

"Only one way to find out, isn't there? I'll support any request you make to interview them. Remember Angus, it's possible there's something going on here that we're not privy to. There could be a whole political dimension that's being pursued without us being told a dicky-bird. We don't know what Steppingham was up to, and nobody's going to tell us, you can be sure of that. Oh, and don't forget those bottles of whisky either. Just when you've time, of course."

The SOCOs were still there, finishing off the food Effie had left, and there was a positive atmosphere in the room, despite Blue's apprehensions, which he kept to himself. Bhardwaj and Craig returned to say they'd found no further sightings of the early-morning cyclist, and needed another cup of coffee. The room was getting crowded.

Jill Henderson appeared by Blue's desk. "Can I have a word, Inspector?"

"Sure, Jill, what's up?"

"I just feel there's something going on here, that we're not being told. That site had definitely been tampered with, there's no doubt about it. And there's something else. We had a good look at the shooting site. The man was well-prepared and well-organised. He had a perfect view of the area in front of the house. So why only wound his Lordship? Why not kill him? I'm sure he could easily have done it if he'd wanted. Like I said before, maybe an inside job."

"That's a good question. I'll agree with you, there's plenty that doesn't add up here. And now they've closed the site down, we can't even look at it again. Let's see what you can get out of the stuff we got. And let me know if anything else strikes you. I value your opinion, Jill. Thanks for mentioning those points."

As she moved off, McCader came up. "Sorry, chief, I forgot to tell you about Fergus, the ferryman, remember. He's on early shift today, finishes at three, then he'll pop up here and see us."

"Good. that's something. Now, time we got those SOCOs on the road."

Ten minutes later the scene-of-crime van lumbered off down the road, with a last wave from Steve out the window. They were looking forward to putting their feet up and then having another meal on the two-hour sail to Kennacraig.

Blue decided to update his report. Moira was making phone calls in the other room, Craig and Bhardwaj were at the PCs, and Alison was reading a book. McCader had gone out to phone his wife. There was a productive silence for maybe half an hour.

Then Moira came in again. "I've been talking to the airport. They'll email me the passenger lists for Friday to Monday. A couple of points they cleared up however. First, Alice Rogers, Eric James and Brian Richards flew on the Glasgow plane at one o'clock on Monday. That's the nurse, the secretary and the co-pilot. Second, there's no record of Ffox-Kaye flying in on a scheduled flight on Monday morning. Nor on a private plane – they've checked the manifests – unless he was travelling under an alias."

"Which is not impossible," said Blue, "but that ties in with him being very shirty when I asked him when he got there."

"Are you thinking he was there all the time?"

"Maybe."

"But why pretend he wasn't? What difference does it make?"

"Remember Jill's idea that it might be an inside job. What if Ffox-Kaye were the shooter? Or if he were there to see that it happened?"

Nicolson frowned. "That's an interesting idea. But then, they'd have to have somebody in the frame for it. They'd have to have it all worked out, wouldn't they? Can't just have it left an unsolved case."

"It wouldn't surprise me if Ffox-Kaye manages to find someone. Maybe that's what this whole parallel investigation thing is all about. Finding the scapegoat. Replacing our jigsaw with theirs. Except that ours has half the pieces missing. Theirs would be complete. And I bet they'll find someone the tabloids will love to hate."

"We'll have to see what happens. I take it we're not giving up."

"No way, Moira. No way. We'll get there."

"If they let us. More coffee, Angus?"

22

Maggie Stillman popped her head round the door. "Someone to see you, Moira."

A short weatherbeaten man with wiry grey hair and stubble, wearing a boiler suit and woolly hat, came into the room, looking around till his eyes lighted on Moira. "Ah! Moira, there you are. Yon Sergeant – I think I saw him out in the car park on his phone – said you were wanting to talk wi me."

"Fergus! Thank you for coming. This is Inspector Blue, from Oban, and Dr Hendrickx, she works with the police too. This is Fergus Ritchie, the ferryman."

Alison put her book down and smiled at Fergus. "Hi, Fergus, can I make a cup of tea or coffee?"

"Aye, lass, that would be grand, a cuppa tea would do just nicely. Milk and two, please."

"Have a seat," said Moira, motioning Fergus to the table. Blue came over from his desk and shook hands with Fergus before sitting down. Tough, hardworking, outdoor hands.

"We're looking at people who came and went on the ferry this last weekend," Moira began. "Were you on then?"

"Oh, aye, I tend to be on most weekends. The lad, Donnie, he's got children. It's easier for me."

"Can we start with yesterday? Do you remember a convoy of three black Range Rovers coming to the ferry, the Jura side, about eight o'clock yesterday morning?"

"Well now, I could hardly be missing them, now could I, Moira? You've given me the easy question to start off with, have you not?"

"I suppose so. What can you tell us about them?"

"Well, first of all, they were in a terrible hurry. We'd not got any of the vehicles on yet. They came right up to the front of the queue and demanded to be on right away, flashing their police badges and aa. Then, once they were on board, they refused to let anyone else on, said it was an urgent matter of national security. What a cheek!"

"Did you see who was in the cars?"

"Just the drivers. The side windows were so dark, you couldna see in. The one who paid – and I'm glad to say they did pay – he was a Sergeant Steele. I looked at his ID very carefully before I let them all on. Tall, sandy-haired lad, a bit officious. The other two never said a word, kept the windows closed too. Both had dark glasses on. I think one had a droopy moustache. Or maybe makes a mess when he eats chocolate, eh?"

"Could you see who else was in the cars?"

"No, as I said the side windows were awfa dark. Though I did try and peer in. Discreetly, of course. There were certainly people in the back of two of them, I could just see the shapes. The other I think just had the guys in the front. The back seats were folded down, there was maybe something in the back, but I just couldna see it right."

"Do you know if they joined the queue for the Kennacraig boat?"

"No. I watched them off. They went up the hill onto the Bowmore road. My guess is that they were making for the airport. Whoever the important people were in there, they werena the sort who'd sit on the ferry two hours just to get to Kennacraig. They'd be flying all right."

"OK, Fergus, I'm going to move you on a bit," Nicolson continued. "About an hour later you would have had a grey people-carrier, possibly driven by a woman. Do you remember that one?"

"Oh aye. Woman driver, looked a real sourpuss. Three teenage girls in the back. One of them opened a window to look out as we crossed. Slightly foreign looking, though I don't quite know what I mean by that. I mean they were white, I think, am I allowed to say that these days? I only saw the others behind the one who had the window open. Maybe they'd been to a party at one of the estates. Anyway, as soon as the girl's feeling the breeze or her face, it lights up. She's pretty. Next moment the old hag in the front's yelling at her. 'Shut the effing window, this ain't an effing holiday!' That's the exact words. Well, the window was shut in no time. She was the one in charge there all right."

"What did the woman sound like?"

"Certainly no from these parts. Like somebody out of *East Enders*, I'd say. Is that London? But pretending to be posh when she spoke to me. To get the tickets. 'One car, one driver, three children, if you please, ferryman.' Well, I said, are you sure they're under 15? 'Oh, yes, of course they are!' Not that I believed her, there's always some trying to get a pound off the fare, but you can't tell nowadays, can you, I mean, how old some of them are "

"Did they go for the Kennacraig boat?"

"Oh, aye, straight into the queue for the 12.00. They'd have a while to wait right enough."

"Thanks Fergus, that's really helpful. Now, here's a third question. Later that morning, maybe about half past ten? Another black Range Rover, two men and a woman in it."

"Hmm. Yes I think I remember them too. The black Range Rover did it, after those three earlier. Young man and woman in the front – I mean under thirty or so. But not a couple, you could tell that. Didn't look at each other at all. No trust. And fear too – I'd say she was afraid of something. Caught my eye once, just the once, and there it was. Fear."

"Fear of the man?"

"No. She just ignored him. No, fear of something bigger, I'd guess."

"Where did they go?"

"They went on up the hill, just like the other Range Rovers."

"Did they have a passenger, another man?"

"Oh, yes, he had the window open during the trip. Thin-faced man, short fair hair, middle parting. Looked like he didn't have anything to do with the other two. Never spoke to them during the trip as far as I could see."

"Did he look afraid?"

"No, I'd say he looked bored. As if he was keen to be somewhere else."

"While we're talking about Range Rovers," said Blue, "do you remember one going the other way, from Islay to Jura, around eleven that morning?"

"Now that doesn't ring any bells with me, what with all the others, I'd have remembered another one. No, I'm sure there wasn't one around that time."

Nicolson took up the questioning again. "Right, Fergus, now cast your mind back before that Range Rover convoy at eight yesterday. Did anyone come on a bicycle?"

"To the ferry?"

"Yes."

"No."

"You're sure?"

Fergus just looked at her. Silly question.

"OK. What about Sunday? Did anyone go over to Jura on a

bicycle?"

"No. A couple of guys came back, they'd gone over on Friday. But that's not what you're looking for, is it?"

"No, you're right." Moira paused.

Blue took over. "What about anyone with a bike attached to the car. On a rack at the back, or on the roof?"

"Aye, there were a couple o them on Saturday. Big cars, two bikes each. One had the bikes stuck on the back, that was an English couple, said they were going to be spendin the week at yon cottage behind the mill. Other one had them on the top – beats me how they dinna fall off up there – aye, that was Mary Buchanan's daughter and her husband, going over for a visit."

"Could someone else have had one of those fold-up bikes in a car?"

"Easily. Most of the cars that go over are on the biggish side. Easy to put the back seat down then cover the bike with a blanket."

"I don't suppose you keep a list of all the cars that go over?"

"Why would I do that, now?" Another silly question.

"But," said Moira, "any car coming off the Jura boat would be caught on the CCTV cameras covering the Kennacraig ferry. Don't worry, Angus, we'll get the footage."

Blue remembered the Euro cent. "Any foreigners come over the last few days?"

"Hmm. There was a French couple, but their car was awfa small. You couldna fit a kiddie's scooter in there. There was another lot, an older man and a girl, late teens, his daughter I'd say. The car had foreign plates, not sure from where, George Petrie's van was right up behind it, but the girl was certainly foreign, though her English was very good. No French, I'd recognise that accent. Or Italian, too quiet. Aye, maybe Mediterranean – their skin was no peelie wallie like us Scots "

"Olive?" suggested Moira.

"Aye, olive, that would do. Maybe even light olive if you pressed me. If it was going to be for a paint catalogue, like."

"Did they offer to pay in Euros?" said Blue. Admittedly a very long shot.

"By the time they're getting to Jura, most people have worked out our currency, Mr Blue! But I'll say this, she did have to rummage about in her purse a while to get the coins she needed. She'd accumulated a lot of change there, kept picking out coins, looking at them and droppin them back in. Should have just paid wi a note. I've always plenty change."

"Can you describe them?"

"He stayed in the car, so all I can say is he looked average, with short grey hair and glasses. She got out to pay and have a look round. Short, slim, long dark hair, glossy, wearing jeans and a red waterproof jacket. And trainers. Nice smile. But kind of sad looking too. Mind you, he didn't look very jolly either, though he smiled at her when she got back in the car. See, she was driving."

"What sort of car was it? Hatchback, saloon, fancy, plain, big, small?"

"Oh aye. Ordinary hatchback. Like a Golf or Astra. But I couldn't tell you what brand it was, there's so many these days."

"Colour?"

"Not white or black. Maybe a brick sort of colour."

"When was this?"

"Sunday morning. Eight o'clock. She said they were just going over for the day."

"When did they come back?"

"You'd have to ask Donnie that. He does Sunday evening, so I can go to the Church. You see, if I go in the evening, that gives Donnie the whole day wi his family. He just covers the last boat: half past six to Jura, twenty to seven back."

"Anything else?"

"Couple of Asians, Indians, or something like that. Men. Fifties maybe. Big car, BMW I think. Came over Friday, back on Monday afternoon."

"Did they sound foreign?"

"Oh aye. Glaswegian."

"Thanks, Fergus. You yourself live on Islay, don't you?"

"Aye, that's right. One of the cottages up the back o Bunnahabhain distillery. You can see them from the boat."

Blue leaned back, a signal that he had no more questions, and Moira thanked Fergus for his help.

"No problem. It'll be whatever's goin on up at Dunrighinn?"

"What have you heard?" asked Moira.

"Oh, nothing much. There's just rumours. Nobody's quite sure what's happened. That's quite unusual for this place!"

23

"He doesn't miss anything," said Alison, when Fergus had left.

"And he's raised a lot of new questions," said Moira. "Who were those girls? What was the nurse afraid of? Did the man and the daughter come back? Who were they? Let me make a couple of phone calls and see if we can eliminate the girls first." She went off to the other room.

Blue noticed his coffee had gone cold, and was thinking about putting the kettle on again when McCader came in.

"Everything OK?" said Blue. "You've been out a while."

"Called the wife. Had a smoke. Came into the building earlier, didn't want to barge in during the interview, but I heard most of it from behind the door."

"And what do you make of it?"

"Man and the girl don't sound like assassins. Hardly covering their tracks. The three girls are worth checking out, though, I've an idea about them. I'd need to chase something up online first." He drifted over towards of the PCs. Bhardwaj stood up to let him use his, headed for the kettle.

Five minutes later, the mugs were steaming again.

Moira came back. "Two of the other estates are closed up just now, nobody there at all. Spoke to the managers at the other ones. Very emphatic that no girls were staying there last weekend. 'What sort of place do you think this is?' Rhetorical question. I'm sure all sorts of stuff goes on."

"Debauchery, eh?" said Alison.

"Just the rich at play."

"Thanks, Moira," said Blue. "What do you want to do now?"

"I'll go over to Port Askaig, and get the CCTV material from the Calmac people, then we can go on to the station and have a look at it. Also need to check everything's OK there. Though Bob can deal with most things. So unless you need them for anything, I'll take Arvind and Deirdra too."

"Actually," this was Alison, "I'm running out of steam now, so I think I'll get along too, unless there's anything you'd like me to do here?" She looked at Blue. Was there a message there? But his mind was a blank, somehow his thinking had ground to a halt.

"Er, I can't think of anything."

"OK. I'll see you tomorrow then. Don't you boys get too drunk tonight, now." She kissed him lightly on the cheek. He felt himself blushing. Were they all looking at him?

Bhardwaj cleared his throat, "Er, see you tomorrow, chief!" he said, grinned, and led the way out.

Blue noticed McCader looking out of the window. "What are you looking at?" he asked.

"No comment, chief. But don't start doing anything just yet."

Blue watched as the others walked over to the cars. Bhardwaj and Craig got into the police car, and Moira and Alison into Alison's. For a minute or two the cars sat there. Then Alison and Moira got out again. Alison opened the bonnet of her car and looked in. Then Bhardwaj got out of the police car and came over, looked in too.

"I think we'd better see what's going on," said Blue.

"Right-oh, chief," said McCader and followed him out and across the road to the car park.

"The car won't start," explained Alison. "She's never given me any trouble before."

"Don't worry," said Moira, "Arvind knows everything there is to know about cars. He'll fix it."

Bhardwaj was poking about at the leads surrounding the engine. "Electrics, definitely. But I can't see what. Have to pull a few things out I think. Need my tool box."

"Tell you what," suggested McCader, "why don't you all go back in the police car. I'll have a look at it. If I don't spot anything Arvind can bring his tools in the morning. It won't come to any harm overnight here."

"That sounds good to me," said Bhardwaj. "Bringing the tools back now and tracing the problem would take a while and we really need to look at the CCTV stuff today if we can. I'm sure we'll have the car fixed tomorrow. If that's OK with you, Alison?"

"Yes, yes, I suppose so. It's not as if we're going out this evening. OK, look after her for me, you two. She's all I've got." She put the bonnet down, pulled a rucksack off the rear seat, then clicked the remote locking, and went over to the police car.

"Just a mo," said McCader, "I'll need the key to have a wee look at the engine."

"Oh yes," said Alison, handing him the keys.

"What time tomorrow?" asked Moira.

"Nine OK?" said Blue.

"Fine, see you then." And they were off.

"Let's have a cup of tea, chief," said McCader, "I've a suggestion to make."

The kettle had been put on before they went out, so the tea was soon made.

"All right, Enver, what's on your mind?" Blue had only the vaguest notion of McCader's previous experience. He'd been sent to him the year before, after doing undercover work on a police operation in Aberdeen. But before that his record was a blank. Blue also knew that McCader had contacts in some odd places. He knew better than to ask direct questions about it.

"This is off the record," said McCader, "deniable if necessary. I'd like to take a little look round Dunrighinn House this evening."

"It's closed up. That would be breaking and entering."

"I'm not planning to break anything. But we do need to know there's no valuable evidence in there, and Ffox-Kaye's not going to invite us in."

"Nothing you find could be used as evidence in court."

"No. But a strong pointer often helps to find evidence that can be used. And we're not being given a fair shot at this one, chief. I think we're being kept out of the house for a reason."

"Have you the skills to do this undetected?" asked Blue. As soon as he asked, he knew it was a stupid question.

"Trust me," said McCader quietly, "I have a lot of experience."

"I can't say I'm happy with it."

"That's why it's deniable. If I get caught, I'll take the rap. And no-one else knows, just us."

"Won't there be alarms? And guards?"

"Hmm, I should think so. Very careless if there weren't."

"What have you got in mind? Do you need me there too?"

"No, no, chief. Not at all. But I would appreciate if you could drop me a mile down the road from the gate, and then pick me up later."

"Won't that police car be a bit visible?"

"Yes, that's why we'll use Alison's."

"But it's broken down."

McCader brandished a piece of wire about six inches long with a bare metal contact at each end. "Nothing this won't fix."

"You disabled her car?"

"Yes, while I was out in the car park having a smoke."

"Surely Bhardwaj would have noticed. He's an expert."

"Yes. I had a little word with him. He's fine. Knows nothing at all about what's planned, just that we're up to something. He'll keep quiet, and be spectacularly successful when he fixes the car tomorrow morning."

24

McCader disappeared for the next two hours, and Blue got on with writing his report.

McCader was back about six thirty, and suggested they get something to eat. "We need to be quite visible, chief, what would you suggest?"

Blue knew there was only one possible answer to that question, so they headed for the Craighouse Inn. Before eating they spoke to the manager, Jan Deventer, a business-like young Dutchman. He confirmed there'd been a party of Germans, twelve altogether, half had gone over to the mainland on Monday morning, the rest were still there. They were due to go the following morning.

"What do they come for?"

"Whisky, walking, fishing. The group still here are doing an Islay and Jura tour. The others were on the Islay, Jura and Mull tour. The minibus picks them up at Tayvallich, takes them to Oban for the ferry to Mull."

"All men?"

"Yes. Good customers. Pay what they're asked, but tell us if it's not good. No beating about the bush. It's very useful to have honest feedback."

"Couple of Asian gentlemen?"

"Oh yes. From Glasgow. They were related to each other, cousins I think. Very nice chaps. Knowledgeable about whisky too. Noticed we had a bottle of Amrut behind the bar. Stayed from Friday to Monday."

"Anyone arrive on Sunday, go off again on Monday morning?"

"No. That would surely be a pointless visit, I think. No time for anything worthwhile."

Being a Tuesday, there was room in the restaurant, and a table by a window gave them a fine view of the bay. The menu looked good too, although the prospect of what they were going to do deprived Blue of most of his appetite. For drinks McCader suggested they order simply tap water. However, as the waiter, Simeon, according to his badge, approached the table with the carafe and glasses on a tray, McCader seemed to stand up without noticing him, and the carafe and glasses fell onto the thick carpet. Nothing broken, but a lot of water about and loud and repeated apologies from McCader. Once Simeon had removed most of the spilt water with a dishcloth and bucket, the meal could continue.

"Now everyone who was eating tonight will remember we were here," McCader whispered to Blue. He pulled out a small plastic bottle from his jacket and quickly filled the two wine glasses that were already on the table. "Cranberry juice. But now they'll testify we were drinking red wine too," he added, as the empty bottle disappeared back into his pocket. "Cheers!" he said loudly, and clinked glasses with Blue.

Blue tried to keep calm, but could only manage a goat's cheese and smoked salmon salad, followed by a whisky-infused *crème brulee*, whilst McCader settled for poached haddock with roast potatoes and a spinach and mozzarella sauce. He declined a dessert, but suggested they both finish with an *espresso doppio*. "Keep us sharp, chief."

They avoided talking about the case, and McCader brought Blue up to date on political and economic developments in Albania, the country of his birth. He lamented the fact that the tourist industry had not developed as had been hoped, due to political instability and fears about crime and corruption. "The crime situation is not so bad now," he remarked. "All the biggest Albanian gangsters live in Switzerland now." He went on to describe the many potential tourist attractions the country possessed: Greek and Roman ruins, mediaeval and Turkish castles, unspoilt countryside, historic towns. Even the Museum of Stalinism, formerly the Anti-Religious Museum.

By nine o'clock Blue's knowledge of that little country the size of Wales was encyclopaedic, but he suspected he'd have forgotten most of it by the next day. Must read a book about the history though, he told himself.

Five minutes later they paid and left, ostensibly going to the lounge bar for drinks. However, they passed on down the passage to the toilet and exited at the rear of the building, then made their way back along the road to the service point. McCader produced the keys and unlocked Alison's car, motioning Blue into the driver's seat. He opened the bonnet and reconnected the wire, signalled to Blue, and the car started immediately. Then he got into the back seat.

"OK, chief, can you drive me as far as the passing place about half a mile short of the gate. I'll give you a shout when we're nearly there. If you can see by the running lights that would be fine, but if any other cars come along, put dipped headlights on."

"Shouldn't we be doing this in the middle of the night?"

"That's when they expect it. This time of night they haven't started concentrating. May not even have switched the alarms on. Anyway, I hate getting up in the middle of the night. Don't you?"

Blue had to concentrate very hard on the driving, and took it very slowly. There was no other traffic on the road, unsurprising since after Ardmenish the road only passed the gates to the estates before coming to a dead end.

On McCader's prompt, Blue pulled into the passing place. Looking round, he thought McCader had gone. Then he saw a vague shift in the darkness and the door opened quietly. McCader emerged from the darkness to stand by the driver's window. He had removed his outer layer, and now wore fairly close-fitting black trousers and top, soft-soled shoes, and a balaclava that completed the makeover. He had become a shadow. A pouch on a strap around his neck, hanging over his chest was the only thing he carried. Blue could not see whether it bulged or not.

"OK, chief, be back here in fifty minutes." And he disappeared into the darkness.

Blue turned the car round and drove it cautiously back to the car park. Then sat in it, in the dark, and listened to the radio. There was a discussion about the National Symbols (Protection) Bill. The speakers, from London-based political parties, all supported the Bill, though the parties in opposition insisted they would 'demand' important adjustments, although unable to specify exactly what these would be. They all agreed however that security of the nation was paramount, and that we must be prepared to surrender temporarily some of our freedoms for the greater good. Once the terrorists had been defeated, as inevitably they would, then things would return to normal. This was where the monarchy had an important role to play in unifying the nation and reminding its citizens of their long and proud history. The monarchy was also above the sleaze and backstabbing of politics, and represented the best qualities of Britishness. Insulting the royal family was therefore reasonably to be regarded as more heinous than if the same calumnies were directed at some private person.

Blue was back at the passing place five minutes early, and exactly on time the dark figure he assumed was McCader slipped into the rear seat again. "OK, chief, back to base."

By the time the car was parked again, McCader had the casual shirt, jacket and trousers he was wearing earlier on again. They hurried back to the Craighouse Inn and slipping in again through the rear and past the toilets, were at the bar in time for a couple of drinks before closing time. Had they been residents, of course, they could have stayed longer.

Blue noticed that Simeon was now behind the bar, along with Karla, whose cropped blonde hair was much shorter than Simeon's mousy dreadlocks.

McCader waved to Simeon, "Same again please, Simeon, doubles this time."

Simeon not unnaturally looked blank. "I'm sorry "

"Sorry, Karla must have served us before. Two of the ten-year-old, please, doubles."

McCader led Blue to a table in the far corner.

"This'll do fine, chief. *Slainte mhath*." He looked around, smiling at the other drinkers as if familiar with each of them, raising his glass in a general sort of way. Several raised theirs in return and smiled back.

"That's our alibi, chief. Even if they question Karla, she won't be able to say for definite that we weren't here all night."

"Surely she'll remember that she didn't serve us."

"No. She'll think it must have been Simeon. Anyway, didn't you see her eyes. Pupils dilated. She's already taken a couple of pills. She'll be on another planet by midnight."

No attempt was made to eject anyone at eleven, the management making the dubious assumption that anyone still in the hotel was a resident. By now the nearest policeman would of course be in Bowmore. Blue and McCader left the inn at quarter past eleven.

"I'll meet you at the base at, say, 8.15 tomorrow, chief, and tell all," said McCader. "I need to think through it now and make a few notes." He waved and was off to his B&B.

Effie was still up when Blue got to the door. "Ah there you are Angus, you've been at the hotel this evening, I'm hearing. Sampling the whisky, I hope."

"Certainly, and it's very good." How did she know that so soon, he wondered.

"But you'll be wanting a wee cup of tea now, to help you sleep. It's just made. And besides, I've something to tell you."

Once sat in front of the fire with a cup of tea, Effie revealed her intelligence.

"Bunga-bunga parties! That's what they call them? isn't it. Like that man in Italy. Only here, well, up at Dunrighinn. Ladies of the night brought in secretly! Decadence reaching lows you wouldn't even want to imagine."

"How do you know this?"

"People talk, Angus, on an island. You can't really do anything in secret. Some of it will always get out. Maybe not all, but some."

"So it's all rumour?"

"Ach, but there's no smoke without fire, Angus, take my word for it. The story goes that since Mr. Steppingham's separation from his wife – that was about four years ago – this sort of stuff has been going on. All sorts of important people taking part too. If I could put a few secret cameras in there I'd be making a fortune from the blackmail."

"Sadly, Aunt Effie, you wouldn't. They'd just have you killed. Do you have any precise details?"

"Well, not as such. But people have seen carloads of young women going in. Sometimes children too. That's appalling."

"Absolutely. Let's hope we can put a stop to it."

Day 3 Wednesday

25

After a hearty breakfast at Aunt Effie's, Blue was at the Incident Room by eight. He made a few amendments to his report, indicating that 'unconfirmed local reports' suggested suspicious and possibly illegal activities involving minors were occurring at Dunrighinn. Then he hesitated, and deleted what he'd just written. His report would inevitably reach Ffox-Kaye's desk, and Blue felt the latter would be more interested in protecting his political charges than in rooting out crime. The only likely outcome of his words was therefore that Aunt Effie or some other harmless local who enjoyed a bit of gossip now and then would be grilled, then accused of spreading malicious rumours, and possibly even prosecuted. Even if he kept it to himself, at least he could see how Effie's information compared to what McCader had found at Dunrighinn.

McCader arrived at exactly quarter past, instantly made himself coffee, and after checking that Maggie Stillman had not yet arrived, and that the doors to the building and to the room were firmly closed, brought it over to Blue's desk.

"Morning, Enver. Well, what did you find? By the way, glad you got back in one piece."

"Thanks, chief. Right. Security wasn't a problem. Two goons watching the telly in one of the outbuildings. Burglar alarm system, but I went in the back door and turned it off. Ditto the cameras. So, what did I find? Three floors. Ground floor. Hallway, traces of a bloodstain on the parquet floor, mostly cleaned up but still visible. Large lounge, well-cleaned. Random selection of expensive whiskies, probably chosen because they're expensive. No foreign treaties lying about. Dining-room, well-cleaned too. Then there's a sort of casual room, big space in the middle, sofas round the walls, not sure what it's used for but have my suspicions. Very well-cleaned indeed. People have taken care to remove all human traces from these rooms. Even the whisky bottles have been wiped to remove any fingerprints. Downstairs bathroom, clean too. Not even a book to read. What I suspect was a study, but couldn't get into – I'd have to get hold of something special to deal with the lock. Kitchen, not so carefully cleaned, but I doubt anyone important went in there. One or two other rooms, nothing interesting. Locked door, looks like an entrance to a cellar, worth a look next time. Utility room by the rear door, fuses, stop-cocks for water and gas"

"Gas! I didn't realise there was a gas main on Jura."

"There isn't. They've got their own supply. Tank out the back, probably propane."

"Go on."

"First floor, six main bedrooms, all en-suite, all cleaned, three more hurriedly than the others, recently used. Managed to pick up a few hairs in each of the bathrooms. Second floor, in the roof, range of mostly smaller rooms, recently used ones carelessly tidied, not cleaned. Cleaners probably ran out of time. Four single rooms used recently. One bigger room, three single beds all used recently, smell of cheap scent, found this in the wastebasket." He pulled out an evidence bag containing a flattened toothpaste tube. "BilkaDent. Bulgarian toothpaste. Got a few hairs in their bathroom too."

"What do you think?"

"I'd say Steppingham and van Kaarsten were getting themselves some entertainment of a kind they wouldn't want publicised. And after the shooting everything had to be cleaned up in a hurry. So much so that they didn't get time to finish off the top floor properly."

Blue shared Effie's reports. "So it does all point in the same direction," he concluded, "and suggests those girls in the people-carrier might be part of it. Could what was going on at the house be connected to the shooting?"

"Seems unlikely on the face of it. It sounds like these romps with possibly underage girls have been going on for a while, without anyone getting shot. That we know of, anyway. It could simply be that after the shooting Ffox-Kaye tried to limit any possible scandal which we might uncover, by getting everybody out of the way, cleaning the place up, and then shutting it down tight."

"We'll need to find those girls. We're not exactly overwhelmed with leads at the moment. Pity we can't send those hairs over to the lab for analysis right now. Too many questions might be asked. But hang onto them, who knows what might be possible."

"One other thing. There's a room at the back of the house on the ground floor, built on at a later date I'd say, not heated, and a stone-slabbed floor. Big marble-topped table, maybe for cutting up large pieces of meat, dead deer, that sort of thing. Wooden shelves on one wall, big hooks on the other. Bloodstain on the floor, could be animal, but I was able to pick up a good sample where it had soaked into the earth between the slabs on the floor. You never know."

Hearing a car door slam, they looked out the window to see Bhardwaj, Craig and Alison Hendrickx, getting out of the police car. Bhardwaj removed from the boot of the car a large toolbox.

"If you don't mind, chief," said McCader, "I'll just nip out and see how Arvind gets on with fixing the car."

Blue could see Alison talking to Bhardwaj, and he shaking his head. He could imagine what was being said: could take a while to sort out the actual problem, notoriously difficult with electricals, no need to wait – I'll give you a shout as soon as it's done. Alison and Deirdra came on in, greeting McCader as he headed out.

"Morning, Angus," said Alison, "Good night last night?"

"Er, oh yes, we went to the Craighouse Inn. Had a meal and a few drinks. Enver told me all about Albania. What about yourself?"

"Did a bit of the Three Distilleries path before tea. I must say I envy Moira. I could easily live out here. I'm feeling healthier already, just breathing the air. Oh, by the way, she's not coming this morning, got stuff to sort out at the station. Arvind and Deirdra are going to look at the DVDs from the CCTV, unless you've anything else for them."

"No, not at the moment. In fact, that's good, we've got a pointer that those girls in the people-carrier are worth chasing up." He reported Aunt Effie's information, but omitted McCader's.

"Hmm. That doesn't sound at all nice. If that sort of thing's going on, I hope you can pin it down and nail somebody. Why don't I give them a hand? I've never scrutinised CCTV footage before."

"Please do, Alison, you'll find it enormous fun."

Five minutes later, they heard a car being revved up. "Great! They've done it," said Alison.

A couple of minutes later Bhardwaj and McCader came in. McCader busied himself with the kettle.

"I was lucky," announced Bhardwaj. "One of the first things I checked. A loose wire had worked its way out. All I needed to do was push it in. Problem solved."

Relief and congratulation followed. "Isn't he a wizard?" said Alison.

Then the two PCs sat at their PCs, and Alison looking over their shoulders, began searching the CCTV images. Blue sent McCader down to Feolin to talk to Donnie on the ferry. He needed to know if the man and the girl had come back.

Blue watched the CCTV-watchers. Looking at the footage was always going to be boring. And give them eye-strain. Endless hours of fuzzy cars in stop-motion. At least there were three of them.

And they had some definite targets. Alison and Deirdra watched Monday morning's footage, while Bhardwaj took the previous day. The camera must have been somewhere near the Port Askaig Hotel, and faced the stern of the big Calmac ferry, where the cars went in and out. The queue was over to the left, and the ramp for the Jura ferry on the right. So vehicles coming from Jura had to pass from right to left across the screen whether they were going to the Kennacraig queue or anywhere else on Islay.

He knew they'd got the three-car convoy when he heard Alison's "Look!" There they were, pressing imperiously across from right to left, disappearing off screen to head up the cliff-side hairpins onto the Bowmore road. Then silence while they watched out for the people-carrier with the girls. There it was. And an hour later the single Range Rover.

"Keep an eye open for anything suspicious in between," he'd said. What did that mean? Man looking shiftily out of the window, cradling a gun on his lap? He was pretty sure if there was anything suspicious, Fergus would have caught it. Sharp guy, no doubt about that.

Then Bhardwaj called out. "Gotcha!" Blue walked over, craned over Bhardwaj's shoulder. He replayed the shot: the car, maybe an Astra, went slowly past, the girl at the wheel, concentrating. Impossible to see if there was anyone beside her.

Now Deirdra had got to the big boat loading, was waiting for the people-carrier. There it was. The camera was well-placed, Blue realised, with a bit of luck they'd get a number. Deirdra saved the screen-shot and leaned back, blinking her eyes. Alison went over to the kettle.

A few minutes later Bhardwaj again. "There she goes." The Astra getting on to the ferry. But the number plate unclear. Daubed with mud, perhaps.

Time for coffee.

"Well done, people," said Blue. "We need numbers and then names for those vehicles. Deirdra, can you enhance the images, Arvind, run the numbers once she gets them."

"I'll phone Oban, check with the SOCOs, see what they've got so far," suggested Alison, getting up to use the phone in the other room.

Blue washed the mugs. Sometimes you just had to wait. The mugs were all white, with YES in big blue letters on opposite sides. He wondered if there were people who refused to drink from them, or demanded a NO mug.

McCader was back. Could he smell coffee from a distance?

"Had a chat with Donnie. He's a lot dopier than Fergus, doesn't notice much. Said the car came back at 6.30, the last boat from Jura, the girl was driving, he'd swear to that. Got tickets for the car and two passengers. Said her Dad was sleeping in the back. Donnie didn't look, why should he check, he says, just his job to sell the tickets, take the boat across. And no, he didn't notice which country the car was from."

"So, it's not clear whether the father was there or not. We need to clarify that," said Blue, "Thanks, Enver. Help yourself to a coffee."

Now Alison came through again.

"Not much news from the lab yet. They've got the blood samples from the site, but they don't have a sample from Lord Steppingham. Don't suppose it would tell them much, after all, we know who got shot."

"What about the hair from the shooter? I should say, possible shooter."

"Hoping to get the analysis later today. Sorry."

His mobile rang.

"Hello, Angus, it's your Aunt Effie. Could you come out to my car for a minute? I'm just outside."

He looked out the window. There she was, standing by her old Fiesta, waving. So he went out. She had brought a slow cooker, full of soup. Goodness knows how she got it into the car. He carried it into the room. She followed.

"You just plug it in, switch it on, in half an hour the soup will be ready. Cullen Skink. My own. I think you'll enjoy it."

"Effie, you don't need to " Blue began, but Alison interrupted. "That's wonderful, Effie, thank you so much. I'm sure it'll be completely delicious. You're so good to us."

"Not at all, you can't be surviving on coffee and chocolate bars."

26

The soup was beginning to bubble when his phone rang again. Moira Nicolson. "Angus, I've got something for you. I'm at Port Ellen, the ferry terminal. Can you come now. It's worth it."

"'Fraid I've got to go," Blue announced, "Moira's got something. Enver, can you hold the fort here. Follow up those vehicles."

"Will do, chief."

"I'll drive you," said Alison. "If that's OK?"

"Great. Thanks. OK, Let's go, then. Don't eat all the soup, please." Cullen Skink was his favourite. He'd had a quick look into the pot. Creamy. Chunks of haddock, and something else too, maybe mackerel. Potato, leek, onion, mushroom. Smelt delicious. But he had to leave it.

As they drove down towards Feolin, she asked how he felt the investigation was going.

"To be honest, not good. No witnesses, hardly any forensics, no suspects, a rival investigation, could it be worse. Don't say it, yes it always could. But we could do with a breakthrough. More than a tube of Bulgarian toothpaste."

"What's Bulgarian toothpaste got to do with it?"

"Er, oh, something I must have seen on telly."

"You don't watch telly."

"Maybe something lurking in my memory. Rerun of Monty Python." Must be more careful, he thought.

"Or something McCader found at the house?"

"What?"

"Come on Angus, you don't think all that play-acting with Bhardwaj fooled me. I always check the mileage when I start the car. It was up 36 miles. That could mean two journeys up to Dunrighinn – I can't think of anywhere else you'd want to go. Using my car rather than the police car. Something underhand, by the sound of it. Do all men think women are stupid? I thought you were better than that Angus. Why the hell didn't you just ask me?"

"Would you have said yes?"

"No, of course not. I love my car. I treat it well. It doesn't like nocturnal adventures. Mind you, this doesn't sound like your idea. Creeping about in the dark isn't your scene. So I'd guess Enver was up to no good. Toothpaste – you'd find that in somebody's bathroom. Even I can work that out. So I'd guess McCader was creeping about inside that house where we're not supposed to be. Am I right?"

"Yes. He wanted to look round the place. I thought there might be evidence there. And there was."

"Bulgarian toothpaste?" She sounded incredulous.

"Those girls were there. The ones in the people-carrier."

"You can't use anything you found."

"No. But we know they were there. We know it's worth following them up. What do you think they were there for?"

"I can guess."

"Look, Alison, I'm really sorry we weren't straight with you. I didn't want you involved in case we got caught."

"Just my car?"

"Your alibi was perfect. You weren't even on the island. We both knew there'd be hell to pay if we were caught."

"Men. You really are assholes. Next time, you ask me first, got that?"

"Yes, I'm sorry."

"All right, you can stop being sorry now, tell me what you found?"

"Well, it wasn't me in the..."

"Yes, that's obvious! You'd fall over the first trip wire. Just get on with it."

So he told her everything McCader had reported.

"Bastards!" was all she said. And after a while, "I wish that shooter had killed them all."

There was no sign of the big ferry at Port Askaig. They drove up the steep hairpins and then onto the long straight to Bridgend. He found the silence too hard.

"I do appreciate you staying, Alison." He hadn't meant to say that, it just came out.

She frowned. "I'm on holiday, I told you. Besides, I want to help you to dig up some more dirt on these upper-class bastards. I'm beginning to think that whoever shot at them had a good reason to do it. Maybe even a Bulgarian father who knew what they'd done to his daughter. If that was it, I'd be right behind him in the queue for the next shot. They deserve all they get."

"Er, yes. Ah, follow the road left here, past Bridgend."

"I know where I'm going! Sorry, I'm getting a bit angry here. I need to calm down, change the subject. Oh, did you see the film?"

"What film?"

"*I Know Where I'm Going*. Powell and Pressburger, 1945. The days when all the characters who mattered spoke with cut-glass accents. Like those bastards in the house, no doubt. But a great film. They cross the Corryvreckan too. Do we go to the police station in Bowmore?"

"No. Port Ellen. Ferry terminal."

The sun had come out, giving vivid colour to places he'd seen the previous Autumn.

Alison was not afraid to drive fast. At one point, she shook her head. "Thank goodness Arvind managed to fix the car! Just a loose connection, eh? Really, you men are like children. But at least you're on my side. I'm glad of that."

They parked by the terminal. There was no sign of the ferry. He couldn't remember the timetable; some of the ferries came in here at Port Ellen, the majority he thought at Port Askaig. You had to know the timetable to turn up at the right terminal.

Moira was waiting just outside the entrance. She led them into the small building by the pier. Inside it was bigger than it looked. A ticket office and waiting room. They went through a door marked 'No Admittance' into a little room with a sink at one end, a kettle and microwave on the work surface next to it. And in the middle, a table and four chairs. A well-built lady with short dark hair and a Calmac uniform rose to greet them.

Moira did the introductions. "Sandra, this is Inspector Blue, and Doctor Hendrickx, from Police Scotland. They'd like to hear what you have to say. Angus, Alison, this is Sandra Morgan. She works on the ferry."

Sandra greeted them. A Welsh voice to match her name. They all sat down. Moira asked Sandra to begin.

"Well, I have to say this is all thanks to Moira. Last winter the company sent us all on a Crime Awareness course she gave in Bowmore. Just half a day, about how to spot something suspicious, and then what to do about it. If I hadn't been on that course, I'd never have spotted this. Or if I had, I wouldn't have known what to do about it. As soon as it happened, see, I reported it. To Bob

Walker at the station in Bowmore."

"OK, Sandra," said Moira. "Tell us what happened."

"This was on the twelve o'clock boat from Port Askaig on Monday. I was serving in the cafe. I was going round the tables collecting the dishes. And giving them a wipe. Otherwise they get very sticky, you know. At this table in the corner, away from the windows, there were three girls, teenagers I'd say, sitting with this older woman. The girls made me suspicious. They didn't look very happy at all. One of them had a big bruise on the side of her face, and it looked sore. I asked her if I could get her some aspirin. She just looked at the woman, I think she was scared of her. I wondered if the woman had hit her. She said to me, this woman that is, 'You mind yer own bloody business, she don't need yer sympathy. Now clear off.'

"Well, I left them to it then, but I kept an eye on them. When I saw the woman go the Ladies, I went over and asked the girls if everything was OK. The one with the bruise looked at me as if she were pleading with me to do something, but one of the others said, 'No, no, we are OK. We are all fine. But please, we mustn't talk to you. We will get into trouble. Our aunt is very strict.' Of course, I didn't believe her. There was no way that woman was related to those girls, you could see that at a glance. And the girl spoke with a foreign accent, not one I recognised. But, see, there was nothing I could do then.

"So when I was a bit further off, I took of photo of them with my phone, when they weren't looking, like. Then I asked Malcolm – he marshals the cars as they leave – to keep an eye out for them and note down the details of their car. Which he did. So on the way back I phoned Bob, Sergeant Walker that is, and reported the matter to him. When I got back here Moira was waiting. She told the captain I had to miss the next trip, as there was an important police investigation going on, and my information could be vital. That's about it then."

"Would you be able to recognise these people if you saw them again?" asked Blue.

"I would, yes, I've got the picture too, I copied it to Moira." Moira produced a printout from a file which had been lying on the table. Three figures round a table. All with long hair, two dark, one dyed blonde. They certainly looked young, thought Blue. He couldn't see the bruise, only one side of their faces was visible.

"So they sounded foreign?"

"Oh yes, the girl who spoke was definitely foreign. Russian maybe. And their faces were very pale, almost pasty I would say. Certainly hadn't been out in the sun much. The woman, though, mutton dressed as lamb, I'd say. Pure *East Enders*. Like Dot Cotton used to speak. Or something like that. I knew what she was up to."

"Sorry?"

"Human trafficking. They smuggle them in from Romania, Russia, wherever. The poor girls are forced into prostitution, and they can't get back home, 'cos they've no money. There was a programme about it on the telly, it was awful. You've got to do something."

"And we will. Thank you so much for your help."

"It was your training, Moira."

Moira handed Blue the folder, as he and Alison left. "You'll need these. I'll email you Sandra's statement, as soon as it's typed up and signed."

Back in Alison's car, Blue looked in the folder. Two sheets. The photo of the three girls. And a sheet with the registration number and description of the vehicle, plus the owner's name from the DVLA: Mrs Gladys Waggoner, and an address in Belfast.

27

As Alison drove, Blue phoned the incident room, reported the vehicle and driver details, and asked them to see what else they could find out about Gladys Waggoner.

"You have to help those girls, Angus," said Alison, "whatever it takes."

"I promise you we will. No-one should be used like that."

They drove on in silence, to the ferry for Jura. As they headed for Craighouse, Blue stared out over the empty moor. This land and its people had been used as much as the girls they sought, used and cast aside by those for whom killing was entertainment.

An hour later they were back in the incident room, and finishing off the Cullen Skink, kept warm in the slow-cooker, and even thicker than it had been to start with. Then Blue called them all round the table.

He began by telling them what Sandra Morgan had seen.

"Enver, does the car tie in with what you got from the CCTV image?" he asked.

"Yes, chief, and there's more on Gladys Waggoner."

"Don't keep us in suspense, please."

"She's known to us all right. Has form, but it's a long time ago. Nothing recent. I found that odd, people like her don't normally suddenly go straight, so I made a couple of calls. I noticed her Belfast address, I've got a few contacts in the police over there. This is strictly off the record, and we can't even repeat it, let alone use it. Apparently, she supplies girls to the rich and famous. Whatever you ask for, she can provide. No questions asked."

"My God, why is she allowed to get away with that?" asked Alison. "Surely it's illegal?"

"She has very powerful friends, I'm told. People who use, or have used, her services, and wouldn't like to see her in court, telling all she knows."

"Is there a reason she lives in Belfast?" asked Blue. "Why not London?"

"Partly, she prefers to keep under the radar. Partly because the border is convenient. According to my contacts, she keeps the girls in a safe house in the Republic, but only does business in the UK.

Harder to pin anything on her that way, even if the police were allowed to."

"Enver, we need to talk to these girls. We need to know what was going on in that house."

"I'd guess they were in Ireland by Monday evening. If they got the ferry from Islay at twelve, they'd be in Kennacraig by two. In another three hours or so they're at Cairnryan, and on the boat to Ireland. The last one's at eight o'clock, so there's plenty of time."

"Do we have any way of knowing where they are?"

"Let me speak to a contact in the Republic. See what he knows."

"Thanks, Enver. So, what else do we have?"

"Been through the manifests from the airport, chief," said Bhardwaj. "Confirms that Alice Rogers, Eric James and Brian Richards were on the scheduled flight to Glasgow at 13:00 hours. I phoned Glasgow and we've got Rogers and James on a flight from Glasgow to Luton at 17:00. Seems they were headed for Steppingham's estate."

"What about Richards?"

"Yes, he was on the 15:00 to Stanstead."

"That makes sense – that's where the company has a base. What about His Lordship and his entourage?"

"Private jet out of Islay airport at 9:10. Manifest withheld for security reasons. Ditto the destination. I only got the departure time from Rhoda at the airport off the record. She reckoned they were headed for one of the London airports."

"Rhoda?" said Craig. "You sound awfy pally wi her, Arvind. Tell us more."

Bhardwaj glared at her. "I just happened to…"

"Children!" said Alison sharply. "Please. Let's concentrate on the case shall we?"

"All right, Deirdra," said Blue, "what have you got for us then?"

"I've been checkin on Lord Steppingham. Turns out he's hardly an old aristocrat. His great grandfather was a butcher in Birmingham, his name was Sidney Statham. Set up a sausage factory, 'Statham's Staffordshire Sausages' became a well-known brand. Made a pile of money, especially selling tinned sausages to the forces in World War One. His son made even more, same sort of stuff: he sold canned meat to the forces in World War Two. It was him, the son that is, bought the Steppingham estate in England, in the thirties. He helped bankroll Churchill into his final period in office, and was paid off with a peerage. Hereditary too. Took the name from his English estate. His son, that's the second Lord Steppingham, acquired the Jura estate in 1958. So our man is the third Lord Steppingham."

"Do they still make sausages?" asked Alison.

"Yes and no. They sold the meat factory to a company called Worldwide Meat Products in 1986. But the family still has a majority shareholding in WMP Universal Holdings, a company based in the Cayman Islands that owns Worldwide Meat Products. WMP Universal Holdings also owns a company called Steppingham Fine Foods. They produce hampers with smoked salmon, fillet steak, guinea fowl, caviar, that sort of stuff. You can get them at upmarket shops or by mail order. They also produce one or two of the ingredients, like 'Steppingham Smoked Duck' and 'Steppingham Venison and Pheasant Sausages.' But Worldwide Meat Products makes far more money, mainly from contracts for meat products with the forces. Seems things dinna change. I guess him being a Defence Minister helps a wee bit too."

"Any particular enemies he might have acquired?" asked Blue.

"Rival meat companies, I suppose. Vegetarians. Political rivals maybe. But he's no been tipped for high office. Probably prefers just milkin the system. He's very rich."

"Personal stuff? Scandal?"

"Well, his divorce was gey acrimonious, and cost him a pile of money. Rumours are he's now seein a model twenty-five years his junior. Two children, Jasper and Tania. Jasper's a banker, Tania designs hand-made wallpaper for the rich and famous. But the ex-wife, Drusilla, says she's very happy with the final settlement, now just wants to get on wi her own life. Now that she's a millionaire in her own right."

"Do I detect a note of distaste, Constable Craig?" said Alison.

"Aye well, I canna be fashed with yon bloodsuckers. I'd like to get rid o the lot o them – the titles, the private schools, their Oxbridge colleges, estates, banks – all of it."

"In short," said Blue, "we don't know of anyone who really wanted to kill him."

"Apart from Deirdra," said Alison.

"Now wait a minute, I didna say anything about killing. I wouldna harm them. I'd certainly take their wealth off them. It was mostly got by rippin off ordinary folk anyway. Then I'd maybe send them out to the Falkland Islands to grow tatties an dig peat. Give them a feel for real work."

Blue allowed them all to enjoy this thought for a few moments, before continuing, "There's also the possibility he was targeted as a political gesture. An act of terrorism. Simply because he was a member of the government."

"There's one thing that's odd about that though," said McCader. "No-one's claimed it. The press blackout is into its third day. If a terrorist group hit him, they won't know he's still alive. They'd have announced the killing right away, and taken responsibility. They do that to stop some other group, who didn't do the shooting, claiming they did. The press blackout gives the group who did it a real exclusive because they can announce the place, date and time. But they haven't."

"So it could still be an inside job?"

"It's possible, but I'm not convinced. There's no obvious reason why he should be got rid of. And if they just wanted to stage a terrorist killing, there are far more prominent ministers they could have bumped off. So I'm sceptical. We need to keep looking. There may be a reason that we just don't know about yet."

"Anything else? What about the car the girl and the older man were in?"

"Yes," said Craig, "unfortunately we couldna get the number very clearly from the CCTV, the rear plate looked like it had been smeared wi paint or mud. We've got a partial identification; we can't see the country clearly, but the first three letters are FSL and it looks like there are four digits."

"Any idea what country that format could be from?"

"Yes, chief," put in Bhardwaj. "Looks like Poland. If so, FSL would suggest the car was registered in the town of Słubice."

"Which is where?"

"Western edge of Poland, on the border with Germany."

"OK, can you chase up the CCTV for the ferries from Kennacraig to Islay? Start with Sunday and work back, see if you can get a clearer fix on the plate. What about the make?"

"Opel Astra. Opel is the European brand-name, Vauxhall is used in the UK. The cars are exactly the same. Very popular small family car."

"Good. Let me raise another question. What if the target wasn't Steppingham at all?"

They all looked at him.

"I mean, what if van Kaarsten was in fact the target, and Steppingham just happened to be in the way? Leaned into the line of fire at the wrong moment. So that we're simply looking in the wrong place for motives or suspects. Deirdra, see what you can find out about him."

"Will do, chief."

"At some point I'll go to Steppingham and try to talk to the nurse and secretary, and any other staff who were up here. But we'll also have to look into van Kaarsten a bit more, if we can And follow up these girls in the people carrier. Another thing I'm wondering is whether we need to retain the room here, now that the site's been closed, or whether we'd be able to work more effectively from the station in Bowmore."

The meeting over, the kettle was on duty again.

Blue phoned Moira Nicolson, and gave her an update. He finished off with the question of whether to move the incident room to the police station in Bowmore.

"Could be a good idea," said Moira. "After all, there's not much else that can be done on Jura, and we've got more facilities here, including a much faster line to the police computer system. And there's something else I just heard. Ffox-Kaye has already set up here. Not in the station. In the Masonic Hall, would you believe? He's got three or four people in there and lots of computers and stuff, and an armoured van with a big aerial on it parked outside. I just don't know what they're doing in there."

"Haven't people noticed?"

"Of course they have. He's saying that he's going to make an announcement soon about a 'major crime' threatening national security."

"Sounds like that'll be the end of the news blackout, and on his terms too. Wonder what he'll say. But you're right Moira, first thing tomorrow we'll get everything shifted to Bowmore. We can get all the data off these PCs here and sent on to you. And we haven't built up a big pile of paperwork so far."

28

He announced the move to the team, then went through to the office to thank Maggie Stillman for letting them use the room. Maggie found him a couple of cardboard boxes into which McCader and Alison Hendrickx put the accumulated paperwork. He was surprised at how rapidly the whole operation could be shut down, everything packed into a car, and the room left as it had been.

He went to the small room next door, and used his mobile to phone Steve Belford.

"Steve, I think you like good whisky."

"Correct, chief. You ask that when you're up to something. What is it you want me to do? Off the record, I'm guessing."

"Just a couple of samples I'd like you to look at, maybe extract a bit of DNA and so on. Is that possible?"

"What's on offer?"

"Bottle of 10-year-old Isle of Jura."

"It's a deal! When do I get the goods?"

"Soon as I can send someone over. Probably Enver. Hopefully you'll get them tomorrow morning."

He leaned in the door of the room, and motioned McCader over. "Enver, can I have a word?" Outside, on the path to the road, he explained. "Those samples you got. I've made deal with Steve. Now, here's forty quid. Go back to Islay with Arvind and Deirdra. Ask them to stop at the distillery shop on the way through Craighouse, and buy a bottle of the 10-year-old. Go with them as far as Port Askaig and get the next boat to Kennacraig and the bus to Oban. First thing in the morning, put the bottle in a supermarket plastic bag, and the samples you got up at Dunrighinn House, and hand the bag directly to Steve. Say to him that it's from me. He'll process the samples off the record, and we'll see what we've got."

McCader handed one of the twenties back. "I'm in on this too, chief. I'm on my way. It's just after four now, so we've plenty time before they close."

The boxes were loaded into the police car, Craig, Bhardwaj and McCader squeezed in too, and the vehicle set off towards Craighouse.

Blue had arranged to see Bhardwaj and Craig at the station the following day, and to phone McCader in Oban in the morning with further instructions. Now only he and Alison remained in the emptied room. Blue plucked up his courage.

"What about a meal before you get back to Islay, Alison?"

She paused before answering. "Yes, that would be nice. I'll phone Moira and say I'll be back later."

Five minutes later she was back. "That's OK. Moira says she'll have a word with Fergus and ask him to run a late boat this evening. They do that on demand for locals only. That would give me till 8.00. She'll text to confirm that."

"Great. Well, it's half past four now. Do you mind if I do a bit of work on my report?"

"Not at all. I'll check my email, then see what I can dig up on Mr van Kaarsten."

An hour of companionable silence ended when Blue's phone rang. The Super. Blue brought him up to date, omitting McCader's nocturnal investigation, and finishing with Ffox-Kaye's setting himself up in Bowmore.

"Yes, that doesn't surprise me. But I don't know whether he'll just try to move faster that you in the same direction, and then claim the credit for your work, or whether he'll move off on a completely different trajectory. These security people can produce terrorist gangs out of nowhere, who often turn out to be nothing of the sort. You need to keep an eye on him. I'd say in that respect, basing yourself in Bowmore is probably a wise move."

"I'd like to interview the members of Steppingham's staff, and in fact his Lordship too, if he's well enough."

"Good idea. I'll put in a request to Ffox-Kaye for immediate access to them. Don't expect an immediate result."

"How are things up there, sir?"

"Chaotic. All hands on deck for this royal thing. But the polls are showing nobody's that interested. There'll be lines of police, with no-one behind them. Now I'm hearing that Downing Street wants all the schools closed and children forced to line up and wave. Huge waste of police time. If they had any sense they'd just call it off, save us a load of money we could use on catching criminals."

"Want to know what I've got on van Kaarsten?" asked Alison.

"Fire away."

121

"Aged 35. His grandfather Abraham van Kaarsten founded AvK Matériel in the thirties in Holland, but moved the business over to London in 1937. He was afraid that if Holland were invaded by the Germans the business would be seized and he, as a Jew, would be sent to a concentration camp. Done well since then. Jason is on the Board, although the Managing Director is his older brother David van Kaarsten. Jason's the youngest of six children, so I guess he'd have had to organise a plane crash to get to be number one."

"Unless he was very able."

"I don't think he's either able or ambitious. He seems to appear more on celebrity gossip than business sites. He's not married, but been linked with several wannabe actresses or idle rich girls. Spends a lot of time enjoying himself. Owns a yacht, house in Antibes, even a banana plantation in the Philippines. Won that in a card game apparently. Only eats his own bananas, according to *Gosh!* magazine. But very charming, his business activities seemed to consist of buttering up likely buyers or influential politicians by giving them a good time."

"And maybe a bit of bribery to get their contracts."

"So not a very attractive character, but there's nothing in there that would make anyone want to kill him. No bitter ex-wife or business rival. Hasn't said anything controversial about anything. Unless our killer simply dislikes the rich and powerful. But then, why choose him? There are plenty richer and more powerful people."

Blue frowned. "I suppose it could be a political thing about who they sell arms to. But you're right, he doesn't look a very likely target. Nevertheless, we'll have to try to talk to him, see what he's got to say. If we can find him, that is."

At six fifteen they went to eat at the Craighouse Inn. Moira had texted Alison that the eight o'clock boat would be waiting for her. There were fewer diners than the previous evening, and Blue explained as they looked at the menu that the six remaining Germans had gone off that morning.

"Of twelve altogether?"

"Yes."

"And six "

"Don't say any more, Alison!" He'd suddenly realised what he

122

should have noticed the previous evening when talking to the manager. Only six Germans had left the hotel for Tayvallich, yet Alex Malcolm had mentioned seven on his boat.

"I think our man went over on the Tayvallich boat on Monday," he whispered. "The man in the Opel. The girl took the car on the ferry on Sunday evening, then drove round to Tayvallich and collected him on Monday when the boat came in. Or if not her, then some other accomplice. We'll talk more about it later."

Like McCader, Alison knew to keep off the current case in a public place. But the realisation that a little bit of the jigsaw seemed to have fallen in to place gave the meal a sense of optimism and even relief that made the conversation come easy and the food taste good.

They talked about archaeology, a subject in which both of them shared an interest, and some practical experience, Alison as a professional, and Blue as a vacation volunteer. She had recently visited Pictish sites in the North East and was keen to share her thoughts about this most elusive of peoples. Carvers of symbol stones, feared warriors who fought off both the Romans and Angles, and yet somehow were willing and able to throw in their lot with the Scots, and join the powerful cultural mix that became Scotland. They talked about the royal and religious site at Forteviot, the Pictish monastery beneath the mediaeval parish church of Portmahomack, and the stones that now rested in the Old Parish Church of Govan. There was time to eat also, for Alison Jura mussels in a white wine sauce with home-baked bread, for Blue a freshly-caught mackerel sautéed in oatmeal, with new potatoes, mashed parsnip and garlic butter. Blue had a bottle of dark Belgian beer, purportedly from an Abbey, but Alison stuck to water. She was driving.

As they sipped their *espressi*, she said, "It's good to see you again, Angus. It always is. Even if it's just a short period, it feels as if it's been weeks, or months. As if every time I see another slice of you. Even as a policeman, there are different bits that come out every time. That's why it's so interesting to work with you."

"Interesting?"

"Fascinating. Layers of you."

"Like an onion?"

"No." She laughed, a laugh that was half a smile. "Like archaeology. The layers of history that make us. The pasts that make our present."

He looked down quickly. She mustn't see the shadow cross his face. "Including stuff we wish we could undo. Pasts that haunt."

"We can't make them disappear, those ghosts, but we can choose how to deal with them. We can choose to be other than our ghosts." She laid her hand on his. "You're not a ghost, Angus. You're constantly remaking yourself, every moment, recombining what you are into something ever so slightly new. We never stay quite the same."

"Everything renewing," he murmured. "Yes, I like that. Let's walk. Have you still time?"

"Oh yes, time enough."

He paid, and they left the inn, and walked out to the end of the long pier. The sun had set now, though its westward fall was not visible from Craighouse, lying as it did in the lee of the humpback ridge of the island. But there remained enough of a glow to see the leaden surface of the dark water.

"Look," he whispered, pointing. A V-shaped trail moved through the water, not far off the pier. "An otter."

They watched the trail until they could see it no longer, lost in the darkness, and looked at the endless sky, everywhere the pinpoints of stars.

"My people came from here," he said. "They watched this water and sky, and worked the land for hundreds of years. They must have stood here too."

"I think if they'd stood right here, they'd have had to swim for it!" And she kissed him. And then a lingering embrace.

As they walked back along the pier, she said, "I guess it's time to go."

Blue was about to speak, when they both caught, somewhere beyond the last twinkling lights of Craighouse and Keils, over the hump of the land before you came to Dunrighinn, a flash in the sky, and a second later the sound of an explosion.

They looked at each other, for a moment, wide-eyed.

"What was that?" said she.

"We'd better look. I guess I'm at this moment the only policeman on the island. Can you drive? I've been drinking. Don't worry. If this is bad, the ferry will be still be running very late. If not, Aunt Effie has another room."

"OK. This is why being with you is such, er, fun."

They drove in her car from the hotel as far as the service point car park.

"Now we'll use the police car. It's got all the kit in the boot. Here's the key."

"Cool. I've never driven a police car before. Can we have the siren on?"

"Absolutely. This looks like an emergency. Fast as you can. But be careful, you'll find the acceleration on this one's quite good. Even Arvind thinks it's impressive."

They set off in the police car. Blue switched on the siren and the flashing lights. Alison put her foot down.

29

The road clung to the side of the hill, and as they rounded the final corner, all at once Dunrighinn came into view. Or rather, what had once been Dunrighinn. For the whole house had become an inferno. Blue was reminded of the final scene of Alfred Hitchcock's *Rebecca*, in which the old house, Manderley, is burnt to the ground, the estate workers and villagers milling about in confusion in front of the flaming edifice. But in this case there were no confused locals scurrying about trying to salvage whatever they could. There was no-one at all that Blue could see. Just the old house, flames pouring from every window. And in colour, too, windows of bright orange and yellow in a furnace that sent flames shooting many yards into the air, with sparks floating further up, to take the fire elsewhere. Blue could already see that some of the buildings round the courtyard and behind the house were beginning to join in the party, issuing clouds of insistent smoke before the flames finally burst out.

They drove up the gate, and saw that it was shut. Blue got out and pushed at it. Locked. He pressed the buzzer. No response.

He opened the boot of the car, calling on Alison to help get the emergency kit out. There was a folding 'Road Closed' sign, which he placed in the middle of the road about twenty yards short of the gates. Then a pile of traffic cones, which he set Alison to laying along the road until she ran out. Meanwhile he called the emergency services. He knew the call would go from the call centre out to Bowmore. Then the volunteer firefighters would be called out, and when there were enough to man the engine, it would rush from Bowmore to Port Askaig, followed by the ambulance and a police car. There, Fergus or Donnie would have to take the convoy over to Jura. Luckily the ferry would be waiting for Alison, so they would be prepared. Then the convoy would have to drive two thirds the length of the island to get to the scene. Blue also knew that the biggest problem would be ghouls rushing to see the blaze, who could easily block the single-track road completely.

"Is there no way we can get in?" shouted Alison. "There might be someone in there."

"Not until that gate's been opened. Shit! Here's the first ghoul already."

A big white Chelsea tractor slid up to the 'Road Closed' sign and stopped a little to one side. There would only be room for a cyclist to get past, let alone a fire engine. The windows wound down. From the driver's seat a large man, multi-chinned, peered at the fire through powerful binoculars, whilst from the back seat a youth filmed with his phone.

"Come on Alison, let's get him moving. Do you have your camera there?"

"Of course." They both carried at all times small cameras with built-in zoom; you never know what interesting thing might catch your archaeological eye.

They walked over to the vehicle, a bloated caricature of a family car. The driver, as obese as his car, lowered the binoculars and frowned at them. The youth, thin with his hair shaved close at the sides and sticking up on top, turned the camera towards them. Blue took out his warrant card and held it up to the driver.

"Good evening, sir. I'm a police officer. Can I ask you what you're doing?"

The man looked at him contemptuously. "Isn't it obvious? Watching the bloody fire, mate."

"Yeah, you tell him, Dad. Bloody fuzz," uttered the youth.

"I'm afraid, sir, as the cones clearly indicate, parking here is not permitted. Would you please move your vehicle away?"

"No way, mate, I was here first, so I get the first row. You can't stop me parking on the roadside."

"How do you think the fire engine is going to get past you?"

The man looked at the road. Thinking took place. "OK mate, I'll give you a bit of room. But I can't turn round here, can I? You'll have to let me past your sign."

Blue moved the sign, and the car drove past, but instead of turning, pulled in at the side of the road opposite the gate, where the road was much wider.

"There you go, now I'm not in the way, am I, mate?"

Blue put the sign back and walked over. He photographed the rear number plate, then approached the driver. "I'm sorry to inform you, sir, that you are causing an obstruction to emergency service vehicles. This is an offence punishable by a fine and a number of penalty points. May I see your driver's licence?"

The man stared.

"Failure to show a driver's licence is also an offence and may result in a further fine and penalty points. I hope driving is not essential to your work, sir."

"Fuckin fascists," the man muttered.

"I'm sorry, sir, I didn't catch that."

The man scowled, but said nothing, with some difficulty fishing his licence from a trouser pocket.

Blue looked at it closely.

"Mr Simon Mather, 18 Wortleberry Road, Bristol. Is that you, sir?"

"Yes. Of course it is. Are you people stupid, or something?"

"And where are you staying at the moment, sir?"

"Cottage at Ardmenish. Called "Sea View". Bloody expensive. Fuck all to do."

"I'm going to ask my colleague to photograph this license, sir." He held it out so that Alison could take the picture. "The resultant file will be deleted if no proceedings are initiated against you. Your actions and words have been witnessed by myself and my colleague."

All of a sudden Blue seized in one swift movement the phone from the youth. "And I'm afraid we must temporarily impound this phone in order to identify and if necessary remove any film which infringes the right to personal privacy of police personnel. If you'd like to drive back to your cottage, as soon as further officers arrive, I will have a receipt for the phone delivered to you. The phone will be returned in due course to the address shown on the driver's licence."

"Dad," said the youth. "We don't live there any more. Not since you and…"

"Shut up, you bloody moron," shouted the man angrily.

"One moment, sir," said Alison. "Have you been drinking recently?"

"I'm fucking going!" shouted the driver, and the electric front window of the car slid rapidly shut. The engine revved furiously and the wheels screeched, throwing up a cloud of dust. Blue and Alison stepped quickly out of the way, and the car shot forward, attempting a very fast U-turn. Unfortunately, this initial advance and turn was too vigorous – perhaps the man was unfamiliar with the power of his vehicle, or perhaps the alcohol had made him less hesitant about wielding it – and the car accelerated across the road and ploughed into the double gates, bursting them open. With a volley of further abuse, audible through the open rear window from which the youth was making V-signs at them, he reversed wildly, crashing into a large rock by the side of the road with his rear, and then roared off back down the road, flattening the 'Road Closed' sign on the way, exhaust gases pumping into the night air.

"Wow," said Alison. "Are they all like that?"

"At least we know where he's staying. We can send someone down there as soon as anybody arrives. Thanks for mentioning the drink, by the way. What made you ask?"

"I smelt it. I have a very sensitive sense of smell, you know, Angus. Sometimes it comes in handy."

"I guess there'll be more of them coming – ghouls, I mean. This'll be visible for miles. I hope that youth didn't have time to post his footage on Facebook."

However, no further cars appeared.

After ten minutes, Blue phoned Moira Nicolson's mobile. "Hi, Moira, what's doing?"

"Hi, Angus, we got the message. The convoy is on the road. Fire engine, ambulance, police car and my car. We're heading for Port Askaig, and Fergus is there with the ferry. Hopefully we'll be there in about half an hour."

Blue and Alison waited for five minutes to see if any further ghouls turned up, but the road remained empty. The house continued to burn, and the flames began to consume the outbuildings too.

Finally Blue decided they should have a look, and pushing the damaged gates aside, they walked into the grounds and headed for the house.

The heat kept them at a distance, and there was no sign of anyone. As they walked past the main building towards the courtyard, there was another explosion behind the house, flinging burning debris into the air over the low buildings round the courtyard and onto the grass, some it landing beyond where they were standing.

"Time to get out, I think, Alison. This is too dangerous, and there's nothing we can do about it."

They made their way rapidly back to the gate.

There was still no sign of any traffic. Blue also wondered why neither Jack Seymour nor Tam McGowan had arrived to check out the explosions. They couldn't have failed to hear them.

30

Twenty minutes later Blue's mobile rang. Moira Nicolson again.

"Hi, Angus, we're almost there. Stuck at the moment just beyond Ardmenish by traffic. Tourists keen to see the free fireworks. We're forcing them to turn and go back, and have had to breathalyse three so far. They're stuck here as there's been a collision on the road. Looks like a maroon Jaguar was moving up towards you at speed, when another vehicle hit it head on going the other way. Also at speed I'd guess. Big white Chelsea tractor type."

"I sent him back about forty minutes ago. He's staying at a cottage called 'Sea View.' Refused to take a breath test and made off rapidly. How bad is it?"

"Very. High speed collision, as I said. Both cars on fire. The next driver to arrive managed to get a teenage boy out of the white car, but the driver was trapped in and the car on fire. He did well to get the lad out. Two men in the Jag, both badly injured, and with serious burns. We've got the fire out, and the ambulance has taken the injured off to the hospital in Bowmore. The helicopter will be waiting there to get them to Glasgow. Donald Ferrier's bringing his tractor up to pull the cars off the road, or at least as far enough out the way to let the fire engine and a police car past."

"What about families?"

"The dead man's wife and daughter are already here. After the father and son went off, they stayed outside the cottage watching the glow from the house burning. So they heard the car crash, and came up to see what was going on. They're pretty shocked, but went off in the ambulance with the boy. That might help him to survive."

"What an experience for them," said Alison.

"They seemed more concerned about the boy than the father. Maybe it hadn't quite sunk in, but the mother said she knew it would happen sooner or later. She was angry with him for taking the son. He'd already had three whiskies. The parents are separated, by the way. Wife said she'd booked the cottage for herself and the children. The father found out and turned up on Tuesday, barged in, insisted on staying with them."

"What about the people in the other car?" asked Blue.

"We're still checking them out. We've closed the road at the service point now. Boris is turning back anyone else who arrives.

What's it like where you are?"

"Nothing on the road at all, but now I know why. The house is well alight and the fire's spread to the outbuildings too. There's going to be very little left of it."

"Any sign of any people there?"

"No, not a soul. I thought Jack Seymour and Tam McGowan would have been here right away, but there's no sign of them."

"That's odd. We'll be there as soon as possible."

Fifteen minutes later the volunteer fire engine swung round the corner, turned in through the open gateway, drove over the grass and parked near the jetty. Two firefighters rushed a heavy duty hose down to the jetty and lowered the bulbous filter into the water. Meanwhile others had unwound two further hoses and were leading one towards the house, and the other towards the courtyard buildings. As soon as the men by the jetty radioed their OK, the pump was turned on and water from the bay was sucked up into the vehicle, then out via the two hoses.

Ten minutes later another police car arrived and parked outside the gates by Blue's. Moira Nicolson got out, and made her way over towards where Blue and Alison were standing, just inside the gate. She wasn't in uniform now, wearing sensible outdoor gear.

"Hi," she said. "Thanks for holding the fort. Deirdra's gone with the ambulance to the hospital in case any of the injured manage to talk. Unlikely, judging by the look of them. Arvind's at the crash scene."

A firefighter came over to them. He nodded to Blue and Alison, and turned to Moira.

"Hi, Graham," said Moira. "What do you think?"

"Too late to save the house, so we're concentrating on the outbuildings at the moment. No sign of any victims so far."

"Are you getting any backup?"

"Two more appliances coming on the first boat tomorrow. Be all over by then, though." He nodded again, then strode back towards the vehicle, silhouetted against the orange roar of the flames.

"There's a price to pay for living on an island," she said to Blue. "I'm going to drive up and see if Jack or Tam are in."

When Moira had gone, Blue and Alison went back to the other

police car.

"Angus," said Alison, "I'm feeling guilty about that crash. If I hadn't asked about his drinking, he wouldn't have driven off in such a rush."

"You weren't to know what he would do. You can't be held responsible for other people's actions. That man decided to drive at the speed he did. He had already decided to drive even though he must have known he was well over the limit. Had I smelt the alcohol, it would have been my duty to say exactly what you did. There are lots of stupid people in the world, and they manage to do plenty of damage to others. Every day there are innocent people killed or injured, or psychologically damaged by the actions of stupid people. Stupidity is not an illness. It's a choice. What you did was sensible. Had he responded sensibly, a life would not have been lost, several others damaged. That was his choice."

"Thank you, Angus. All this. It feels like we left reality behind somewhere."

Moira returned to report no response at the homes of Jack Seymour or Tam McGowan. It was by now clear there was nothing they could do at the fire scene until the fire was out, so they returned to the service point, passing on the way the two smashed and burnt-out cars by the roadside, the dead marked off from the living by a line of plastic cones.

The two police cars parked at the service point car park, next to a yellow Lada, the property of PC Wayne 'Boris' Blackett. The tall, cadaverous figure of PC Blackett himself stood by the *Road Closed* sign. Any driver would be persuaded to turn back by the strangely penetrating gaze and the oddly hollow voice which seemed to emanate from somewhere above PC Blackett's head. His skill in dealing with angry or drunken individuals or mobs was legendary. He turned as Inspector Nicolson approached and his hand, as if under its own control, made a jerky movement up and down, vaguely resembling a salute.

"Good evening, ma'am." The slow voice seemed to issue from the darkness beyond him.

"How's it going, Wayne?" asked Inspector Nicolson.

"Very good, ma'am. No traffic with reason to go further so far. Nor any with reason to loiter."

"Well done. You know Inspector Blue and Dr Hendrickx?"

The dark shape made a slight bowing movement, as if hinged at the waist, in Alison's direction. "Oh, yes, ma'am. One wouldn't forget." He gave no indication of having noticed Blue.

"I see that Tatiana has recovered from her dip in the harbour," said Alison.

"Oh, yes, Doctor Hendrickx. Touch and go for a while, but she pulled through. She's brave, that one. Sturdy. Made when cars were cars, designed to run for ever on the endless steppe."

"Is Arvind here?" asked Inspector Nicolson.

"Oh, yes, ma'am. He's for fetching drinks right now." He didn't move any part of his body, and yet something made them all turn to look at the service point building. A dark shape stood in the doorway, silhouetted by the light from inside. As it moved out onto the path, it resolved itself into the form of PC Bhardwaj, bearing two mugs of steaming liquid. He approached and gave one to Blackett.

"Evening, boss," he said to Nicolson, "I've coned off the crash scene, so we can examine it in the morning. I also phoned round to find out where those guys in the Jag were staying. First time lucky – I didn't think anyone with that kind of motor would be in a B&B, so I tried the Craighouse Inn. Two work colleagues from somewhere in Essex, the manager said. Got the details in my notebook." He carefully set his mug on the ground and fished out the notebook. "Yes. Geoffrey Denholm and Tim Grandoaken. I've got addresses and phone numbers too." He tore out the page and passed it to Inspector Nicolson.

"Are you sure these are correct, Arvind? I don't want to give bad news to the wrong people."

"That's the details Mr Deventer gave me. But I phoned Bob, er, Sergeant Walker, and got him to check the reg. number in the vehicle database. It's registered to a Geoffrey Denholm, same address as here."

"Thanks, Arvind," said Nicolson, "I'll phone them as soon as I get to the station. Can you and Wayne keep the night watch here? I'll send Bob or Deirdra to relieve you in the morning. Any problems, ring me at home."

"No problemo, boss," said Bhardwaj.

"I don't anticipate there being need for that, ma'am," a metallic voice somewhere near Blackett added, "but it's a comfort. Knowing, that is." The disconnected saluting motion reoccurred, as if a tic, and not a conveyance of meaning. Blackett turned again to stare into the darkness towards the pinpricks that were Craighouse.

"There's nothing we can do here till tomorrow," said Nicolson to Blue, "so I'll get off. I'll go to the station and phone those families from there, and check with the hospital too."

Alison touched Blue on the arm. "I'm going back now, Angus. Moira's got the ferry waiting for us. Not sure what I'll do tomorrow. Maybe go for a walk. If you're really short-staffed, let me know. I'm sure I'll see you soon." She stroked his cheek briefly with the back of a finger, and was off. In five minutes the two cars had disappeared into the darkness on the road south.

Blue said goodnight to Blackett and Bhardwaj and walked back towards Craighouse. As he turned off the road up the lane to Effie's house, he looked back up towards Dunrighinn. There was still a bright orange glow, and occasionally a flame shot up over the horizon.

31

Effie had a mug of tea ready as he opened the door. "Come in, Angus, you've got a visitor."

Tam McGowan was sitting in an armchair in the living room, a mug of tea on a coffee table beside him. He pushed himself with difficulty out of the chair as Blue came in, and shook his hand.

"I'm awfa glad to see ye, Mr Blue. I need to speak wi ye."

"I'd better leave you to it, then," said Effie, making reluctantly for the kitchen.

Blue waited till the door shut. "All right, Tam, what's the problem?"

"There's somethin no right up at the house. I wanted to tell ye. I wis at the Hotel this evening, in the bar for a wee drink. I seen you an the young lady, an I thought I'd get a wee word with ye later. But then we hear the bang, and next thing someone says it's the house gone up. I came through to see if I could find ye, but ye were awa. So I had a couple more, then came roun here to see if Effie knew whaur ye were, an she says jist tae wait on ye. So I did."

"OK." Blue took a small digital voice recorder from his coat pocket and set it on the coffee table. Tam looked at it uncomfortably. "I'm recording you just so I don't miss anything. Don't worry, this won't be used in court."

"Aye, awright then."

"So what is it you want to tell me?"

"It's no been a good place, since his lordship's divorce, aye well, maybe afore too, an his wife kept awa. She kent what was gaun on. The parties. Drink, drugs, women, sometimes they were awfa young. God knows what they were daein. Sometimes it was the men wha'd paid fur the shootin – aye, through the nose too, but they could afford it. Arab sheiks, they were the worse – aa the things they couldna dae in their own country. And the next day out onto the muir tae kill the deer. Or the grouse, or mountain hares, or whatever they could find tae shoot at. One day they shot a sea eagle. Beautiful bird. The Arab, he was disappointed they couldna trap it, said he would have used it for huntin, you know, like a falcon, only bigger. It was an American that shot it. He wanted to take it home to have it stuffed, but his lordship persuaded him it would be too dangerous to try an take it out the country. So he asked me to get rid o it, so's there's not a trace left. Which I did. But I didna like it, I can tell ye. They had a camera on its nest, so the wildlife folk knew soon enough it was killed. But they never found wha did it."

"So is it sex with minors or illegal shooting you want to report?"

"Naw, neither o them. There's something funny about yon shootin o his lordship."

"What do you mean?"

"There was something special last weekend. It wisna the usual thing."

"In what way? How did it differ from what usually happened?"

"Well, for one thing, I was told to keep well awa from the whole place, and no tae come back till after the helicopter was aff on Monday mornin. Usually I was just supposed to keep awa from the house. There'd be stuff needin done roun the courtyard, or just tools that needed fetchin. That's how ah'd get a keek now an then o who was here. And then, there was a lot mair security, yon Ffox-Kaye and his sidekick, the one that looks like a bull terrier."

"Plaistow?"

"Aye, that's him. Thinks every Scot's called Jock. Or disna care what they're called."

"When did they arrive? Did they come together?"

"Aye, taegither, on Thursday mornin. A whole gang of them, in thae black Range Rovers. Always rushin like they was in a hurry tae get tae a funeral."

"How many men do you think they had altogether?"

"I couldna tell ye exactly, but I'd say at least a dozen. Plus a couple of women too. I mean security women, no the other sort."

"Did you see any of the other sort there?"

"Aye, there was a woman brought in three lasses, in a big grey car. Thursday afternoon sometime. Awfy pale they were, and no very old, I'd say. I saw them standin out on the grass havin a smoke. I was in the tackle room, the one you left yer bags in, remember?"

"So did you see Lord Steppingham and Mr van Kaarsten arrive?"

"Naw. Thursday afternoon, about five, I was repaintin the bollard on the jetty, when Plaistow comes up and says I'm to clear off and no come back till Monday. That's his own words. 'Time for you to clear off, Jock,' he says, 'and don't show your face inside this fence till after eight o'clock Monday morning. If I see you anywhere near here,' he says, 'I'll effin kill you. And I mean that, Jock, I can make you disappear. For ever.' I can tell ye, I'm no a coward. But I knew he meant it. I was off right awa."

"And you didn't come back till Monday morning?"

"Aye, that's right. And as soon as I arrived, Ffox-Kaye says to me that if any other policemen come, I've to say nothin to them. Not a word. Do you remember that you were talkin to me in the tackle room?"

"Yes."

"Well, just after that, I'm checking the gas tank."

"Gas tank? What sort of gas?" Blue remembered McCader's mention of a gas tank.

"Propane. They use it for cookin and heatin. There's no gas main on the island, so they have a tank out the back. Gets filled up every couple a months. Any way, I've checked the valves an I'm checkin the level – that's routine on a Monday mornin – and everything's fine, it was filled up just a couple a weeks ago. All at once Plaistow appears, out the blue, grabs my arm, real tight like, an he says, 'You've been talking to them plods, eh? You were warned about that." Then he punches me in the stomach, real hard. I couldna breathe, I just fell down, then he kicks me in the ribs and stamps on my ankle. Then he says, 'If you want to stay alive, Jock, eff off right now' – he used the actual eff word – 'and don't come back here till yer told.' I got out of there as quick as a could, I was real scared, I can tell ye. He coulda killed me easily. And he'd have enjoyed it, ye could see it in his eyes. I'm tellin you, Mr Blue, there's something real bad up there."

"Do you know anything about the explosion?"

"Nothing at all. Like I said, I was down at the Hotel when it happened. And I'd not been inside the perimeter since Plaistow hit me. But I do know it was a big one."

"Why do you say that?"

"I was a firefighter for about ten years, that was a while back. In Paisley. We did a few explosions. I can tell ye, it takes a lot o work to make an explosion that big."

"You're saying it wasn't accidental?"

"No way. The only accidental event that would produce an explosion that big is a gas leak, and I checked the valves and even the pipework. There was no leak."

"Problem with the central heating boiler?"

"Naw, it's got a detection device, switches off if the gas pressure drops."

"Someone forgot to turn the gas off on the cooker rings?

"They'd have to have all the rings on for a long time to build up enough gas for a bang that big. See, propane's heavier than air, so it sinks. Every time somebody opened the kitchen door, some would pour out, and they'd notice the smell."

"So what do you think happened?"

"The place was blown up. Nae doot. Someone opened the valve, maybe even opened up the pipework to let the gas in faster. If they opened the cellar door, they could fill the cellar full of gas in a couple a hours, then if it were left runnin with the doors shut it would fill up aa the ground floor a few feet deep. Open some of the ground floor windows too, get some oxygen in tae mix wi the gas. Then set off a wee timed charge and boomph!"

"There was second explosion a while later. What would that be, do you think?"

"Hmm. Coulda been the tank goin up. Unless there's other stuff we dinna ken about."

"Would there be evidence of it? I mean if it were deliberate."

"Aye, well, if the explosion was gas, there'll maybe be chemical residue they can find. But showin it's *definitely* deliberate, as opposed to *probably* deliberate, aye, that could be trickier. The pipework's copper, coulda melted. Best bet would be the timer for the detonation charge. That's what they'll be lookin for. Once the ruins are cool enough, that is."

"One other thing. You haven't seen Jack Seymour recently? We noticed that he didn't turn up to see what was going on, though he must have heard the bang very clearly, and realised it was the house."

"Naw, I've no seen him since Monday. That's odd right enough, him no comin out to see what's goin on. Did somebody try his house?"

"Yes. No answer. Could he have gone off somewhere?"

"Aye, that's always possible. Or they coulda told him tae clear aff, like they did me."

"OK, I'm glad you shared that with me, Tam. I'll need to take a statement at some point, maybe in the morning."

"Aye, but I'm no goin home the night, Mr Blue. I tell ye, I'm real scared now. I'm gettin awa for a few days."

"Hmm. Tell you what we'll do. I'll ask Effie if she can put you up here for the night, and we can pay for it from the witness protection fund, then in the morning we'll take you up in a police car to check your cottage and get any stuff you need. Where would you go?"

"I've a pal over in Fife, no far fae Dunfermline, used to be a firefighter too. We get on fine, it'll be OK. I'll stay there a couple a weeks, till this business is all over. Then I'll be lookin for another job, as far frae here as a can get."

"That makes sense. One final thing. Not a word of this to anyone. That includes Effie, and your pal in Fife. Keep a low profile till it's clear this case is closed."

Effie was happy to put Tam up, no doubt hoping for some juicy gossip from Dunrighinn, and absolutely refused to accept any payment for it. "Tam's been here long enough to be a Diurach, Angus, you can't be asking your neighbours to pay for staying on their own island. I'll go and get the other room ready."

Superintendent Campbell answered his mobile after one ring. He listened in silence to Blue's report.

"Seems it's all happening down there, Angus. At least that'll end the press blackout and the newshounds'll be over tomorrow. I suggest you point them at Ffox-Kaye."

Blue relayed Tam's views about the explosion.

"Well, if there was something fishy there, it's good way to get rid of the evidence. And if you're having a bonfire, you may as well chuck anything else you want to get rid of in there too. I'll talk to the fire people here, make sure they send a good investigator. Denise Rankeillor if we can get her."

"How's the royal progress going?"

"Ha! It's a joke. They were in Glenrothes today. More police than spectators."

"What about the schoolkids?"

"Bit of a problem there they hadn't anticipated. Parents need to give permission for their kids to be taken out of the school premises during school hours. Some of the teachers wouldn't hand out the forms – said it was a political event – so they were posted out by the council, but most parents never returned them. A lot of parents kept their children off school for the day, just in case. Then the teachers were advised by their union not to leave the school precincts. So it was council officials who came to collect the kids. Then the Heads refused to let them take the kids, as they hadn't had their Disclosure Checks certified."

"So who did turn out?"

"A few neds, old ladies, a few guys from the Orange Lodge in bowler hats and sashes, people who happened to be there for some other reason. Even a couple of tourists. And a good crowd of demonstrators, asking how the royals can live in luxury while the rest of us suffer austerity. The only trouble we got was people complaining about the main road being closed. Someone told me today there's a warehouse full of paper Union Jacks on sticks they couldn't give away. Maybe at some point it'll just blow up too!"

Blue said good night to Effie and Tam, who were now deep in conversation. He declined a whisky and retired to his room to update his report, and get some sleep.

Day 4 Thursday

32

Blue was at Dunrighinn by 7.30 am. The house was still burning, though in a more subdued way, and the buildings round the courtyard were simply smoking. The volunteer firefighters were still there. He asked the man they'd spoken to the previous evening, who seemed to be in charge, what was happening.

"There was nothing we could have done for the house itself, but we've managed to save some of the outbuildings. Not that I suppose that matters very much. It'll either stay a ruin, or they'll bulldoze the lot."

"When will it be safe to examine the wreckage?"

"Not till tomorrow I shouldn't think, maybe even the day after. The other buildings are out, so we're concentrating on the house now. But it'll still be a while. And even then, it'll be a dangerous place to go into."

"Are you getting any help?"

"Oh, yes, two appliances are on the way over on the first boat, one from Lochgilphead and one from Oban. Then I expect the fire investigation officer will be over at some point. They'll determine how it started, and if it was accidental or deliberate. If the place is insured, the insurers will send somebody too."

"If?"

"Old building, miles from anywhere, empty for substantial periods, I wouldn't be keen on insuring it. I'd worry that the owner would be tempted to leave the gas on and go to the South of France for a fortnight. Then collect the insurance and put up a more suitable building. And pocket the difference."

"You think gas might have been involved?" Blue didn't mention what Tam had told him. A second opinion would be useful.

"That was just an example. But in this case, the violence of the initial explosion and the speed with which the whole place caught, would suggest gas to me. But I'm no expert."

"What do you normally do?"

"I work at the malting plant over on Islay. Transport co-ordinator. Graham Telfer."

"Angus Blue." They shook hands.

"Are you thinking there was some skullduggery, Mr Blue?"

"There have been some unusual events here recently, we need to check out every possibility."

"Someone getting rid of the evidence, eh?"

"Who knows? I mustn't keep you, Graham, good to have met you. But do give me a shout if you see something suspicious. When everything's cooled off, we may want a closer look too."

It was a sunny morning, though the forecast was for showers. Blue found a folding chair in the boot of the police car, and sat himself on it on the grass. He wasn't sure what to do next. There wasn't much he could do at Dunrighinn until the building was safe enough to go into. Then he'd see what the fire investigator thought. At some point he would need to get over to Bowmore, and see if they could follow up the leads on the Polish car, and on the three girls, but he'd also have to talk to Alex Malcolm about the extra German on the Tayvallich boat. And buy that whisky for the Super.

He decided to phone McCader first.

"Hi, Enver, how are you doing?"

"All the better for a night back in my own bed, chief. Just having breakfast now."

"Anything to report?"

"Gave the bottle and the samples to Steve. No problem there, he'll find a way of slipping them through. Couple of days before he'll have any results, though. He obviously can't give them priority status, they have to be treated as simply routine."

"Anything from your Irish contacts?"

"Not yet, I've a call to make later this morning. I'll get back to you then."

"One other thing, Enver. Can you see if you can squeeze a ballistics report out of Kevin? He's notoriously slow at putting anything on paper."

"Will do, chief."

Just after eight a black Range Rover swept through the gates and parked on the grass. Ffox-Kaye sprang out of the passenger door, followed by the driver, a man whom Blue did not recognise. Not one of the goons who'd been at Dunrighinn earlier. He opened the rear of the vehicle and pulled out a camera bag and a tripod.

Meanwhile Ffox-Kaye simply stood contemplating the burning building. His face showed no emotion. He paid no attention to the firefighters.

Eventually he turned and seemed to notice Blue. He strode over, as if about to marshal his troops for a battle. Blue stood up as he approached.

"Who opened those gates? I should have been called to authorise it."

"A Mr Simon Mather. Address in Bristol. He used his car to ram them."

"I assume he's been arrested? That's clearly an offence, and there are security implications too."

"He won't do it again, I can assure you. He's dead."

Ffox-Kaye ignored this news. "Why wasn't I informed of the fire?"

"I don't think anyone was aware that a house fire was part of your investigation. Didn't you leave people to look after the site?"

"They left yesterday. The gates should have kept anyone out."

"What about Jack Seymour? Wouldn't he have reported it to you right away? He just lives up the road."

Ffox-Kaye's jaw twitched. "Well, he didn't."

"And he wasn't here last night. Inspector Nicolson checked his house, but he didn't seem to be in."

"So even the plods were here!" said Ffox-Kaye. "Have you talked to these fire chaps? What are they saying?"

"They've saved some of the outbuildings, but there was no hope for the house."

"Shame. Fine old building. Still, I suppose it was an accident waiting to happen. An absolute tinder-box. All that panelling, and wood everywhere. Floors, walls, ceilings, all wood, you know. All those stuffed deer heads, I suppose they'd go up too." He chortled.

"How do you think it might have started?"

Ffox-Kaye warmed to the subject. "My money'd be on electrical. Wiring in these old places is all very dodgy. Wires connected to old fitments that are ripped out, but stay live. Gnawed through by mice, rats, weasels, what have you. And I suspect up here there are no qualified electricians either. All the work was probably done by that handyman. Jock whatsisname."

"Tam."

"Whatever. You'll certainly need to look at his qualifications."

"When was the last time you talked to Jack Seymour?"

"Jack Seymour? Why do you want to know that?"

"Are you sure he hasn't gone to Lanzarote for a fortnight?"

"What the hell are you talking about?"

"It seemed odd to me that all the witnesses to the shooting suddenly found they had to be somewhere else."

"I'm not sure I like what you're suggesting, Blue. Seymour wasn't even a witness to the shooting – I can assure you he saw nothing. As I said before, I understood that he was at home, and I was therefore very puzzled to find that he hadn't informed me last night of the fire."

"So when did you learn about the fire?"

"Not until this morning. They were talking about it at my hotel. Said there'd been a fire at one of the estates. I eventually asked which one. Then I came straight up here. The ferryman was reluctant to take me across here ahead of his schedule. No wonder Giles never hired the locals." Ffox-Kaye seemed irritated at being asked questions. He kept smoothing the ends of his moustache with his thumb. An odd habit, thought Blue.

"By the way, Phil," he said, trying to sound more light-hearted, "how's your investigation coming on?"

Ffox-Kaye smiled smugly. "I think we're making a lot more progress than you are. But then, we've got access to data from the security end that makes things a lot clearer. I think we'll have it tied up in a few days."

"I'm glad to hear that. I'd still like to interview Lord Steppingham's employees who were in the house at the time of the shooting, if you are able to facilitate that?"

Ffox-Kaye stroked his moustache again, striking a pensive expression, as if weighing many possibilities. Finally he nodded, as if reluctantly granting a favour. "I'll see what I can do. Just give me a moment, if you will." He took out a mobile and walked away from Blue, poking at the screen as he did so.

Blue sat down again and waited till Ffox-Kaye returned, two or three minutes later. This time he didn't stand up.

"Yes, Blue, that should be no problem. I've just talked to Matt – he's down there at the moment, and will make all the arrangements. He'll have to be present, of course, to cover security matters, you understand. And naturally the local police will be there too. We can't be stepping on toes, can we? Tomorrow morning do you?"

"Er, yes, fine." Blue had a feeling he was being used. Ffox-Kaye's ready agreement was suspicious. But it was an opportunity he couldn't turn down.

"Good. Tell you what, I'll get Matt to give you a buzz later this morning, soon as he's got everything fixed. Hope you find it useful."

"Thanks. I hear you're making an announcement soon."

"Yes, sometime this morning. Just a routine press briefing. Got to keep them onside, once the news is out. Why don't you come along? Anyway, I'm going to nip up to Seymour's place now, see if he's in. See you later." He strode off towards the Range Rover, got in, and drove off. Blue noticed that the other man was over by the helipad, taking pictures of the fire.

As Blue was folding up his chair, he heard the sound of sirens, and a moment later two red fire engines rushed through the gates and drew to a halt by the local appliance. People got out, and he saw Graham Telfer shake hands with one of them, and lead him round the vehicles, presumably to explain what was happening. Blue returned the chair to the police car, and drove back to Craighouse.

33

He parked at the car park by the pier and walked over to Alex Malcolm's hut. It was shut. Blue glanced at his watch. After half past eight. When did the boat leave for Tayvallich? He hurried down the pier, and spotted the catamaran moored to a pontoon half way down, three or four people sitting out in the open area at the rear. He couldn't see into the cabin, but he was clearly visible from it, as Malcolm himself came out onto the rear deck and waved to him, then stepped nimbly onto the pontoon and up a stone stairway onto the pier itself.

"Good morning, Inspector. If you're in a hurry for the mainland, you're just in time. We're off in five minutes."

"No, I just wanted to ask a question. Have you a couple of minutes?"

"For you, Inspector, three minutes. But I take a pride in leaving on time, so please don't delay me."

"I'll try. Let me explain. On Monday morning you carried seven Germans. However, only six of them were in the party from the hotel. One wasn't. Can you tell me anything about him?"

"Sorry. Weren't all seven from the hotel?"

"No, only six. So if those six were paid for as a group, the other one must have paid you individually."

"Good question. Yes, the group from the hotel were pre-paid, Jan from the inn gave me the voucher for the group when they arrived at the boat. To be honest, they arrived at the last minute, I didn't even look at the voucher, just counted the guys as they got on. Shit! That guy got away with a freebie."

"So you didn't speak to all of them?"

"No, they were all talking to each other in German. I just chatted to one of them for a moment or two. He said they were from Berlin, and they'd had a great time. That's all."

"What did the others look like?"

"That's a tall order. Well, if it's not being racist, I'd say they were all white, although a couple were quite red. In the face that is. Mind you, one looked a bit, how can I say, not quite as well-heeled as the others. They all had top-brand gear on. His stuff looked a bit more ordinary. But he wasn't standing apart, he was chatting away with them."

"What did he look like?"

"Hmm. I'd say not quite as tall and definitely slimmer than the others. More sunburned or weathered, gave the impression of being fit. I'd say his gear was for use rather than show."

"What was he carrying?"

"Was he armed? I didn't see. OK, just a joke. I think he had a rucksack. All the Germans piled their gear in the cabin, I guess he put it in the same pile. But he had it on his back when he got off. I remember that. Quite a bulky one. The others had holdalls or suitcases."

"How old do you think he was?"

"Fifties, probably. Same as the others."

"Glasses?"

"No."

"Beard, moustache, clean-shaven?"

"Moustache. Just ordinary, you know, not Hitler, Kaiser Wilhelm or Pancho Villa."

"Hair colour. Light? Dark?"

"Darkish. Not black, maybe dark brown. And his hair cut fairly short. Maybe a number 4 clipper."

"Could you describe him to a police artist if we can get one to you?"

"Sure. I think so. Mind you, I only glanced at him, I never really studied him."

"One other thing. Did he go off with the others at Tayvallich?"

"Yes. They all went together towards the car park. That's where their minibus was waiting."

"Then did he get into the minibus with them, or go to another car?"

"I don't know. To be honest, I was more preoccupied with Marie and Annette. My car was parked beyond the boat sheds. And I had to tie up and check the bookings for the return journey before I could drive them to Lochgilphead. So that's all I can tell you." He looked at his watch. "Can I go now? Feel free to talk to me again, I'll see if I can think of anything."

"OK. I don't want to spoil your punctuality record. Many thanks for your help."

Malcolm couldn't be that concerned with punctuality, thought Blue, as the boat pulled away from the pontoon, if he ferried a couple of *mesdemoiselles* to Lochgilphead before doing his return journey on Monday.

The village shop stood by the entrance to the pier. Blue went in. He was surprised how much bigger on the inside it looked, and also at the extensive variety of goods on offer, including fishing and camping materials. A bookshelf was well-stocked with classics in addition to the latest best-sellers, and a thick paperback about Jura. Blue flicked through a copy; it looked fairly comprehensive. He took it to the counter, where a smiling grey-haired lady awaited.

"Ah, Mr Blue, you'll be buying Mr Youngson's book. You'll not regret that. I'm thinking you'll find your own people mentioned a few times in it. I know my own are."

Blue thought hard, and remembered. "You'll be Mary Buchanan, am I right?" He remembered Craig and Bhardwaj's report of the witnesses to passing vehicles.

"Touché, Mr Blue, as they say in the films. Though my maiden name is McIsaac, which is why we're in the book. He lists all the main families you see."

"Wait a minute, I think my great-grandmother was a McIsaac. Anne McIsaac."

"Aye, that would be right enough. She'd be a sister of old Duncan McIsaac. He lived to be 102, just died a few years ago. So I guess we're related somehow. Your aunt Effie was saying she was real pleased to see you again. It's good you've come. It'll be about that business up at Dunrighinn. No wonder it's burnt down. It had a reputation, you know, as a house of evil. Not that we heard any details, but enough to give a sense of it. Secret comings and goings, lights on at all hours of the night. Other things too, that I won't repeat. Aye, maybe the place is better in ashes right enough."

"Did you ever meet the owner, Lord Steppingham?"

"His Lordship? Aye, he'd sweep in now and then, like the laird dipping his toes in the common folk. Never spoke to me, just talked to that fawning secretary as if I didn't exist. 'Get some wine, Eric, the best they've got. Half a dozen bottles. I don't suppose they have champagne.' He got a surprise when I told him we did, but he just looked at it and said, 'Oh dear, well, Eric, we'd better have a few bottles of this stuff. Looks like rubbish, but us poor beggars can't be choosers, what?' Next night the secretary was back for more, said it was really good. I told him, 'Forget France, Georgia's where the best wine comes from.' He thought I meant America." She shook her head in wonder at this stupidity.

"I think you were very helpful to our constables in reporting a couple of vehicles you saw passing on Monday morning?"

"Arvind and Deirdra. Such nice young people. If only they were all as polite. Yes, I do tend to notice traffic that's out of the ordinary. Especially outside of July and August, that's when we have a lot more than usual."

"Think back to Monday morning. Did you happen to see a man, about fifty, on a bicycle, a small fold-up one."

She pursed her lips and thought. "Hmm. Now that you mention it, there was a chap with a wee cycle. I'm over here at seven in the morning, to get everything ready – we open at eight, you see – and I must have glanced out of the window, and I saw him, walking past the shop wheeling the bike."

"What time was this?"

"Oh, maybe about half past seven, maybe a bit more. At eight, he came in and asked if we had the day's papers. I said to him, no, not till Alex, Alex Malcolm, that is, gets in from Tayvallich, after eleven. He asked if Alex's boat was running as usual, I think he was planning on getting it. He bought a bar of chocolate, I think he felt he had to buy something. And a cup of coffee, from the machine. He was very pleasant. Very polite. Foreign, but I couldn't say where from. Nicely dressed too, not expensive but sensible, somebody who takes care of himself, I'd say. I hope you're not after him for something?"

"No, no, just routine. He might have seen something. Can you tell me what he looked like."

"About average height, quite slim, dark hair, quite short, moustache but no beard, kind eyes."

"Kind eyes?"

"Yes, you can tell a lot from eyes, you know. Kind, but there was pain in there too. A man you would trust, I think. Rather like yourself, Mr Blue."

Blue looked at the floor, then the shelves, then out the window, at the dark sea. Clouds had obscured the sun now, and it felt colder. He felt Mary's gaze on him.

"It wasn't him that left the bomb at the house?" she said suddenly

"What bomb?"

"They're saying there was a bomb at the house. Blew up the whole place. Even blew a car off the road at Ardmenish. People killed. That's awful. I do hope you get them."

Blue left the shop, and walked round to the rear, where a couple of yards of grass separated him from the rocky beach abutting the pier. So the mystery man bought a cup of coffee and might have been waiting for the boat to Tayvallich. What if he'd come round here, sat somewhere out of the way, waiting for the boat? He may have seen the group come from the inn, and decided to mingle with them on the walk down the pier. Was he German too, or did he just have a good command of it, enough to converse freely?

And what did he do with the bike? He didn't take it with him onto the boat, Alex would have noticed that. Blue began to wander around looking behind rocks and among the discarded pallets littering the grass. Nothing there. He walked over to the pier. At the landward end was a small car park, empty apart from a couple of big wheelie bins, a green one marked 'Recycling' and a grey one marked 'General waste'. He lifted the lid of the grey bin. Nothing. Then the green one – and there it was. A folded up bicycle, the metal parts painted over black. Blue took out his camera and photographed it *in situ*. Then he extracted a handkerchief, put one end through the corner of the frame, and holding the loop thus formed, lifted the bike out of the bin. He suspected there would be no prints on it, but you couldn't make assumptions. He carried it carefully, at arms length, over to the police car, opened the back, and lowered the bicycle in. Another valuable piece of evidence. He took out his notebook and noted when and where he'd found it.

The distillery was just across the road from the inn, which was situated by the pier, on the other side from the shop. A stocky young woman, with brown hair swept back into a braid, was just opening the shop, through which the general public had to pass to gain access to the distillery itself.

Blue greeted her. "Good morning. Are you open?"

"Yes, yes. We don't usually get customers till mid morning. You're the first."

Blue showed his warrant card. She looked shocked. "Is it about my visa? It's completely legal. Are they sending us away already?

150

People from the EU?"

"No, no, nothing to do with that. Where are you from, by the way?"

"I'm from Lithuania. My name is Milda. It's the name of the Old Lithuanian goddess of love."

"That's a long way away. So what brought you all the way out here? Are you a whisky fan?"

"Ha, not me, but you are close to the truth. My boyfriend is big whisky fanatic. He got the job here, driving the truck. So then I came also, and got work here. I do not have the taste for whisky. But that means I am less likely to drink on the job, eh?" She laughed.

Blue laughed too. "Can I ask you a question, Milda? When you were opening up on Monday, did you see a man walk over from somewhere behind the shop and join the people getting on to Alex Malcolm's boat?"

She thought. "No. I'm very sorry. I didn't take any notice. I think people came from the hotel. Oh, and two French girls. They came in here on Saturday. They tried the whisky but did not like it. They still bought a little bottle each, to present to family when they are home."

"That reminds me. I'd like to buy some. The 21-year-old. One *Time* and one *Tide*."

"Yes, they are very popular. But I think we have still a small number of bottles in the store. I'll be back in five minutes. By then it will be ten o'clock and I can sell alcohol to you legally."

"How much are they? Er, I'm buying them for my boss."

"You mean to bribe him?" she said seriously.

"No, no, not at all, he'll give me the money when I see him. Honest!"

"OK. I believe you. Two hundred and eighty pounds only. Each bottle is one hundred and forty."

Blue gulped. He knew the Super's tastes were expensive, but it was still hard for him to pay so much for two bottles of alcohol.

When Milda returned he also bought a bottle of the *Diurach's Own*. Milda added to the bag – "just for you" – a whisky glass and a couple of miniatures.

Effie opened the door before he'd reached it.

"Come on in Angus, are you wanting a cuppa now? The kettle's just boiled."

Over tea and a chocolate digestive, he asked what Effie had heard about the fire at Dunrighinn.

"Well, now, I heard something from Yvonne, at the cafe. I'm just back from my morning coffee there. I'm there every weekday, you know. We have to keep up with all that's going on. Mind you, I don't know where she got it from, but she's got a pal over Ardmenish way, maybe from her. Is that right, that it was a bomb?"

"I can't tell you that, Effie. Once the fire's died down, the investigators will go in and see what caused it."

"Tam was thinking it was gas." So much for keeping his mouth shut, thought Blue.

"Where is Tam?"

"Och, he was up and away just a moment after you'd left yourself this morning. He said to say to you that he didn't need anything at his house, so he'd just go straight off on the first boat. I think he was frightened to go up there, even with a police escort."

Blue wasn't surprised at that; it was probably sensible for Tam to get off the island as soon as possible. He explained to Effie that he'd have to be going himself, to stay on Islay while the investigation continued. Effie would accept no payment, even from Police Scotland. Not for family.

"And I hope you'll be coming back to see me before you're finished on Islay?"

"Of course, Effie." And he meant it, too.

34

An hour later he parked outside the police station in Bowmore, an Edwardian villa not far off the main road through the town, and went in. Sergeant Bob Walker was on duty at the reception desk, and greeted Blue like an old friend.

"Good to see you again, chief. You'll be wanting to use the office upstairs you had last year?"

"Is the furniture still there? I thought the council would have reclaimed it."

Bob grinned. "Well, chief, no-one asked for it back, so it's waiting for you."

Blue went through the door alongside the reception desk, along the corridor past the workroom, and up the stairs. The room on the right was just as he had left it, and he was happy to put his bag on the worn-out armchair and sit at the well-used desk that had once graced a classroom in the secondary school. He sat for a moment, then knocked on the door to the next room, at the end of the corridor.

Moira Nicolson opened it. "Angus, you made it. Coffee?"

"I'd love one. I see you're eating your sandwich. Do you mind if I join you?" Effie had insisted on making him a sandwich before he left, smoked salmon with soft cheese and finely-sliced shallot.

Over lunch he brought Moira up to date on what had happened that morning.

"So it's looking like the bicycle man could be the shooter?"

"Could be. But I also need to talk to Steppingham's staff, and follow up those three girls, to find out what was going on at the house, and whether they saw anything."

"The only thing that's happened here is Ffox-Kaye's press conference. I went along to see what he had to reveal."

"And?"

"Well, he did reveal that there had been a shooting. That Lord Steppingham was the target, and was badly wounded "

"I thought he wasn't that badly injured. Anyway, sorry to interrupt, go on."

"And that he believed it was a terrorist attack, which was why there had been a news blackout. He went on to say that Dunrighinn House had since been destroyed. The cause of the fire was yet to be established, but he considered that also might be a terrorist atrocity."

Blue frowned. "Did he use the actual word 'atrocity'?"

"Yes. Why?"

"Atrocities usually involve people being killed. As far as we know, that's not the case. Maybe he's trying to create a so-called 'moral panic'?"

"What do you mean?"

"The term was invented in the seventies for the process whereby something that isn't in itself a problem is made out to be a threat, and righteous indignation is whipped up, usually against a particular group. Then there's public demand for action, so that whatever the authorities do against the target group is welcomed and accepted without any criticism. People who do criticise can then be branded as troublemakers or even traitors."

"So why is he doing that now?"

"I don't know. He may already have identified a scapegoat, and just be preparing the ground. We don't know what he's doing, what leads he's chasing. All we can do is follow the trails that we've got."

Back in his office, he phoned McCader, and asked him to go to Tayvallich and see if anyone remembered a lone, middle-aged, fit and weatherbeaten possible German coming off Alex Malcolm's boat, being picked up by a car with Polish registration, or getting a bus or taxi. McCader had hustled Dalvey for his report and was still awaiting a call from Dublin.

Ten minutes later the phone rang.

"Police Scotland. Inspector Blue here. How may I help you?"

"Cut the shit, Blue." Inspector Plaistow. "Re your trip, I'll meet you at Steppingham station at ten tomorrow morning. Got that?"

"Yes, I…" The line went dead. Not much hope of developing a working relationship with Plaistow, then.

After updating his report, he went downstairs to the workroom on the ground floor to see if Bhardwaj and Craig had anything to report. As he turned from the stairs into the corridor a voice called out, "Hi Angus, what's doing?" John Striven, reporter for *The Nation*, and an old friend of Blue's from university days, was standing by the reception desk in the foyer.

"Wait there, John," Blue called back, and mounted the stairs again to fetch his coat.

They walked out of the town to the Gaelic Centre, overlooking Loch Indaal, around which Islay huddles like a sleeping giant. There was a good cafe there, and Blue didn't want their conversation overheard. He didn't think any of Ffox-Kaye's henchmen would have made it this far. They talked over coffee and home-made carrot cake.

"So you've been to Ffox-Kaye's press conference?" asked Blue.

"Yes. Got over here as soon as the news of the shooting was released."

"What did you make of it?"

"Strikes me he's already got some poor sucker fingered for it. Probably an immigrant or refugee. He was very vague about details. Only that Lord S. had been shot by a single gunman and was rushed to London for treatment. And then his house is completely destroyed by fire. Believe me, something stinks there. He's only telling us what he wants us to hear. He did mention, rather reluctantly, that local police were involved, said they hadn't made any progress, so a more competent agency had to step in. I don't believe that, so that's why I've come to you. What can you tell me?"

"Unfortunately, very little at the moment. We were called in a few hours after the shooting. We've located the shooter's position and have some evidence from that. I can't say more till it's been examined. It looks like there was a single shooter, and he probably made off as soon as the shooting was over. We're examining some important leads at the moment, but I can't give you any more at this stage. Sorry John, I really can't. But, as soon as we have something to say in public, you'll be the first to know."

Journalists could often go where police officers couldn't, and John Striven had helped Blue in the past, so he needed to keep him onside. "Here's something you didn't hear from me, John. Rumour has it locally that parties were held here involving drugs and under-age girls. I can't confirm these rumours of course, but…"

"Say no more, Angus. I'll have a chat with some of the Jura folk and see what we can dig up. Anything I think you ought to know I'll pass on. Now, let me pay for this. It's on expenses."

When Blue got back to the police station, he went straight to the workroom on the ground floor. Bhardwaj glanced up from behind a PC.

"Hi, chief. Think we've got something interesting here. Deirdra was going through the film Laurence Mather – that's the youth who was in that car – had on his mobile. Some footage of the fire, as well as the encounter with Dr Hendrickx and yourself. And this."

He pointed at the PC that Craig was sitting at. Blue stood behind her and watched the screen as she set the video footage running. The noise was the first thing that struck him, the sound of a helicopter. The picture showed Dunrighinn House, filmed from some considerable distance away.

Craig paused the film. "It's Monday morning, chief, and the chopper's just coming in. We reckon he must have been up early, gone for a walk round the shore at Ardmenish. If you get far enough round, there's a rocky knoll from which you could get this distant shot of the house. He must have heard the chopper and started filming right away. See what happens next."

She clicked to run the film. Nothing was immediately visible, but the noise was clear. Then the helicopter came into view and landed on the pad. A tiny and fuzzy figure ran out to the chopper and disappeared behind it. "That'll be Plaistow," said Blue. "He said he checked the flight details with the helicopter crew."

Then the figure went back towards the house, and more figures, so distant as to be individually indistinguishable, emerged and headed for the aircraft, led by the one they'd identified as Plaistow. They were half way to the pad when things went awry. Some of the figures fell over, others ran to pick them up and get them to the house, then three emerged again and started pointing to where they presumed the shooter was. "They're shooting back," said Craig, "but the shots aren't audible on the film."

Then the figures seemed to give up shooting and all disappeared into the house. "That's all we've got, chief," said Craig.

"Run it again," said Blue. "I need to just confirm what I think I saw."

"We ran it several times," said Bhardwaj. "There are definitely two people shot there. Not one!"

It was true. Two of the little figures were hit. It was not easy to see at first, as three people were walking together towards the aircraft. But once the shooting started, they could see that one figure staggered a few paces then fell over, then the figure next to him fell to the ground. The third figure threw himself to the ground. Other figures ran to them and two were lifted up and carried into the house. The third picked himself up and ran, crouching low, back to the house.

"What is going on?" said Blue to himself.

"Should I ask Inspector Nicolson to have a look too?" asked Bhardwaj.

"Yes, yes, the more eyes we've got on this the better. Deirdra, have you tried to enhance it?"

"Aye, but it just pixelates, we'll no get nice clear images. Sorry, chief."

"That's OK."

"Aye. But they've some software at Paisley Uni that might help. It's for enhancing satellite images. I know one o the folks workin on it, I could gie her a call."

"Yes, great idea. Soon as you can, Deirdra. Good work."

Moira Nicolson was called, and they ran through it again. There was no doubt at all. The shooter had claimed two victims.

"One of them, we know," said Moira. "Lord Steppingham. But who was the other?"

"A security man?" suggested Bhardwaj. "The fact that all three victims were so close together could still mean that only one was the target. Probably Lord Steppingham. The shooter had to take the other one out to get to him."

"It could be another guest, that we don't know about," put in Moira.

"Deirdra," said Blue, "can you slow it down, and see in what order the victims get shot?"

"Aye, I'll give it a go, chief. I'll phone my pal at Paisley first."

"Right," agreed Blue. "There's no point in speculating till we've got some more work done on the film. But at least we know there were two victims. And Plaistow and Ffox-Kaye were both lying about it."

"And the pilot, too," said Bhardwaj. "I took his statement. He's clear there was only one victim."

"What are they hiding?" said Moira.

"I don't know," said Blue, "but it makes me keener than ever to see Lord Steppingham's staff. I'll need to book a flight."

"When do you need to fly?" asked Moira.

"Six o'clock plane this evening. Then I'll need a flight from Glasgow to Luton tomorrow morning first thing."

"OK. I can ask Bob to fix the flights now. Last minute, they'll not be cheap. I hope your Super's happy to sign the expenses." She disappeared into the corridor.

Back in his office, Blue phoned his cousin Janice, and asked for accommodation for that night. Janice and her husband Bill Muir lived in Bearsden, north of Glasgow.

"No problem, Angus. The dog's got a cold, so make sure he doesn't sneeze on you while you're in your bed. What time will you be arriving? Not the middle of the night, like last time, I hope."

"Plane gets in at 6.30 this evening."

"That's great. I'll come and meet you. See you later."

He thought of doing a bit more work on his report. But he was aware that as soon as he saved the latest version to the Police Scotland hub, Ffox-Kaye would have access to it. And for whatever reason, Ffox-Kaye didn't want Blue to know that there were two victims. So he left it for the moment.

35

At 4.30 there was a knock on his door. Alison.

"Hi, Angus. I've come to take you to the airport. Then I can wave my handkerchief as you fly away."

"I'll be back tomorrow."

"Ah. That's what they all say," she smiled. "Now, are you all packed?"

As they drove to the airport, he told her about the film.

"It's getting murky, isn't it?" she said, without taking her eyes off the road. "Be careful. Will you be safe down there, with Plaistow? I don't want you to be the next victim."

"I don't think that's likely at the moment. As far as they're aware I don't know very much, and I'm certainly going to keep quiet about what's on that film. I suspect they're letting me talk to the staff simply because they think it won't get me anywhere. Maybe just to get me out of the way for a day."

Alison parked the car at Islay Airport, with its sand-blown runway disappearing off into the sea, and they waited together in the single room that served every airport function. They knew better than to talk about the case.

"What have you been doing today?" asked Blue.

"I went to Finlaggan. An island in a loch on an island. Quite a secure spot for the Lords of the Isles to hold court. And for all their power, how modest it is."

"I'd like to see it."

"I'll take you, if you've time. With free lecture thrown in."

"I'll hold you to that."

"I hope you do." She stroked gently with her fingers the back of his hand.

As the plane climbed, he watched from the window as the island shrank beneath. As the plane turned, he saw the Paps of Jura rising grey and bare from the faded brown moors. Then it drifted away as they crossed the water towards the ragged coast of the mainland.

Janice Muir was waiting at Domestic Arrivals when Blue came through at 6.40.

"My long-lost cousin flitting past again. It's nice to see you." She gave him a hug. "Come on then, I've a lot of catching-up to do. And I want straight answers."

In the car, she asked, "Are you involved in this shooting business on Jura?"

"There are plenty of shooting businesses on Jura."

"Ha, ha, very funny. Lord Steppingham. It was on the news as I was waiting for you. Big announcement by some guy with a double-barrelled name."

"Yes, that's Ffox-Kaye. Special Branch. I'm just on the edge of it." No need to give too much away. "I need to interview a couple of people down south. Routine stuff."

"I'm not sure I believe that. Let's go, anyway."

Janice drove Blue back via the Erskine Bridge. Bill Muir was waiting at the house, and an evening meal was ready. Conversation didn't focus on the case, as Janice was more interested in Blue's personal relationships. "Come on, Angus, you've been on your own too long. You'll turn into a grumpy old man. What about Alison Hendrickx, she's your type isn't she?"

"What do you mean by that?"

"You know what I mean. Pleasant nature, intellectual, shared interests, you could do a lot worse."

"She brought me her drone to play with."

"Well, that's a conversation-stopper."

"That's the idea," said Blue. "How are things at the FE college, then?"

"Point taken. Crazy. We were ordered to have the day off to-morrow, so the students could wave flags as the royal party parade through Glasgow. All the Chinese on the Hotel Management course were very excited. At least they'll be out with their Union Jacks. The other students thought having a day off was a great idea, but I doubt they'll be lining the streets. Apparently there's a 'Royal Festival' in George Square on Saturday. They're going to unveil a new statue, and there will be pipe bands and stalls and glüwein."

"Glüwein?"

"They couldn't think of a typical royal drink. But the stalls from the Christmas Market can easily be set up."

"They were going to invite some Rangers players to appear," said Bill, "but the club refused to let them. Said they wanted to keep clear of politics. Very sensible. Now, what about a nice glass of Talisker?"

Day 5 Friday

36

Next morning Janice drove Blue to the airport. His flight to Luton was without incident. Since he had all he needed in his backpack, he didn't have to wait for any baggage. From the airport, he got the train from Luton Airport Parkway, through Luton itself and on into the countryside, passing what had once been villages, but were now commuter suburbs masquerading as rural communities. Harlington, Fledgwick, Kempstone, Markingley, and another couple before Steppingham. As the train came into Steppingham itself, he saw an estate of modestly sized detached houses, with the occasional block of flats, by an artificial pond.

It was not yet nine when the train pulled into the station, and as he stood to get off, he saw the platform on the other side was packed with people. How long did the commuter rush last, he wondered. As he stood on the platform, getting his bearings, the London train arrived, already packed, and he watched the crowds squeezing themselves into the bulging carriages. Despite the announcement that another train was coming in ten minutes, the crowds were desperate to force themselves into the one that was there. Blue suspected the next train would be just as full.

As he came out of the station a voice shouted. "Hey, Blue, over here!" Plaistow, calling from the rear window of a police car parked opposite the station entrance, in a disabled parking space. Blue went over and got in at the other side.

"I wasn't expecting you till ten," said Blue. He'd been hoping to have a look round Steppingham before meeting Plaistow.

"Checked with the airport, knew when you'd arrive. Still this way you'll get away quicker. This shouldn't take us very long."

Blue noticed the front seats of the car were both occupied. The driver was a uniformed female officer, all he could see was short blonde hair and ears with rings in them. The other was a man in plain clothes. Blue assumed him to be one of Plaistow's creatures. The man gave directions to the driver, who nodded, and they set off. The man then turned round in his seat. Light brown curly hair over a smooth and slightly chubby face. A serious expression.

"Hi. Inspector Blue, I assume. I'm Inspector Geoff Rackham,

Bedfordshire Police. I guess we're your hosts today. Though Mr Plaistow's in charge, as I'm sure you're aware."

"Rackham's here as a local police officer," said Plaistow, "whereas you're here simply as a visitor, Blue. This is a security-sensitive interview, so there are some rules that you two will observe. First, no recording of anything said, either by digital or manual means. Second, you can ask the questions, Blue, but the interviewees will wait for me to indicate whether they can answer or not. For security reasons some questions may be blocked. Rackham, your job is simply to observe on behalf of the local force. So keep your mouth shut from start to finish. Third, this is not an official interview, it is merely a consultation. Therefore nothing that is said may be used in any court proceedings. Is that clear?"

"Christ!" said Rackham. "What have these people got to hide?"

"Shut your bloody trap, Rackham! Another word from you and the whole thing's off. I'm sure our colleague from Jockland won't want to have a wasted day." Plaistow paused to savour his words. "Finally, I must remind you that this event is covered by the Official Secrets Act, and any infringement of the Act will result in immediate action, which could include arrest and prosecution. Now Rackham, get WPC Plod to move her ass – I'm sure it's nice one – and get us there a bit faster."

Rackham didn't turn round but spoke in a toneless voice, as if addressing someone outside the front windscreen. "My driver will naturally adhere to the guidance for safe and considerate driving issued by Bedfordshire Police."

"Well, that's a pity, mate," said Plaistow to Blue. "I'm including this journey in the time available for the interviews."

Blue chose not to respond, and for the next five minutes there was silence in the car. They passed a number of commuter estates, before turning a sharp left between two stone gateposts and onto a long drive, edged by a six-foot wooden fence. Blue noticed the houses over the fence on either side of the drive. At some point in the recent past, Lord Steppingham must have made a lot of money selling land to developers.

About a quarter of a mile up the drive, they stopped at a gateway which reminded Blue of Dunrighinn. Black metal gates were firmly closed, and a metal fence topped by razor wire stretched away to left and right. Plaistow got out and spoke to someone on the intercom set into the faux stone gatepost. The gates swung open. Plaistow got back in and they entered a drive which curved round the edge of a wide lawn before arriving at the front of a large classically-styled building of the late-18th or early-19th century. Everything was in good condition. Blue could almost see money oozing out under the wooden front doors and dribbling down the wide staircase that led from the portico down to the drive.

"Special treat today, lads!" said Plaistow jovially. "We're going in the front door. Normally it's the tradesmen's entrance for you lot." He poked the driver in the back. "Once we're out, Sweetie, take this vehicle round the back, and stay with it. Your boss'll phone you when it's time to go." Without another word, he got out, and Blue and Rackham followed suit.

A man in a cheap dark suit, evidently one of Plaistow's men, opened one of the tall polished wood front doors, and let them into a spacious and largely empty reception hall. He led them from there through an almost invisible doorway hidden in a corner of the hall into a corridor, and thence to a small square room looking out onto a courtyard which Blue assumed was at the rear of the building. It contained only a timeworn dark wooden table and four matching upright wooden chairs, with upholstered seats. Plaistow arranged the chairs so that three were on one side of the table, and one on the other. Blue noticed that whoever sat on the single chair would have their back to the light, making it difficult for the other three to see their face clearly.

"Excuse me a moment, gentlemen," growled Plaistow, and left the room.

Rackham looked grim. He said nothing and sat down in the left hand chair. Blue sat in the middle one.

The door opened, and Plaistow entered, motioning Eric James to enter, then sit on the single chair. He himself then moved the other chair, which was next to Blue, round to the narrow end of the table. Blue realised that by not aligning himself with the policemen he was making it plain that he would mediate between the interviewee and Blue. He would control the interview.

Eric James was a thin man with dark hair carefully combed from a middle parting, a pointed nose and small moustache nestling beneath it. He wore a neutral expression, but Blue could tell immediately that he was tense. He was concentrating hard.

"Mr James has kindly agreed to this consultation," began Plaistow, "on condition that it is moderated by me. I will bar any question that I think is unreasonable or irrelevant, or could impact on security issues. Please begin, Mr Blue."

"Thank you for agreeing to talk to us, Mr James. I'd just like to ask some questions about recent events at Dunrighinn House. But first, could you give me some idea of your role in Lord Steppingham's household?"

James looked to Plaistow as if asking for confirmation that he should answer. Plaistow scowled at Blue, and nodded to James. "Just keep it short," he said.

James nodded. "I am Lord Steppingham's secretary and office manager. As such, I organise his diary and his correspondence. I arrange transport and accommodation, and other facilities required from time to time."

"So you spend a lot of your time with Lord Steppingham?"

"I'm not sure what you mean, Inspector. What is 'a lot'?" said James.

"Do you see Lord Steppingham every day, to receive instructions or make arrangements?"

"Yes, of course."

"Can you tell me what happened on Monday morning?"

"Certainly. I had a brief consultation with Lord Steppingham at 6.20, since he was due to take the helicopter out at seven. I was to go later in the morning with other staff members to Islay airport to get the plane to Glasgow and then on to Luton. After the consultation, which lasted perhaps ten minutes, I went to the kitchen to have my breakfast. I believe I had a bowl of cereal, followed by a poached egg on a bed of rocket, and wholemeal toast with low fat spread and low-calorie marmalade. And tea. Rogers was also there, and Mrs Gregg, who had cooked for us. Rogers was having breakfast too. I heard the helicopter land as I was eating my toast. Then, just after the engine noise died down, there were some loud cracks, three I think, but I could be mistaken.

"Naturally, we wondered what was going on. We couldn't see anything, as the kitchen is at the back of the house, so I went through to the lobby. When I got there I saw the front door was open, and a moment later Lord Steppingham was brought in by two of the security people. One of them said, 'He's been shot. Get the nurse!' I ran back to the kitchen and called Rogers through. She grabbed the first-aid kit and came through. Meanwhile Mr van Kaarsten had got in. He wasn't hit, I believe he'd thrown himself to the ground as soon as the shooting started."

"Army training?"

"Yes, how did you know that?"

I read the script, Blue felt like saying, but instead said, "Do carry on, please."

"Well, Rogers immediately examined His Lordship's shoulder – that's where he'd been hit, you see."

"Did you hear any more shooting?"

"No. I think it was all over by the time I got through to the lobby."

"OK. What happened after that?" Blue felt that James was presenting a well-rehearsed account.

"Rogers removed the bullet, cleaned the wound, and bandaged it. And gave him some pain-killers. She said her bandage would be OK till he got to a hospital to have it properly looked at. X-rays and so on. Then Inspector Plaistow said that we should get His Lordship away as fast as possible, in case there were more shooters up there. He was taken to a car, and driven I believe to the airport. I went off with Rogers later in the morning, as planned, and got the plane to Glasgow, then Luton. I reached the house here at about seven o'clock in the evening."

"Do you normally stay at Steppingham House?"

"I normally stay wherever Lord Steppingham is residing."

"Not at the moment?"

"Obviously not," growled Plaistow. "'Is Lordship's in 'ospital. Ask a sensible question."

"Can you tell me how many people were staying in Dunrighinn House on Sunday night through to Monday morning?" James glanced at Plaistow, and Blue caught uncertainty in his eye.

"Why do you want to know that?" asked Plaistow suspiciously.

"I'd like to rule out the possibility of other potential witnesses."

"I've done that. There weren't any. Next question."

"Mr James, can you think of any other member of staff who may have witnessed the attack?"

"I just told you," grunted Plaistow, "there weren't any. Are you bleedin' deaf?"

"Mr James, can you confirm that you drove down to the Islay ferry, with Miss Rogers?"

"Yes."

"Who was driving?"

"I was."

"Did you see anything suspicious on your way to the ferry?"

"Again, I'm not sure what you mean, Inspector. Do you mean like someone polishing a rifle or carrying one of those round black bombs they used to have in silent films?" He smiled. Plaistow snorted.

"You're right," said Blue, "silly question. Did you happen to see three girls, possibly Eastern European?"

James's mouth dropped open, but nothing came out. Plaistow was caught out too, gasped briefly and was in control again. "What are you bloody talking about, Blue?" he shouted.

"A witness reported them on the ferry. We don't know where they were staying, or why they were on Jura. I wondered if Mr James might have seen them."

"Well, whoever they were, Blue, they weren't at the 'ouse. I never saw them. Neither did Mr James. Did you, sir?"

"No, no, not at all," gasped James.

"Right, time's up," said Plaistow. "You can go now, Mr James. Thank you."

James breathed a sigh of relief as he rose from the table and made for the door. It had been harder than he'd anticipated, thought Blue.

"Is there any point in talking to Miss Rogers?" said Plaistow, with a look at his watch. "She'll just tell you same as him."

"Nevertheless," said Blue, "now that I'm here, I'd like to hear it from her own mouth."

Alice Rogers had shoulder-length mousy hair, and a sympathetic face, though she was dressed like someone twice her age. But she was not as self-possessed as Eric James, and looked very nervous.

Plaistow began again. "Thank you, Miss Rogers for agreeing to talk to us." He turned to Blue. "Miss Rogers has had something of a shock from Monday morning's events, and I'd ask you to be careful what you ask. Please don't waste our time repeating some of the stupid questions you asked Mr James." This warning to Blue

166

was no doubt meant to reassure Miss Rogers, but the aggressive tone in Plaistow's voice seemed to make her even more nervous.

"Thank you for speaking to me, Miss Rogers," began Blue. "I'm of course aware that you're a nurse, but can you tell me what your duties are in Lord Steppingham's household?"

"Yes, well, a lot of it is, er, routine examinations. For instance "

"No need for examples!" cut in Plaistow.

"No, of course not," said the nurse. Blue could see her hands quivering. She's scared stiff, he thought. She went on, "Em, well, I also advise on general health topics like exercise and nutrition. And I'm available 24/7 in case anything should happen."

"Which, of course, on Monday it did."

"Yes." She looked down at the table.

"Did anyone else at the house need your help that weekend?" Miss Rogers opened and shut her mouth.

Plaistow spoke before she could say anything. "That's not relevant, Blue. Monday morning's what you want to know about. Stick to it."

"So, at just before seven on Monday morning, Miss Rogers, where were you exactly?"

"I was in the kitchen, er, having breakfast." Her voice had sunk to little more than a whisper.

"Who else was there?"

"Eric, Mr James, he was having breakfast too, and Mrs Gregg, she'd made it for us."

"Was anyone else there?"

"She just told you who was there, didn't she?" sneered Plaistow. "You ain't listenin'."

"Just tell me what happened."

"Well, we were eating, and we heard the helicopter. Then it stopped, and there were these bangs. Maybe two or three. Eric went to see what had happened. A few moments later he dashed back into the kitchen and said I'd have to come right away. His Lordship had been shot. Well, of course, I got the first-aid kit – it's a big one, it's kept in a cupboard in the kitchen – and rushed through. Two of the policemen had just helped him into the house. I could see right away he'd been wounded in the shoulder. But he was conscious and in some shock I think. I gave Lord Steppingham a local anaesthetic, then got the bullet out. Then I cleaned the wound and bandaged it, gave him some pain-killers. Co-codamol, 30/500."

"She did a great job," added Plaistow. "Carry on, Miss Rogers." He was clearly pleased with her performance so far, and the nurse began to look more relaxed, and spoke a little more loudly.

"The chief inspector asked if he was fit to travel. He "

Plaistow cut in again, "Thanks for the promotion, Miss Rogers, it's plain old inspector. For the moment, anyway." He'd spotted the slip.

"Yes, of course, sorry about that. Yes, Inspector Plaistow wanted to get him away from the danger as quickly as possible. I said, yes, as long as they kept him comfortable, and got the wound looked at properly, you know, by his own doctor, as soon as he got home. He'd need to go to a hospital too, get it X-rayed, in case the bone was fractured."

"So the wound wasn't a particularly bad one?"

"Nurse Rogers ain't a doctor," Plaistow sneered. "It's not up to her to say how bad the wound was. Next question."

"Sorry, Miss Rogers. What happened next?"

"Well, we got him into a car, and made sure he was comfortable, and off he went."

"How many cars were there? In the convoy with Lord Steppingham."

Miss Rogers hesitated, eyes wide, looked at Plaistow.

"That's not relevant," he growled, "And we agreed to talk to Miss Rogers, Blue, not to harass her."

"That certainly wasn't my intention, Miss Rogers, and I apologise if my questions are making you upset. I'm almost finished. You're Lord Steppingham's nurse. Why didn't you go with him?"

"Don't answer that!" barked Plaistow. "Reasons of national security. That's all you need to know, Blue. You've five minutes left."

"OK. Was anyone else hit, apart from Lord Steppingham?"

"Yes, no. No, only Lord Steppingham was hit."

"What about Mr van Kaarsten?"

"Van Kaarsten wasn't hit," snarled Plaistow. "You know that already. He got himself into the house. He'd thrown himself to the ground."

"Of course," said Blue. "Army training."

He addressed the nurse again. "Did you check Mr Van Kaarsten for injuries?"

"Yes. I checked him over, but he hadn't been hit. Had a bit of a bruise on the forehead from when he hit the ground. That was all."

"So after Lord Steppingham had been taken off, what did you do then?"

"Well, nothing really. I got packed."

"And during this time, did you see anything suspicious? Anyone you didn't recognise, for instance."

"No, no. I knew them all, you see. Even well, no, nobody suspicious. I packed."

"Then you went off with Mr James, to get the plane to Glasgow."

"Yes, that's right."

"You don't expect to have to treat gunshot wounds, do you? Must have been quite a shock."

"Yes, it was. I…" She stopped, looked down at the table.

"Time's up!" snapped Plaistow.

"Miss Rogers, thank you so much for your help," said Blue. "If you do remember anything further, you can contact me on this number." He took out a card and offered it to her.

She took it, with a shaking hand, but Plaistow snatched it from her. "I'll take that, thank you. If you do remember anything, tell me about it. If it's relevant, I'll pass it on to Mr Blue. Thanks for your time, Miss Rogers."

Miss Rogers almost staggered as she made her way to the door.

"She'll take a while to get over it," said Plaistow. "They all do, sooner or later."

"Could I talk to Mrs Gregg?" asked Blue.

"Sorry, Blue, she ain't here," said Plaistow. "Gone to visit her daughter, in Australia. For a month. No point going all that way just for a week, is there, eh?" He laughed loudly. "And don't even think of asking to speak to Van Kaarsten. You won't get near him. Reasons of national security. Right, Rackham, get the floozie to bring the car round. Time we were off."

37

The car dropped Blue at the station, and he was surprised to see Plaistow get out too.

"I'm coming with you to the airport, Blue, so I can see you onto a plane. Don't want you hanging around here getting into trouble, do we? You're too curious for your own good. Look what happened to that cat." He laughed. He found his remark very amusing.

Blue already had his return ticket to the airport. Plaistow had a ticket too – he didn't tell Blue where it was for. The next London train was due at 11.30, so they crossed the bridge to wait on the platform. It was already crowded. Who goes to work at this time, wondered Blue. Maybe the crowds were now shoppers or tourists. He looked at a man in a dirty raincoat, and recognised immediately that he was a professional beggar. He would leave his nice suburban house at the same time each day, take the train to London, and sit in a doorway for six hours. Long enough to make a comfortable living. His wife probably left for work before him, never realised what 'something in the City' actually meant.

Plaistow stood close to him, breathing heavily. Blue noticed that his breath smelled of onion.

When the train arrived, it was as full as the earlier ones. Plaistow didn't wait to see if anyone was getting off, but bulldozed his way into the mass of people. "Stay close," he growled to Blue. Was that an invitation, an instruction, or a threat?

Even to speculate about an empty seat was pointless. The seats were probably all filled up at the train's point of origin, wherever that was. Plaistow had stationed himself in the standing area by the door, but Blue squeezed past him into the aisle, where there was slightly more room to breathe. Plaistow nodded, reassured. Now Blue couldn't get off without passing him.

At the next station more people crushed themselves in, and Blue was carried further down the aisle by the press of bodies, towards the end of the carriage. At the following station he let himself be pushed to the very end of the carriage, and found himself by the door through to the next one. Several tall people and a grey bundle balanced on someone's shoulder interrupted his line of sight to Plaistow. As the train rattled through a cutting and the light dimmed, he slipped through the door and gently closed it, then drew his breath in the space between the carriages. As he felt the train slow down for a station, he entered the next carriage, pushed his way through the crowd, and got off the train. On the platform, he stayed close to the train, and moved towards its rear, just in case Plaistow was looking out the window. As the train pulled out of the station, he turned his back, and filled his lungs with fresh air.

He went to the ticket office, and bought a return ticket to Bedford, then crossed the bridge to the other platform. The train was due in ten minutes. There was a stall on the platform which sold coffee, snacks, magazines and newspapers. He bought a copy of the *Bedford Observer*, and found on page 9 a list of 'Useful Contact Numbers.' He phoned the number for Bedford Police Station, and asked for Inspector Rackham. He heard the girl shouting, 'Is Red around?' and various muffled and incomprehensible ripostes. Suddenly it stopped and electronic muzak took its place. He was about to cancel the call, when just as suddenly the muzak stopped and a voice was there.

"Bedfordshire Police. CID here. Inspector Rackham speaking. How may I…"

"This is Blue. I need to talk to you."

"Blue? Where on earth are you?"

Blue glanced around to see the station's nameboard. "Luddford Parva. At the station."

"When's the next train in this direction due?"

"Three minutes."

"OK. Get it. Don't get off at Steppingham, wait till the next station. Gillingford. Get off there. Out of the station, same side, turn left, 200 yards, pub called 'The Golden Rail.' Wait in the bar."

"Will do."

"And one other thing. Take the battery out of your phone. Right now." The line went dead.

As Blue put the phone battery in one pocket and the phone in another, the train drew up. Surprisingly, there was plenty of room, and he could sit down and look out the window. They passed several fields full of plastic tunnels. Long sheds which he thought might contain pigs or chickens. And more housing developments.

How long would it take Plaistow to notice that he'd absconded, he wondered. The airport station at the latest, at 11.55 when the train got there. What would he do then? He would undoubtedly come back to look for Blue, and call up whatever resources he could muster. Blue guessed he would probably put a watch on all the stations down the line, so the quicker he got away from the station at Gillingford the better. And Rackham's advice to take the phone battery out was wise. Of course, they would have the technology to track his phone, and pin him down maybe very quickly if it was working. He was feeling nervous.

At 11.50 the train arrived at Gillingford. Blue got down, feeling very conspicuous, casually strolled through the waiting room cum ticket office, and reached the road. No-one! He walked more rapidly up a slight incline between hawthorn hedges. At the top, an old house, red brick so dark it was almost burgundy, and the sign 'The Golden Rail,' above a painting of a gold-coloured railway track heading towards a distant rainbow.

The bar was dark-wood-panelled, with cushioned benches and rustic tables. Sepia-tinted pictures of old railway engines hung on the walls. The place was empty.

A plump blonde behind the bar looked at him expectantly. He could hardly sit without a drink. He ordered a half of mild.

"You ain't from these parts, eh?" said the barmaid.

"No, well-spotted. I'm here for the conference in Bedford. 'Plasterboard in the 21st Century'. Starts tonight. Should be exciting. You wouldn't believe what they're doing in Latvia."

She'd already lost interest and returned to the magazine tucked under the counter.

He sat down at a table in the corner and drank two-thirds of his beer in one gulp, he was so thirsty. Glanced at his watch. 11.59. They'd be on to him now. Where was Rackham?

At 12 the door opened and Rackham came in. He greeted the barmaid – "Hi, Margo, how's the dog doing?"

"Mr Rackham, I'm fine, since you didn't ask. And Pinkie's good too. She'll get used to just having three legs. What can I get you?"

"Nothing at the moment, thanks, I've just come to collect my colleague." He glanced round the room and waved to Blue. "Ah, there you are, Dave, time we were off."

"You going to the plastering conference too, Mr Rackham?" said Margo, as Blue got up and swallowed the rest of his beer.

"Can't miss it," said Rackham, holding the door open for Blue to pass. "By the way, Margo, if anyone asks after me, I've not been in today."

Parked on the road was a dark blue Vauxhall Zafira. Rackham pointed to the passenger door, and got into the driver's. Once inside, he said, "Let's get away from the railway, that's where they'll look first." He took off at speed and soon they were racing along a deep hedged lane that every so often turned a sharp right angle. It emerged into another village, which turned out to be a small town with a wide market place at the centre.

Rackham parked here and led Blue over to 'Cindy's Flower Box and Tearoom'. They entered the flower shop and climbed the stairs to the tearoom. They sat at a table overlooking the market place, and ordered coffee. Several of the other tables were occupied, mostly by pairs of elderly women, deep in earnest conversation. They both knew to keep their voices down.

"OK, Blue, what's this all about? That bastard's told me nothing at all. There's clearly something nasty going on – that guy James was lying through his teeth and the nurse was scared out of her wits. Has Steppingham got something to do with it? Said on the news last night he'd been shot, somewhere in Scotland. And his house torched too."

"Yes, that's it. I'll tell you what Police Scotland know. Plaistow can't arrest me for sharing normal police information. By the way, it's Angus Blue."

"Geoff Rackham. They sometimes call me 'Red.' No idea why."

Blue gave the details of the shooting, and the cars which had sped off afterwards. He left out the man on the bicycle. That needed chasing a bit further before he could share it. Or Laurence Mather's film.

"Well, well," said Rackham. "We've had the same sort of rumours about goings-on at Steppingham House, and also been warned off following them up. "

"What was going on at the house may well be relevant to the shooting. That's why I wanted to talk to Mr James and Miss Rogers. But it looks like Plaistow's coached them. They're all giving the same line."

"James stuck to the story pretty well, but he was plainly caught out when you mentioned the girls. They didn't know you knew about them. Getting witnesses who'd seen them on the road was good work."

"Have you come across a Gladys Waggoner? The car the girls were seen in was traced to her."

"Oh, yes. 'Bad Glad' they used to call her. In and out the nick. Then nothing. A few years later she's a madam for the rich and famous."

"What did you think of what Miss Rogers had to say?"

"She was a lot more shaky. I thought she might have been hinting that more people had been injured."

"We have evidence that suggests one other person, whose identity is still unknown, may have also been shot."

"A secret guest at the party. High-up in some foreign government perhaps. If they were talking about an arms deal, that is. If we pulled Miss Rogers in and sweated her a bit, I'd be surprised if she didn't break down and tell all."

"I doubt Plaistow would let you get close to her. Is there anything you've got that might be relevant?"

"There is one thing, a case we had last year. A sixteen-year-old girl claimed she'd been invited to a party at the house, and then was raped. Unfortunately she couldn't identify any of the male guests – there were about a dozen altogether, of whom four were involved in the rape – as they were all wearing animal masks, and only spoke to each other in animal names: Lion-o, Lynx-o, Panthro, and so on"

"Thundercats!"

"Sorry?"

"An animated series that was on the telly a long time ago. Go on."

"Lord Steppingham admitted, via his lawyers, there had been a party, said it was a private event, there was no rape, and all the girls invited knew what to expect. Everything was consensual. He refused to name any of the guests or say anything more 'in the interests of national security.' Anyway, we'd recovered some semen from the girl, and ran a DNA analysis, then tried the DNA database. The result pointed to a guy living in Bedford who'd done time for two indecent assaults on schoolgirls."

"What was he doing at the party?"

"He wasn't. He'd topped himself six months previously."

"How do you explain that?"

"Well, the semen was genuine enough, so the problem had to be with the DNA database. Here's how they do it. And by 'they' I mean the upper class rapists who frequent his Lordship's parties. They could just refuse to have their data on the database. Then we'd get a 'sample unknown' result, but we'd keep looking for evidence. So instead, they put their data up, then add some software that, if theirs is flagged, the database points instead to some local whose form might be relevant. The ID number attached to the sample can be linked to the case file, so the software can identify what type of crime is suspected. If the guy who's pointed at doesn't have a cast-iron alibi, he goes down for the crime, and the toffs are in the clear. If he does have an alibi, the case usually collapses because we've obviously fucked up with the DNA."

"Neat."

"These people are bastards, Angus. An elite that thinks it's above the law. Trouble is, most of the time they are. And they can always change it if it's inconvenient. Take Steppingham. Eton, Cambridge. Two mediocre A-levels and a third class degree, but joined the right clubs and met all the right people. And they run the country for their amusement. The crazy thing is, they can only get away with it because enough people are willing to be their creatures. Like that thug Plaistow. Sorry for the rant, Angus."

"I don't disagree with you. So what happened then?"

"Just what I said. Our SOCOs were branded as incompetent. CC closed the case down, suggested we charge the girl with wasting police time, which I refused to do. So Steppingham got his lawyers to harass her, threatened to sue for slander, gave her a mouthful of abuse in the House of Lords. She had a nervous breakdown and her family emigrated with her to New Zealand."

"Can you send me the file on that case?"

"Leave that with me, and if there's anything else I can do, let me know. Here's my card. Now we'd better get you out of here. I'll drive you to the airport."

Rackham dropped Blue at Luton airport not long before two, well in time for his mid-afternoon flight to Glasgow. As he arrived at the departure gate, he saw a man at the edge of the seating area look at him, then pull out his phone. Five minutes later Plaistow arrived, puffing as if in a hurry.

"Where the hell have you been, Blue? I told you to stick with me," he growled.

Blue offered a puzzled expression. "I'm not sure what you're talking about. Those crowds on the train pushed me through to the next carriage. I looked for you when I got out, but with all those people, I couldn't spot you. As it was, I'd got off at the wrong station. Luton, rather than Luton Airport. I'd plenty time, so I walked out to the airport. Hardly fresh air, with all that traffic, but at least there was a pavement to walk on, and I got some exercise. Even had a cup of coffee on the way."

"I phoned your mobile. Why didn't you answer?"

"I wasn't aware of that. Maybe the battery's run down." Blue took out his phone and tried to activate it. "No, doesn't seem to be working. I'll need to recharge the battery. You don't have one of those portable recharging things, do you?"

Plaistow waved the other man over. "Make sure this gentleman gets on the Glasgow plane. Even if you have to cuff him and drag him on. Any problem, call me."

"Yes, sir," was all the man said. Plaistow turned on his heel and walked off.

"You better sit down over here, sir," said the man, pointing to two empty seats next to each other. Blue sat down, and the man took the adjacent seat. Blue's attempts at conversation elicited no response. When the flight was called, the man accompanied Blue as far as the gate, then watched from the tunnel as Blue greeted the attendants and went on into the plane to find his seat.

38

When the plane touched down in Glasgow, he put the battery back into his mobile. There were still two and a half hours until his flight back to Islay.

Almost immediately the phone beeped. A text from McCader. Call ASAP.

"Hi, Enver, what've you got?"

"Hi, chief. I got hold of Kevin's report this morning. Confirms all the bullets came from the same gun."

"That's something, I suppose. Confirms one shooter. Any progress re Tayvallich?"

"I drove over there this morning. Found a witness – guy in the chandlery shop – saw a foreign car parked in the car park, can't remember much about it. Thinks it was pink or orange. There was a woman in it, he's fairly sure of that. But doesn't remember anyone getting into it and didn't see it drive off."

"That could be them. At least suggests they were there. If it were, the question is where they went next."

"On the basis that a foreign car would attract some attention at this time of year, I went over to Lochgilphead and asked around in the cafes. No luck there so I moved on to Inveraray. Finally got lucky! They had lunch at the 'Tartan Kettle' – it's on the main street, next to the whisky shop. Arrived about half past eleven. Left not long after twelve."

"Yes, I know the whisky shop. Impressive range of stuff. Go on."

"I can confirm they're not vegetarians. She had a Chicken Caesar salad and he had a haggis baked potato. They both had coffee, and he had a glass of cognac with his. People don't often order cognac there. The waitress did hear her call him 'Pappy'. I guess that means Dad but in what language? She heard them talking in a foreign language, but couldn't say which one – except that it wasn't Spanish. That's where she goes her holidays. No-one saw the car, they probably parked it at the big car park by the church, it's free this time of year."

"Sounds like they were headed east, but where then?"

"If they're going home, let's assume for the moment that's Poland, they'd have to get a ferry. There are several options. I checked."

"What if they wanted out of this country as fast as possible.

What's the nearest one?"

"That would be Newcastle to Amsterdam. DFDS. They'd have to drive quite a bit further to get the boat from Hull to Rotterdam or Zeebrugge, and even further to get Harwich to Hook of Holland."

"Could they have made the Newcastle boat on Monday?"

"Easy. Check-in's open till five pm. If they're not booked, they'd have to get there earlier than that, but I reckon if they left Inveraray at twelve, and kept moving, they could be at the ferry terminal in North Shields around four. Any of the other routes, they'd be pushing it to get there in time for the Monday evening boat. I could contact them, see if they've got CCTV footage. Maybe they booked in advance."

"Hold on for the moment. What else have you got? What about your Irish contact?"

"Had a chat, off the record. They know all about Gladys, would love to have an excuse to raid her safe house. But our request for assistance would have to be official. We'd need to go via the Super."

"Right. I can get onto that. But I'd need a word with your contact first."

"His name's Ruaraigh Ó Fiachan. Inspector with the Garda CID. Here's his number."

Blue copied the name and number into his notebook. "Thanks. Where are you now?"

"I came on down to Tyndrum. I wasn't sure where you'd want me to go next. From here I can go up to Oban or down to Glasgow. I've got an unmarked pool car. I'm in a cafe. Plenty parking and convenient for whichever road I need."

"Good. Stay there for the moment. I'm still at Glasgow Airport. I'll call Inspector Ó Fiachan now, then the Super. Then I'll get back to you. Can you try the ferry people at Newcastle, see what they can do?"

"Will do, chief."

Blue bought a cup of coffee and a sandwich, and typed in the number McCader had given him.

"CID. Ruaraigh Ó Fiachan." Definitely Irish, by the voice.

"Hi. Angus Blue, Police Scotland. Sergeant McCader gave me your name."

"Angus, good to hear from you. Call me Ruaraigh. I thought

178

you'd be wanting to call me as soon as you could. Enver's put me in the picture. He's a good man by the way, you're lucky to have him. Got a few good tricks up his sleeve, I can tell you that. So you're wanting to get hold of these three girls, so to speak?"

"Yes, we want to know what was going on at Dunrighinn House last weekend, and who was there. I don't suppose we'd get much out of Gladys Waggoner."

"Don't even think of going there, Angus, you'll not even get to speak to her. A lad in the Cheshire vice squad tried to nail her. He's now running the police force in the Falkland Islands. Not quite the promotion he wanted! You're very sensible. Far better to go for the girls, especially as they're not in the UK."

"Do you know where they are at the moment?"

"That's no problem at all. They're at Gladys's safe house in Dun Laoghaire – that's just a few miles south of Dublin, on the coast. Nice Edwardian semi not far from the front. Dun Laoghaire used to be a popular resort, up to the sixties. Then everybody went off to Spain."

"Any reason Gladys has the house there?"

"Gladys wouldn't be for doing anything without a reason. The ferries used to run from there over to Holyhead, right up to 2015. She could drive from her place in Belfast down there, pick up her girls and get onto the boat. Nice thing about the boat is, there's not so much security as a plane. Much more anonymous, and a lot less hassle."

"How many girls does she keep there?"

"We don't rightly know now, but there'd be a fair few of them. We're keen to be finding out. So a request from your end would just give that final nudge to our bosses here to give us the wee nod to raid the place."

"How do you know the girls we're interested in are there?"

"That's an easy one. We've been watching the place 24/7 the last three months. Gladys got there just after eight o'clock on Monday evening, went into the house with three girls. Half an hour later she came out on her own and drove off, probably back to Belfast. They've not left the place since."

"Who looks after the house then, and keeps them there?"

"There's a couple who run the place – Gerald and Sharon Winsor. Nasty pair – I'd think they run the place like a prison camp. Even if we can't find any evidence implicating Gladys, we'd love to pin something on that pair. And the place is not just a hostel for call-girls. We suspect there's illegal immigrants moving through there, people-trafficking, and we suspect some of the girls are under-age. So, are you up for it? You'd need to get your boss to express an interest in talking with some of the occupants of the house with the head of CID here – that'll be Superintendent Brian Ó Mallaigh – and Brian will give us the go-ahead."

"Thanks, Ruaraigh, I'll see what I can do."

"Then you'll need to be coming over here to talk to them as soon as we've got them. If they're EU citizens and over eighteen, we may not be able to hold them for very long. No doubt Gladys will be on to her lawyers pretty fast. Oh, and I hope Enver'll be coming with you. It'll be great to share some craic with him again. And you'll be wanting to try some Guinness yourself too, the real stuff, that is."

Blue drank some coffee. Then he called the Super.

"Angus, you're lucky you weren't in Glasgow."

"Why, what happened?"

"Nothing at all. Just about every policeman in Scotland lining the streets, for the royal progress, and hardly anyone turned out to see it. It was a huge waste of money for us. And whatever idiot organised the parade had included a fife-and-drum band from an Orange Lodge. Must have thought a pipe band would be too Scottish. Luckily there was no trouble, thanks to the lack of spectators, but the Orange band did arouse a lot of hostility. They had to stop playing when a group pelted them with onions and bananas. That was the only work our people had, telling the Orange guys, who looked like they were ready for a fight, to pack up and push off. Anyway, where are you with the Steppingham case?"

Blue brought Campbell up to date on the case.

"Hmm. So your main leads are the folks in the Polish car, and these three girls? What next?"

"The Garda are keen to raid Gladys Waggoner's safe house, and if we were to add our backing, they'd do it. But you'd need to speak to the Garda CID chief, that's a Brian"

"Ó Mallaigh! Yes, I know him all right. Met him at the Celtic Nations Police Conference in 2017 – a lovely man. And a great whiskey connoisseur. Did you hear the extra 'e' Angus? I didn't think that stuff was up to much till he gave me a few pointers. More than a few. Yes, I'll certainly speak to Brian right away."

"Will you need to run it past the DCC?"

"No, no, I don't think so. We're not asking for any specific action on their part, just expressing an interest in these three girls. It's up to them to decide what they do about it. Leave it with me."

As Blue ate his sandwich, his phone rang.

"Hi, Angus, Geoff Rackham here. Those bastards have taken that file! The hard copy's gone from the basement and the digital stuff's been wiped from our server. All my own case notes were in it. I got onto our IT guys, but they said it's a professional job – nothing left behind. The only other thing I can remember is that the most violent of the rapists had a scar on his left thigh – claimed it was a bullet wound. I hope that helps."

Blue thanked him, and finished his coffee in silence. Then he phoned Moira Nicolson, reported his experiences in Steppingham, and asked if any progress had been made in Islay.

"Not a great deal. Deirdra's got the software from her pal now, and is setting it up. It works by deciding how to clarify the fuzzy bits on the basis of clarifications to other parts of the picture provided by the user. So if we can supply clear pictures of Steppingham, Van Kaarsten and even Plaistow, the program uses the differences between their fuzzy and their clear images to decide how to tackle the remaining fuzzy bits. Arvind has sourced pictures of all three – he got the first two off the web, and Andy McGuire had a good one of Plaistow he'd taken while photographing the crime scene. Deirdra's entered them – that took half an hour as they had to be converted to a special format – and now it's churning away. But she reckons it could easily take a good while before an optimised result appears. Apart from that, nothing. The fire investigator will be here tomorrow morning, so we'll get an initial report from her."

"Anything from Ffox-Kaye?"

"Not a peep. But I'm sure he's not idle. And the fact he hasn't shown any interest in what we're doing suggests he's pursuing a line of his own."

"OK. Thanks Moira. I'll get back to you as soon as I know what's happening about Dublin, and when the raid's likely to be. So I may or may not be back on Islay this evening."

"By the way, Alison says hello."

"Oh, uh, yes, do say hello back. Er, talk to you later." Why did he feel so discomposed?

He flicked through *The Nation*, and noticed in item on page four about the Jura shooting, written by John Striven. After giving the facts as known and adding quotes from Ffox-Kaye's press conference, Striven reported that he'd talked with residents on Jura, no names given, and noted strong rumours that in recent years Dunrighinn House had been the scene of wild orgies where politicians, businessmen, celebrities and rich foreigners had been 'entertained' by young women. He quoted one anonymous local who said that, 'Every weekend carloads of women were driven up to the house. We could all imagine just what was going on there.' Striven promised his readers more in the days to come.

He was on to the football pages when a text from Campbell arrived: 'OK for Dublin.' So, time for action. He phoned Ruaraigh Ó Fiachan immediately.

"Angus! Glad to hear from Brian that your boss is supportive. The raid is on for first thing tomorrow. Five am. Catch them in their beds, eh?"

"Sounds good. Any chance we could be in on it?"

"Sorry, Angus, that's not going to be possible. Too politically sensitive, apparently. But we'll hold on to the girls for you, so you just get here when you can."

"Where's here?"

"Oh, sorry. NBCI, that's the National Bureau of Criminal Investigation, we're based in the Police HQ building on Harcourt Street. Near the Iveagh Gardens. South side."

"We'll find it. Not quite sure of the travel plans, but we'll see you sometime tomorrow morning. That's myself and hopefully Sergeant McCader."

"That's really great, Angus. I'll see you tomorrow now."

Next he phoned McCader.

"Enver, where are you?"

"Dumbarton. I hoped you might get the OK for Dublin, so I came on down the road a bit, just in case it was a goer, and you wanted me there too."

"Well, it is a goer, and I think we both need to be there. Can you pick me up at the airport and we'll make for the ferry at Cairnryan?"

"No problem, chief. I'm only ten minutes from the Erskine Bridge. Half an hour at the pickup point OK?"

"That'll do nicely."

That gave him time to cancel his flight to Islay, and then let Moira Nicolson know his movements, and that he hoped to be back in Islay the following day.

"Don't worry," she concluded, "Alison'll still be here. You must come round for a meal, when you've time."

He mumbled goodbye and hung up.

39

At half past five McCader arrived at the pickup point on the ground floor of the multi-storey car park opposite the terminal building, driving a black Škoda Octavia. As they set off down the M8 and then the M77 towards Kilmarnock, the sergeant went over the information he'd got at Tayvallich and Inveraray.

"The waitress at Inveraray," said Blue. "Could she give us a detailed description of the pair?"

"No problem, chief. Might be worth trying for a photofit or getting the artist in."

"Good idea. We could then take it to Fergus. He had a good look at the girl on the Jura boat. By the way, Enver, what about the DFDS people at Newcastle?"

"They were very helpful. They'll courier a couple of disks to Oban – I thought that was quicker than sending them to Islay, some of the courier companies are a bit iffy when it comes to islands. Plus they'll have a look through the bookings, see what they can find."

"Yes, that's fine. I'll ask Jill Henderson to take a look at the disks. She doesn't miss a thing. By the way, I've just had an idea about the Polish car. I'll contact Tadeusz Piłsudski. I'm sure he'll be able to help us."

Blue had known Tadeusz Piłsudski a few years back when he was sent by the Polish police on a training placement with Police Scotland. Some sort of EU project, Blue remembered. Piłsudski had just been promoted to Sergeant at that point and was keen to learn, and to get involved, which he did. Blue's vivid memories were of the darkness and the noise of the water slapping against the walls of the sea-cave, and then the burning boat drifting away from the island, a beacon on the black water.

"Good idea, chief. I met him early last year, just before I was transferred to Oban. He was liaising for the Polish Criminal Police in a case I was involved in. He remembered you well. Told me I was lucky to be able to work with you. He's now a *komisarz* – I think that's equivalent to an inspector here. I'm sure he'd be able to track down that car for us. Quicker than the official route."

"Do you know where he was based then?"

"Somewhere in the west of the country. Wrocław maybe."

"That would certainly be interesting. To talk to him again."

McCader's driving was swift and assured, and they made good speed down the M77 and the A77 dual carriageway. But their progress slowed once they'd passed Ayr, and the dual carriageway gave way to a narrow and congested rural highway snaking its way through the towns and villages of the Ayrshire coast. Overtaking was only an option for those who did not expect to live long. It was twenty past seven when they finally reached the ferry terminal at Cairnryan. Theoretically check-in for vehicles had closed at 7.15, but their warrant cards eased that issue aside, and they were waved into the queue.

As they waited to drive on, Blue checked his email on his phone. A message was there from Ó Fiachan indicating that he'd provisionally booked them into a B&B in Dublin. Easter Rising House. McCader would know it.

"Oh yes, I know that place all right. We used it quite a lot. The owner's a Mrs Connolly."

"Any relative? Of James Connolly?"

"Oh, no. Common enough name. But it might have suggested the house title. It's a good place. And I know exactly how to get there. I'll give her a ring, if that's OK, chief."

McCader used the number Ó Fiachan had emailed to Blue, and called Mrs Connolly, who, judging by the squawks Blue heard from the phone, was immensely pleased to hear from him.

They had something to eat on the boat and Blue permitted himself a glass of beer. Then he set up his laptop and updated his report. He noticed that McCader was reading a thick paperback, a history of the mafia. When he'd done the report he checked the news on the internet. Attendance at the royal progress through Glasgow was described as 'thin' and the Scottish Government was blamed for not ensuring that people turned out in droves. 'Drunken louts' were blamed for attacking a flute and drum band. The Secretary of State for Scotland was quoted as deploring the disturbance, and praising the 'loyalty and enthusiasm' of those who had turned out to greet the royal personages. He himself had been 'immensely humbled' at the opportunity to salute the party as they passed the City Chambers. The item concluded with a phone number being given where any organisation could obtain free paper union jacks on sticks, for supporting the royal progress as it continued the following day visiting Loch Lomond and the Trossachs.

"How's the book, Enver?"

"Pretty interesting. I hadn't realised it all started in the lemon groves in Sicily. Supplying lemons to the British Navy."

Before Blue could respond his phone pinged. A text from Ó Fiachan: '4.45 Seapoint Ave, N end. Observe only.' He showed it to McCader. "Looks like we can watch."

"Better than nothing. We'll have to get up early."

The boat got into Larne at ten, but it was ten to twelve by the time McCader pulled up outside an anonymous villa on Dublin's south side. A small metal plate on the gatepost bore the legend 'Easter Rising.'

"There's no B&B sign," said Blue.

"It's very exclusive. Only take people they know. Personal recommendation."

"Do I need a password?"

"I'll handle that." Was he joking? Blue couldn't tell.

McCader rang the bell, and the door was opened by a large and jolly lady of advancing years, her grey hair in a bun, and glasses hanging from a chain around her neck. She thrust the glasses on and stared at them. Recognition dawned.

"Enver! Sure, and it's wonderful to see you again." She gave McCader a big hug. "How're you doing, my wee laddie? And the family, how are they?"

"All doing just fine, Teagan, just fine. Good to see you too."

"And this'll be your friend Mr Blue. It's nice to meet you, sure it is …"

"Angus."

"Well, Angus that's a strong name now, I do approve of that. Well, come in, the both of you. Will you be wantin a cup of tea now, before you go to bed?"

Blue declined the tea politely, sensing that Mrs Connolly and McCader had some catching up to do. His room, on the first floor at the back of the house, was large enough to hold a single bed against one wall, a comfortable armchair and coffee table, and a table below the window large enough to make a good writing desk with an upright chair. The bathroom was ensuite. There were tea and coffee making facilities, and little packs of shortbread. And a miniature of whiskey: Bushmills 10-year-old single malt. After a mini-feast of shortbread and whiskey, Blue set his alarm and slept.

Day 6. Saturday

40

He was up at four, showered, dressed and went downstairs. McCader and Mrs Connolly were sitting in the dining room chatting. Had they been there all night?

"I'll be with you in a tick," said Mrs Connolly and left the room, returning with a poached egg sitting on a slice of black pudding on toast. "I thought you'd be needing something quite light, since it's early. But you've got a long day so you'll want a bit of building up too."

McCader was onto toast and marmalade, but an empty plate in front of him showed smears of tomato sauce. "We'll need to be away by half past. It's not far, but we'd better be on time."

In the car, McCader drove through streets only just beginning to come to life as the light grew.

"Do you know Dublin well?" Blue asked him.

"Oh, yes. I was around here a few years. Both sides of the border." He didn't elaborate.

Dun Laoghaire seemed to be a comfortable suburb of Dublin. Blue suspected the houses would be pretty expensive now.

McCader swung the car to the right, off the main road, onto a street of what looked like semi-detached bungalows from the 1920's.

"There they are," muttered McCader, and drove slowly for another fifty yards before stopping behind a row of parked cars. In a few seconds a tall well-built man walked down the row of cars towards them.

"That's Ruaraigh," said McCader.

Blue wound down his window as Ó Fiachan approached. Dark hair, greying, and sleepy eyes. A relaxed walk.

"Alright, it's only yourselves," said Ó Fiachan, shaking hands with Blue. "You're not armed, are you?"

"No," said Blue. He hoped that applied to both of them.

"Now listen, lads. I shouldn't really be doing this at all now. Strictly speaking, you're not here. So no heroics. Follow us in the car, but don't get out till we've gone into the house. Is that clear?" They both nodded, and Ó Fiachan went off.

Five minutes later the convoy, of six cars, moved off, making two turns into a street lined by substantial Edwardian semis, red-brick faced with stone blocks down the corners, square bay windows, and palm trees in the gardens. They drove slowly about half way down, then suddenly stopped, and men leapt out of each vehicle. Apart from the last, that is. Men in plain clothes, men in uniform, men with helmets and guns. In seconds the house was surrounded and a helmeted officer rang the doorbell, other armed officers behind him on either side of the door. Nothing happened, and ten seconds later two men charged up the stairs to the front door clutching a battering ram between them, and with a splintering crash the door was open, and the armed officers rushed in shouting warnings.

Blue and McCader got out of the car to see what happened next. They could see neighbours peeping from behind curtains, and in one upstairs window opposite a man in pyjamas was filming the events on his phone. Blue wasn't the only one to spot that, and the next moment a uniformed Garda officer was rapping at his door.

For a few minutes there was peace in the street. Then two dark blue vans drew up right outside the house, and they could see figures being led out the house straight into the vans. Two uniformed officers appeared round the side of the house, leading a man and woman, jackets draped over their heads to cover their faces. Blue assumed they had tried to escape out the back. They were taken past the vans and placed in the rear of a car. The car immediately left, followed by the vans.

Five minutes later Inspector Ó Fiachan came out of the house, and over to their car.

"Was that not a nice bit of work, now?" he exclaimed. "We've netted the whole lot of them!"

"Well done!" said Blue. "How many did you get?"

"We got thirteen girls altogether, including the three you're after – thanks for sending the picture, by the way. The Winsors tried to make off out the back way, but we got them too. We just need to search the house now and see what we'll find. We'll get the computers back to HQ as fast as we can. The more we can do before Gladys gets a lawyer in, the better. If you get over to Harcourt Street right away, you might be able to talk to those girls before the lawyer arrives. We'll separate them all as soon as they're at HQ, and we'll keep the Winsors well away from the girls."

"Many thanks for inviting us here, Ruaraigh," said Blue.

"Not at all. I had to go through the motions of saying you couldn't come, so remember that you weren't here. Hopefully that moron up there was the only one trying to film it, and we've confiscated his phone. See you at HQ. Just wait for me there." He turned back to re-enter the house.

McCader drove them back to Dublin, and into the car park at the rear of the seven-storey office block that housed Dublin's Metropolitan Police HQ, as well as its National Crime Squad. Blue explained at reception that they were to see Inspector Ó Fiachan, and were sent up to the fifth floor, sat in the corner of an almost empty office, and offered a coffee. As they waited, more officers came in, including those carrying cardboard boxes and large plastic bags. Others came in who looked as if they'd been summoned early from home, looking fresher than those who'd been on the raid. Blue could feel the sense of purpose and determination building up in the room. They'd been waiting for a while for this to happen.

Ten minutes later, Ó Fiachan came into the room. Applause broke out. He held up a hand.

"Well done, all of you! I know we've waited a while to spring this trap. Now let's get to work and see what we can nail the merry Winsors on. And if someone can bring me the head of Gladys Waggoner, that would do nicely too." The atmosphere in the room raised another notch. He noticed Blue and McCader and raised a hand for attention. "Just one more thing. These are our friends Inspector Blue and Sergeant McCader from Scotland. Their request helped us get this show on the road. Give them every help you can whilst they're here."

Five minutes later, he came over. "Well, now, lads, we're just processing the girls at the moment, so you'll be able to see yours shortly. But you understand I'll have to question them first about what was going on at the house. We'll be as fast as we can."

Another cup of coffee and two chocolate biscuits later, Ó Fiachan was back. "OK, lads, you can talk to them now." He looked carefully at a sheet of paper in his hand. "Their names are Radina Ivanova, Nadezhda Hristova and Bilyana Radova. They're from Bulgaria. Radina and Nadezhda say they're eighteen, Bilyana says she's nineteen. We've yet to see their passports. Their English is not good, but that may be a pretence."

"Have they said much so far?" asked Blue.

"Apart from personal details, nothing at all. I guess they're scared. Or they've been instructed, just in case this might happen. Half the time they pretend not to understand the questions. Do you want them together or one at a time?"

"We'll start off with them together, see how they relate to each other. Then we can talk to them individually afterwards."

"Right-oh. One of my people will have to sit in with you, to make it legal here. That'll be Sergeant Ó Dálaigh. She's just coming along now." A tall young woman with black hair in a pony-tail and startlingly green eyes was approaching. "Sinéad, can you take Inspector Blue and Sergeant McCader here to interview room three to interview the Bulgarian girls?"

After introductions, Sergeant Ó Dálaigh led Blue and McCader down a corridor and into an interview room. The three girls were led in by a female uniformed officer, who remained standing by the door.

Sergeant Ó Dálaigh set out the digital voice recorder, then introduced herself, Blue and McCader, and asked the girls to identify themselves. All three gave their names willingly enough. Blue noted their distinguishing features on his pad. Radina Ivanova was the youngest-looking, small and slight, with lank brown hair, freckles and round eyes, one of them disfigured by black and yellow bruising. Bilyana Radova was taller, with a thin face framed by long bottle-blonde hair, and a fuller figure than Radina. Nadezhda Hristova was shorter and plump, with a round face and light brown shoulder-length curly hair. Radina looked nervous, Bilyana bored and Nadezhda thoughtful. Blue could see immediately that Bilyana was the dominant figure of the three; he suspected they'd get little out of her. With the other two, he wasn't so sure they'd keep quiet.

Sergeant Ó Dálaigh indicated that Inspector Blue would begin the interview. She put a pad and pen on the table in front of her, and smiled at Blue. He was momentarily distracted by her eyes, but pulled himself together rapidly, and turned to the girls.

"Thank you for speaking to us," he began. "We'd like to ask you about some events of last weekend."

"Excuse please," said Bilyana, "we no understand. English very bad. We need interpreter."

McCader leaned forward as if to ask a question, but at that moment the door was thrown open, and a fat man with a bald head and an expensive suit burst in.

"Stop this right away!" he shouted. "I'm legally representing these ladies, and I need to advise them of their rights before they can be interviewed."

Sergeant Ó Dálaigh stood up and gave him an icy stare. "And you are?"

"My name is Eamon Raffin, of Raffin, Radleigh and Gilks, Dublin. As I'm sure you well know. And I demand a moment alone with my clients."

"You may need an interpreter."

"I've brought my own," said Raffin, motioning someone in from the corridor. A large, pudgy woman, perhaps in her fifties, thrust herself into the room. Blue could immediately see her as a warden at a Siberian camp. "This is Miss Olga Karpova."

"Do you speak Bulgarian?" asked Ó Dálaigh.

"I speak all these languages," said the woman, contemptuously. "I have interpreter's certificate from University of Minsk."

"We'd like some time without police personnel present. Thank you," said Raffin, with a professional smile.

Ó Dálaigh led Blue, McCader and the female officer out of the room. In the corridor, they met Ó Fiachan.

"Sorry, lads, we ran out of time too fast. Gladys was quick off the mark. They've had a procedure in place, right enough. Called her as soon as they saw the cars outside. We've got three lawyers here, all from Raffin, Radleigh and Gilks. They'll surely slow everything down."

"What about police interpreters?"

"We're trying to get some of the people on our list, but it's not proving easy, we've already had a few excuses, and the one we've managed to get an OK from won't be here till after ten. So I guess you're going to have to wait a while."

"Let's go with their interpreter, and see what happens," suggested McCader. "She may be as competent as she says. But it's odd that they managed to find her so fast. Could suggest that she's part of the operation. The one who talks to the girls when they need talking to."

"That sounds ominous," said Ó Fiachan, "but you may be right, Enver. We'll check her out, and interview her later. Is it OK with you, Angus, I mean, to talk with them right away?"

"Yes, it's worth a try," said Blue. "I'd rather we do something than nothing."

Ten minutes later they were back in the room, now a lot more crowded, with the portly form of Seamus Raffin squeezed at one end of the table, and the solid bulk of Olga Karpova at the other. The atmosphere had also become more stuffy, the powerful aromas of Raffin's expensive but overdosed aftershave combining with a waft of onions from Karpova to create a sickly miasma in the room. Blue wished he could pull out a pipe, stuff it with aromatic Turkish tobacco, and fill the room with a thick fog suggestive of the 1930s. On the plus side, he, McCader and Ó Dálaigh had plenty of room on their side of the table. The female officer stood again by the door.

Sergeant Ó Dálaigh commenced the session by repeating the introductions, but now there was a pause while her words were translated for the girls. Karpova spoke to them very slowly, giving emphasis to every word. Watching, it was clear to Blue that the girls knew her, and feared her. Ó Dálaigh went through the process of personal identification again, but this time it took three times longer. Then she asked to see their passports. The interpreter spoke very briefly to the girls, then announced, "They say they gave them to Mrs Winsor for safekeeping, and insurance."

"What do they mean by insurance?" asked Blue.

Raffin interrupted, "What she means, Mr Blue, is that the passports were retained by Mrs Winsor as a *surety*, in case they absconded without paying their rent, or caused damage to the premises. 'Insurance' was not quite the right word. Mrs Winsor is in legal terms their landlord, and has the right to ask for a deposit or other surety." He leaned back with self-satisfied air, and waved for Blue to continue.

"Thank you for the clarification, Mr Raffin. As you know, Sergeant McCader and I are here with the permission of our Irish colleagues, in connection with a case we are currently investigating. I should stress here that we are interviewing Misses Ivanova, Radova and Hristova purely as possible witnesses to an assault, and not in connection with any other events or activities."

Raffin nodded, then remembered the voice recorder, and cleared his throat. "Yes, that is understood, Mr Blue. Your questions will be confined to your own current case." The translation of these remarks seemed to Blue to be delivered with an expression of warning. He noticed McCader frown. He had spotted it too.

"I'd like to begin," Blue went on, "by asking Misses Ivanova, Radova and Hristova where they were last weekend. From Friday until Monday. I don't mind which of them answers." He had spoken very clearly, and saw how the girls reacted as he spoke. Radina and Bilyana understood him. Radina's eyes opened wide, whilst Bilyana looked sharply at the interpreter. Nadezhda just looked at Karpova, waiting for the translation. Karpova took her time with the translation, and seemed to Blue to say a lot more than he had said. Only Bilyana spoke in response, and after an interchange with Karpova, the interpreter at last spoke to Blue.

"They say they visited a house on a Scottish island."

"You said 'they' but only Miss Radova spoke."

"Bilyana speaks for all of them."

"Can Bilyana tell us where the house was."

"She told you already. On an island in Scotland."

"Which island?"

"She doesn't know."

"Will you ask her, please, if she knows which island they were on?"

Karpova made an exasperated sigh, and spoke again to Bilyana, who replied, shaking her head vigorously.

"She repeats, she doesn't know."

"When did they go to the house and when did they return?"

There was another interchange with Bilyana.

"She says they went on Friday and returned on Sunday."

Blue noticed Radina frown at the interpreter in puzzlement.

"We know that they went to the house on Friday and returned on Monday," he said. "Please ask Bilyana to tell us the truth." Karpova was caught out by this, and paused to think, before speaking sharply to Bilyana.

"I have told her always to speak the truth," she said. Now Raffin began to look worried, and stared meaningfully at the interpreter.

"Thank you," said Blue. "Can Bilyana tell me who took them to this house?"

After another discussion, which as far as Blue could tell, did not include the words 'Gladys Waggoner' or anything resembling that, Karpova spoke again. "They do not know the name of the lady who took them to the house. They think she was a friend of Mrs Winsor. She was a very kind and helpful lady."

"Did this lady stay also at the house?"

Again the consultation. "No, none of them stayed in the house itself. They stayed in a *dacha*, in the forest, some way from the house."

"And why did the girls go to the house? What were they doing there?"

Bilyana spoke again. Then Karpova: "They are entertainers. They sing and dance. They were hired to entertain guests at a private party."

"Who hired them?"

This time Karpova made no pretence at consulting Bilyana. "They do not know who hired them. It was arranged by their manager."

"What is the name of the manager?"

"Their manager is Mr Winsor."

Ó Dálaigh raised a finger. "Just a moment, there. Let me get this clear. So Mr Winsor is their employer, and Mrs Winsor is their landlord. Is that correct?"

Raffin intervened. "I think what I heard Miss Karpova saying is that, whilst Mrs Winsor is indeed their landlord, Mr Winsor is their *manager*, and not their employer. I think that for tax purposes they would be regarded as self-employed."

"Thank you, Mr Raffin. I'm sure our tax authorities will be keen to speak to the girls about their status, as well as to Mr and Mrs Winsor." Blue caught a flash of anger in Raffin's eyes.

Ó Dálaigh went on. "Can Bilyana tell us some of the songs which form their repertoire?"

"I don't understand your question," said Karpova. "What is 'repertorr'?"

Raffin intervened again. "I'm not sure this question is not frivolous. In fact, it seems a little unhealthy to me."

"Not at all, Mr Raffin. I'll be blunt with you, now. We wish to establish that these girls are in fact legitimate entertainers, and not simply prostitutes. I think you'd agree it would be in their interests to help us establish that."

Blue noticed that the word "prostitutes" drew a gasp from Radina.

Raffin shuffled uncomfortably in his chair, before replying. "I will obtain as soon as possible, either from them or from Mr Winsor, a list of the items they perform, and have it sent to you."

"Thank you, that's noted," replied Ó Dálaigh. "Mr Blue, would you carry on now?"

Blue nodded his thanks. "Ms Karpova, can you ask them how many guests were at this party? And who they were?"

After another consultation, Karpova replied. "There were only two guests. No names were mentioned, and the girls did not recognise them."

"It sounds a strange party. Didn't the girls find it odd?"

Again Raffin cut in. "Asking my clients' opinions is hardly going to help you. I suggest you stick to the facts."

McCader nudged Blue, and leaned close to him. "Can we talk for a moment, sir? Outside."

"I'd like to ask Sergeant Ó Dálaigh to suspend the interview now," said Blue. "I'll indicate in a short while whether we wish to continue."

The sergeant formally suspended the interview and switched off the recorder. As Blue got up, he saw Radina looking at him. She wants out, he thought.

Raffin stood up too. "If you're not wanting to speak to these girls now, Miss Karpova will be needed to sit in at other interviews, and I need to talk to Mr and Mrs Winsor. So if you need to reconvene here, you'll need to consult me as to when would be convenient."

In the corridor, Blue asked McCader what he thought.

"It's hopeless, sir. The interpreter is coaching them. Right at the start she told the other two to keep quiet so that only Bilyana spoke. She said that if they tried to talk they'd be punished later. 'And you know what that means' were her exact words."

"You can speak Bulgarian?" asked Ó Dálaigh.

"No, not really. But I do speak Russian, so I can follow quite a lot of it. Can I suggest that we interview them one at a time, and I do the interpreting."

"What about the lawyer?"

"In fact, the girls being over eighteen, he needs their consent to represent them, and that wasn't specifically mentioned in the interview. So we can still ask them whether they want to be represented by him, or someone else, or no-one at all."

"That's right enough, Enver," said Ó Dálaigh. "Who would you like to see first, Mr Blue?"

"Let's take Radina."

Five minutes later the uniformed officer led Radina back into the interview room. She immediately noticed that neither the lawyer nor the interpreter were present. She looked questioningly at Blue, but it was Sergeant Ó Dálaigh who spoke. "Ms Ivanova. I think you understand me if I speak simply. You are over eighteen years of age?"

"Yes?"

"Then it is your right to decide whether to be represented by Mr Raffin, or by another lawyer, or by none at all."

She looked puzzled. "I do not completely understand."

McCader immediately spoke to her in what sounded like Russian to Blue. Radina's jaw dropped. Then she recovered herself, and asked McCader a whole series of questions. After five minutes of rapid exchanges, McCader turned to Ó Dálaigh. "She's naturally surprised that I speak Russian, and asked if I understood what Karpova was saying to them. She doesn't want Raffin or Karpova in the room. They are both involved. She doesn't want legal representation at this point. She hates these people, and will tell us everything she knows, if we can get her away from here and out of Ireland. She is afraid the gang will come after her if she talks."

I've no doubt they will, thought Blue. So we better nail them. "Tell her we'll take her back to Scotland with us and ensure she's protected." He noticed Ó Dálaigh's raised eyebrows. "We'll naturally run that eventuality past Inspector Ó Fiachan." He hoped the long words would prevent Radina from following their conversation too closely. "What do you think, Sergeant Ó Dálaigh?"

"Sure, the boss can be very flexible when he wants to. Especially for someone he knows. Sorry, a personage of his acquaintance." She smiled.

"Thanks," said Blue. "I felt we had to table something substantive at this juncture. Do you mind if Sergeant McCader does the questioning, the translating takes too long?"

"No problem."

"OK, Enver, start with what was going on here in Dublin, then move onto that weekend."

McCader spoke fluently, and the conversation proceeded rapidly. It occurred to Blue that Radina could probably speak Russian as well as Bulgarian. He could see that McCader was gaining her trust, and that she was telling him everything she knew.

After ten minutes, McCader summarised: "All the girls at the house were brought over from Eastern Europe with promises of work in hotels or restaurants. Then they were forced into 'entertaining' and then having sex with men. The boss of the operation is Gladys Waggoner. The Winsors and that interpreter work for Gladys. Karpova explains to the girls what's what, and what'll happen if they don't co-operate. They are paid a fee for each piece of work they do, and have to pay rent to the Winsors. Then Mr Winsor registers them with the tax people as self-employed entertainers, so it all looks above board. They aren't thrown onto the streets of Dublin to tout for business. This is a much more high-class operation. Gladys offers services to top people, we know that already. So they are trained for each visit. Her clients don't want sluts off the street."

"But they want to do the same thing to them," put in Ó Dálaigh.

"Exactly."

"Are they forced to stay there?" asked Blue.

"The money is calculated so that they never make very much once 'board and lodging' are paid for, but they're told they can make lots if they stick with it. However, once, when a girl did decide to leave, she was badly beaten up, and then disappeared. Karpova told them she'd had an 'accident' and the same thing would happen to anyone else who thought of going off."

"OK, what about Jura?"

McCader and Radina talked again, and Blue could see that the more the girl talked, the more she wanted to say. He could sense the relief in her that she could share her story. The worry would come later.

"OK, sir. She says Gladys told them they were going to entertain some very important people. Three of them."

"Three?"

"Exactly. Unfortunately they weren't told who these people were, only that they were very important. Gladys herself collected them at the house first thing on Friday, and took them on the boat to Cairnryan, then drove them up to Kennacraig and then via Islay to

Jura and Dunrighinn House. Though they weren't told the name of the house. But she's not stupid. She knew they were on the island of Jura, she could see the signs. They were required to entertain on Saturday and Sunday evening. This involved doing a bit of erotic dancing and then pairing off with each of the three men and doing whatever they wanted."

"What did she say about each of the three men? Could she describe them?"

"Yes. The three men – and it was three men – all wore masks. Steppingham and van Kaarsten were fairly identifiable from their physical descriptions. The third man less so; he was athletic, well-built, young, but he had a scar on his left thigh"

"Like our man in Steppingham Hall."

"Yes, he told her it was a graze from a bullet. This man was very demanding, she says. Also liked violence."

"Hence the black eye."

"There's more you can't see. Much more."

"Did she hear them speak to each other. How did they address each other?"

McCader spoke to Radina again, and reported. "The masks were animal masks, and they addressed each other as 'Piglet' – that was Steppingham – 'Wolfie' – that was van Kaarsten – and 'Lion-o' – that was the third man. Only once she heard van Kaarsten refer to the third man as 'A.G.'. The man immediately snapped at van Kaarsten, 'Lion-o, fuckhead!' and punched him hard on the arm. It was a nasty punch – she says van Kaarsten was rubbing it for a while afterwards."

"How about the way they spoke. Accents?"

"She's not good on identifying accents in English-speakers, she felt from their behaviour that they were upper class. One other thing. She says that Ffox-Kaye was there when they arrived and right through the weekend. He was in charge of security, she thought."

"Where were they kept?"

"In the top-floor room, with Gladys next door. They were brought down the servants' stairs to the kitchen for their meals by Gladys, then escorted back up to the room as soon as they'd finished. Apart from that, and the evenings, they had to stay in the room."

"OK. Did they see anything on Monday morning?"

McCader and Radina talked again. "She says they weren't going down for breakfast till eight, so they were in the room when it happened. They had the window open to let some air in, so they heard the helicopter coming. They watched it from the window, and saw the people coming out, then two of the men were shot. These two had to be carried into the house. The third man wasn't hit at all. He fell to the ground, but after a short while got up and ran into the house. That's all they saw. They were afraid, they didn't know what was going on. They kept away from the window then, in case anybody spotted them. After maybe half an hour, Gladys came into the room, told them to pack up, and that they'd have to hurry to get the boat. She asked them if they seen anything, and all three denied it – they aren't stupid. They asked her what had happened. She said there had been an accident, but they shouldn't say anything to anyone about it. Not even the Winsors. On the way back, in the car, she also told them that if anyone asked, they should say there were only two men there, 'Piglet' and 'Wolfie'. No-one else."

"Thanks, Enver." Blue addressed Radina. "Many thanks, Ms Ivanova. Don't worry. I promise we will look after you. We'll take you away from here as soon as we can. Hopefully later today." The girl nodded as McCader translated. She seemed satisfied. But Blue knew if they kept her waiting too long she would stop trusting them. They had to move fast.

Sergeant Ó Dálaigh terminated the interview and turned off the sound recorder. Then she nodded to the uniformed officer, who escorted Radina out of the room. "Don't worry," she said to Blue, "She'll be kept away from the others now."

"Thanks, Sinéad," said Blue. "That confirms the account given by the Special Branch men, Ffox-Kaye and Plaistow, the difference being there were three men there, not two. The question now is, who was the third man?"

"There's the scar on his thigh," put in McCader. "Not everyone's got one of those."

"That might come in useful. Do you think it's worth speaking to the other two?"

"Bilyana, I doubt it. She wants to toe the party line. She may even have some sort of senior status among the girls. Worth a shot, but I doubt we'll get much out of her. But Nadezhda, I think we should certainly speak with her. She looks a simple country girl who's in this too deep and doesn't know how to get out."

41

Blue knew he had to make a deal with Ó Fiachan to get Radina out, so he left McCader and Ó Dálaigh to interview Nadezhda, and then Bilyana, and went to find the Irish Inspector. They talked over coffee. Ó Fiachan was not averse to a deal, provided his superintendent, as well as the girl herself, agreed to it. Her evidence could be used to unlock the testimony of the other girls too.

"Once they know someone has spilled the beans – and we won't say who – most of them will be relieved to endorse it. After all, we can get them all out of here if they want it. And the poor girls aren't the ones we're after. We need as much as we can get on the Winsors, and maybe we'll even get something on Gladys Waggoner. By the way, we've detained that interpreter for questioning – I'm glad to say our own has finally got here."

"Did you get much in the house?" asked Blue.

"A treasure trove. Mr Winsor we have to thank for his meticulous record-keeping. He should have been an accountant. He did train to be one, in fact. There's enough to put the Winsors away for a long time. Especially if the girls can testify to the human effects of their activities."

"What about Gladys Waggoner?"

"Not so easy. If the Winsors can be persuaded to talk, we'll have her. If not, it'll depend on what the girls say. And it looks like she kept the thing at arms length, apart from when she delivered girls to a job. To be honest, I think she's just too well protected. But if we leak enough of the stuff to the media, it could make her life very unpleasant, and her protectors will soon want to drop her. At least it might put her out of circulation for a bit. Anyway, I'll talk to Brian now, see what he thinks."

Blue went back along the corridor and slipped into the interview room. McCader was talking to Bilyana. She kept a very straight face and was, it seemed, either saying no or that she didn't know to everything she was being asked. McCader soon terminated the interview.

"Any luck?" asked Blue, once the girl had been led out.

"Nadezhda just wants to go home. She confirms Radina's account, but can't add to it. She says she wasn't with the third man at all, and her English is much poorer, so she didn't overhear anything."

"And Bilyana?"

"Denies everything. Says the Winsors are great people and she wants to go back to stay with them. Says if the others say anything different, they're lying. Won't say anything more without a lawyer."

Blue and McCader thanked Sergeant Ó Dálaigh for her help, then went down to the canteen for coffee and something to eat. Blue switched his phone on. A text from Moira Nicolson to call her.

"Moira, hi, what's doing?"

"Angus, Ffox-Kaye's made an arrest. Says he's solved the case."

"What? Who's he arrested?"

"A Syrian called Ahmed Salebi. He worked as a cleaner at the hospital here in Bowmore."

"What evidence has he got?"

"None that he's willing to share. Says that secret intelligence from the Anti-Terrorist Squad enabled him to focus on Salebi, and he's been arrested under anti-terrorism legislation to prevent him fleeing the country. Says evidence is still being collected. Where does that leave us?"

"Not sure. Better call the Super. I'll talk to you later. Hope to be back later today."

Next he phoned Campbell.

"Angus, glad you phoned, all getting a bit odd here. I assume you've heard about Ffox-Kaye's arrest."

"Yes. Moira just told me. Do you know anything more?"

"Not any more details. I got a call from the DCC, wondering whether it was time to close your side of the case. I said it wouldn't be appropriate until it was clear whether Salebi was going to be charged with the shooting. But I suspect that'll happen quite soon. People like Ffox-Kaye don't let little problems like evidence get in their way. How are you getting on in Dublin?"

Blue updated him on the raid and their interviews with the Bulgarians.

"Hmm. This other man is a rum business. Ffox-Kaye still insists there was only one victim. I'm getting a bad feeling about it. If it does turn out to be somebody important, the whole thing could get very unpredictable. Oh, by the way, my whisky?"

"Yes, got it, chief. I'll get it to you as soon as possible."

Twenty minutes later Ó Fiachan came over to their table.

"Alright, lads. Brian has agreed that you can take Radina, as long as she's happy with that, and provided that we can recall her to give evidence if we need to. I don't anticipate that being necessary, but you never know."

"What about Nadezhda?" asked McCader.

"She's not going to be so much use to the case, given her poor English. We've got her statement, and two of the others are giving us a lot more even as we speak. We've also had orders from above to repatriate as many of them as we can. The confiscated criminal assets fund will pay for it. Given the possibility that Gladys was tapping into a bigger network, I'd be happy to get them all out of Ireland before somebody decides to get rid of possible witnesses. So if she wants to go, we'll have her out in the next couple of days. Don't worry, Enver, I'll personally make sure that Nadezhda gets out."

"Thanks, Ruaraigh, I owe you one."

"No, I owe you lads for helping us get this operation moving. That's why I couldn't have you missing the raid. You deserved it. By the way, are you waiting for a pint of Guinness this evening?"

"Sorry," said Blue, "we've to be back on Islay as soon as we can."

McCader explained to Radina what her options were, and that it would help their work on Islay if she could come there, even if only for a few days. She would be given board and lodging and a daily allowance. If she preferred to be flown to Bulgaria immediately, that was also possible. He strongly advised her against remaining in Dublin.

She readily agreed to come to Islay. She had no desire to return to Bulgaria – she admitted that she felt her own father had colluded with the traffickers, that they had paid him money for her. Ó Fiachan had told her that eventually she would receive a payment from the Criminal Compensation Scheme, but for the moment she was destitute, and therefore the offer of help to survive in the short term was welcome. Besides, it was clear to Blue that she trusted McCader.

In view of the news that Ffox-Kaye had made an arrest, Blue felt it imperative to get back to Islay. McCader checked the ferry and the news was not good; the 10.30 had long gone and the next wasn't until 4.30 pm. The car had to go back to Oban, so McCader had no option but to drive. Blue therefore asked him to bring Radina along, and had himself booked onto the next flight to Glasgow.

42

Ó Fiachan organised a car to take him to the airport, sirens blaring, and he made a flight at twelve fifteen, reaching Glasgow an hour and a half later. Unfortunately, he now had three hours to wait for his flight to Islay. He came through domestic arrivals and went back up the stairs to the café near the entrance to the security gates. Here he found a reasonably secluded table, and got himself some lunch. Then he set up his laptop and plugged the power cable into a nearby socket. Plenty of time to update his report. And get his thinking straight on what was happening.

Before starting he phoned Moira and reported what was happening with Radina. He asked how they could best manage her stay on Islay.

"Leave Radina's accommodation with me, Angus, I'll get something sorted out. We don't want her standing out like a sore thumb. Especially if there are people who might come after her. But about the shooting, this third man could be an important witness, if he's still alive, that is. What do we know about him?"

"Youngish, fit, strong, likes violence, was addressed as 'AG', and has a scar on his left thigh, possibly a bullet wound."

"Hmm. If he's well-known, there could be mention of him in celebrity or gossip mags, or on the web. I'll ask Arvind and Deirdra to see what they can find."

"Any luck with that program to clarify the video footage?"

"Well, it made it a bit clearer, but not so's you could see what he really looks like. And he was wearing a baseball cap, which covers part of his face. Van Kaarsten was wearing one too, and the program tried to make them identical twins, so Deirdra had to take Van Kaarsten out of the algorithm."

"Anything else over there?"

"Yes. This morning, the firefighters found a body at Dunrighinn, in a room at the back of the house. Badly burnt, not clear who it is yet, but John Seymour's still missing. I've asked the SOCOs to come back, they'll be on the ferry this afternoon. The area's cold now, and I've had the body cordoned off, and tented. And I've got it guarded. The fire investigator was over this morning too, she'll send me her report as soon as it's done. On the phone she said, off the record, it looks like a gas explosion. To get a blast that big, she reckons there would have to be a big leak, which is less likely to be accidental. But she can't be more specific till she's had some tests done. The body doesn't prove anything one way or the other, till it's been examined more carefully too. It could have been someone trying to fix the leak, when it went up."

"Lit a match to see where the leak was." Blue knew of accident victims even more stupid.

At 3.30 he got an email from Ó Fiachan to say that Nadezhda was now on a plane to Amsterdam with three of the other girls. From there she was booked on a flight to Sofia, where her parents would meet her. They were overjoyed she was coming home.

Only Bilyana had turned down the offer of repatriation. On being given her passport back, she had left the police station in the company of Eamon Raffin.

The case was building up steadily against the Winsors, as the computers and files from the house were examined. Drugs had also been found at the house, as well as a couple of Canadian passports in the name of a Mr and Mrs Delaney. The pictures were of the Winsors, the passports fake. The couple had now been charged with multiple offences and the inspector was confident that bail would be refused.

Unfortunately, there was very little which could connect the crimes of the Winsors to Gladys Waggoner. She would no doubt claim to be a simple-minded dupe who'd been used by them to ferry young women around the country to their entertainment venues.

Ó Fiachan was glad to have cleared up one criminal operation, but was aware that what the Winsors were doing was linked to wider networks extending well beyond Ireland. Still, every little success counted.

Blue phoned McCader to pass on the news from Ó Fiachan. McCader and Radina were now at Larne, waiting for the ferry to Cairnryan, which would sail at 4.30.

43

At five, he flew out to Islay. Alison Hendrickx was waiting for him at the airport.

"Alison. What a surprise."

"What did you expect?"

"That I'd get a taxi to the police station."

"Poor you. Don't be so sorry for yourself. I had to fight the others off for the chance to meet you. And don't let that go to your head either! By the way, you look tired."

"Got up quite early this morning. Lot of excitement earlier on. Long day yesterday too."

They got into Alison's car and headed off towards Port Ellen.

"You're going to check into your hotel first," said Alison, "then you're coming over to Moira and Alasdair's for a meal. You can go into the station in the morning. I'm sure Moira will fill you in on everything this evening. An earlyish night will do you good. Sharpen you up."

Blue didn't object. The last time he'd been at Moira's, the previous autumn, he'd almost fallen asleep over the meal, and he didn't want that to happen again. Besides, Alison was right. A good sleep would make him more effective the next day. He'd known cops to make some bad mistakes, just because they'd been awake far too long.

He'd been booked into the same hotel as last time, the white-painted Victorian one on the way into Port Ellen, with the classical portico in the middle and the Gothic towers at each end. Alison said she'd wait for him, as she didn't want him to fall asleep in his room and forget all about going to Moira's. She walked in with him, taking a book from her bag, and sat down in the foyer to read.

He had a shower and put clean clothes on. It made him feel much more awake. He resisted the temptation to open up his laptop and check his email.

When he came back to the foyer, Alison was still reading.

"What are you reading?" he asked.

"Hubert Valkerius, *Lost Dogs in the Imperial Sunset*."

"What a title. It'll go far. I've heard of him, haven't I?" Blue decided not to mention that he'd got to page 1 of one of Valkerius's books in German, before being sent to Jura.

"Yes, we talked about it when you came to Moira's last time. It's the series that Alasdair's translating from the German. Inspector Brack? In pre-World-War-One Austria-Hungary."

"Er, yes. Is that the first one in the series?"

"Yes. Thankfully the publishers decided to publish the series in English in the same order that it came out in German. That makes the character development much more intelligible."

"So what's it like?"

"Pretty good so far. Page 57, that is. Don't you think the cover is rather expressive?" She held up the book to show the cover. A sepia photo of two rows of army officers posed for the camera. One row seated, and another row standing behind. The uniforms were fantastical, no two the same. The only common features were the shiny riding boots and the neatly trimmed moustaches. Blue would also have said the self-satisfied smiles, but he noticed that two of the figures were not smiling. They were at the right hand side of the standing row, and while one gazed at the photographer with a completely neutral expression, the one on his left, at the end of the row, had a more worried look. Was he hiding some personal tragedy, or did he know what was coming to his kind? The picture became darker further down, so that the feet of the officers seemed to be lost in darkness, already sinking into the past.

Blue took it from her and turned it over. On the back, close up and faded, was the face of the worried man.

"The story good?"

"Yes. Brack's father is a Calvinist pastor somewhere to the north of Budapest, who ensures his son has a good education, and, through influence of a local aristocrat, a place in the Imperial Gendarmerie – that's what the police were called then. He's sent to Salzburg as a corporal, but through an error in the official posting notice – the word 'von' has been mistakenly added – he's thought to be an aristocrat, and immediately promoted to lieutenant. That gives him the opportunity to lead his own cases, and, well, it goes on from there. You should read it."

"I should really read it in the German. My German used to be quite good, but I've let it slip. You have to keep reading to maintain it. But you're right, it does sound interesting. And that period, the decrepit empire clinging still to its fantasy of European domination, whilst all the bits were waiting for the chance to escape. Much like Britain today."

"So, the political commentator as well as a linguist. How multitalented."

Blue felt himself blushing. What he'd just said sounded pompous. He deserved the put-down.

"Sorry, I didn't mean it to sound that way. It really does sound an interesting book, and I will try to read it. Even in English."

"OK, professor, let's go. The food will be waiting."

Moira and Alasdair Nicolson lived just at the edge of Port Ellen in a former manse, a generous but difficult-to-heat Victorian building, with a big and unruly garden. Alasdair, a tall man with white hair and beard cut short, greeted them at the door.

"*Hallo, Aonghus, ciamar a tha thu?*"

Blue had been put on the spot by the Gaelic welcome the last time, but this time he was ready, and had revised in his head his very limited knowledge of the language on the way round. He had spent a year at an evening class in Oban a few years back. He couldn't deny that it had been very useful.

"*Tha gu math, tapadh leat, Alasdhair. Agus thu fheinn?*"

"I'm fine too," said Alasdair. "I won't prolong your agony. But I'm glad you still remember some." The soft Hebridean drawl of his voice was always calming.

And the meal was a good one too, as he knew it would be. Pan-fried salmon coated in oatmeal with home grown broccoli and potatoes, and a hollandaise sauce, followed by a dessert of fromage frais, raspberries and banana on a bed of crushed shortbread infused with Madeira. Alison sat next to him, and every so often he felt her hand on his arm, or caught the subtle scent she used.

He apologised for asking Moira about the case, but needed to know if there had been any new developments. He knew Alasdair would be discreet.

"I went round to the hospital this afternoon, to try to find out about the chap Ffox-Kaye arrested, Ahmed Salebi. Apparently he used to be a teacher in a secondary school in Aleppo. English was his subject. He took part in some of the early demonstrations against the regime. Later on his family, who were staying with relatives in Damascus to be, as they thought, safer, were killed in a bombing raid, no-one knew by whom. He managed to get out of the country, and made his way here. He told them he wanted to be as far away from Syria as he could get. Hoped eventually to go to Canada. I think he has a cousin there."

"What did people think of him?"

"He was nice, that's the word they used. Quiet, always polite, never complained. Did a good job. But always sad. And no family to take up his case now."

"Could he have done it?"

"His colleagues at the hospital didn't think so. Far too gentle. In terms of opportunity, I asked about his shifts. The only way he could have done it was by having access to a boat. He didn't go over to Jura at the weekend on the ferry, Fergus is sure of that, nor did he come back on Monday morning. He works evenings, so he could have theoretically taken a boat across on Sunday night, and then back on Monday morning. I sent Bob over to ask around, but no-one saw him on Jura. Ffox-Kaye will say that's not surprising if he used a boat, he would have gone straight to the shore near Dunrighinn. But we've no evidence he had access to a boat of any kind."

"I suppose Ffox-Kaye will just say there are plenty lying around he could have borrowed."

"Quite."

"So no-one can prove he didn't do it, but neither can they prove he did?" put in Alison.

"That's about it, yes."

"Where is he now, Salebi I mean?" asked Blue.

"I don't know. Not here, anyway. I tried to see him early this afternoon. I was told at the Masonic Hall that he'd been moved to a 'Secure Interview Facility' in England. This was supposedly in order to prevent bids by terrorist groups to free him. They refused to tell me where it was."

"What'll happen to him?" asked Alison.

"I've a nasty suspicion," said Blue. "The best way for Ffox-Kaye to avoid having the evidence, or lack of it, examined, is to get a confession."

"How can he do that?"

"I'm guessing he wants to tie this one up quickly, and pin it on the right sort of perpetrator. I'd bet in a secret facility with no-one watching, he can be as persuasive as you can imagine. And without leaving a mark."

"Torture! That's appalling!"

"I couldn't agree with you more, Alison. Unfortunately, if Salebi's gone, we're not likely to see him here again."

"Surely he'll have to appear in court?"

"Yes. In an anti-terrorist tribunal somewhere in England. Just a couple of judges to decide his fate. People from the same background as Ffox-Kaye. People who probably share his world-view. And with a confession sitting in their desks."

"Unless you can prove someone else did it, Angus. What about the suspects you were after?"

"Well, we do have something positive. Our suspect, Bicycle Man that is, got the boat to Tayvallich on Monday morning, and was picked up by his putative daughter there. Then they drove to Inveraray where they had lunch, then on to Newcastle, where they took the boat to Amsterdam on Monday evening."

"So they got clean away!"

"Not quite. I'm hoping Jill Henderson will have some information on them from DFDS tomorrow. And remember we know where their car's registered. We'll track that down eventually. And them too. I'm not giving up on this."

"We don't want to talk about the case all night," said Moira, "but there's just one more thing. The body in Dunrighinn House, or at least the ruins of. Our SOCOs got there this afternoon and got the body out. Dr Halsetter certified it dead. She also had a look at the teeth, so we might have an identification tomorrow, as long as he, or she, went to a dentist in this part of the world. I'm still waiting for the fire investigator's report – that should come in tomorrow too."

Blue's phone rang. He excused himself, went through to the living room, and took the call. It was McCader, on his way to Kennacraig to get the last ferry to Islay. He hoped he'd make it.

Blue went back into the dining room. "That was Enver. He and Radina should be on the Islay boat soon."

"Good," said Moira. "The girls are looking forward to meeting her." She noticed that Blue was looking blank. "Our girls, Angus. We have two, Eilidh, she's seventeen, and Anna is sixteen. You didn't see them last time you were here, and they're up in their living room in the loft now. They keep out the way when we have guests. We can put Radina up for a while, till she's worked out what she wants to do."

"That's very kind of you both," said Blue.

"Another one up there won't make a lot of difference," said Alasdair.

"Hopefully she'll be able to identify the mystery man pretty soon," observed Alison, "then she can get on with her life." Was she looking at him significantly?

"Yes," said Blue. "Time we were getting on with ours too, so no more talk about the case. Alasdair, how's the translation going?"

"Angus, I really thought you were never going to ask," Alasdair smiled. "Very well. Inspector Brack moves on. He's at the eve of war now. 1914. He's had a tip-off about a Serbian gang wanting to kill Archduke Franz Ferdinand, but the authorities believe it's just a distraction, that the real target is another member of the royal family, Archduke Charles, who's second in line to the throne, but is younger, more dynamic, more likely to try and revamp the empire. Can Brack persuade them in time that they're wrong? Well, no, sadly, because we all know what happened at Sarajevo, but it makes a gripping story nevertheless. You almost believe as you read that it can be prevented, that somehow history can be different. That killing one royal"

"And his wife," said Alison. "Don't forget her."

"Sorry, and his wife, can make such a huge difference to world history."

"Don't you think if that hadn't happened," said Blue, "something else would have triggered it? All the big powers wanted war, it was just a question of when. They all thought they could win. All those aristocrats were getting bored with peace. They wanted a more exciting game to play."

"What happens to Brack, then?" asked Alison.

"He gets to Sarajevo, but just too late, and is then arrested himself because he seems to know about the plot. Needless to say, the top brass in Vienna deny that he warned them about it, and try to make him a scapegoat. I won't tell you any more. I wouldn't want to spoil it for you."

And the discussion moved to other topics, along with coffee, liqueurs and good whisky.

At half past ten the doorbell rang. As Alasdair got up from the table, rapid footsteps on the stairs and voices in the hall told them that Eilidh and Anna were still up. A few moments later, McCader came into the dining room and greeted them. He looked tired, and declined a whisky, saying he needed to get over to his B&B. Blue felt it was time he left too. A wave from Alison and a kiss blown across the room left him with a warm feeling as he walked back to the hotel.

Day 7. Sunday

44

Blue was up at seven. He needed to get back on top of the case. If there was still a case, that is. He couldn't see Ffox-Kaye permitting another investigation to continue, once he had 'solved' it himself. However, that instruction would have to come via the CC and the Super, which might give him a few more hours. And the body at the house raised a new case altogether. Unless Ffox-Kaye claimed the killer had also burnt down Steppingham's house.

He phoned the station and asked if someone could pick him up at twenty to eight. On the dot, Bhardwaj was outside his hotel. As they set off, Blue asked him what he'd been up to the last couple of days.

"We spent ages on that program that Deirdra's pal sent us, but it looks like we really didn't get much from it in the end."

"Could you see anything of the mystery man?"

"He was wearing a baseball cap, which covered most of his face, but you could see he was clean-shaven, and his hair was cut short. Colour could have been light brown, blond or ginger, depending what settings we tried. But not black. He was quite well-built too, fit-looking. Just one thing caught my eye, which might be useful. I think he had quite a prominent chin, bit like Kirk Douglas. If we had a database of chins, we could probably find him in five minutes."

"That might be helpful, nevertheless. Anything else?"

"Not related to the case, chief. We had to arrest a serial dogshitter yesterday."

"You arrested the dog?"

"Wish we had. Big fat creature, overfed on cheap dogfood. Produced gigantic droppings – all that sawdust just passing through. The owner – that's a Barry Cawthrop, he's a driver for the Co-op – got into a dispute with his next-door neighbour, said the neighbour – that's a Mrs Clarke – was letting her cat shit in his garden, and make holes in his vegetable beds."

"And did she?"

"Probably. Says where the cat goes at night is none of her business. A spiteful and cantankerous old woman, chief, that Mrs Clarke, we've had trouble with her before. She's deaf, and last year Mr

Cawthrop complained about the noise of her TV. It was very loud, everyone in the street could hear it. Her daughter came over from Glasgow, and got her some wireless earphones. The obvious and simplest solution, except she wouldn't wear them. They had to get the noise pollution man from Lochgilphead to come and record it, then the council served an enforcement order on her. The family – none of them are on the island – were furious, said they were picking on a harmless old woman, but they made her use the earphones."

"So what was Barry doing with his dog, apart from overfeeding it?"

"He decided to get his own back for the cat's business, so he made a habit of getting his brute – called Caesar, by the way – to do his work right outside Mrs Clarke's front gate. Every day. If it had been me, I'd have gone up the path and got the stuff dumped on her doorstep. Out on the pavement, other people soon noticed it. Matters got worse when somebody lifted one of the monster turds in a doggie bag, then chucked it into Mrs Clarke's garden, thinking she was to blame. So she, thinking that Mr Cawthrop had done that, picked up the bag and stuffed it through his letter-box, causing it to burst. As it happened, he was in at the time. We were soon called by another neighbour. They were shouting at each other, and the dog was barking too. We had to arrest them both. Charged them with affray and disturbing the peace, plus Mr Cawthrop with dog-fouling with intent."

"What'll happen, do you think?"

"They'll both be up before the Sheriff next month in Loch-gilphead. They'll probably just get a warning each, and told to keep out of each other's way. Maybe a fine for the dog-fouling, though."

At five to eight they drew up outside the police station.

"Good to see you again, sir," said Sergeant Walker at the reception desk. "Nasty business, this fire up at the house."

McCader was already in the workroom on the ground floor, working at a PC.

"Morning, chief. Good time to chase stuff up on the web, first thing Sunday morning. Before the late risers clog the wires."

"So what have you got?"

"Just checking out newsfeeds. They've all got the Salebi arrest. The London papers are talking as if its all over."

"What do you think they'll do to him? Salebi, I mean. Down there in deepest wherever."

"Oh, they'll persuade him to confess, no doubt about it. Here's the way it works. They'll have kept him awake since they got him, then put something in his food so he sits on the toilet for a few hours. Dehydrate him a bit. Then they'll pull him out of his cell and take him to a room stinking of goodness-knows-what where a couple of unpleasant-looking bruisers will hold him down. Then another guy will come in, who looks like he's completely insane – keeps laughing to himself, strokes the bruisers, the prisoner doesn't know what's going on. Then the mad guy starts the waterboarding – you can't imagine what it feels like."

"Can you?"

"I don't need to. I went on a course. It's bloody awful, chief. Anyway, the mad guy will be screaming at him to confess, and poor Salebi thinks he's going to die, when suddenly the door bursts open, and a plump middle-aged man with glasses and a moustache, wearing a suit, rushes in. 'Good God,' he'll say. 'What the hell are you chaps doing? Rufus, I warned you about this. Bloody savages! Let him go at once!' Well, the bruisers look disappointed but they let him go, Rufus snarls in a corner, and the man shepherds our prisoner out of the cell, into the lift, and up three storeys to a pleasant room with a nice carpet and a view of the countryside.

"Now the man in the suit, let's call him Mr Woolley, apologises profusely, and offers Salebi a cup of coffee. It comes with a chocolate biscuit too, top quality. Then he explains. There's a bit of a problem. Salebi's work permit has been revoked because he's in police custody. If he doesn't confess to the shooting, sadly he'll have to be returned to Syria, handed straight over to Mr Assad's secret police. Well, obviously he doesn't want that any more than Salebi does, but he can't do anything about it. Unless, that is, Salebi were to confess to the shooting. Salebi will say that he didn't do it. But Mr Woolley says, 'Well, old chap, you see, nobody will believe that. Everybody thinks you're guilty simply because we've arrested you. But if you think about it, it's not so bad, really. Go back to Syria, you'd be tortured to death, probably over a period of several days. Wouldn't you agree? Here in the UK, well, you haven't killed anybody, and the fact you confessed will lighten your sentence, especially as your confession will express profound remorse. You'll be presented as a gullible refugee, grieving over his family, and therefore prey to the wiles of the real terrorists. You could easily get away with just four or five years for attempted murder. You'll be sent to a place for non-dangerous prisoners, quite comfortable conditions, and you could be out in a couple of years, by which time everybody will have forgotten about you. Because of your good behaviour, your residence and work permits will be restored, and we'll even find you a new job.'

"It's a tempting offer, and Salebi doesn't have many options. There's no way a lawyer will be allowed within a mile of him, so he's no idea what legal avenues he's got. And he's still sleep-deprived and feeling like shit. Mr Woolley probably put another laxative in his coffee, so he sits on the toilet, feels sorry for himself, and then signs the confession. Who'd blame him? A couple of days later a swift trial at a Terrorism Tribunal. He pleads guilty, the confession is read out, all over in twenty minutes, he gets seven years and he's taken off to begin his sentence."

"But?" Blue detected something hanging, incomplete, at the end of McCader's speech.

"Yes, you're right, there's always a but. They know he didn't do the shooting, so can't have him talking to the other prisoners about it, even if they are only swindlers and shoplifters. So they put him in solitary. Then, after maybe a year or so, when the case is well off the radar, one day he's found hanged in his cell. Oh, they'll say, if only they'd realised he was a suicide danger, they would have taken his belt and his tie and his scarf and the cord from his dressing gown away. But he was such a nice man."

Blue knew not to ask how McCader knew all this. The only positive he could see in that account was that Ffox-Kaye might be unwilling to shut off Blue's investigation until he'd got a confession from Salebi. Then there'd be no counter-argument.

"How long do you think it'll take them to get the confession?"

"Not long. Maybe a day, two if he resists. Mostly they don't."

Blue called a case meeting for nine, then retired to his temporary office. At 8.30 Moira Nicolson arrived, and popped her head round his door.

"I guessed you'd be in at crack of dawn," she said. "That's the trouble with murder, I suppose. Much more interesting than dogshit, but you have to get up earlier, and spend your Sundays on it."

"You didn't need to come in at all."

"I thought it was worth dropping in for the meeting, see where we are. Anything you'd like me to do?"

"No. Get home after the meeting and enjoy the rest of the day. Wish I could. Anything planned?"

"Have a leisurely breakfast, go for a walk, frame a picture, read a book, talk to my daughters. Not necessarily in that order. What about you, what would you be doing if you weren't here?"

"Maybe the walk and the book. Breakfast never lasts, does it? You'd think somebody would invent toast that stays hot."

"I think it's called porridge."

Round the table in the workroom at nine were Nicolson, McCader, Bhardwaj, Craig and Sergeant Walker, along with Steve Belford, Andy McGuire and Jill Henderson. Blue brought them up to date on his visits to Steppingham and Dublin. He omitted to mention that Radina had come to Islay. He made it clear that the arrest of Salebi did not mean their investigation was ending just yet, and they were going to keep focused on the couple in the Polish car and the identity of the mystery victim. A second case might be opened in connection with the fire at the house, but they'd have to wait for the fire investigator's report and whatever the SOCOs could find at the site before jumping to any conclusions. He asked Bhardwaj and Craig to focus on celebrity gossip sites that might reveal the mystery man's identity, and McCader to go up to the house on Jura with the SOCOs, and take a look round himself.

"And if Ffox-Kaye and his goons aren't hanging around, get up to John Seymour's house, and have a look round. Maybe Tam's too if there's time."

"We'll make time, chief."

Jill Henderson reported that the security people at the North Shields ferry terminal had sent an image which showed the car's registration number clearly. The plates were Polish, as Bhardwaj had suspected. They'd promised to send some video footage and check to see if there was a booking linked to the car.

Blue set another meeting for four that afternoon. On the way out, Steve mentioned to him that the results of "those extra samples" weren't back from the DNA lab at Gartcosh yet. He'd let Blue know as soon as he had them. "And by the way, that whisky is very good."

After the meeting Blue composed an email to Inspector Piłsudski. He'd not been in touch with him for a while, and hoped he'd get a positive response. He wasn't sure of his current email address, but found on the web the Wrocław police headquarters, and sent his message to the general contact email given. It simply asked Piłsudski to get in touch and gave his email and phone numbers.

45

At ten, he borrowed one of the police cars, and drove to Port Ellen to attend the morning service at the little Baptist Church just off the front. The service began at 10.30, and he was able to park nearby and arrive with just a couple of minutes to spare. He slipped in, and since the entrance was at the rear of the seating area, he was able to look around without being too conspicuous. The pews were well-populated, but he recognised one figure immediately: Alison Hendrickx was sitting in a pew right at the back. She glanced round, and seeing him, waved him over to join her. Blue then saw that Radina Ivanova was next to her, on the side away from him. He smiled and nodded to her, and got a wary smile in return.

Then the service began. The minister, David Sempleton, Blue recognised from his previous stay on Islay. A tall man with thick glasses and long dreadlocks, clearly committed to Islay and its people, of whatever persuasion. The prayers were heartfelt, and included a prayer for Ahmed Salebi, the hymns were singable and addressed with gusto, and the sermon was clear and not too long.

After the service Mr Sempleton headed immediately for Blue's pew.

"Mr Blue! How good to see you again. And this time I see you've brought your family too." He shook Blue's hand heartily. Blue felt himself blushing.

"Er, this is my friend Alison, and er "

Alison immediately cut in. "Oh, hi, this my Slovak friend, Renée. She's over here for a few months."

"Oh, sorry," said the minister, "you just looked so family-like. Well, do come and have a cup of tea and some cake." And he led them through the door at the other end of the church into a smaller room where other members of the congregation were already queuing for cups of tea and slices of fruit cake.

Radina stuck very close to Alison, but once they'd got their tea and cake, she spoke quietly to Alison, who then spoke to Blue.

"Angus, you know the minister here?"

"Yes."

"Radina, I mean Renée, wants to know if he is a good man. Maybe she means godly, I'm not sure."

"Yes, you can tell that he is."

"Then she wishes to speak with him. In private."

"OK. I'll see if I can find him. How much can I say about her?"

"You can say that Renée isn't her real name, but ask him to keep that to himself. And that she's been involved in some bad stuff. But leave it at that. Radina will tell him as much or as little as she wants."

Blue saw David Sempleton at the other side of the room, went over and apologised for interrupting him, and explained that Renée would like to speak with him.

"Of course," said the minister, "I'll see her right away. I think Sam should come too." Samantha was his wife, at that moment serving tea at the table in the corner.

Blue introduced Sam to 'Renée', and the Sempletons led Radina through a door which Blue knew led to a small vestry.

"What do think that's about?" Blue asked Alison.

"She asked if she could come to a church this morning, and I knew you'd been to this one. I think she wants to make her peace with God. Get her soul cleaned out and start again, and this time live a normal life."

"She'll find a welcome here, for herself, not what she's done. But I hope she can forgive herself. Your own guilt is the worst thing to deal with." He forced himself to focus on Radina.

"None of it was her fault, though."

"I doubt she'll feel that."

Alison caught the sadness in his tone. For a few seconds they were silent. She laid her hand on his arm. "Well, Angus," she said softly, "we'll have to help her as much as we can. Those people can't be allowed to ruin her life."

"Yes, you're right. Getting her over here will have helped. How's she getting on with Eilidh and Anna?"

"Early days, but seems good so far. She's keen to learn, too. It's lucky her English is not bad, that's helped too."

They were now greeted by some people who'd recognised Blue from his visit the previous year, and plied with more coffee and fruit cake. Once again Blue noticed he and Alison were treated as a couple. He felt good about that.

It wasn't until half an hour later, as people were drifting off and the cups and plates being washed that the Sempletons reappeared with Radina, more red-eyed than when she had gone to talk to them.

She was holding tightly on to Sam's hand.

"We've had a good chat," said Dave. "And prayed together. God's grace abounds, for those who will accept it. And we hope Renée will be coming back this evening. You know the evening service is in Bowmore." This to Alison.

"Er, yes," said she, "If Renée's happy with that. We'll see how it goes today."

46

Back at the station, Blue found it hard to concentrate. He was itching to do something. He knew they didn't have a lot of time, but it seemed that right now all they could do was wait. Not good enough, he said to himself. He asked Bhardwaj and Craig how they were getting on. No luck so far. He phoned McCader up at the house. He had nothing to report either. He walked down to the pier, filled his lungs with the sea air, then walked out to the Gaelic Centre just along the coast and ordered a sandwich and a coffee. As he sat down at a table, he remembered a meal he had shared there with Alison back the previous autumn. Where was their relationship going? He had to admit to himself that he wanted something more permanent. Being your own boss was all very well, but sharing was so much better. He'd have to do something about that.

His thoughts were interrupted by his mobile. International. He didn't recognise the number.

"Police Scotland, Insp…"

"*Cześć*, Angus, *dzień dobry*! How are you? Don't worry, I know your Polish is not existent."

"Tadeusz! Good to hear from you. How are things?"

"From good to better, Angus my friend, I do well here. Wrocław is a very beautiful city. You must come visit soon."

There was a lot of catching up to do, and then Blue gave an overview of the case, before broaching the subject of the car.

"Is not a problem! For you, my friend, anything. In that cave on Skye, you saved my life. This is nothing in comparison. Nothing! I am on it at once. I get back to you later today, I promise. *Do widzenia!*"

This was encouraging. He glanced at his watch: three fifteen. He got a choc chip muffin to go with his coffee, and tried to do some thinking. He felt sure that Salebi was innocent, but what could he do about it? He decided to try to see the accused man. The phone number he had for Ffox-Kaye took him straight to voicemail, so he left a message, asking permission to interview Salebi.

Then he phoned Steve Belford's mobile.

"Hi Steve, anything there?"

"Hi, chief. Nothing dramatic to report. Lots of ash and burnt stuff. Just what you'd expect in a house fire. But several downstairs windows look like they were open. Could be just a coincidence."

"But maybe arson. And maybe murder too. When will we get a cause of death?"

"PM's tomorrow morning in Oban."

"OK. What about those extra samples I gave you?"

"Ah yes. The hairs were from two different people, both female. No matches with anyone on record. But the blood, that's another story."

"Don't keep me in suspense, then."

"Well, I'm not really sure what's happened. I sent it up to the lab at Gartcosh in amongst a pile of stuff from other cases. The database then delivered a match, with a guy who lives in Stornoway who was done for poaching in 1993. Enver tracked him down, and gave him a ring. He's now 67 and in a wheelchair. Claims he's never been to Jura in his life. Does that mean anything to you?"

"Yes, but not quite what you think. Thanks for that, Steve. Enjoy the whisky."

Back in his office, he considered Steve's information. He remembered what Inspector Rackham had told him, about the switching of DNA matches. There was no point in hiding Steppingham's identity, that would have merely delivered a no match. But here was a deliberate attempt to hide the identity of the other man who had been shot on Jura. Not that he could prove it.

The phone buzzed. International again.

"Angus, hello! I have success for you. The owner of the car lives here in Poland, in the town of Słubice. It's a very nice place, there are some historical buildings by the river. It used to be German, you know, part of Frankfurt on the Oder, but since 1945 all this side of the river is now Polish. Anyway, the car owner is a Dariusz Kowalski."

"Like the sergeant?"

"Which sergeant? There are many Sergeant Kowalskis here in Poland. It's very common name, in English I think it is blacksmith."

"Sorry, I was thinking of American films about World War 2. There's always a Sergeant Kowalski. He never gets to be an officer, but is always there when he's needed. And usually dies saving the youngest soldier in his platoon. Anyway, what about Dariusz Kowalski?"

"OK. I must watch these films. So, I called *Pan* Kowalski on the telephone. But he says that he owns the car no longer. He asserts that he sold it to a Turk two months ago. But he did not complete the papers for the vehicle. He claimed that he was not certain what a person must do when he sells the car to another country. So he does nothing. He will be imposed a large fine for that."

"So who was the Turkish gentleman who bought the car?"

"No, not Turkish, a Turk. A German with family origin in Turkey. The car was advertised on a Polish website. The man phoned him and asked to see the car. He came to Poland a couple of days later and examined the car. Then he offered a good price, and paid immediately, in euros. Cash in the hand, and better than *złoty*."

"Did he give a name and address?"

"Oh yes, of course, this is the law here. A form must be filled in by the present owner, which must include the details of the purchaser. But *Pan* Kowalski did not complete the form, although he says he got the details from the Turk. Ahmet Inonu. An address in Berlin. I checked with my German colleagues, but there is no record of the car on their vehicle database. Or of Herr Inonu either."

"A false name."

"Exactly put! But all is not lost, my friend."

"Like Poland."

"Ah, yes! Indeed, you know our national anthem. Well, just so, as your Mr Kipling would say. I will tomorrow morning at once sent an officer to *Pan* Kowalski's dwelling, and we will obtain a description of Herr Inonu. My officer will also get any further details from *Pan* Kowalski, and these may help us too. Do not worry, my friend, we will track down this varmint. We talk again soon!"

It became clear almost as soon as the four o'clock meeting started that they weren't much further on. The SOCOs had plenty of samples of ash and various charred objects and unidentified substances, but it would be a day or two before they could get results from the lab. If there was trace of an accelerant, then that would point to a cause of the conflagration, and suggest foul play.

"Any point in staying the night and looking again tomorrow?" Blue asked.

"Don't think so," said Steve, "not till we've a clearer idea what we're looking for."

"OK, call it a day there. You've still time to get back to civilisation this evening. We can lock up the site gates, and keep an eye on the place. Hopefully we'll have the Fire Investigator's report soon, and that may point us further. And a result from the PM on the body. Arvind, Deirdra, any luck with the celebs?"

"Not a sausage, chief," said Craig.

"We'd have got him by now," said Bhardwaj, "if we had access to the chin and scar database." No-one laughed.

"Right, you can have another go tomorrow. Enver?"

"Jill and I went up to Jack's and Tam's places. Both had been done over. Not clear what was being sought. If they had computers, they don't now, no sign of laptops, phones, tablets, all that sort of stuff…"

"But I did get a few fingerprints," added Jill. "Probably Jack and Tam's own. Except we don't have either on record to eliminate. I got some from the crockery in their kitchens, which we could presume are theirs, but it's not definitive."

"I think I can get Tam's," said Blue.

"Well, we can check what we got on the database tomorrow, but if the places were done over professionally we won't get much."

The meeting was over five minutes later, the SOCOs heading for the ferry and the local officers home. McCader had already secured the gates at Dunrighinn with a chain and large padlock, so there was no need to send anyone back. It seemed to Blue that the investigation was already winding down.

It was with a sense of frustration that he tried to update his report. He realised that the report on the shooting was more for his own benefit than that of Police Scotland, since he expected the case to be closed the following day. And on the fire, there was little he could say until they had some results from the lab and the report from the fire investigator.

At ten past five the phone rang. The Super.

"Angus, have you heard the news? Just breaking."

"No. I don't have a…"

"That Syrian. He's confessed. Ffox-Kaye held a snap press conference at Scotland Yard at five, and announced it. I watched it live.

Waved his statement around like Neville Chamberlain back from Munich."

"Where does that put my investigation?"

"Not in a good place. It would certainly look odd if we carried on whilst the brightest and best have already solved it. I gather from your tone that you're not convinced about Salebi."

"Let's just say I have serious doubts about it. We can't prove he didn't do it, but we've no proof that he did. Ffox-Kaye will no doubt say that he has secret intelligence information that led him to Salebi, plus a confession. I'm sure he's very persuasive when it comes to extracting a confession."

"Sadly, that may be true. But I'm afraid there's not a lot we can do. You'd need to produce something pretty conclusive to affect the case now, maybe a signed confession from the killer would do. But they've got one of those already, so you'd have to prove yours was better. To their satisfaction. However, this is where official channels might help us, because we only have to close the case at this end when we've been told officially from London that they've solved it. Official channels tend to be the slowest form of communication. But even so, I'd guess that by this time tomorrow I'll have to tell you to stop. Sorry Angus."

47

At 5.20 he walked over to the little Baptist church on Bowmore's main street for the evening service. Many of the faces he recognised from the morning. Radina was there again, along with Eilidh and Anna and their mother. He was disappointed not to see Alison again. The service was more informal than the morning's, consisting of prayers and songs, followed by a lively discussion on a Bible reading. After that tables were set out for a soup-and-roll supper.

Blue sat himself by Moira, and noticed that Mhairi, the fiddle player who had joined the piano to accompany the songs, perhaps in her mid-twenties, had invited the girls over to join her and a couple of other younger folk.

"Good day?" asked Moira.

"Not much progress. And it looks like we'll be shut down tomorrow."

"So, not a good day. I won't mention mine then, you'll only be jealous."

"Tell me anyway."

"I built a bench, for the back garden."

"That sounds impressive. I'm glad something creative has happened today."

"Oh dear, you'd better tell me how things went."

That didn't take long.

"So what you're saying is, you might make more progress tomorrow, but the case will be shut down anyway. You obviously don't think Ffox-Kaye has solved it."

"No. I suspect he's just picked on someone who fits his terrorist paranoia. But he's got the power to shut us down. I'm getting closer to the guy who actually did the shooting. We've linked the Polish car to a German of Turkish extraction, but he gave a false name and address. There's no way we can tie it all up in the few hours we have left."

"No luck then on the celebrity websites. What'll you try next to find Mr X?"

"Not sure. Any suggestions?"

"The dentist. Not her personally, I mean. But the waiting room is notorious for the gigantic pile of old magazines there. Might be worth flicking through them. Sometimes what you see on paper is clearer or sharper than how you see it on the screen."

"Thanks. We might give that a go. Can I ask you something else? Do you think Radina might be willing to help there? Looking though the mags might prompt some recollection she's not mentioned yet."

"Hmm, leave that with me. I'll talk to her this evening, and let you know. But we can't push her if she doesn't want to. She may want to be clear of all of this."

"OK. How's she doing?"

"Fine. Gets on well with the girls. Even persuaded them to come to church. She's talking about going to school with them. But there's a slight problem there. How much should we be advertising her presence here?"

"I'd say, as little as possible. She could be called as a witness in Dublin, and there are people who may want to stop her from talking. At the moment we need to keep her presence here as discreet as possible. Is she aware of that herself, do you think?"

"Yes, we had a chat about that this morning before she went to church. And got her a cover story. Her name's Renée, and she's a Slovak student who's been an au pair for a cousin of Alasdair's and has come over to improve her English, and maybe learn a bit of Gaelic."

"That sounds good. The school might want a bit more though."

"We'll have to work something up for that. I've suggested she chills out for this week and thinks about starting a week tomorrow. So we've got a bit of time."

As Blue left the church, he walked into a thick mist of persistent drizzle, seemingly far wetter than any straightforward rain. Even the weather was hiding something. He drove carefully back to the hotel and took a glass of 12-year old Talisker – from Skye rather than Islay, but dense enough to fit there – to a table in the lounge, and a chance to think things through.

Whatever the truth of the matter, Ffox-Kaye had effectively sewn the case up. Salebi was innocent – of that he was sure – but that seemed to matter little when political interests demanded the case be tied up and put away. As indeed, Salebi would be, as the perfect fall guy. The second victim and the mysterious German would just be swept under the carpet. Was that why it had to be tied up quickly? Lest the identity of the second man came out?

It was clear to Blue that sometime on Monday his investigation would be closed. How soon would simply depend on when the CC got the official notification from London, and when he got round to passing that on to Superintendent Campbell. With luck they might still have the morning. Perhaps telling Police Scotland would not be Ffox-Kaye's top priority.

He had hoped the German couple could be tracked down, but it seemed they too had slipped through his fingers. Without them he had little else.

The TV was on in the corner of the lounge, not too loudly to intrude into anyone's conversation, but enough to be a comfort to those for whom silence was oppressive. He stared at it without taking in what was being shown, then began to wonder what it was. Persons whom he did not recognise but were evidently famous were being taught how to make their own soap. The celebrities were concentrating as much on getting in their pre-scripted quips and smutty allusions to the viscosity or otherwise of the mixtures they were producing.

Next came the News. The main item was the abrupt cancellation of the royal tour of Scotland. The reason given was the royals' concern for Prince Arthur, a grandson of the queen, who had fallen off his horse during a hunt, and been taken to an exclusive hospital somewhere in Kent. The extent of his injuries was not specified. This all sounded too convenient to Blue, a great excuse to get out of a Progress that wasn't making much progress.

The next item was Salebi's confession to the Steppingham shooting. Ffox-Kaye clearly relished being interviewed by a reporter keen to lay out for the public the details of a terrorist atrocity. He described how, while local investigations were going nowhere – "not that I'm blaming our regional colleagues, they were doing their best" – secret intelligence sources had led his team fairly quickly to the door of the shooter. This was an Arab who had made his way into the UK masquerading as a refugee, with the sole purpose of killing a key member of the Cabinet. That he failed in his attempt, only wounding his target, showed a lack of professionalism which was typical of the Middle Eastern mindset. A photograph of Salebi was shown, and Blue noted that the description he had of Salebi was of a man who was neat and clean-shaven, yet the man in the picture had a day's growth of dark stubble and bags under his eyes, enough to make him look like the suspicious foreigner we were right to take him for.

There followed an interview with the Home Secretary, who emphasised that these events demonstrated exactly why it was crucial for the well-being of our population that much stricter controls were applied on who could come into the country. "And only Britain is competent to determine what those controls should be," she concluded.

When the report moved on to a celebrity divorce, Blue switched off and went to bed.

Day 8. Monday

48

He was at the police station at 8 am. Bhardwaj was on reception.

"Hi Arvind."

"Morning, chief, are we still on the case?"

"For the moment. But it's only a matter of time before we're shut down."

"And back to dogshit patrol for me."

"You won't be here for ever, Arvind. Enjoy it while you can. You'll get your weekends back."

"Ah yes," muttered Bhardwaj to himself. "Must phone Rhoda." Then to Blue. "I was thinking of asking her to come with me, to walk to that plague village you mentioned."

"Solam? Yes, it's well worth it. You…"

The phone rang. Bhardwaj grabbed it after one ring.

"Hello. Islay Police…"

He stopped and handed the phone to Blue. "The boss, I mean, Inspector Nicolson, for you."

Blue took the phone. "Hi Moira…"

"Angus, we've got him!"

"Sorry? Who?"

"The mystery man. He was on the news this morning, on the TV. We were having breakfast. We normally listen to the news on the radio, but to help Radina with her English, it's better with the pictures. She recognised him right away. Something about his chin, she said. She was frantic, I had to give her something to calm down. Well, a mug of Baileys was all I could find. I guess that's safer than pills. Alison will stay with her. She's scared out of her wits."

"Who is he?"

"Didn't I say? That royal who's in hospital. Supposedly fell off his horse. Prince Arthur."

"Shit! No wonder they wanted to keep it quiet. Is she sure about it?"

"Absolutely. Then Alison found his picture on the web, and she confirmed it again. HRH Prince Arthur is our third man."

"So he may have been the target rather than Steppingham. This isn't good."

"Got to go now, Angus. But I'll be in before nine. I guess you need to do some thinking now."

He handed the phone back to Bhardwaj, who put it down.

"Sounds like they've identified our third man. Anyone we know?"

"His Royal Highness Prince Arthur."

"You mean that one who's in hospital?"

"That's the one. Listen, Arvind, not a word of this anyone, understand, till you hear more from me. We'll meet as soon as everyone's in. Meanwhile, can you find anything out about this Prince Arthur?"

"OK, chief, no problem. I'd better not phone Rhoda just yet then."

"I think you can assume that next weekend's OK. This makes it even more likely we'll be closed down in a hurry."

At nine he met with Nicolson, McCader, Bhardwaj and Craig in the upstairs room he'd used as a base the last time he was on Islay. The table and chairs were still there, though somewhat dusty. The door was firmly shut.

"OK, people, we have a breakthrough. We know the other victim was Prince Arthur."

Given that three of the five present already knew this, it was only McCader and Craig whose reactions were spontaneous.

"Jeezes," gasped Craig.

McCader stared thoughtfully at the table.

"Arvind," said Blue, "Tell us a little about Prince Arthur."

"OK, chief. He's ninth in line to the throne. Also the Duke of Stratford and Earl of Skye. Now aged 27. Usual upbringing. Prep school then Westminster, a year at Cambridge, then Sandhurst. Two years in Germany as a lieutenant, then promoted to captain and in Afghanistan for six months, came back a major, now assigned to staff duties, at the army base on Salisbury Plain. Occasionally travels round the world promoting British companies, mainly arms manufacturers. Unmarried. Dogged by scandals surrounding his private life: drugs, wild parties, hints of violent sex. Hobbies: fox hunting, shooting animals of any kind, likes to watch cage-fighting. Rumours that he liked shooting people in Afghanistan. Enjoys holidays at our expense in the Caribbean, surrounded by girls of a pneumatic disposition. Provides a good argument for the abolition of the monarchy. The last bit was my opinion."

"Thank you, Arvind. A good summing-up, brief and to the point. And you wisely identified the bit that was your own personal view. Any comments?"

"This is real trouble, chief," said McCader. "It's political, it was from the moment HRH was shot, we just didn't realise that."

"What do you mean?" asked Moira Nicolson.

"This isn't a crime investigation. It's about protecting the ruling class and its totems. They've tried from the start to prevent us knowing that the prince was a victim. No wonder they weren't happy with us sniffing about. May I offer some advice, sir? I have some experience of how these people – I mean the security services – work. Drop everything right now. Close the case yourself, if you can."

"Flee to South America?" said Bhardwaj.

"I'm not joking, Arvind. This is serious. Right now, we know too much. If they think we suspect, it could make us targets too. The hunting injury story is a cover. For whatever reason, they don't want it known that he was shot."

"You mean it might have been an inside job?" asked Moira.

"That doesn't automatically follow. There could be all sorts of reasons. If it were a terrorist thing, they wouldn't want it known that a royal had been taken out. That would be too much of a coup for the terrorists, even if the shooter was caught."

"But we're not sure it was a terrorist thing," said Blue.

"No, you're right there, chief. I suspect if it were, whoever did it would be shouting to the world what they've done. But there's been nothing. An inside job? No, I doubt that too. They'd have made it look more like an accident."

"He really would have fallen off his horse?" said Craig.

"Yes, something like that."

"But they still don't know who did it, do they?" said Blue. "They've got hold of Salebi, and will pin the Steppingham shooting on him. But they're not bringing Prince Arthur into it at all."

" That can be easily explained," said McCader. "It could simply be a matter of keeping the royals away from controversy, sustaining the myth that they have nothing to do with real life, that they're above all the humdrum stuff, and especially crime and politics. They're world celebrities, after all. Plus, if one got shot, it shows the

231

police failed to protect him, and heads would have to roll."

"But we still don't know who the target of the shooting was," said Bhardwaj. "I mean, maybe it was still Steppingham, and the prince just happened to be there for a dirty weekend. Wrong place, wrong time."

"If that were the case," said Moira, "Even more reason to keep him out of it. Enver's right. These are special people. If he just happened to get in the way of someone else's shooting, that would hardly do his celebrity ratings any good. Every part of their lives has to be a drama, with them as the stars. So if he's injured, a dramatic fall from a horse, as he springs over a hedge, leading the hunt..."

"And the fox disnae realise how privileged he is," added Craig.

"Quite," put in Blue. "I think we have to assume for the moment that the prince, as the bigger fish of the two, was the target. But there could be another explanation for leaving him out of the story. What if the reason for the shooting is nothing to do with terrorism? What if it's something else, that publicity about the prince being shot would drag into the daylight. And it's that something else that has to be covered up."

"Taking bribes to endorse products, maybe," said Nicolson. "Not directly, of course, but by being accidentally photographed using the product. Or mentioning it to someone who passes that titbit on to the celebrity mags. Big companies would pay a lot of money for a royal endorsement. Not like the old 'By Royal Appointment' thing you used to see on pots of jam.

"There's another possible angle," said McCader. "Van Kaarsten worked for an arms company. Maybe they were working out some deal. If that came out, it wouldn't look good at all."

"Could that be a motive for the shooting?" suggested Bhardwaj.

"One thing about the shooting still puzzles me," said Moira Nicolson. "Whoever the target was, the gunman failed. Surely a professional assassin would have got his man."

"Maybe he did!" said McCader. "What if the prince were the target, and he is in fact killed? It's Steppingham who gets in the way. The prince's body is then smuggled off the island along with Steppingham. It's kept on ice somewhere until they can think up a story as to what's happened to him."

"So sooner or later, they'll announce that he's died of his injuries?" said Craig.

"Exactly. After a valiant struggle and tremendous efforts by heroic surgeons to save him. Then someone purporting to be a nurse at the hospital will leak to the media a graphic account of it all. The prince's bravery as they operate without anaesthetic."

"If that leg has to come off, do it now, doc, just gimme another slug of whisky," added Bhardwaj. The joke relieved the tension that had been building up as the discussion went on. They leaned back in their seats, letting the whole thing settle into their heads.

Blue broke the silence. "OK. We've opened up a whole can of worms here. The question is, what do we do about it. Or what can we do about it?"

"We've got be very careful," said McCader. "As I said, we could become targets."

"Are you serious?" asked Moira.

"Absolutely. If the falling off the horse thing is going to be the official story, anyone who knows the real story is in danger. They need to be kept quiet. It wouldn't surprise me if we start to see people who witnessed the shooting having unfortunate accidents. And if they know we know the prince was involved, it makes us targets too. The very first thing we have to do is to keep absolutely quiet about it."

"And you think I should close the case?"

"Yes. Admit defeat, announce that Ffox-Kaye got it right after all. I know you won't like that, chief, but the sooner we revert to the part of dumb plods, the better. If they think we're idiots, they're more likely to forget about us."

"I'll have to think about that," said Blue, "But Enver's right. Certainly for the moment, we have to keep this to ourselves. Moira, who else knows at your house? Apart from Radina, that is?"

"Only me and Alison. Alasdair was already in the study working, and Anna and Eilidh were upstairs getting ready for school. Nothing was said to them before they went off."

"OK. Phone Alison now. Make sure she tells Radina not to say anything to anyone, not even the girls. But you should tell Alasdair. He needs to understand what Radina's going through. And he's your husband."

"Thanks, Angus, I'll do that now." Moira immediately got up and went off to her office.

"Let's break for half an hour," said Blue to the others, "I need to think about this."

Blue's mobile had been on silent, and as he took it out in his office, he noticed the alert light winking. A text from Jill Henderson: "call when conv." Once he had a cup of coffee steaming on his desk, Blue phoned Jill.

"Hi, chief. I've confirmed the Polish car was on the boat from North Shields."

"Good."

"But I've also got from DFDS a name. He had to give his name and passport number when he made the initial booking. This was checked when he arrived at the terminal in Amsterdam. Hanno Attmann."

It didn't sound very Turkish to Blue, but he wasn't sure what a Turkish name should sound like. If the man was in fact Turkish, or of Turkish origin, that is. He only had Piłsudski's informant's word on that.

"OK. So unless he has a false passport, that's his real name. Did they have an address too?"

"Yes. Let me read it out: Bauernstraße 67, Frankfurt-Oder, Germany." She spelled out the street name.

"Did they check the address?"

"No. He paid online, and they sent his ticket by email. Do you think the address is false?"

"We'll need to check it out. But it could well be genuine. After all, if he had to give his real name and passport number, there wouldn't be any point lying about his address. Thanks Jill, well done."

"Shall I email you that information, so you've got it spelt right?"

"No, don't do that. In fact, destroy any bits of paper with that information on it, and delete your correspondence with DFDS. Given that the Met have solved the case, they won't take kindly to any work we've done subsequent to their announcement of that."

He asked to be passed on to Steve Belford, and instructed him to suspend any scene-of-crime analysis related to the shooting or the fire, until it became clear whether they should proceed with the cases.

He now knew that he had the name and address of the shooter in front of him. He pulled up a map of Germany on his laptop. Frankfurt on the Oder. Right on the eastern edge of Germany. And just over the border was Słubice, in Poland.

He called Piłsudski.

"Tadeusz, we have a name and address for the man who bought the car. Hanno Attmann, Bauernstraße 67, Frankfurt-Oder."

"Ha! The man is clever. He gives a far away address to *Pan* Kowalski, so that we don't suspect he lives just across the river. Leave it to me. I will personally have a look at this address. Don't worry, my friend, I will do nothing to alert him. After all, it is not in my jurisdiction. I'm just a jealous Pole who drifts up the street looking at how our wealthy neighbours live."

The meeting reconvened. Blue began.

"I know that Enver has advised us strongly to close the case, but I'm not going to do it right away. As Enver hinted, that would be out of character for me, and that might just make them pause to think, why do I give up so easily. Then they might begin to suspect we know something. I don't know how paranoid they are, but we shouldn't take the risk. Instead, however, we'll continue with our current lines of investigation until we've told to stop. Then I'll grumble about it, but do it."

"That seems reasonable," added Moira. "But won't they start to worry too if they think we're on to the guy who actually did it? They might suspect that if we identify him, and reach him before they do, that he might reveal to us his motives, and that might involve revelations about the prince that they don't want to come out."

"That's a good point, Moira. Thankfully I haven't put my report onto the police hub for a couple of days, so they don't know how far along we are with that. I'll keep it that way."

"Doesn't it really annoy you, Angus, having to slow down, even stop, when you've got good leads to follow?"

"Yes, it really does, Moira, it really does. But we all know from the case of the Peat Dead last year how far these people will go. I can't risk any of you. We have to be realistic, and know our limitations. It's especially irritating that Ahmed Salebi will be jailed for something he probably didn't do. That the reputation of the upper class will be put before justice. That a man who is probably innocent will suffer."

"Chief, I don't mind going on with it," began Deirdra Craig, and Blue could see Bhardwaj next to her nodding vigorously.

"Don't say any more!" he interrupted. "I know we've all worked hard on this one, but there comes a point where it gets foolish to poke an ants' nest too much. Whatever we do, we can't kill all the ants. No more active work on this case, and that's an order. Can you two start organising all the paperwork and other material we've got and put it in cardboard boxes. It'll have to go to the basement in Oban where all the dead cases live."

"It won't survive there long," said McCader. "Ffox-Kaye will borrow it, to 'reconcile it with his own work', and it'll never be returned. Then one day all reference to it will magically disappear from the Police Scotland databases. It'll never have happened."

"One other thing," said Moira, "During the break I, as the local police commander, got an email from Ffox-Kaye's office. He's had the fire investigation report diverted to himself 'as it seemed clear the fire was a terrorist act'. He's also ordered all the scene-of-crime material and reports to be transferred to his unit, and has had the site placed under close guard, in case of further incidents."

"Interesting," commented Blue, "But after what we've been talking about, I'm not surprised. Everything to do with this business is going to be off limits to us. And we need to go along with it."

"Even if somebody was killed?" said Deirdra, it doesna seem right."

"It's not, Deirdra. But I'm not putting our lives in danger."

"Do we know who the dead man in the house was?" asked Bhardwaj.

"My suspicion is that it was Jack Seymour. He's probably seen too much, or knew too much. Perhaps he was killed then left in the building. Ffox-Kaye will conclude that the fire was accidental, and that Seymour was trying to put it out and got caught up in it."

"Or that he was the instigator," added McCader. "They could easily produce fake testimony suggesting Seymour had very radical views. That would wrap it up nicely."

The meeting ended. Blue could tell they were all dissatisfied. Not with him, but with the way in which the case was being interfered with by those whose concern had nothing to do with justice.

49

Blue made a few additions to his report on the Police Scotland Hub. It would look odd if he was completely silent, when he normally updated regularly. But he added very little to the one he had submitted three days previously. He indicated that his visit to Steppingham only confirmed facts already known, and that the trip to Ireland had proved a dead end, throwing no light on the events at Dunrighinn. He mentioned the fire at the House, noting that it was still a case for the local police until a crime had been proved. He concluded that, having been informed of Ahmed Salebi's confession to the shooting, he had immediately suspended his team's activities on the case.

At half past eleven, Superintendent Campbell phoned.

"Hi Angus. I'm sorry to say that the order has just reached me from the CC. The Steppingham Case is now closed. I was glad to see in your report this morning that you've suspended work on it already in view of the confession. And it won't surprise you to learn that the closure also applies to the Dunrighinn Fire Case."

"Yes, sir, I heard that from Inspector Nicholson. What's the reason they're giving?"

"National security. The case will be taken over by the anti-terrorist division at the Met. Inspector Plaistow will be in charge. All the physical material on both cases has to be handed over to DCI Ffox-Kaye by five o'clock this evening. Or rather, to a couple of his creatures who'll come to Oban to collect it. And I'd like a word with you in my office tomorrow morning sometime. We all need to be singing from the same sheet on this one."

He went down to the workroom and informed Bhardwaj, Craig and McCader that the cases were now closed, and asked McCader to check the material as it was boxed, and shred anything that he felt might give the impression that they knew too much.

"I think I should take out any reference to Radina and the other girls, sir. We wouldn't want any comeback on them from this."

"Yes, good idea. No point in clogging the files with irrelevant information, is there?"

"One further thing, sir, if I could have a word in private."

Ten minutes later, he knocked on Moira Nicolson's door.

"Hi Moira. I'm sorry we've hit the buffers on this one. But I think I need to talk to Radina before I go. Would you like to come too?"

They drove over to Moira's house. On the way Blue repeated to Moira what the Super had said to him.

"Is he on our side?" Moira asked.

"Oh, yes. I trust him. You told me once your exile was here. His is Oban."

They met Alison and Radina in the big high-ceilinged living room at the front of the house. Motes of dust floated in the wedge of sunlight resting on the carpet by the window. There was a distant sound of the sea. Steam drifted lazily upward from their mugs of coffee. To Blue this peacefulness was absurd. In a film of these events the music would be discordant, threatening, hinting at the troublous nature of the point they had reached, at the danger they might all be in.

For a few moments they sipped the coffee in silence. The tension grew.

Radina spoke first. "It was him, this prince. I know it. I am sure. But I am frightened. I know too much. Now they will surely try to kill me."

"Radina," replied Blue, "your information has made this case a lot clearer for us. But your identification of the prince has not been revealed, and the case is now closed. You will not be required to testify about it. Only a very small number of people know about your identification of the prince, and they will say nothing. Very few people know you are here, and we'll keep it that way."

"But what happens when Radina goes to school?" said Alison. "Surely her identity will come out then, and questions might be asked."

"This is between the four of us," said Blue. "Sergeant McCader has offered to obtain, from sources known to him, a passport and other documentation for Radina, under a suitable name, depending on which country she prefers to come from. He suggests that a Slovakian passport could be obtained quite quickly. We will have to work carefully to construct an identity for her that can be shared with everyone. Is that OK with you, Radina?"

Radina nodded apprehensively. "Then I must speak the correct language."

"Slovak is a Slavic language, like Bulgarian," said Moira. "So the general structure will be familiar. But there will be differences in grammar and especially vocabulary. You wouldn't need to speak like a native, especially on Islay. English with a foreign accent will do fine. But it would certainly be worth knowing some Slovak, and coming out with a phrase now and then."

"I'll get a copy of *Teach Yourself Slovak* as soon as I get back to Stirling," said Alison, "and post it here. I think that would be more discreet than Moira ordering it locally. This is a great opportunity, Radina. Very few people get the chance to become a new person."

Whilst Moira talked further with Radina, Blue and Alison walked out the front door of the house and sat together on a home-made wooden bench on the lawn, with a view down to the road and then on to the jagged rocks, above which the occasional shower of spray marked the edge of the never-still waters in which Islay sat. Blue related what had happened that morning.

"So it's all over?" said Alison.

"I don't know," said Blue. "I know the case is closed. But the game they're playing, that isn't over yet. It will play out over the next few days."

"But what about you, Angus? Is it over for you?"

"What do you think, Alison?"

"I'm getting to know you quite well, Angus. I don't think this is over for you. I think you want to see justice done. But it isn't clear how you can do that, is it? Without putting others in danger, I mean."

"I think you do know me. Yes, there's a worry inside me about this case, but I know that right at the moment I have to suppress it. Though not for ever. I'll think of something."

"We'll think of something," said Alison, letting her hand slip into his.

50

Blue invited Alison, Moira, Enver, Arvind and Deirdra to lunch at the Chinese restaurant. They all knew not to mention any details of the case in a public place. Blue thanked them for their work on the case, and wished them all the best for the future. He could still sense the frustration at having to give up the work before it was completed, and took pains to assure them that these things happened.

"Life isn't always like crime stories on the telly, where at five to nine the detective inspector announces the name of the guilty party, explains how it was done and ties up all the loose ends. Sometimes you work your ass off, and then it's all chucked in the bin, because somebody contaminated the crime scene, or a witness is too scared to testify, or somebody's name was mis-spelt in the court papers. Or, as in this case, because somebody higher up decides for reasons of their own, to close it down. Sometimes the case goes to trial and right through to a conviction, and then the judge decides to give the villain a lenient sentence, because he was taken in by the crook's weeping remorse, or because he plays golf with his father.

"But what makes the job worth while is that a lot of cases we win, and we see justice being done. And there's nobody but us whose job it is to make that happen. While the judges and advocates focus on the law, our job is about good and evil. It's about catching people who do bad things, because they're stupid or drunk or crazy, and trying to persuade them not to do it again. And occasionally it's about catching people who are just plain bad, evil right through, and trying to put them away for ever.

"There's never an end to the battle, a point where all the bad guys have finally been defeated. But we win enough to make our society a safe-ish place for ordinary people to live in. And all of you will play a part in that. You are colleagues that I'm proud to work with. So let's drink to us!"

After the meal several cardboard boxes were packed into the pool car McCader had brought from Oban several days previously, and Blue and McCader set off for the ferry. Alison had decided to stay on with Moira for a couple more days, to help Radina flesh out her new identity.

They talked very little on the journey. The boxes were left at reception at the Police HQ for collection by Ffox-Kaye's men, and they went home, McCader to his family and Blue to a poached egg and a slice of Stornoway Black Pudding on toast. And page 1 of *Die Toten ohne Schatten*.

Day 9. Tuesday

51

Blue was at his office at nine, and was called up to the Super's office at ten-thirty.

"Angus, come in, sit yourself down, like some coffee? Did you hear the news?"

"Thanks, chief, yes I would, and no, I haven't. What'd happened?"

"It seems Lord Steppingham has just died of his wounds. It was announced at ten-fifteen by a Home Office spokesperson."

"I thought he was recovering. Alice Rogers said it was a fairly straightforward shoulder wound, and a bit of hospital treatment would sort it out."

"He never left the hospital. Apparently it got worse, and blood poisoning set in. There were complications because of his underlying medical conditions, and they couldn't save him. It looks like that nurse will be investigated for negligent treatment at the scene. Not cleaning the wound sufficiently."

"Do you believe that, sir?"

"Do you, Angus?"

"Is this just between ourselves, sir?"

"Fire away."

"My impression of the nurse was that she was pretty competent, and I can't imagine someone like Steppingham hiring somebody without checking them out thoroughly. I just feel that Ffox-Kaye and his crowd are tying up loose ends on this case. It suits them to have his Lordship dead."

"That seems a bit extreme." Campbell looked appraisingly at Blue. "Is there something else you know, Angus? Don't answer that. If there is something, and it's not supported by cast-iron evidence, don't tell me. There won't be anything I can do about it, and that'll be another person you'll have to trust not to spill the beans later on. What I do realise perfectly well is that there's more to this case than meets the eye. But we'se firmly out of the loop now, and if we raise any new issues about it, we won't be thanked for it, and there'll be trouble. Stay safe, Angus, keep quiet. In fact, the best thing you can do now is get on with some routine stuff. We've had a tip-off about some illegal fish landings down in Tarbert. Immature mackerel, tons of it, apparently. Can you look into that?"

"Yes, chief, of course. Right away."

Blue was back in his office, staring out the window at the back yard of the Scotia Hotel, when his mobile rang.

"Greetings from Wrocław, my friend! How are you?"

"A little down, Tadeusz. Our case was closed, by order from above. They got a confession, but I don't think he did it."

"Yes. It's not easy to argue against a confession. And sometimes dangerous. From what you've told me, it seems these political policemen want to make a tidy parcel of the affair. A rotting fish in a plastic bag has no smell. You know that in Soviet Poland plastic bags were in short supply. The smell was everywhere. So maybe you don't want to hear about my little trip to Frankfurt on the Oder."

"Tell me anyway."

"Bauernstraße is a street near the edge of the town, quite long, and with separate little houses on it. Each one in a little garden. Some big, some small. Some well-kept, others not so good."

"And number 67?"

"A small house. The garden is large, but a little overgrown. One level, with an extra room in the roof."

"A bungalow?"

"Quite so. Exactly. Bungalow. The condition is OK, but perhaps it needs painted."

"Any sign of occupants?"

"I think there is only one man lives there. I saw him in the garden at the back. An older man, maybe fifty or more, but slim and fit. The way he holds himself, I would say he has been a soldier. Very upright. I called to him, said I was trying to find my cousin who lived in that street, or maybe the next one. He was very courteous. His German is very good, I think he has grown up there. I would guess his father came from Turkey, maybe married a German girl. His eye is sharp, he is an intelligent man. But I believe there is a sadness too, his garden speaks of it. He tends it, but without pride. To employ himself."

"You think he could be our shooter?"

"It's possible. There is nothing about him that makes me think he is not suitable. What would you like me to do next? Perhaps I drive by with *Pan* Kowalski and see if he recognises him."

"No, I'd rather we left it there for the moment. I'll have to think about what can be done. If anything."

"OK, my friend, just let me know, and I act immediately. And if nothing happens, well, why not come and see me anyway? Have a holiday."

The news that evening on the internet reported that Lord Steppingham had died, following complications to his wounds. The impression was given that he had been hit by several bullets. Questions of competence were being raised regarding the nurse who had treated him at the scene of the shooting. Consequent to his death, the investigation into the shooting had become a homicide enquiry, and Ahmed Salebi, who had confessed to the shooting, would now be charged with murder.

Meanwhile, His Royal Highness Prince Arthur remained in a stable condition in hospital. He had suffered serious head injuries when he fell from his horse, and the staff were doing everything they could to save him. His brother, sister and father visited him in hospital, but would not comment when they emerged. Later a royal spokeswoman stated that the whole family were encouraged by the Prince's courageous struggle despite his very serious injuries, and they would continue to hope that a recovery might be possible.

Later that evening he phoned Alison. Eventually he came to the point.

"Er, Alison, there was something I was going to ask you, and I…"

"Yes, Angus I'd love to.

"But you haven't even heard it yet."

"It took you so long to get round to it that it must be something that you're nervous about asking. You're afraid I might say no. So you're not just going to ask me to go to the pictures with you. My guess is you're going to suggest we go off for a few days together. To a quiet hotel somewhere scenic. A walk during the day and a cosy evening, just us together in front of an open peat fire. That's what I'm hoping anyway."

"Er, yes, that was it. And you'll come?"

"You haven't said where yet."

"Berlin."

"Wow! Yes, that wasn't quite what I was expecting, but I'm sure it'll do nicely. Though I'm wondering why Berlin. There's an agenda here and I'm beginning to suspect what it is."

"Well, there is something I need to do there, and…"

"And you thought you'll kill two birds with one stone. You're such a romantic. If it wasn't that I suspect I know what you're up to, I'd tell you where you can stuff your little break. But I'm curious. And I like you. So I'll come. On one condition."

"What's that?"

"That I come along with you on whatever it is you 'need to do' there."

"It might be dangerous. Or get you into trouble."

"Take it or leave it."

"I'll take it, I mean, you. Thank you."

"One other thing, Angus, I'm sure you're wondering about. I think one room will do for us. But make sure it's a good one. I need space for the dog."

"But you don't have a dog."

"That's just as well then, isn't it?"

Days 10-16. Wednesday-Tuesday

52

The rest of that week, Blue had busied himself with the illegal fish landings. Tarbert is now a picturesque village with a large quayside that had once seen large quantities of fish landed. In the off-season it's very quiet, and even a white van creeping about during the night would be spotted from behind a dozen twitching curtains, and become a topic of conversation for days. A battered long-wheelbase transit van with a dodgy gearbox, defective silencer and a refrigeration unit stuck on top could hardly advertise itself more, and was soon identified and traced to a freelance fish dealer, who was selling the mackerel on to a factory in an industrial estate near Lochgilphead that made fish cakes and paté for budget supermarkets. Faced with some difficult choices, the dealer decided to tell all.

On the Friday Blue had asked the Super for a few days off, in the following week, to which the latter immediately agreed. "I rather hinted you needed to get away for a bit when I saw you on Tuesday," he said. "I'm glad you've taken it on board. Where are you off to? The Western Isles, I'd guess."

"Berlin, actually."

"Oh. Ah, yes, of course, lot of history there, isn't there? That's your thing too, isn't it? Do you speak German?"

"Just a bit. Thought it would be good to polish it up."

"Anything in particular you want to see there?"

"Thought I might take a look round Tempelhof Airport. The terminal is the largest fascist building still standing. I'm told it's enormous. The airport's where the planes flew into during the airlift. Then there's the villa where the Wannsee conference took place. You know, where the Nazis discussed the practicalities of ex-terminating the Jews. The DDR Museum. And the house where…"

"Sounds like you've plenty to see, then. But don't overdo it, Angus. You need to chill out a bit too."

"Yes, you're right. I've heard there's good walking in the Spreewald, and then…"

"Great! Well, no problem with those dates. Make sure you enjoy yourself."

He worked on Monday, and packed in the evening. As he was relaxing with a glass of 14-year-old Oban whisky and page 6 of *Die Toten ohne Schatten*, his mobile rang.

"Angus, hi, Geoff Rackham here. Got some news for you, but you didn't hear it from me."

"OK. Fire away."

"It's not good, I'm afraid. Alice Rogers, the nurse who had treated Lord Steppingham's wounds."

"Yes?"

"Found dead this morning, in her room at Steppingham House. Looks like suicide. Paracetamol and codeine washed down with vodka. Probably yesterday evening sometime."

"What do you think?"

"Looks like she did it herself. No disturbance in the room. Suicide note in her own handwriting. Says she couldn't take the stress of the negligence inquiry. Phone records show several calls to her mobile between 8 and 10 pm last night from an unknown number. Pay-as-you-go mobile that couldn't be traced. We've checked with her friends and relatives. No-one says they called her that evening. I would guess somebody put a lot of pressure on her, enough to tip her over the edge."

"Is it possible that someone could have got into her room and forced her to write the note and take the pills?"

"It's just possible, though there's no evidence to suggest that. And she states again in the note that she wasn't negligent. I think if she'd been forced, they'd have made her confess to it."

"She wasn't negligent. She simply knew too much."

"What do you mean?"

"She knew Steppingham had only one wound, and that he was likely to recover. Once she'd dressed the wound, she didn't even need to go with him in the car to the airport."

"You're suggesting that something went wrong while Steppingham was in hospital."

Blue knew he had to be careful what he said. "It does seem that way. She knew that he wouldn't have died from the injuries he had, and she would have asserted that at the negligence inquiry, and given the precise medical details. The implication of that could be that something happened to him in the hospital, so they needed to shut her up."

"Like an infection or something. Yes, I can see that that would look bad in view of the government's underfunding of the NHS. But driving her to suicide. That's abominable."

"So what are you going to do on Alice Rogers then?"

"Nothing. We've already been told from higher up that it's an open-and-shut case of suicide, and that's that. I tried to set up an interview with Steppingham at the hospital, but I got put straight through to someone in the Political Protection Unit who told me in no uncertain terms that I was poking my nose into security matters. An hour later I got a bollocking on the phone from my CC, for interfering with the business of other forces."

Blue set off at seven-thirty on Tuesday morning from Oban, and drove to Stirling, where Alison was waiting for him outside her flat near the town centre. They then went on to Edinburgh Airport, left the car in the long-stay car park, and checked in for their flight with a German budget airline. They were in Berlin's Schönefeldt Airport, having gained an hour on the clock, by 3 pm. They took a bus from the airport towards the city centre, Blue studying the public transport map, and got off on an anonymous boulevard with blocks of modern flats on both sides. The hotel faced the bus stop, a white modern building of four or five floors, with regular square windows. There were however, four semicircular bays jutting out from each floor, at regular intervals, giving the impression of four towers set into the structure. The room Blue had booked was of the 'Superior' type, a bright and spacious area that included one of the bays.

"Right," said Alison, when they'd put their bags down, "the room is fine. I'm relieved to find that I like it. Now I'm going to have a wash. Then I'd like for us to go for a walk, to get some fresh air. Then we'll go for a meal, and it would be nice then if you were to tell me exactly what we're doing here."

Later that evening, they ate in a Mexican restaurant not far from the hotel. All the patrons seemed to be locals, and the staff spoke only German and Spanish. They sat at a corner table. There was no-one nearby. Everyone spoke quietly. Blue hated loud people in restaurants, who made with their own egoism everyone else's meal a torture.

"All right," said Blue. "Can you guess why we're here and not in Barra or Berneray?"

"It's about the man in the Polish car, isn't it? He gave an address in Berlin. And you want to visit him, don't you? Let me think. You just want to have a chat with him, see what he says, see whether you think he's the shooter. Just for your own satisfaction, of course, nothing official. Am I right?"

"Am I that obvious?"

"Only to me, Angus. I'd like to see what he says too. But I'd also like to enjoy this trip, and not have you focused on the case all the time. Part of me wanted to tell you where to get off when I realised why we were coming here, but another part of me wanted to see where the Polish car led. And there's also a bit of me, and I'm not sure yet how big a bit, that doesn't mind where I go if it's with you. So assure me that there's some space for us here."

"Alison, I do appreciate you coming here despite your misgivings. I want to be able to share the case with you, and see what we can find. But that's not all we'e here for. Visiting this guy will take one day, that's Thursday. That means we've got tomorrow and then Friday and Saturday completely at our disposal."

Day 17. Wednesday

53

The following morning, about 10.45, as they sat in a boat on the river Spree, passing the government buildings, Blue's mobile rang. He listened for a few minutes, responding in monosyllables, then thanked the speaker and rang off.

"Who was that?" asked Alison, "Some new development?"

"That was Geoff Rackham. Eric James, Lord Steppingham's secretary, has vanished. Geoff tried to get hold of him yesterday, but they couldn't find him at the house. He went round first thing this morning and found he's done a runner. Taken as much of his stuff as he could get in his car, and driven off. Reckons it was not long after they found Alice Rogers."

"Did he kill her?"

"Geoff doesn't think so. He believes Mr James was scared the same thing would happen to him. That he'd be 'persuaded' to commit suicide."

"Will he get away?"

"I doubt it, not unless he's very clever. These people can track his phone, his bank cards, and his passport, and that's just for starters. His best bet would be to have a stash of cash ready, bin his phone and bank cards, drive to Luton Airport and take the first flight out, preferably to South America. Then he can change his name and set himself up as a teacher of English in some small town, and hope to make a modest living. But always with the fear that sooner or later they'll track him down."

"Maybe they already have."

"That's possible. If that is the case – say they were already watching him and picked him up as soon as left the house – then he could easily disappear for good, and we'll never find out. He'd be just another guy who ran away."

"It's like the Kennedy assassination," observed Alison. "You know, all the people who died in freak accidents in the months after the shooting. There are people who claim they were all killed."

"It could be they want to clear the decks, so to speak, just get rid of anyone who was actually present at the shooting. Except, of course, themselves."

"Can't we warn them, you know, to look out?"

"Who'd believe us? We'd just be branded daft conspiracy theorists, or mentally unstable. Then we'd become the target. Suspension from work, disciplinary charges, breaches of the Official Secrets Act. Or worse."

"Who do you think will be next?"

"All depends who knows who was there that weekend. The only other people who saw the shooting were the pilots. Helicopters can crash so easily. But today we're not on the case. Would you like another hot chocolate with rum?"

Day 18. Thursday

54

The news was in all the papers, German as well as British, that morning. The previous evening HRH Prince Arthur had died, after a desperate struggle against terrible injuries. It was revealed by a Palace spokeswoman that in the fall from his horse he had broken his back. Despite the prospect that if he lived he would have been paralysed at least from the waist down, and maybe even from the neck, he had faced the future with unbending fortitude and constant good humour.

No comment was yet forthcoming from the royal family themselves, but the prime minister had early that morning given a statement outside 10 Downing Street. Statement was the wrong word, thought Blue as he watched it, performance a more accurate description. At times the premier's voice faltered with perfectly honed emotion, and at one point he took out a neatly folded and ironed white handkerchief and dabbed the corner of one eye. Politicians and celebrities alike queued up to air their practised grief in the public arena. The morning chat shows would no doubt echo with weeping and wailing. The BBC had cancelled all programmes for that evening apart from news bulletins, and would broadcast a two-and-a-half-hour documentary on the prince's life. It would be followed by a reshowing of the charity episode of *People Can Dance*, in which the prince, despite tripping over his partner's feet a couple of times and elbowing her in the face, won the contest with a spirited rumba, and raised £20,000 for good causes.

The state funeral was scheduled for the Saturday of the following week, with kings, queens, presidents, sheiks, sultans and other heads of state expressing their eagerness to attend. Only the leaders of Iran and North Korea were not invited. The London hotels were over-joyed at this unexpected bonanza, and raised their prices accordingly.

Blue and Alison had seen the news before breakfast, and did not mention it during the meal, taken in the hotel's self-service buffet area.

"Thank you so much for yesterday, Angus," said Alison, "I really enjoyed it. All of it."

"My pleasure," responded Blue, blushing.

"So what's the plan for today?"

They left their mobile phones in the room, and left the hotel at eight o'clock. It was cloudy; maybe later it might rain. They walked the 200 metres to the nearest U-bahn station, and travelled to Berlin-Alexanderplatz. Here, at a kiosk, Blue bought a cheap pay-as-you-go mobile. After ten minutes they picked up the express to Frankfurt on the Oder at 9.28. The train stopped at Berlin-Ostbahnhof and then at four small towns. The landscape was flat, fertile and peaceful. An hour later, just before the train was due in, Blue sent a text message. As the train neared the station they could see low whitewashed blocks of flats, and lots of trees. There was a sense of spaciousness. They flashed past an Aldi supermarket.

The station was bright, clean and efficient, with a short covered mall of shops leading to the exit. Here they bought a plan of the city, and then came out of the station building, red and white painted with a steep tiled roof, into a small plaza with stances for buses and taxis, fringed by discreet and tasteful eating establishments. As they stood looking around Blue's phone pinged. He read the text message, then pointed to a wide archway between two redbrick buildings, which seemed to be apartment blocks. "I think we go this way."

He led Alison through the archway and onto a terrace which overlooked the town. From this high vantage point they could see the river Oder, wide, shallow and sluggish, oozing its way between Frankfurt below them and Słubice beyond. The river was something of a disappointment, lacking the forceful movement of the water and the busy barge traffic of some of Germany's other waterways. The bridge linking what had been before 1945 the two halves of the city was clearly visible, a neat concrete span replacing the old bridge destroyed during World War Two. There was a lively traffic across the bridge, now linking Germany with Poland, both cars and pedestrians. The town had suffered substantial damage towards the end of the war. Nevertheless, some of the older parts had survived, and they could see the ornate Gothic-revival facade of the Town Hall below them, and the tower of the mediaeval Marienkirche beyond. Behind the church rose a monument to the soviet era, a bland concrete tower block overlooking, no doubt deliberately, the church tower.

A paved path led from the left-hand end of the terrace onto a road which made a steep and winding descent towards the streets parallel to the river. On the way down they passed a ruined archway of glazed brick, once the entrance to some grand villa, beyond it now only rubble. Further down they came to tenements from the Imperial era, pock-marked by gunfire, interspersed with attractive and pristine modern blocks. Finally they reached the bottom of the road and emerged onto a street faced on both sides by large nineteenth-century villas, many again still bearing signs of the old conflict.

"We'll wait here, maybe a few yards away from the corner."

"This must have been the posh end of town," said Alison. "I wonder why they didn't fill in the bullet holes."

"Maybe they would have looked worse filled with cheap cement. Perhaps they were also making a political point, that we shouldn't forget the war."

A silver BMW slid past them and came to a standstill. The driver's door swung open and a man got out. A large man with a thick moustache and black hair cropped short. He could have been taken for a pirate on leave. He grinned broadly at Blue, advanced rapidly, and grasped him in an all-enveloping bear hug. On releasing him, he smiled again. "Ah, Angus, my friend, it is so good to see you again! I have waited for this moment many years. How was your trip?"

"Very good. It's good to see you too, Tadeusz."

"Aha! And this is your very lovely, er, assistant?" He raised one bushy eyebrow.

"Yes, this is my friend, er, and colleague, Dr Alison Hendrickx. Alison, Tadeusz Piłsudski."

"*Pani Doktor*, it's my very best pleasure." He bowed slightly, took Alison's hand and kissed it. "But we have no time to waste. Business first, then enjoyment. My wife will meet us later for a meal over in Poland. But first, we visit *Herr* Attmann. So, we get in the car."

Angus got in the front and Alison in the back, and they set off.

"Bauernstraße is about ten minutes from here. We go north and then west."

"There are so many trees," said Alison.

"Yes, there is much greenery. A lot of the city was destroyed during the War. Some of the rebuilding was good, some bad."

"Are you coming with us, Tadeusz?" asked Blue.

"Very much I would like to talk again with this assassin. But if I'm discovered it would be very bad, our German colleagues will be very upset that a Polish officer comes to Germany without telling them. Even if our enquiry is 'off the record' as you say. So I will drop you near the house, then wait elsewhere in the car. You will text when you're finished and you find me nearby. That is clear?"

"Absolutely."

"By the way, my friend, are you armed?"

"No."

"Do you want a pistol? I have an anonymous one here."

"No, thanks, Tadeusz. This is an unofficial visit, and if *Herr* Attmann doesn't want to talk, then we won't try to force him."

"Yes. That's good. We're nearly there."

They were now proceeding slowly along a street, on either side of which were detached houses which looked like they'd been built in the nineteen-twenties or thirties. Some of them were bungalows, others two-story family houses, some well cared-for, others more dilapidated. Each house was set in a garden, or rather a patch of land, and behind the houses could be seen bushes and stunted trees.

Towards the end of the road, the car drew to a halt.

"Here you get out. We are next to number 53. So 67 is just a little way further on."

There was no-one in the street. Were some of the houses un-occupied? It was very quiet; maybe the traffic noise from the other streets was absorbed by the trees.

Number 67 was a bungalow, in need of a good coat of paint, set back in a patch of grass and weeds. Blue noted the foliage was not overgrown; someone was cutting it every so often. A small wooden plaque by the door read 'Attmann'. Blue rang the bell. Soon a light went on the hallway, and through the frosted glass they could see a figure approach the door. Not the sort of door to have if you feared assassination, thought Blue. This wasn't the house of a professional criminal.

The door opened, and Blue recognised the description provided by Tadeusz. The man was not tall, but held himself upright, so that he seemed tall. The eyes which appraised him were sharp. The hair and moustache tallied with Alex Malcolm's description of the man who had travelled to Tayvallich on his boat. This was the man, Blue felt sure.

"*Ja? Kann ich Ihnen hilfen?*"

"Herr Attmann?"

"*Ja.*" The man waited. He had not slammed the door.

"*Er, guten morgen. Ich bin...* "

"Please, I speak some English. You are not German, so it may be easier."

"Thank you. I am Detective Inspector Angus Blue, Police Scotland." Blue showed his warrant card. "This is my colleague Dr Alison Hendrickx. We would like to ask you a few questions."

"So. At last. You have come." The man seemed almost relieved. "I knew that sooner or later someone will be here. Please, go through to the kitchen. At the back." He indicated the narrow corridor that led from the left side of the small hallway, then, as they passed him, he turned to shut the door again, and follow them.

The corridor had doors opening off it, one on the right, which, the door being ajar, looked like a bathroom, and two on the left, perhaps bedrooms, the doors shut. Blue suspected there was a living room to the front of the house, probably the door he had noticed at the right of the hall.

They came into an airy kitchen, with windows to the left and at the back. Through the rear window he could see a garden with several raised beds, and beyond that the trees behind the houses. There was a table with a scrubbed wooden surface in the centre of the room, four upright chairs surrounding it. Attmann came into the room behind them.

"Please, sit down. But of course, please, I introduce myself. I am Hanno Attmann." He shook hands with both of them. A firm, dry handshake. "Now I make some coffee for you, OK? I already made one for myself before you came."

"Thanks, that would be great," said Blue.

"Yes, please," added Alison.

They sat themselves down as Attmann busied himself with a cafetière. The kitchen was neat, neither old-fashioned nor modern, nothing that was shiny and new, but everything in working order. A mug of coffee already sat steaming on the table, next to a German newspaper, open at the puzzle page.

Attmann put the cafetière and two mugs on a tray, added a little bottle of cream, a box of sugar cubes, and a couple of teaspoons, and put the tray on the table. "Please. You will serve yourselves."

As Alison poured the coffee for them both, Blue noticed that the mugs were clean, with no staining inside. A man who took care of himself, and kept his things in good order.

Attmann sat down, took a sip of his coffee, then folded the newspaper and leaned over to put it on the counter. He turned back to face them. "You are police from Scotland?"

"Yes, that's correct," answered Blue.

"But you are here without German colleagues. This would be usual, I think, in a country where you have no, ah…"

"Jurisdiction?" suggested Alison.

"Yes, thank you, *Frau Doktor*. Is your visit known to our police, then?"

"No," said Blue. "We are not here on an official basis. As such, any answers you give to our questions will carry no legal weight. It will be as if you had not spoken with us."

"If this is so, then why do you ask?"

"The information you can give us will help us to understand the case we are working on. This is the case of two men shot on the island of Jura seventeen days ago." Blue noticed a gleam come into the man's eyes, before he looked hastily down into his coffee.

"Oh yes, I've read about that. But I thought only one man was shot. An English Lord, yes?"

"That's what the papers have said. But I think you know, as I do, that not one, but two men were shot that day. And that you shot them."

Attmann leaned towards the counter and tapped the newspaper. "I read here that another man has confessed to the crime."

"Yes, a confession has been obtained. The case is closed. We are not seeking any other persons. We only seek to understand what really happened. We hope you will tell us."

"What makes you think it was me?"

"Here's what happened. A woman, perhaps your daughter," – he noticed an intake of breath at the word – "brought you over to the island on the Sunday. She dropped you off near Dunrighinn House. You left a folding bicycle hidden near the shore, then you walked onto the hillside and concealed yourself for the night at a spot overlooking the house. In the morning you packed up your sleeping bag, and prepared your weapon. You waited until Lord Steppingham and his party were walking towards the helicopter. Then you took aim and fired. Your target was not Lord Steppingham, but he moved into your line of fire, took the first shot. So you had to fire again, and this time you got him. Your real target. Prince Arthur."

Blue noticed Attmann stiffen, and stare at him. "Perhaps you needed two shots, we haven't seen the body, so we don't know. Anyway, you finished off with a shot into the helicopter's rear rotor mechanism, to disable it. Then you packed up the rifle and crept off the hill, assembled the bicycle and rode back to Craighouse. There you left the bike in a waste bin and tagged onto a group of German whisky tourists heading for the boat from Jura to Tayvallich. Over there, your daughter picked you up again and took you on to Inveraray. There you had lunch. You finished with a glass of *schnapps*. Then you went on to North Shields, from where you travelled with the ferry to Amsterdam. And from Amsterdam you drove back here. I'm guessing that's the car out at the back, with the tarpaulin over it."

"That's a very detailed story, *Herr Kommissar*."

"We have good evidence for all of it. As I said, and say again, the case is closed. What you tell us will not be attributed to you, unless we have your explicit permission."

Attmann paused for a long moment, as if considering his options. He glanced across the kitchen towards the rear window, and Blue saw there was a picture of two smiling girls in a frame there.

"Yes, it's true. I did it, exactly as you say, *Herr Kommissar*, yes, you have it all. But my daughter, she is innocent. She wanted to help, but I said she must only drive me over and collect me later. The shooting is my responsibility. Mine alone."

"Why did you do it?" said Alison quietly. "That's what we'd like to know. We want to understand what led you to kill the prince. Would you tell us?"

"Hmm. Yes. I will do it, on one condition."

"What's that?" asked Blue.

"That you record my words."

This was a surprise. "Yes, that's no problem. But why?"

"When only the English lord's death was mentioned, I realised that those in power do not wish it to be known that Prince Arthur was a victim. When the other man, the Syrian, confessed, I knew they had found a, how do you say in English, *Sündenbock*, to blame for the killing."

"A scapegoat," said Blue.

"Yes. A scapegoat. I knew there were only two possibilities regarding my part in this event. First, that they had not tracked me down, that I had, as you might say, got away with it. Or two, that they knew it was me, but they did not want me to tell my story in the court. I now believe that it is something in between. They have not identified me yet, but sooner or later they will. And then they will come for me, to kill me quietly, because I know the truth."

"You may be right. They certainly want to keep the truth about Prince Arthur's killing hidden. I have tried to avoid passing your information on. But what we have done, they can do too. I agree with you, that you are in danger. Maybe you should get a sturdier front door."

Attmann laughed. "Yes, that is very good. Ha! Then they must shoot me through the back door."

"It sounds to me," said Alison, "That you feel that the prince's death was deserved."

"You are right, *Frau Doktor*, and I want all the world to know it. I have left two other statements, one with my daughter, who lives in Berlin, by the way. And the other, with a *notar...*"

"A lawyer."

"Yes. A lawyer. If I am killed, he will make this public. My daughter will also send the statement anonymously to several newspapers."

"You sound as if you expect to be killed soon," said Blue.

"Yes. I think that is true. When you rang the bell, I thought that was them. That's why I don't replace the door. Also, you must know that I will die soon anyway. I have the *krebs*, how do you say it?"

"Cancer."

"Yes, cancer, in three places now. It is only months, maybe even weeks. So it was essential to me that I carry out my plan before it was too late. This is also why I tell the story to you too. I think you are not the political police?"

"You're right. We're interested in justice, not politics." Blue took his digital voice recorder from his jacket pocket, put it on the table, and pressed the red button. "*Herr* Attmann, perhaps you could tell us your story now."

55

"Thank you. My father was Turkish, you know, he came to West Germany not long after the World War. He worked hard, and married a German girl. He was keen that their children should be Germans, Europeans, so me and my brother and sister, we all had German names. He even changed our family name, to make it sound a little more German. His name had been Ataman, so it didn't need a big change. We are German citizens. I joined the army, served for twenty years. I was a good shooter, I won many competitions, though I never shot anyone during my army service – all our service overseas was on aid and reconstruction missions. I married a wonderful German girl and we had two daughters, Magda and Annike. I retired from the army and got a job with the Deutsche Bahn, the railway company, in Hanover. We brought up our girls to be good girls. They did well at school, both wanted to go to university. Life was good.

"As you know, there are British bases near Hanover. One evening our eldest, Magda, she was then only sixteen, went out with some of her friends. We thought she had gone to the house of a friend, to talk and listen to music. But one of them had met a young officer from the base and he invited her to a party. He came with a jeep and took five of them to the base. Only four came back.

"When we contacted our daughter's friend, she said that she didn't see what happened to Magda, she had assumed she'd come home separately. It was clear to me when I spoke to her that she was frightened. But she would say nothing. I understand now that she had been threatened, she feared for her life. We never saw Magda again.

"We asked the *Landespolizei*, the state police of *Niedersachsen*, to find her. For weeks we heard nothing. Then another policeman came to the house, a man like yourself without uniform, from a federal agency that was not familiar to me. A *hauptkommissar*."

"Chief inspector."

"Yes. He told me he had spoken to the British military police, and it was clear that Magda had never been to the base. He suggested she might have run away, and began to question me about whether I beat her. 'You Turks know how to deal with women, eh?' That's what he said to me. When I denied it, he said if I pursued the case, I will be arrested for child abuse. 'Once you're labelled a paedophile,' he said, 'people will always think that. You'll never prove them wrong. So keep your mouth shut and forget your daughter ever existed. Tell the neighbours you sent her back to Turkey for an arranged marriage.' He laughed. This man was like someone from the *Stasi* in the DDR. Or the Nazi secret police.

"But I found out what happened. Part of my Turkish background that I cherish is the connections we maintain with family. I had a cousin who was a clerk at the headquarters of the *Landespolizei* in Hanover. This was two years after Magda disappeared. She was told to sort some files which someone had discovered in a cellar, to classify them, and place them in the correct location in the *Archiv*. She saw among these files one with Magda's name on it. She did not dare to take the file away, but she read it carefully and as soon as she got home wrote down all she could remember.

"The file was marked 'Highest Security'. It was written by a *komissar* of the *Landespolizei*, and recorded that he had visited the British base and interviewed some of the officers. It was clear they were hiding something, and he reported this to his superiors. He was later told that an arrangement had been made with the British Government, that no-one would be prosecuted for this crime, provided that we were told the truth. Germans, you must know, like to keep records of everything, even if we keep them secret for eternity.

"Magda and her friends had indeed been taken to the party. It was a small party hosted by young officers at the base, an elite group of young men from backgrounds of great wealth or position. These were young men who expected that they could do just whatever they wanted, that no act, however bestial, could be denied them. Their title or wealth would always see them absolved. These were creatures without morality or humanity, I assure you, *Herr Kommissar*. Their leader was this Prince Arthur, a member of the English royal family, and therefore completely above the law. Had he been a decent man, that might not have been a problem. But he is, he was, not a good man. He was I think a psychopath, someone who has no feeling for the joys or the sufferings of others. He enjoyed inflicting pain, he needed more and more from every sexual encounter to gain satisfaction, and he felt he had a right to take any woman he liked. His favourite phrase while he was stationed in Germany was '*Frau, komm!*' Have you heard this phrase?"

"Yes," said Alison, "I have. It was what the Russian soldiers in occupied Germany said to a woman, when they wanted to rape her. It was an order, not an invitation…"

"Just so. Prince Arthur raped, tortured and finally killed my daughter. He could not be interviewed by our police, but *ein Untertan…*"

"An underling, a creature," said Blue.

"Exactly, this underling explained to the policeman that the prince was sorry that he had killed the girl. He had only intended to intensify her pleasure – I think by that he meant his own pleasure – but that she had collapsed and he had not been able to resuscitate her. She must have had a weak heart. Maybe she had drunk too much also, or been taking drugs before coming to the party, he said. The policeman did not believe this account. He had heard rumours of the prince's behaviour, and suspected that drugs had been administered to the girls at the party without their knowledge. One of the other British officers confirmed this, and, on condition of anonymity, described the bestial acts which the prince had carried out. This was supported by the evidence of one of the other girls, who had been taken from the party and dumped outside a hospital. She needed several operations and will never be able to have children. The British commanders refused to say what had been done with Magda's body. The policeman suspected that it had been swiftly cremated on the base. The final entry in the file stated that the matter had been passed to a federal agency to be resolved. The man who came to me was from this agency.

"So now I knew the truth. I tried to contact the policeman who had written the report, *Kommissar* Heidefeldt. I said I was an old friend who wanted to meet him again. But I was told he had left the police, and emigrated to New Zealand. He had left no forwarding address. Then I decided that I myself must be the agent of justice, that my daughter's memory called for it."

"How did your wife take it?" asked Alison.

"Very badly. Six months later, she stepped in front of a tram, and was killed instantly. I don't know whether it was deliberate, or whether she no longer looked where she was going, often it seemed that she was in a dream, as if her mind was somewhere else."

"You said your daughter was sixteen when this happened?" asked Alison.

"Yes," Attmann whispered. "Just sixteen." Attmann stopped. They could see him forcing the thoughts out of his head, before he went on. "Our other daughter, Annike, she was one year younger at the time, that was eight years ago now. She agreed that we must find justice, for Magda and for my Francesca too. She had been killed also by the prince, albeit at a distance.

"After Francesca's death, Annike and I moved away, and came here to Frankfurt, as far as we could get from Hanover and the British bases. Annike has made a life, she studied at university, and is now a sound engineer and works in Berlin. I worked again for the Deutsche Bahn, but three months ago the cancer was detected, and I retired. I needed to finish the work before it was too late.

"I had studied the prince in great detail. I could write a biography of him, except that no-one would publish it. I have a thick file on him with much detail. I keep it here" – he pointed to a red box-file sitting on a shelf between two bags of sugar – "to remind myself to remain focused. I found websites which adore him, and others which hate him. There is a lady on Facebook who is a big fan and notes down all the prince's actions, all his plans and future movements. This was very useful, it told me he will be on Jura staying with the lord. Annike was keen to help me, and it went just as you have described. You are a good detective, I think."

"I have good people who assist me," said Blue.

"Yes, good support is necessary too," said Attmann, smiling wanly at Alison. "But now I am satisfied. Justice is done. It is only necessary now that the prince's deeds are made public, that not only his life, but his reputation is ended. This is why I am happy to speak to you. And if you want to arrest me, and take me to Scotland for trial, I am happy to go with you. As long as Annike is left alone."

Blue switched off the recorder and put it back in his pocket. "Thank you very much for your co-operation, *Herr* Attmann. As I explained, this meeting is unofficial, and I am not empowered to arrest you. Indeed, even if I did arrest you, I could not guarantee your personal safety. I don't have the authority to stop our own political police from getting hold of you. If that happened, you would simply disappear. They already have a better culprit for the shooting, and everyone believes that the prince fell off a horse."

"Is *Herr* Attmann in danger now, Angus?" said Alison.

"I suspect so. *Herr* Attmann, I have kept most of the information about you out of the police database, but I suspect there may be enough there to lead others to you. Be careful. Maybe you should move to another town."

"There is no more any point, but thank you for your advice, *Herr Kommissar*. As I said before, I know they will come for me, and if they get me, I think that will be the end, they won't follow Annike. I'll tell you a secret." He pointed to a bulky waterproof jacket hanging on a hook on the back door. "In the pocket of my coat I always carry a powerful explosive device, a high-blast hand grenade, NATO issue. If they come for me, I intend to take some of them with me. So maybe you're right, I should replace the door. I need them to come into the house."

"I think it's time we were going now," said Blue. "Thank you again for your help. I don't think we'll be coming back."

Alison got up and gave Attmann a hug. Now he wept freely.

And the doorbell rang.

56

Attmann wiped his eyes. "Please, wait a moment, I see who is here."
He went out, closed the door, and padded off up the corridor.

There were no shots. Blue heard the door open and then indistinct
voices. One was Attmann, but there was something about the other.
Maybe just the intonation, but he knew they were speaking English.
That didn't sound like good news.

Footsteps approached along the corridor and the door opened.
Attmann came in first, followed by a gun, and an arm, and a man.
Plaistow!

"Blue! What the fuck are you doing here?" Plaistow came into the
room, followed by two other men. Had Blue seen them at
Dunrighinn? He couldn't remember.

"Just visiting," he replied. "What about you, Inspector Plaistow?"

"Oh yeah, just visiting, my arse. With your tart in tow too." He
leered at Alison. "Very nice. I wouldn't mind getting my hands on
your assets, love. Sadly, I've got work to do at the moment. But
maybe we'll get a minute or two later, eh?" He stuck his tongue out
and wiggled it from side to side. Then turned the gun on Attmann
again. "All right, Fritz, you're Attmann, ain't you, eh?"

Attmann didn't respond.

"Well, no need to answer, I've got a pic and it fits. We just want
a few words that's all. In private, like. Trouble is, with these two
here, we'll have to go somewhere more discreet."

"What questions?" said Attmann. "I'm just a retired railway
worker."

"We thought he was someone else," said Blue, "but we were
mistaken. He's harmless."

"How many times do you think I've heard that one before, Blue?
'Honest, mister, I'm really harmless. And I promise never to reveal
anything to anybody.' You just keep your trap shut, matey. After
me and Mr Attmann have had our chat, I'll be back to deal with you
and the skirt. Gary, you keep an eye on these two. Don't let them
out of your sight. We need to ask them a few questions, find out
how much they know, so if they try to get out, don't kill them. Just
take out a kneecap each, we don't want them too damaged.
Especially the skirt, eh?"

One of the thugs produced a pistol and leaned casually against the sink at the other side of the room. "No worries, boss."

"Don't worry, Mr Attmann, the guns are simply to keep you focused. All we want are answers to some questions. We'll bring you back in ten minutes. Lee, you stay with me."

"May I put my jacket on?" asked Attmann. "I suffer much from the cold."

"Of course you can. We ain't gonna kill you. We're your pals." The two henchmen chortled. "But just do it slowly, eh? We can get very jumpy."

Attmann raised his hands slowly to show they were empty and walked slowly over to the door. He took the jacket off the hook and put it on. "Thank you," he said to Plaistow, then to Blue and Alison, "It was good to meet you. I'll be back soon, so please wait for me. *Auf wiedersehen und bitte hinlegen Sie sich. Sofort.*" He walked out of the room followed by Plaistow and Lee.

As the door shut behind them, Gary pushed himself upright, and waved the gun at them. "All right, you two, the party's over. Get onto the floor, in that corner." He pulled a set of handcuffs from his left pocket with his free hand.

"No problem," said Blue, and to Alison, "Quick as you can!" They threw themselves down onto the floor, against the wall and away from the doorway. "And keep your mouth open!"

"What the…" shouted Gary, then the penny dropped. "Shit!" He flung the door open and ran down the corridor. "Boss! Boss! The jerry, he's got a…"

He never finished. The explosion blew the door off its hinges and shattered the glass in the back door and the rear window. The mugs, cafetière and sugar box were swept off the table. A kettle, a food mixer, a bread bin and a microwave oven crashed off the counter. Something landed with a thump on the floor by the door. Plates and dishes in the cupboards rattled and clinked. A wisp of smoke drifted into the room along with an acrid and unfamiliar smell.

Blue felt dizzy. He couldn't hear anything, and swallowed several times before he felt his ears pop. "Alison, are you OK?" He grasped her arm.

She nodded, said something, but he couldn't hear it.

He glanced over towards the doorway. An arm lay there. Without a hand and without a shoulder or the rest of a body. Just a naked arm. With a tattoo, an SAS dagger. He got up carefully, leaning against the wall, made his way to the doorway and peered into the corridor. He could see as far as the hall. The walls were splashed with blood, the floor littered with body parts. Something round and bloody was still rolling about. There was a draught running through the room. He guessed the front door had been blown out. Maybe the front of the house too.

Alison was replacing her glasses, shaking her head as if to get a lot of dust out of it.

"Alison, time for us to get out of here. I think the neighbours will have noticed the bang." He helped her up. "And there's nothing we can do for *Herr* Attmann. We don't want to get caught here. Let's get out the back."

"I can't hear what you're saying, Angus. What should we do?"

"Wait a moment!" On the floor near the rear window was a pile of sugar and on top of it the red box file, held shut by a cord tightly tied around it. Blue grabbed the file, then took Alison's hand and led her towards the back door. The glass panel filling it had been blown out, so they carefully stepped through the gap into the garden. There was no fence at the back of the property. Blue set off towards the trees at the rear. He pulled her after him into the wooded waste ground, and headed back in the direction from which they'd come. Once they'd passed the rear of two of the houses, he pulled out the mobile and sent a short text. Then they set off again, until they'd passed the back gardens of perhaps eight or nine houses, he wasn't counting exactly.

Alison followed him, poking at her ears and shaking her head. "Say something," she said loudly.

"Keep moving! Did you hear that?" said Blue as distinctly as he could, without shouting.

"Yes, there's an awful whistling, but I heard you. What now?"

"Let's get through one of the gardens and onto the road. He's on his way."

Since there were no fences at the rear, it was easy to move into one of the more run-down gardens, in which a disintegrating caravan was parked, surrounded by long grass. They paused behind the caravan, saw there was no sign of life, and slipped down the side of what seemed an empty house.

They were nearly at the front of the house when a dog started barking loudly.

"Shit!" said Blue.

The next moment a Rottweiler came bounding round the back of the house and stopped facing them, snarling and salivating.

Alison walked towards it very slowly, singing a low, soft, Gaelic song. Was it a lullaby? The dog stopped snarling and looked uneasy, pawing the ground as if unsure what to do next. Alison slowly rested her hand on the dog's head, and whispered to it. It lay down with its head on the ground, then closed its eyes and relaxed. A moment later it emitted a gentle snore.

"Come on," she whispered. "He won't sleep forever."

"How the hell did you do that?" said Blue.

"It's an old skill, passed through the family, from my father. It's more useful with horses, but works with most reasonably sized domesticated animals. I almost managed it with a deer once. Small animals are too nervous to pay enough attention."

They crept on to the wooden fence separating the garden from the road. There was a wide gap in it, giving entry to a hard standing at the front of the house. In a few seconds they were on the road, and walking along like any couple out for a stroll. Except they didn't quite feel like that. And they looked a little dishevelled.

They reached the other end of the road from number 67, and turned right onto a wider street, with shops on one side, apartment blocks on the other. A couple of minutes later they heard sirens, and a police car, followed by an ambulance, raced past them and skidded round the corner into Bauernstraße. A minute after that they heard another siren, and this time a fire engine rushed past. As they passed a Lidl supermarket, Blue's phone pinged. The silver BMW was waiting in the car park.

"Tell me about it later!" said Tadeusz as they got in. He drove carefully through the town, and was soon on the bridge over the Oder, taking them out of Germany and into Poland.

"Now we are in my jurisdiction, my friends," he announced, as they passed the sign welcoming them to Słubice. "Now you may tell me everything. Then I can decide whether I need to get you to the airport in a hurry!"

57

An hour later, they sat in a small restaurant in the town of Kostrzyn nad Odra, 30 kilometres further north, with Tadeusz and his wife Justyna. Diminutive and slim, with dark hair braided and fixed round her head, she was a lawyer, specialising in forestry and environmental issues. In front of them, plates of *Bigos*, sauerkraut mixed with fresh cabbage, chunks of meat, and small doughballs.

"I hope you don't have to go all the way back to Wrocław this afternoon," Blue apologised. "It must be quite a way."

"A few hours driving, yes," replied Tadeusz, "But no, we don't do it today. Justyna's sister lives not far away, so we stay with them till Sunday, and have a little holiday."

Once they had moved on to coffee and *Sernik*, a cheesecake with cherries on top, talk turned to the events of the morning.

"So, Angus," said Tadeusz, "What do you plan to do now? I think we do not mention our part in this incident to anyone."

"Yes. What I'd like now is to get Attmann's story, and the stuff about Prince Arthur in the box file, out into the public gaze. Once it's clear what actually happened on Jura, they'll have to release Salebi."

"Ah, my friend, I'm sorry," said Tadeusz. "There you are too late." He held up his phone. "My newsfeed just tells me this man is dead. The report says he killed himself by hanging, in his cell. A police official suggests that this was because he feared he would disclose under interrogation the names of his terrorist associates, and their future plans. This proves he was a fanatic, they say."

"He was an innocent victim," said Alison. "He came to Islay to find peace, and instead he became a pawn in a cover-up. Used and then cast aside by those to whom lives are merely playthings. Living toys for boys who never grow up. It makes me sick."

"It reminds me very much of the soviet times," said Tadeusz quietly. "I was young then, but I heard of the things that could happen. When the policy of the state becomes more important than the lives of the people. My parents marched in the street to end that regime."

"We may have to do the same in our turn," said Blue. "Maybe sooner than we think."

"Could they still go after Attmann's daughter?" asked Alison.

"She can be edited out of Attmann's text," answered Blue. "But I think that coping with all the stuff about Prince Arthur that comes out will make them reluctant to proceed with the shooting investigation. They'll want to shut it down fast. They may just stick to their original narrative: Salebi killed Steppingham, confessed, then killed himself, end of story. They'll claim Attmann's story is just fake news, made up by the terrorists, and fallen for by the stupid foreign media. They'll play up his Turkish background, try to turn him into a Muslim fanatic with a grudge against all things civilised."

"Rather than simply a father seeking justice for his child."

"None of Attman's material will appear in any of the UK papers. I doubt if even *The Nation* will be allowed to print anything."

"So it needs to get plenty of airing outwith the UK," put in Alison. "Even if the mainstream media in Britain pretend it doesn't exist, many people there now get their news from the internet or social media. The truth will get around."

"I know someone who can help," said Justyna. "The editor of a magazine here. It's a celebrity magazine, but they are not just sycophants. They print the bad as well as the good. The stuff in the box, they will print some of the more lurid things. That will attract other papers, more serious ones. The Polish papers will have no fear in printing these things, they have no love of royalty. Our government will not object, it will distract people from problems within our country."

"Then the Germans will take it up," added Tadeusz, "And the French. And then it's everywhere."

"Leave the box with me," said Justyna quietly. "I'll take good care of it. On Monday morning I'll have a complete copy made, and meet with Henrik, he's the magazine editor. He'll be keen to see me when he knows what I've got. I also have the copy of Attmann's statement from your recorder on a USB stick.

"Remember what Attmann said to us," added Alison, "That the lawyer will also release his statement, as well as his daughter. Shouldn't we try to stop Annike from getting involved? She could attract unwelcome attention to herself."

"Do not worry," said Tadeusz. "I will find her address, and Justyna will speak to her. She is very good at talking sense. But soon you must go. From the station here, you can get a train directly to Berlin. Then you still have time to visit a few sites, be seen enjoying yourselves, put some pictures up on Twitter. Go to the Tiergarten, photograph yourselves returning from a day in the park. And I pay for this meal, so then you have no *złoty* in your pocket. The railway station will take Euros. Now I wish you to enjoy the rest of your vacation."

"I can't thank you enough," said Blue.

"No worries, my friend. You can thank me even more by coming, with your lovely lady here, to visit us in Wrocław later this year."

"We'd love to," said Alison, her hand resting on Blue's arm. "We really would."

From the World's Press

Aktualnosci: "Gwalt i Morderstwo: Ksiaze Oskarzony"

Die Zeitung: "Sexskandal und Mord im Königshaus: Prinz beschuldigt"

Nouvelles du Monde: "Le Prince du Déshonneur"

Melbourne Telegraph: "Veteran's Confession reveals Prince's Secret Crimes"

Washington Mail: "UK Government denies Royal Cover-up"

The Nation: "This blank space is where our main story would be printed. But legal action by the UK government has silenced us. Look on the internet or social media, and you'll find the story they don't want you to read."

The End

About the Author
Allan Martin

Allan Martin worked as a teacher, teacher-trainer and university lecturer, and only turned to writing fiction after taking early retirement.

He lives in Glasgow and with his wife regularly visits the Hebrides and Estonia.

He has had several short stories published, notably in *iScot* magazine and *404Ink* magazine.

He has also translated from Estonian a closed-room mystery, *The Oracle*, originally published in 1937.

His first novel, *The Pead Dead*, will be printed in Estonian in 2021.

The Peat Dead
Allan Martin

Shortlisted for the 2019 Bloody Scotland McIlvanney Debut
Scottish Crime Prize.

ISBN: 978-1-910946-55-8 (Kindle)
ISBN: 978-1-910946-54-1 (Paperback)

On the Scottish Hebridean Island of Islay, five corpses are dug up
by a peat-cutter. All of them have been shot in the back of the head,
execution style.

Sent across from the mainland to investigate, Inspector Angus
Blue and his team slowly piece together the little evidence they
have, and discover the men were killed on a wartime base, over 70
years ago.

But there are still secrets worth protecting, and even killing for.
Who can Inspector Blue trust?

"A mystery so redolent of its island setting that you
practically smell the peat and whisky on the pages." –
Douglas Skelton"

This atmospheric crime novel set on Islay gripped me from
the start. A book that shows decades-old crimes cast long
shadows." – Sarah Ward

In The Shadow Of The Hill
Helen Forbes

ISBN: 978-0-9929768-1-1 (eBook)
ISBN: 978-0-9929768-0-4 (Paperback)

An elderly woman is found battered to death in the common stairwell of an Inverness block of flats.

Detective Sergeant Joe Galbraith starts what seems like one more depressing investigation of the untimely death of a poor unfortunate who was in the wrong place, at the wrong time.

As the investigation spreads across Scotland it reaches into a past that Joe has tried to forget, and takes him back to the Hebridean island of Harris, where he spent his childhood.

Among the mountains and the stunning landscape of religiously conservative Harris, in the shadow of Ceapabhal, long buried events and a tragic story are slowly uncovered, and the investigation takes on an altogether more sinister aspect.

In The Shadow Of The Hill skilfully captures the intricacies and malevolence of the underbelly of Highland and Island life, bringing tragedy and vengeance to the magical beauty of the Outer Hebrides.

'...our first real home-grown sample of modern Highland noir' – Roger Hutchinson; West Highland Free Press

Madness Lies
Helen Forbes

ISBN: 978-1-910946-31-2 (Kindle)
ISBN: 978-1-910946-30-5 (Paperback)

When an Inverness Councillor is murdered in broad daylight in the middle of town, Detective Sergeant Joe Galbraith sees a familiar figure running from the scene.

According to everyone who knows him, the Councillor had no enemies, but someone clearly wanted him dead.

The victim's high profile means the police want a quick resolution to the case, but no one seems to know anything. Or if they do, they're not prepared to say.

This second novel of Highland Noir from Helen Forbes continues the series with a crime thriller that moves between Inverness, North Uist and London, reaching a terrifying denouement at the notorious Black Rock Gorge.

'You would expect Helen Forbes to write well of an exile's experience of Sollas, Vallay and west side of North Uist, and she does. She evokes the machair, the changing sky and sea, the flowers, birds and waving grass, the dunes, the people and above all the peace.' – Roger Hutchinson; West Highland Free Press

The Birds That Never Flew
Margot McCuaig

Longlisted for the Polari First Book Prize 2014
ISBN: 978-0-9575689-3-8 (Kindle)
ISBN: 978-0-9929768-4-2 (Paperback)

'Have you got a light hen? I'm totally gaspin.'

Battered and bruised, Elizabeth has taken her daughter and left her abusive husband Patrick. Again. In the bleak and impersonal Glasgow housing office Elizabeth meets the provocatively intriguing drug addict Sadie, who is desperate to get her own life back on track.

The two women forge a fierce and interdependent relationship as they try to rebuild their shattered lives, but despite their bold, and sometimes illegal attempts it seems impossible to escape from the abuse they have always known, and tragedy strikes.

More than a decade later Elizabeth has started to implement her perfect revenge - until a surreal Glaswegian Virgin Mary steps in with imperfect timing and a less than divine attitude to stick a spoke in the wheel of retribution.

Tragic, darkly funny and irreverent, The Birds That Never Flew is a new and vibrant voice in Scottish literature.

"Not Scandinavian but dark, beautiful and moving, I wholeheartedly recommend" – scanoir.co.uk

The Deaths on the Black Rock
BRM Stewart

ISBN: 978-1-910946-47-3 (Kindle)
ISBN: 978-1-910946-46-6 (Paperback)

It's been a year since Rima Khalaf died in a fall from the Black Rock, deemed to be a tragic accident by the police.

But her grieving parents are dissatisfied with the police investigation, so DS Amanda Pitt is sent north from Glasgow to the small town of Clachdubh to re-examine the case.

Despite the suspicions of the distraught parents, all the circumstances seem to confirm Rima's death was indeed a tragic accident, until another woman is also found dead in the town.

Frustrated by the lack of any real evidence, DS Pitt pushes the limits of legality in her quest for the truth.

Stewart writes with a gritty intensity that places the reader in intimate contact with the darker side of society, in a way that forces you to empathise with the uncomfortable idea that sometimes the end justifies the means for those who are supposed to uphold the law.

Toxic
Jackie McLean

Shortlisted for the Yeovil Book Prize 2011
ISBN: 978-0-9575689-8-3 (eBook)
ISBN: 978-0-9575689-9-0 (Paperback)

The recklessly brilliant DI Donna Davenport, struggling to hide a secret from police colleagues and get over the break-up with her partner, has been suspended from duty for a fiery and inappropriate outburst to the press.

DI Evanton, an old-fashioned, hard-living misogynistic copper has been newly demoted for thumping a suspect, and transferred to Dundee with a final warning ringing in his ears and a reputation that precedes him.

And in the peaceful, rolling Tayside farmland a deadly store of MIC, the toxin that devastated Bhopal, is being illegally stored by a criminal gang smuggling the valuable substance necessary for making cheap pesticides.

An anonymous tip-off starts a desperate search for the MIC that is complicated by the uneasy partnership between Davenport and Evanton and their growing mistrust of each others actions.

Compelling and authentic, Toxic is a tense and fast paced crime thriller.

'...a humdinger of a plot that is as realistic as it is frightening' – crimefictionlover.com

Shadows
Jackie McLean

ISBN: 978-1-910946-29-9 (Kindle)
ISBN: 978-1-910946-28-2 (Paperback)

When DI Donna Davenport is called out to investigate a body washed up on Arbroath beach, it looks like a routine murder inquiry. But then the enquiry takes on a more sinister form.

There are similarities with a previous murder, and now a woman connected to them both has also gone missing. For Donna, this is becoming personal, and with the added pressure of feeling watched at every turn, she is convinced that Jonas Evanton has returned to seek his revenge on her for his downfall.

Fearing they may be looking for a serial killer, Donna and her new team are taken in a horrifying and unexpected direction. Because it's not a serial killer - it's worse.

Moving from Dundee to the south coast of Turkey and the Syrian border, this is a fast paced novel about those who live their lives in the shadows, and those who exploit them.

"With sensitivity and honesty, Jackie has written a thriller that will shock and grip the reader in equal measure."

Run
Jackie McLean
ISBN: 978-1-910946-65-7 (Kindle)
ISBN: 978-1-910946-64-0 (Paperback)

RUN THE GAUNTLET

DI Donna Davenport and her team are under pressure.

With the hunt on for the country's most notorious cop killer, and an ongoing complex international investigation, the murder of a local thug during a football match is the last thing the police need.

But as more incidents overload the police, and fear brings vigilante mobs onto the streets, suspicion grows that the mayhem is being orchestrated.

CUT AND RUN

One man can make it stop. With the city heading towards chaos and disaster Donna prepares to abandon caution and the rules, even if it means she is ostracised by her own team.

"A superbly plotted and gripping police procedural that will leave you breathless. McLean has excelled herself with Run"
– Tana Collins